A BOOK OF PROJECTS

By Derek Waters
A Book of Festivals
A Book of Celebrations
A Book of Assemblies (in preparation)
Creative Work with Found Materials

A Book of

DEREK WATERS and
MARGARET BRANDHAM

*Illustrated by Greta Kinder with
title pages by Janet Swiss*

MILLS & BOON LIMITED, LONDON

First published in Great Britain 1972 by
Mills & Boon Limited, 17–19 Foley Street, London W1A 1DR

ISBN 0 263.05004.1

Made and printed in Great Britain by
Butler & Tanner Limited, Frome and London

CONTENTS

ACKNOWLEDGEMENTS

The authors are grateful to Mrs Joan Bryant for her advice on the presentation of this material; to Greta Kinder for patient work with the drawings to illustrate suggestions for art and craft work; and to Janet Swiss for her supporting art work.

We are indebted to the following for use of certain photographs:
Kentish Times
Evans Brothers
Henry Grant AIIP
Ron Weston of Pace Ltd
National Dairy Council
Forestry Commission
British Waterways Board and
The BBC.

PART I

LEARNING THROUGH PROJECTS

INTRODUCTION

At a time when there is so much educational ferment, experiment and reaction to it, we would like to discuss the relevance of the project method as a means of learning for the 7–13-year-old children in our schools today.

We have used this method ourselves for some fifteen years in a variety of situations – semi-rural, old urban and new estate with classes of various sizes, ages and abilities. During this time various ways of working have been developed and consolidated. Modifications and adjustments were made to suit different situations, and to ensure that the process did not become too stereotyped. The increasing availability of audio-visual aids, building and furniture improvements, less rigid time-tabling, the new possibilities opened up by the adoption of an integrated day and team teaching, all influenced our pattern of working.

A description of the philosophy and practice of the project method takes up the first part of the book; by way of illustration we have devoted the second part of the book to outline schemes of a variety of projects of which we have singly or jointly had experience. We have deliberately taken a broad look at each of the topics because we are aware of the bias that can occur in working in this way, because of the nature of the subject or the particular interests and enthusiasms of the teacher. We would ask the reader not to regard these outlines as recipes but rather as suggestions or guidelines from which selections can be taken, and modifications made.

Inevitably new suggestions will come from a class sufficiently stimulated, and topical and local points will be taken up so that the theme becomes unique to the group. In some examples, a smaller topic can be extracted to suit the needs of a young class or where there is a limit on the time which is available. Also, where a teacher is new to this way of working or to the profession, he or she may decide not to start on an over-ambitious scheme. Success is very important when embarking on any new way of working. The time for boldness is usually when one is experienced. Risk the failures and disappointments then, and learn from them. It is only from some setback that one realises some drawback in a procedure, and can make some alteration to avoid repetition. One story told of Dr W. G. Grace was his reaction to a player who said he had never scored a duck. He put him last in the batting order, because it would seem that the man had not played much cricket!

We have included mathematical and scientific work wherever possible because these two subjects are notoriously difficult to integrate within most schemes, without appearing to have been pulled in by the scruff of the neck. Religious education, perhaps the most controversial aspect of the curriculum, is another subject which suffers particularly because it is so often taken in isolation, and so where there is a natural extension from the main theme in this direction, suggestions for activities have been included.

This book has been written by two primary school teachers, but as we see encouraging signs of the project method being increasingly used in the first and second years of secondary schools, often under grander names such as integrated and interdisciplinary studies, we hope our colleagues there will find the suggestions useful. By the adoption of these methods already familiar to the children the transfer from the primary stage should become much smoother, and also will suit the mixed ability groups which are becoming increasingly a feature of some of the lower forms of many comprehensive and other secondary schools. In Middle Schools which form part of many local authorities' new plans, specialisation is not likely to be a predominant feature, and it is probable that the best practice from the more progressive primary schools will be adopted. We believe that an active and hardworking atmosphere can be engendered when the project method is employed, and so we would like to offer our suggestions to the staffs of these schools too.

Students who are frequently advised to work in this way may find that in their school practices they are tossed into classes and even schools which are quite unused to this approach. We hope that they will find useful guidance here.

Margaret Brandham and Derek Waters

1. THE PROJECT AS A WAY OF LEARNING

Plate 1 *The rearranging of tables and other furniture may be necessary to encourage group activities and movement within the classroom.*

We want children to become involved in their own learning. They will not do this to any great extent if they have to sit passively on their chairs all day and every day. We believe that the great merit of the project method is that it develops the habit of active learning, and to ensure this a relaxed and informal atmosphere is desirable.

The rigid arrangement of furniture which inhibits any attempts at co-operative learning will require some alteration. In fact, a great deal of thought will need to be given to the layout of the room, and some suggestions are given in Chapter 3, 'Resources for Learning Inside the School'. To provide more working space and access, some of the chairs may have to be disposed of! In the case of group activities, which involve self-discipline, responsibility and questions of leadership, some movement and talking will occur. These activities will need to be encouraged, and not merely tolerated.

There should be an abundance of opportunity to develop the imaginative side of a theme, and so equal value needs to be placed by the teacher (and headteacher) on drama, poetry and other writing, art and craft activities.

Some educational philosophers make much of the undifferentiated day. But even within that kind of organisation, when the child may appear to have a completely free choice of activity, there needs to be a pattern, and in fact some limitations on the options available. The sensitive teacher will prepare the classroom environment and provide stimulus and information, and in this carefully prepared situation, the child can prepare his own programme. In such situations as this, the teacher will be realising her true role – as guide, adviser and senior planner. There is nothing casual about this way of working. It requires a great deal of energy, imagination and determination, if it is going to succeed. In this kind of integrated day approach, we have found that the project is a unifying activity. It provides the class with a sense of security, continuity and orderly progress towards some ultimate goal. One of our responsibilities as teachers is to see that we help children to take care of their talents. We need to see that, once they have embarked upon a task, they see it through to the end. We must, ourselves, see it through to the end. There is nothing more depressing for a child than to discover that there will not be time to complete his task, and that at the completion of the period of study there is no satisfactory end-product.

Group and individual work fit quite easily into the integrated day, and where, under this enlightened approach, each child has a measure of freedom of choice of activity, so must he fulfil a certain contract of work each week, or fortnight – the terms of the contract determined for each individual. In addition to this personal commitment, a portion of the working week can be given over to group enterprises, and there is likely to be a variable amount of time required for general discussion, preparation, appraisal, films, excursions, music and story. This is not only economical but desirable from the social point of view, in which all or almost all of the class can engage.

Under such an arrangement, art and craft, music and other creative activities will be going on during each day, so that there will be a steady output of illustrative material. This will contribute towards the ever-changing scene of a lively classroom, and by careful display, it will act as a further stimulus to the class.

Team teaching and co-operative learning situations are on the increase, and within such situations there is very much a place for project work. The topic may be at the instigation of one member of the team, or may arise from some topical issue which is likely to be suggested by the children. By sharing ideas and responsibility for certain aspects, the topic can be explored in depth and breadth.

Whether in a school built to encourage this kind of work or one modified to make it possible, decisions will need to be made about areas within the working space which can be designated for particular tasks – art and craft, quiet corners, etc. Some decision needs to be reached about the particular responsibilities of various members of the team. Where these cannot be completely resolved, a compromise must be found if any advantages are to be had from the co-operative situation. For instance, where two members are keen to follow their personal interests in art and craft, an area could be created in each bay to accommodate some aspect of this creative element of the topic. The planner's ideal of a clean area and a dirty area may not work out as conceived originally.

Another compromise solution is possible, where the language work is dealt with by one teacher during one thematic study, and an equally enthusiastic teacher will agree to take over the leadership for the following project. In this way each will have a turn in a subordinate position, and later as leader. Ideally a fully co-ordinated and collaborative plan should be aimed for. Frequent consultation is inevitable and necessary when working in this way, and time needs to be set aside for planning meetings at least once a week, in addition to the lunchtime, and after-school, informal exchange of views. The keeping of records is essential, particularly because of the larger number of children involved and their freedom to move around in the various teaching and learning bays and areas, so possibly avoiding attention.

It is interesting to note how children, while being able to appeal to any member of staff in a team, will soon get to know the unofficial specialists.

Co-operative teaching has featured in a number of our projects. In one such situation, the topic was 'Waterways and Canals', and the co-operation of the two authors was requested in this, because of their enthusiasm for this way of working and their special-interest skills in the creative fields of art, craft and music.

In another project, three classes combined to study 'Russia' (and later 'America' – both topics described in *A Book of Festivals*). One teacher took responsibility for the overall planning, and the other two adopted particular features of the work which appealed to them, the art work, writing, etc. Mass viewing of information films, listening to music and drama work was possible, releasing one or even two others to take some aspect with a very small number of children.

In yet another type of situation, two classes worked co-operatively for part of the day only, mixing for the project. In addition to responsibility equally shared for most aspects of the study, specialisation occurred in the areas of music and literature.

At the other end of the educational spectrum, we have found that the project method can be used within a formal organisation. One part of the syllabus can be explored in depth, with the agreement of the head-teacher. Some other time-tabled subjects can be associated with this study in history or geography or science, written English, literature, drama, art and craft, thus allowing a considerable amount of time, per week, which can be given over to the study. Similarly, a specialist taking music, drama and a subject such as history can be invited to 'adopt' the theme (and enjoy the 'instant' interest of the class).

We have found in practice that there is a need to continue basic work outside the project. During the study, the various skills of reading, writing and number are applied frequently, and are improved, not only by the practice, but also by the interest engendered by the theme. The children, so involved in this type of work, readily see the reasons for learning and practising skills, and will work harder to improve their performance for the right reasons. But a sound basic scheme in such skills is vital if they are to take full advantage of the opportunities the project method offers.

Standards are of great importance, and the fact that there is a large output of material throughout a project does not excuse slovenly, untidy work. The majority of children will feel a great sense of pride in their project work. Certainly they will be stimulated by the feeling that each aspect of the work in which they are involved is a contributory part of the whole study. For any one piece of work to be below standard affects the quality of the total presentation. If, by our example, they see the importance that we attach to written work, careful trimming of pictures, thoughtful display of models, then the project will be a very worthwhile experience for all of them

BIBLIOGRAPHY

Ash, B. & Rapapone, B.: *Creative Work in the Junior School*
(Methuen).

Bates, E. & Bartlett, P.: *Impetus to Integrated Studies* (Ginn).

Black Papers, One, Two & Three (primary sections) edited by
Cox, C. B. & Dyson, A. E. (Critical Quarterly).

Brown, M. & Precious, N.: *The Integrated Day in the Primary School*
(Ward Lock).

Ferguson, Sheila: *Projects in History* (Batsford).

Freenan, J.: *Team Teaching in Britain* (Ward Lock).

Hammersly, A. *et al.*: *Approaches to Environment Studies*
(Blandford).

Hilton, A. C. & D. A.: *Projects in Biology* (Batsford).

Hoare, Robert: *Topic Work with Books* (Geoffrey Chapman).

Holt, John: *How Children Learn* (Pitman).

Kent, Graeme: *Projects in the Primary School* (Batsford).

Layton, E. & White, J. B.: *The School Looks Around* (Longman).

Pluckrose, Henry: *Creative Themes* (Evans Brothers).

Rance, Peter: *Record Keeping in the Progressive Primary School*
(Ward Lock).

Shaplin, S. T. & Olds, H. F.: *Team Teaching* (Harper & Row).

Summerfield, Geoffrey: *Topics in English* (Batsford).

Walton, Jack: *The Integrated Day in Theory and Practice* (Ward Lock).

2. A PLAN FOR THE PROJECT

Plate 2 *Small groups of between three and eight children can be invited to carry out assignments within the project.*

We are particularly concerned in this book with the type of project which involves everyone in the class. However, many of the points discussed will apply equally to those individual studies chosen by the children.

The choice of project is a matter of importance, and what is soon apparent is that almost anything can be adopted for study. The main criteria for selection are that there should be sufficient opportunities for work for a whole class over a prescribed period of time; that the subject matter will be of interest to the class; that the teacher feels an enthusiasm for the theme, because without this, it is unlikely to last for very long or produce many worthwhile results. This does not necessarily mean that the initial idea needs to come from the teacher, but where it does not, it must be one which excites her imagination.

Where this method of working is within the regular pattern of learning in school, the children will be curious at the end of one project to know what the next one will be. In conversation with a small group, or in a full class discussion, the teacher can invite suggestions for future work. In such a situation a dominant teacher can, in magician's parlance, 'force a card', but if the democratic principle is fully at work, the ideas will come from the children. These can be listed on the blackboard, the teacher grouping them and adding lines of contact between them, as suggestions are volunteered.

In the course of the discussion, two or three main ideas are likely to emerge, and gather to them support from groups within the class. A vote can always be taken if one of the factions does not wish to concede defeat. It may be necessary for the teacher to exercise some prerogative when an inappropriate suggestion is made. For instance, the choice of a project on the 'Seashore' might be unsuitable because the chances of fine weather for fieldwork might be poor; it would be unwise to follow one history-biased theme with another in the next term. The class (or many of them, where there has been a reorganisation) may have recently carried out a project on the same or a closely related theme. The teacher may be particularly attracted towards one of the suggestions, and so may select that one, but a promise can always be made – and kept – that the other theme be adopted later in the school year.

Often during the classroom discussion, the skilful and imaginative teacher can suggest a suitable 'umbrella' title under which a great diversity of interests and suggestions can be gathered. For example, when the following list of ideas was put forward by a class: football, TV, films, dancing, puppets, acting, motor cars and costume, the project 'Entertainment' was born, and everyone was satisfied. By making the project cover the study of a country or continent, a large cross-section of interest is possible. By the adoption of this broad look at a region, a comprehensive study is clearly possible.

The spectacular event, whether it be a single-handed voyage around the world by boat, or a journey to the moon in a more sophisticated craft, presents the teacher with a situation which can turn into a stimulating project. Such occasions are well reported in newspapers and magazines, and on television. This is most valuable because the usual resources to encourage learning may not be present. Compare this with the situation when the hardy annuals – 'What We Drink' or 'Transport' – are chosen. Here the problem today is one of selection and discrimination when there is so much information available in various media.

The approach of some regular international event such as the Olympic Games is accompanied by a build-up of publicity. Since interest is already aroused for many of the children, they are likely to be very receptive to the suggestion that the sporting occasion forms the core of their study. Links with Ancient and Modern Greece, and the host country, can extend the interest of the theme. In this particular project there is almost the unique opportunity to integrate physical activities, and a considerable amount of mathematics.

Often in the classroom an interest is sparked off for one or two children who have read something, or been asked to do a piece of work. The teacher becomes involved in the follow-up work and recognises it as a situation which can develop into a class theme.

Many of the projects carried out in school are those which are teacher-inspired. They are on themes of fundamental interest to most people including teachers and they enjoy therefore the merit of previous consideration. Before the subject is introduced to the class, the teacher has taken time to think around the subject, build up her own background knowledge and enthusiasm, and plan the particular approach she would like to adopt.

The germ of the idea may be born a long time before the actual project takes place – a year or even longer. For instance, a teacher on holiday in Wales travelled across the Pont Cysyllte Aqueduct which spans the River Dee. Eighteen months later this blossomed forth as a remarkably successful project on canals and waterways, already mentioned. Between the inspiration and the realisation, there was a great deal of preparation, which included the assembly of a variety of aids, a lot of reading, preparation of assignment cards and planning of a three-day field exercise.

An important event such as the 900th anniversary of the Battle of Hastings was well heralded, and for this, the teacher was able to undertake a similar careful programme of planning which included a comprehensive reading about the events leading up to the invasion, and the subsequent effect of the Norman victory. Such anniversaries occur with remarkable frequency, and by early preparation a well-planned project can be carried out simultaneously with the national or local celebrations.

When deciding to adopt a theme, the teacher will bear in mind the age range, ability and experience of the children so that the whole exercise is conducted at the right level. While it is important never to underestimate the ability of young children to become enthusiastic and knowledgeable about a subject, it may be necessary to avoid a subject obviously more suited to older children. If there are too many elements in a project which are unsuitable, it is better to postpone it until a more appropriate group is available to work on it. The ideas and information continue to accumulate, and once the teacher has lodged an idea in her head the scheme will continue to grow, and so be that much better when used.

The length of time a project is planned to run is obviously very important. The programme can be as short as a fortnight, and this time may be appropriate to very young children or where the subject matter may be an important happening like the 1969 Investiture of the Prince of Wales. Quite young children are capable of sustaining an interest for a longer period of time than this, but certainly older pupils, provided they are given the right stimulus and direction, can work on a theme for a whole term. If this unit of time is adopted, it is advisable to introduce a new aspect after the half-term break. Thus in making a study of North Wales, the main emphasis in the first place might be agriculture with particular reference to sheep farming, while after a half-term break the quarrying for stone and slate could provide the main feature for study.

Sometimes a radio or television series can be used to provide stimulus and information for the project. Some of the series are divided into small units, but others, such as 'Man' on radio and 'A Year's Journey' on BBC TV, run for twelve months. Occasionally such prolonged series can be 'suicidal' in that there is often so much follow-up work that some classes have to miss out some programmes, or abandon the listening or viewing and complete the study without it.

One of the writers adopted a number of annual studies with upper junior classes. Each of the themes was closely related to the seasonal cycle, and by taking the project over a year, direct observations were possible throughout so that the study within the classroom could be directly related to changes outside.

Each of the studies on farming, fishing and forestry ran alongside the syllabus in a formal school, and the additional time required for such large subjects was available by making such extended studies. At the end of each half-term, there was a small presentation, which provided the necessary climax needed when part of a study had been completed.

At the end of each year of work there was a full exhibition. Certainly after a study of this length, the children knew and understood a great deal! Details of the work on 'Agriculture' were given at a joint conference of teachers and farmers, and one countryman, on hearing the length of time the children had been working on the project, remarked, 'Poor devils.' Contrast this with the comment from one of the children – 'My mum says I'm farming-mad.'

One can say with some certainty that, providing the topic is made exciting enough for them, the majority of children will be interested. Obviously this enthusiasm will fluctuate with different people at different times. But once the class has been stimulated, it is very hard for any member to resist the infectious enthusiasm of a group hard at work. One of the most testing features for any teacher working in this way is the way in which the less able, the difficult and the unconfident child is persuaded to become involved, and make a contribution to the work.

Where there is a lack of discipline within the classroom, the children may not be ready to benefit from working in this way, and a teacher would in these circumstances be unwise to embark on such a scheme. It is obviously an advantage for the new teacher to come into a school and take over a class already accustomed to carrying out projects, but she needs to establish her attitude at the beginning to such matters as standards of work, noise level, and other aspects of classroom dynamics.

At this point a notebook or file should be brought into use, and in it details of the organisation can be set out. A page can be given over to jottings of the various aspects of the project as they occur during the preliminary thinking. At this stage, the degree of importance, order of presentation, and bias of the ideas or ways in which they can be used are not matters of great concern. If we take 'Fire' as an example, we might make the following notes . . . 1666, Pepys, Evelyn, 1940 Blitz, Fire Brigade, Fire the Master, Forest Fire, Prairie Fire, Fire Down Below, Fire Prevention, Insurance, Nero, Fire Balloons, Fireships, Beacons, Firearms, Fire the Servant, Making Fire, Matches, Baking, Heating, Cooking, Lighting, Fuels, Engines, Bricks, Pottery, Glass, Ores, Fireworks,

Guy Fawkes, Bonfires, Handel's Fireworks Suite, Ritual Fire Dance, Firebird Suite, Prometheus, Shadrach, Meshach and Abednego, Fireflies, Salamanders, Phoenix, Fireplaces . . . How many more 'thoughts' could you add to this list ? Now try a different theme, 'Water' for instance, and compare the list and developments with one of the projects on this theme in Part II.

By mentioning the theme to colleagues and other friends outside school, the teacher will probably find that another page for the further suggestions is required.

Now, it is necessary to provide a framework, to group certain closely related features together. Some of the ideas will fall into traditional subject headings, while others defy any such inclusion in a category. If we take 'Mountains' as another example we can see how this sorting procedure develops.

Geography
Mountain forms
Glaciers

History
Hannibal
Famous climbs

Literature
The ascent of Everest
The first ascent of the
Matterhorn

Human activities
Sheep farming
Forestry
Climbing
Winter sports

Religious instruction
Moses
Elijah

Art
Swiss landscapes
Mountains of the Moon

P.E.
Rope and apparatus
climbing
Wall climbing for older
pupils
Expeditions for hill
walking
Dry-skiing
Survival training

Drama
Hall of the Mountain King
The rescue

Craft
Imaginative
mountainscapes
Contour modelling

Writing
Alone on the mountain
Avalanche

Natural history
Eagle
Wild cat

Excursions
School journey to
N. Wales; Scotland
Winter sports –
Switzerland

Each subject area needs a section in the planning file, and within it every idea needs some evaluation on how it can be used. Each one needs classification as to its potential for class, group or individual use.

A film chosen for use within the topic, and the follow-up discussion, would be a class exercise, although certain other follow-up work from it might be handed over to groups; a story selected because of its close links with the topic would probably be heard by all the class; a lesson on the use of the compass prior to a field trip would be required by every child in the class.

Group work ideas are assessed as to their value in stimulating and employing some half-a-dozen people under a democratically chosen leader. The important feature of all group work is that it is a study in depth by a team whose final aim is to bring all their findings together and in some way communicate them to others. The varied ways in which this can be done are given in a later chapter.

For much of the project time, children will be working individually, discovering facts and figures for themselves and forming impressions concerning particular aspects of the work. To help the children to do this research systematically, workcards are prepared for every resource that is available. Examples of these are given in the section on 'Resources for Learning Inside the School'.

In the file, the week-by-week activities need to be planned, including the use of various audio-visual aids, excursions and the date of project presentation. This programme will provide a solid framework around which the project can be built.

There needs to be great flexibility in the scheme, so that new opportunities can be taken, and time taken to develop particular aspects which have so gained the attention and effort of either individuals, groups or the class, that extended time needs to be allowed for adequate study. Indeed, it is a poor plan that admits of no alteration or improvement. Fresh ideas and facilities are

Project title _____ _____

Class or group _____ Average age _____

Year _____ Term _____

Intended duration _____

 Brief description of project

Particular aspects to be covered

Details of resources to be used within the school

Any special requirements (audio-visual aid material, books,
   visiting speakers, space, etc.)

Excursions

Form of final presentation _____

                  Class teacher _____

(Appraisal of the project, and details of particular contributions
by children, to be written overleaf)

always coming to one's notice, especially when one's whole concentration is upon a single theme. What might appear to the outside observer as luck is usually no more than opportunity allied to planning. In this same context, one can also say that discovery favours the well-prepared mind, and that the class will also be finding unexpected material which can be turned to good use within the classroom.

A summary plan of the project should be offered to the head teacher for comment. This is particularly important where the method is new in that school, and where some different form of activity is being proposed.

Opposite is a form the summary can take.

Alternatively, the teacher may prefer to develop a flow diagram of the project, which will give an indication of the scope, sequence of the theme and the interconnection between various elements. If the teacher chooses a particular colour for her flow-chart ideas and adds those from the children in a different colour, both will see how the project is growing and moving in particular directions. The display of such a chart in the 'workshop' should pay dividends in terms of worker-management co-operation. Overleaf an example of a chart is given for a topic on 'Animals'.

How to begin work is the next matter to consider, and on the introduction may well depend the fate of the project. The initial arousing of interest is of paramount importance and needs to be thought out carefully. Unless the class are completely blasé, the very mention of a new topic should make them sit up and take notice. However, since we need to sustain this curiosity for a long time, the method employed to launch the topic should be stimulating and different from other beginnings which have been tried.

Here are some ideas which have been used.

1. A straightforward statement about the project, giving a general account of the work to be carried out, mentioning a number of

A plan for an animal project

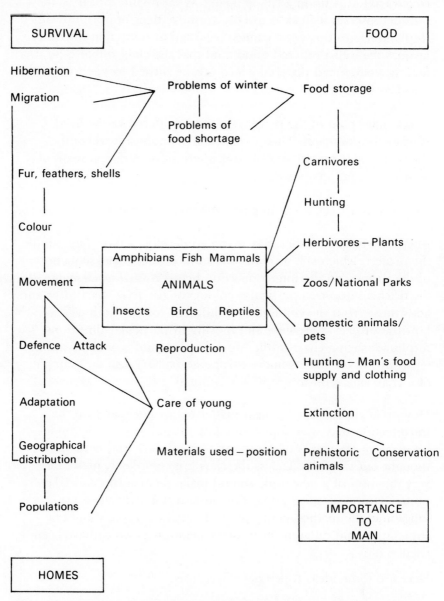

Music, poetry, stories, writing, drama, movement, art and craft are some of the activities that can be developed within this project.

the aspects to be covered, with just sufficient details to whet the appetite. If one can get the 'oohs' and 'aahs' of pleasurable anticipation, then the signs are favourable for a successful project!

2. A conversation with the children to produce two lists. One which shows all the things which are known about the subject, and the other which will give details of everything which is unknown. As the project proceeds, the aspects dealt with can be transferred from the second column to the first.

3. Still too often one hears of schools where a single notebook is issued to the children who have to write the geography notes (probably from the blackboard) at the front and the history notes at the back – having turned the book upside down and reversed it. Do try to issue a notebook or a file and folder to be used for the work of the project – the title of which has been stencilled on the front.

4. A series of attractive pictures about the project, with short captions, can be displayed in the classroom. For example, 'The Story of Lumberjacking in Canada'.

5. The showing of a film giving a general account of the theme of the project – the story of a particular river.

6. The first transmission of a TV or radio series which will be used to introduce the main theme.

7. The reading of the opening chapter of a story – or an exciting incident from a tale. For example, Cynthia Harnett's *The Load of Unicorn* for a topic on 'Printing' or 'Communications'.

8. An invitation extended to an authority on the subject. A teacher who has been on exchange in that country could introduce with film, slides, tape recordings, 'Life in New Zealand'. A postman, in uniform, can be invited to meet the class and answer questions about his work. Such an introduction would be appropriate for a Post Office project, or 'People Who Serve Us'.

9. An invitation to a drama group, from another school, or an adult amateur or semi-professional group, to give a performance on the subject of the project, for example, 'The Story of the Thames', told as a series of dramatic episodes to initiate a project on the river; a re-creation of a medieval

feast, in an appropriate outside location, to introduce a topic on the Middle Ages.

10. A visit, after a short introduction, so that the class capture the feel of the place. For instance, an excursion to an abbey which is 'alive' today as an introduction to a project on the monasteries. A visit to the ruins of an abbey priory would be more appropriate later in the project.

After any introduction, the class will wish to ask questions, offer suggestions, promise to bring things from home and so on. Such excited reaction should be regarded as normal. It might be argued that some projects have foundered because there was an over-stimulus at the beginning followed by a quick run-down of enthusiasm. The important thing is to be able to control this group of children who are at this moment in time anxious to get on with the job.

There will be noise and bustle as the group swings into action. Providing the required materials are to hand, the majority will be able to make their preliminary moves in the first assignment. There will be some indecision on the part of a few children; there may be what you feel is excessive noise from others. So it may be necessary after just a few minutes to call the class to order – a very useful test of the response to a teacher. The aims of such a signal are to remind everyone that he has a particular task to do, and that some of the excited conversation needs moderating. A certain level of work-noise is necessary. Children seem to thrive on it, although some teachers find it rather wearing. Indeed, in the organisation of a project, consideration needs to be given to the siting of certain activities because of their distracting but inevitable noise. Woodwork and music-making come within this category, and extensions from the classroom need to be looked for, so that some activities can be out of earshot. An unused classroom, a corridor, a cloakroom, a stage in a hall, a medical waiting room and the playground are all possibilities. Another solution, where the school does not have any such extra features, is to limit some activities to particular parts of the day and note when some rooms are vacated by classes at the swimming pool or in the hall. Or put up with it – if you

want to have a full range of creative activities associated with
the project!

The role of the teacher in the project is a difficult one. Apart from
a great deal of preparation before and during the study, the work
in the classroom is very demanding. It is not a desk-bound position
but rather a busy itinerant one. Whatever method of working is
planned, the teacher needs to move around from individual to
individual, and group to group, encouraging effort. This requires
a positive approach. It is not enough merely to pat a few heads
and mutter 'well done' to each and every one. Each piece of work
must be looked at carefully, and while in many cases commenting
on good features, critical discussion must be entered into,
suggestions made and so on. Children need help in deciding on
the method of presentation; they want advice on how best to
mount their pictures and written material; they need to be shown
new and different techniques in art and craft.

A record book needs to be kept, reporting on the progress of the
project, and the various contributions that individuals and groups
are making to the work. A summary of the workcards successfully
completed is important to keep. Later a summary of each child's
reaction to and contribution towards the success of the project
should be transferred to the school academic record.

It would be little short of tragedy to even contemplate the
foreclosing of a project. An inexperienced teacher embarking on
such a method of working would be well advised to start on a
project of quite modest proportions, and certainly one should
always choose a subject and consider it in terms of one's ability
to control it. Certainly children new to this method of working
often need to be brought slowly towards accepting and utilising the
unaccustomed freedom. Going in at the deep end has not always
produced the best swimmers and so with teachers attempting the
project method of working.

Doubts may be felt about the progress of a project. Who does not
entertain such doubts from time to time about the success of their

work ? A cooling-off period is quite useful on such occasions, when for a few days formal or different work is given a larger share of time. A discussion with the head or another sympathetic colleague can be as useful as a self-analytical look at the situation. Merely to discuss the problem often provides the solution. A new direction may be required and perhaps part of the project postponed or abandoned, and some heed taken of Wellington's advice when he commented that he learned more from his defeats than his victories! Looked at from that point of view, it is unlikely that the same errors will be repeated.

Whatever has been achieved in a project, and it may only be a little, it is important for the morale of the class (including the teacher) that all the work is brought together in the form of an exhibition. Often the display of work may act as the spur for a lethargic class, or to bring to life a not very imaginative project.

Scope and sequence diagram of a project

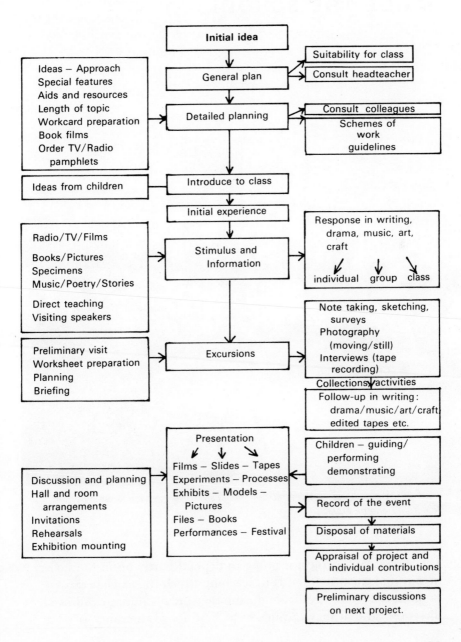

Initial idea

General plan
- Suitability for class
- Consult headteacher

Ideas — Approach
Special features
Aids and resources
Length of topic
Workcard preparation
Book films
Order TV/Radio
pamphlets

Detailed planning
- Consult colleagues
- Schemes of work guidelines

Ideas from children

Introduce to class

Initial experience

Radio/TV/Films

Books/Pictures
Specimens
Music/Poetry/Stories

Direct teaching
Visiting speakers

Stimulus and Information

Response in writing, drama, music, art, craft
- individual
- group
- class

Preliminary visit
Worksheet preparation
Planning
Briefing

Excursions

Note taking, sketching, surveys
Photography (moving/still)
Interviews (tape recording)
Collections/activities

Follow-up in writing: drama/music/art/craft, edited tapes etc.

Presentation
Films — Slides — Tapes
Experiments — Processes
Exhibits — Models —
Pictures
Files — Books
Performances — Festival

Children — guiding/performing demonstrating

Discussion and planning
Hall and room arrangements
Invitations
Rehearsals
Exhibition mounting

Record of the event

Disposal of materials

Appraisal of project and individual contributions

Preliminary discussions on next project.

3. RESOURCES FOR LEARNING INSIDE THE SCHOOL

Plate 3 *The setting up of a central, comprehensive resource area is an important feature for a large project.*

The success of a project is going to depend partly upon the variety, quality and quantity of aids to learning which the teacher can organize and make available during the study. Children will need direction, so that they can make the best use of the range of resources. The amount of help they will need will depend upon their age and experience. How effective the learning is, through the use of the aids, will be the great test for the teacher.

Books occupy a unique position in schools because of sheer numbers, and because they must stand as the main source of information and inspiration. Since the project method requires a wide range of reference and other books, the needs of a school are often best served by the creation of a central library. For the period of each study, block loans of books relevant to the subject matter can be arranged. Some authorities have a large loan collection of books which can be used and returned afterwards. Some public libraries will also co-operate with loans of books while a particular project is in progress. The fact that one can dispose of books no longer required when the project is complete is important for a school where bookshelf space is at a premium. Encyclopaedias are often in short supply in schools, and in great demand, and it is better to leave those sets in the central collection for everyone's use. It is obviously an advantage for each teacher to know of other current topics, so that books and aids can be shared amicably where there is an overlap of interest. In some such situations a form of co-operative teaching may be possible. Certainly an exchange of ideas would be profitable, and where specialised knowledge and skills are involved, some kind of collaboration could be envisaged. Where a project has been carried out by a colleague some time in the past, her experience can be drawn upon, and advice sought on sources to use. Many teachers who attend in-service courses are finding such discussion and swopping of ideas immensely helpful.

Class textbooks have a special place within a project. Although a full set is unlikely to be needed at any one time in the classroom, there are many occasions when a few copies from several sets are invaluable. For instance, in a topic on homes or costume several copies from a course series, chronologically arranged, could form a basis for the whole study.

The criterion, when choosing any books for the project, should be the quality of the information. This should be reliably and

attractively presented with plentiful accurate supporting illustrations.
An index is desirable, but if this is lacking, then chapter and
paragraph headings should be present.

For much of the project, the children will be working individually,
discovering for themselves facts, figures and impressions of and about
the subject. To help them to work systematically, in using books
and other aids, sets of workcards are required. For a class of forty
children, at least sixty cards will be needed. They should be designed
not only to suit a particular age group, but to accommodate slow
and fast workers, gifted and less able children. Most projects will
have a number of aspects, and as these are introduced, new sources
should be introduced along with workcards to make their use more
effective (see Appendix 1).

The preparation of workcards demands a great deal of effort and
skill from the teacher. Not only must she have a full knowledge of
all the books and other resources to be used, but the teacher needs
to be able to phrase questions to make the child think out the
answers. This is necessary so that a systematic process of learning is
achieved. The cards may be numbered or lettered and succinctly
titled. A system of colour coding can be adopted to suit a particular
way of working, or to introduce different aspects of the topic to
children. Colour cards can be adopted, or a series of coloured
transparent plastic wallets (e.g. as available from Philip and Tacey
Ltd, Fulham, SW6). This wallet ensures that the card stays in mint
condition. The alternative, when using coloured card, is to cover
with a contact adhesive sheet as used for library books.

For example, blue cards might cover the whole topic - and
every child would be expected to work through these – alone
or with a partner.
Yellow – simplest cards – only for the less able readers.
Red – more advanced cards.
Green – very advanced and only the most able would be able
to use these. They would require sustained work for one week
or even longer.

Or a system might be adopted where a variety of aids was in use.

Blue - picture material
Green – simple comprehension type of card using books.
Yellow – cards require use of index and contents page.
Red – requiring use of other aids – tapes, loops, slides, etc.

The success of the venture will hinge upon the organisation of the classroom work. There needs to be a resource area within the room, where books and workcards are displayed. Monitors can be delegated to keep this section of the room in good order at regular intervals, so that available material can be found immediately.

Records need to be kept of workcards successfully completed. Once again the teacher will need to look frequently at the children's files, work folders or notebooks, and discuss with them not only short-comings but further extensions of the work.

We have come to the conclusion that children who are average or below average need a great deal of structuring, so that by practice and progression they learn how to learn successfully. When the teacher becomes more experienced, and the children more able to master the various techniques of classroom research, then the work proposed can be much more open-ended. General guidelines are all that need to be provided for the most able children. Various types of stimulus cards can be provided which will allow, and in fact, encourage, the child to move in a number of directions, and exercise a great deal of personal choice in the form his response might take. If the right enthusiasms have been engendered, many, if not all, children will wish to pursue their own researches at home. In some homes, where there is good parental support, this kind of extra-curricular activity knows no bounds, extending to museum visits, purchase of resource material, production of models and so on. Examples of the Stimulus Cards are given in Appendix 2 at the end of the book.

The books available for the project should include story material because the project should not be considered in terms of a number of facts to be assimilated. The mind and imagination need feeding too. More and more authors are writing stories for young children. Such books can be used as serial reading for the duration of the project. Extracts from others can be used to provide background information in a very palatable form. Thus readings from *Elephant Bill* by J. H. Williams and *The House of Sixty Fathers* by Meindert De Jong would be useful during a study of SE Asia.

Newspapers, magazines, colour supplements and children's illustrated educational journals frequently include information and illustrations which would be useful to the class. These will frequently be brought in by children who have been stimulated by some aspect of the project. They can be used in personal files or to make up display material. Once again, some care, and time, need to be given to the making and mounting of these aids, with suitable captions, if they are to compel the attention of the class.

There are many commercially produced charts, some free and others at nominal cost. Occasionally in an effort to give value for money, too much data are given, and so it is better to be able to preview charts before offering them to the class.

A number of organisations have set up educational departments within their public relations sector to meet the needs of schools enquiring about their products and services. Often a variety of aids is offered, some free and others at small cost. Sometimes sets of pamphlets are issued for use by pupils, and many of these have been imaginatively produced. Children should be encouraged to write for information, but it is important to check such letters not only for legibility but for courtesy and relevance. The use of the school's headed notepaper is sometimes required by firms, and this should encourage the children to produce a satisfactory letter. A note of thanks from the class for such help received is a gesture likely to be appreciated.

Reproductions of works of art, sets of photographs, postcards of scenic views or museum exhibits, pictures from the *National Geographic Magazine*, the *Geographical Magazine*, *History Today*, *Child*

Education, are examples of other material which is valuable for the teacher to collect, and use at appropriate times.

Many museums and libraries provide, at reasonable cost, photostat copies of archive material. The Jackdaw series (published by Jonathan Cape) has made an important contribution to this kind of aid by their facsimile documents issued in wallets, and older juniors are able to gain much from these studies of events and persons of the past. Some universities, e.g. Newcastle and Sheffield, have produced similar material which has local interest as well as national appeal.

A growing museum service, especially valuable in areas remote from the great national collections, is the loan service of exhibits to schools. In recent years the British Museum has reproduced some of their valuable items, and schools may wish to purchase such articles for their own collections. Provided that such storage and display space is available, there is much to be said for collecting samples of rocks, soils, fossils, pieces of pottery and artefacts, for use in illustrating certain aspects of future projects. In the same way, other aids made for one study can be usefully stored to provide the raw material for another later project.

Maps have an important part to play in many topics, both those of geographic and historical nature. In the latter case photostat copies can be obtained from county archive sources. Supplies of the Ordnance Survey sheets, Dark Ages, Roman Britain and Monastic Britain can be purchased through a bookseller. For local geographical studies the $2\frac{1}{2}$ inches to 1 mile and 6 inches to 1 mile scale versions are useful ones to purchase. The aerial photograph offers an unusual and valuable viewpoint not only of geographical features but also of places of historical interest. Oblique shots as well as vertical photographs can be obtained.

The teacher with photographic interests may wish to make a collection of coloured slides for use during topics. She may be able to borrow transparencies taken by friends. Some organisations make sets of slides available, and the teacher can make a selection for use in class. Similarly museums and other places visited by the public produce some excellent slides at reasonable prices. Often a teacher will prefer to cut up a purchased filmstrip and put the shots into frames so that a personal arrangement can be made. It is not necessary for such aids to be used by all the class at one time. The slide projector or a hand viewer can be used by an individual or small group who have been invited to carry out some workcard questions based on transparencies.

The loop projector is admirably suited to small group use, and an increasing number of cassettes are being produced by commercial firms. Previewing of these is important before purchase. A number of teachers, often working at centres, have begun to produce their own loops for only a few pence more than the initial cost of the movie film. Such teachers also make films for more conventional use in the classroom, and with careful editing and commentary, spoken live or tape-recorded, the use of these has a special personal appeal, like the home-produced chart. Since there are standard 8 mm and super 8 mm films, cameras and projectors, a check on the school equipment needs to be made before going into production. (There are some dual-gauge projectors available, and perhaps the purchase of one of these is the ideal solution.)

There is now available a large number of 16 mm educational films of high quality, and the teacher can include a series of these in the project because of the information and stimulus that they will provide. A preview of the film, as well as a study of the printed synopsis of the film, should be made.

Some authorities maintain their own film libraries while others have a favourable booking arrangement with the Educational Foundation for Visual Aids. In addition there are large numbers of sponsored films available free or for a small handling charge from many organisations. Educational television on the national network or in regional closed-circuit systems, and schools radio programmes, can be used to provide the inspiration and information core for a project. Annual and termly programmes are issued by the various organisations which give general details of transmissions, while teachers' notes and pupils' pamphlets give more information. Whole series, short units or even a single broadcast can be taken in the classroom. In the case of radio, it may be found more convenient to tape-record broadcasts. This can be used at a later date, and the tape can then take its place in the school resource centre for use later. Details will need to be recorded on the tape box. The day is not far distant when video tape-recording will be a regular feature. Incidentally tape-recordings can be kept until the end of the school year without violation of copyright. Broadcasts made out of school hours can often be used in this way, and if the tape-recording of these is not possible, pupils can be advised to listen at the appropriate time, or view, if it is a TV programme which is being recommended.

Schools may well have an extensive collection of records of music for appreciation, or use in drama or movement work. There are now many recordings of poetry, ballads, stories, plays, sound effects, archive material, etc., both on record and tape, and these can be purchased or borrowed from local authority libraries.

An exchange of letters between schools can be of mutual interest to both parties where the theme is common to both. Such links depend upon teachers' personal contacts, but local authority education officers can sometimes help. An advertisement placed in one of the educational journals will often produce results. Where a class link has been made, the exchange of letters between teachers will also be of great value. Another form of exchange can be of taped talks by the children and where possible other sound effects can be added to enliven the recording. While such tapes are of great interest to the class which makes them, it is important that they are carefully and interestingly made, especially where they may be going overseas where English may not be the first language.

During a project it is often possible to engage the attention of an expert who could be persuaded to link with the class through letters, tape-recordings and personal visits. As well as straightforward letters and reports, the introduction of a question and answer service is also of value.

The actual visit to a class by an expert is an important occasion, and some thought needs to be given on how to make this a valuable educational experience. If possible some indication of the present knowledge of the class in the subject matter needs to be given, as well as the size and age group of the children concerned. The visitor should be encouraged to bring things to show, and handle if possible. He may have a set of transparencies, which are always valuable to focus attention. Some indication should be given of the length of time you wish the visitor to have, and where there are signs that he is about to dry up, some appropriate questions should be asked or invited to get him under way again.

Foreign travel, often to unusual places, is so common today that people (e.g. parents) with such experience can often be persuaded to come into school and talk about their visits. Once again some tactful help may be necessary if such an occasion is going to be fruitful.

There are some organisations which specialise in providing experienced speakers, e.g. the Commonwealth Institute, and few problems should arise with these travellers.

It is obvious that not all these aids can or should be employed within any single project, but by bringing some of them into use, new and valuable dimensions can be given to a project.

There are some important points which should increase the effective use of aids. Working in such a way does not mean that books and equipment do not require looking after. But fair wear and tear must be expected, if maximum use is going to be made of all the available resources. No child should be permitted to maltreat any piece of equipment or other school property. An early example may need to be made of anyone who infringes this rule. A short period of time will be needed at the end of each day to see that the room is returned to some kind or order, and this is everyone's responsibility. The keeping tidy of certain areas of the room can be the task of a number of children in the class and there is usually no shortage of volunteers who will perform such jobs.

If possible all books should have some plastic covering either on the dustjacket or boards. This keeps them in mint condition for much longer, and therefore attractive to handle and use. Small tears, which do arise, should be reported immediately and repaired (or the books withdrawn until time allows the repair to be done). Charts and other picture material should only be used if in good condition. Storage in cardboard tubes in a special area of the stockroom is worth while, and corners and holes strengthened with linen washers or cellulose tape. A damaged chart can sometimes be cut and re-made. The careful hanging of charts will set a good example to the class, and a regular check should be made to see if any pins or staples have become dislodged during the day. Frequent changes of all displayed material should be made before they seem to become part of the wall. Nothing is likely to breed apathy quicker in a class than a wall which has been unchanged for more than a fortnight.

The projectors and tape-recorders should be got ready before they are required, e.g. at playtime, and checked to see they are in serviceable condition. The threading up of a film (by a colleague if necessary) does take a few minutes, and if this is done and the film inched through, such aids become as easy to use as a piece of chalk. It is as well to check early with visiting speakers what equipment they require. It is irritating to find that you have the filmstrip carrier on the projector when slides are being used or that the tape-recorder is a two-track machine playing at $3\frac{3}{4}$ i.p.s. when a four-track machine is needed with a speed of $7\frac{1}{2}$ i.p.s.

The tape-recording of a broadcast is sometimes overlooked if the teacher takes it on herself to remember. Such a job can safely be left to a child to do, once the procedure has been explained to him. For live broadcasts on the radio, a child can be delegated to check the time of transmission and switch on the programme. The volume can be reduced before the actual programme commences and the class collect together around the speaker. In the case of educational TV a five-minute period should be allowed, so that the set has time to warm up, and any adjustments made to contrast, brilliancy, line-hold, etc. Too often one hears of broadcasts being taken with the first few minutes lost because of this lack of foresight.

For electrical equipment in a school, there is usually at least one person who becomes expert at correcting small faults, and where a problem occurs he or she should be informed so that the situation can be assessed as to whether outside help is needed. Many authorities are appointing local visual-aids assistants to service the growing numbers of pieces of equipment which are now in use in schools, and these can be contacted to give early help. A supply of fuses and projector lamps should be kept in school, when such first aid is required. Most authorities lay down regular times for servicing of aids, and where a school makes regular and full use of them, then the equipment will need such attention.

Sometimes equipment is in great demand within a school. In such cases the head teacher should be able to requisition for more. Since there are regrettably some schools which do not make full use of such aids, the local adviser may well be sympathetic to such appeals. It may be necessary to time-table the use of the popular aids, and the audio-visual aids room, where this exists. Usually, this may still mean a generous portion of time in the week, but it is a safeguard to know when a tape-recorder or film projector is available for use. In the same way the hall time is often at a premium and some allotment of periods is required, but usually colleagues are flexible enough to accommodate a request for additional use where the situation demands it.

SOURCES OF INFORMATION
General aids
Barker, R. E.: *Photocopying and Tape Recording of Educational Material* (The Publishers' Association, 19 Bedford Square, London WC1).

BTA, Lofthouse, Wakefield, Yorks: *British Trades Alphabet* (issued annually with a particular theme and details of a project competition).

Burston, W. H. & Green, C. W., Eds.: *Handbook for History Teachers* (Methuen).

Cutforth, J. A. & Battersby, S. H.: *Children and Books* (Blackwell).

Department of Education and Science: *The Use of Books: Pamphlet 45* (HMSO).

Hedley, P., Ed.: *The Treasure Chest for Teachers* (Schoolmaster Publishing Co).

Historical Association, 59A Kennington Park Road, London SE11: *Guide to Sources of Illustrative Material for Use in the Teaching of History* and *Recent Historical Fiction for Secondary School Children.*

Institute of Education, University of Southampton: *Teaching Geography, History and Related Local Studies.*

Library Association, Ridgmount Street, London WC1: *Readers' Guides.*

Long, M.: *Handbook for Geography Teachers* (Methuen).

Morris, Helen: *Where's that Poem?* (Blackwell).

National Book League, 7 Albemarle Street, London W1: *Historical Fiction, Readers' Guide No. 11; School Library Books: Non-Fiction.*

NCVAE, 33 Queen Anne Street, London W1: *Visual Education Yearbook* (also monthly magazine *Visual Education* and series of frequently revised visual-aids catalogues).

Osborne, C. H. C.: *Using Books in the Primary School* (School Library Association, 150 Southampton Row, London WC1).

Purton, Rowland: *Surrounded by Books* (ESA).

Saunders, Dennis: *Puffins for Projects* (Penguin).

Topic Records Ltd, 27 Nassington Road, London NW3: Series of leaflets, e.g. *Topics for Juniors* and *Topics in History.*

Unesco Source Book for Geography Teachers (Longman).

Correspondents

Association of Agriculture: 78 Buckingham Gate, London SW1 (for printed letter service with British and Commonwealth farmers).

British Ship Adoption Society: HQS *Wellington*, Victoria Embankment, London SW1 (for ship correspondence).

Central Bureau for Educational Visits and Exchanges: 91 Victoria Street, London SW1.

Commonwealth Friendship Movement: 6 Broadway Mansions, Brighton Road, Worthing, Sussex.

Correspondence Scolaire Internationale: 29 Rue Dohn, Paris 5 (for French links).

English-Speaking Union: 37 Charles Street, London W1 (for USA contacts).

International Friendship League: Correspondence Bureau, 21 Wyndham Road, Birmingham 16.

Museums

School Loan Services: 33 Fitzroy Street, Fitzroy Square, London W1.

Aerial photographs

Aerofilms Ltd: 4 Albemarle Street, London W1.

Aero Pictorial Ltd: Redhill Aerodrome, Surrey.

Air Ministry: (Room 54 E) Whitehall, London SW1.

BEA: (Chief Photographer) London Airport North, Hounslow, Middx.

BOAC: (Photographic Section) Stratton House, Piccadilly, London W1.

University Curator in Aerial Photography: Selwyn College, Cambridge.

Films

Educational Foundation for Visual Aids: Brooklands, Weybridge, Surrey.

Rank Film Library: PO Box 70, Great West Road, Brentford, Middx.

Guild Sound and Vision Ltd: Wilton Crescent, Merton Park, London SW19.

4. RESOURCES FOR LEARNING OUTSIDE THE SCHOOL

Plate 4 On a visit children should be encouraged to work in small groups on assignments proposed by the teacher.

Since it should be possible to relate a project to the world outside school, if it is to have any reality, the question of organized excursions needs to be considered in the original planning. Once again a new opportunity may arise during the project, and this should be taken where possible. Thus visits might be made to a mediaeval castle, a performance of a ballet, the underground railway, the National Dairy Centre for a cooking demonstration, or an airport, all by way of illustrating some feature of a particular project. While the children will regard these occasions as the highlights of their studies, they are not merely an escape from the classroom. It could be said that in a sense the project is a long and careful preparation for an excursion. Since we would like to assume that the children are interested in their study, they are most likely to enjoy this important aspect of it and gain much from it.

It was suggested earlier that a visit could be used to stimulate interest in a new theme, but in most cases excursions will be taken near to the end of the work when the maximum knowledge has been gained and enthusiasm is at its height. In most schools outings will have to be financially self-supporting, and so it will be necessary to have the expense in mind when the programme is being planned. Where this way of working is accepted by parents, they will appreciate the importance of the outside visit, and so few difficulties should arise about payments for coach and entrance fees.

If a large amount of money is required, i.e. over 25p, then an early letter announcing the outing, its purpose and details should be sent out. The opportunity to pay by instalments is appreciated by some parents, especially where there are a number of children in the school, all engaged on work likely to include visits. Children of families in need should have their expenses covered from school voluntary funds.

Often a second or even third visit is desirable. It may be impossible to complete all the work in a single day, e.g. in visiting a large market town, different aspects of work may need to be decided upon for two separate excursions. Market Day may be chosen as one day's study, with all its related activities – tradesmen with stalls, increased bus and rail services, catering problems, etc. The other occasion would be used to look at general aspects of the town. Two visits to a farm may be necessary to observe the different seasonal activities. Where the expense of these multiple outings proves to be excessive, the school fund can be used to subsidize them, or the proceeds of a jumble sale or funfair used.

Local opportunities for visits are often overlooked by teachers. There may be a stream, which provides several features of a river in miniature; a museum which in one room features local historical finds; a craftsman who still plies his trade; a small bakery. These may be within walking distance or no more than a short journey on public transport, and because of this they are more appropriate for younger children.

Another advantage of a local journey, especially those in the open air, is that the occurrence of rain on the chosen day makes the postponement an easier proposition to accept. Since a new arrangement can easily be made, even for the next day, there is not such a keen sense of disappointment when such a decision has to be made. Everyone enjoys a fine day for fieldwork, and in one of our year-long topics, on trees, the monthy field trip to the local park could always be taken on a fine day – even in winter. There are of course certain critical times for trees, when the flowers are forming or the leaves are flushing, and a few days either way could mean that an opportunity would be missed – so at certain times the best of a poor lot of days may need to be chosen. Where something even more definite than a change in a tree occurs, e.g. the running of the highest tidal bore on the Severn, or the release of a set of racing pigeons at a local station, then you must decide on how important the event is to the class. Most people survive a soaking!

Where the group is fully committed to the excursion, it is valuable to have alternative plans when the day turns out to be disastrously wet. The London Zoo suggests an itinerary for such occasions, and part of this can be used to fit in with the particular purpose of the class visit, e.g. a 'Cat Family' or 'Animal Camouflage' theme could both be followed very easily under cover. Where a coach has been hired, there is usually no problem, uncomfortable as it is, to eat one's packed lunch inside, and with a co-operative driver the class can be taken as close as possible to the places one intends to see.

It may be possible to make some local arrangement to obtain shelter, for instance, a village hall, community centre, local school, railway station waiting room are all worth considering. Such places, while serving as a temporary refuge from the rain, can become a classroom and a base from which sallies can be made to carry out various assignments. A gratuity to the caretaker, and a responsible attitude about litter and furniture, will be appreciated.

It should go without saying that adequate clothing ought to be worn on all outings. The weather in this country is rather changeable and so preparation for rain ought to be made. Strong footwear should be worn. While encouraging children to look smart on outings, these occasions should not be used to launch the latest fashions or to wear slingbacks – and new at that – when the farm walk is the first part of the programme. It is often cooler at the coast, and always on a boat, so extra woollies should be carried. Often very casual clothes – jeans, wellington boots and an old sweater – for children and staff are quite the most sensible things to take.

But let us return to the beginning again. The success of an excursion will depend upon the planning which has gone into it, and this includes the preliminary visit by the teacher. No guidebook, letter, or even conversation with anyone who has been before, will be an adequate substitute for a personal visit in advance of the children's excursion. Funds should be available to cover the out-of-pocket expenses of the teacher making such trips, and if the local authority is not sympathetic to this principle, then the school funds should be used.

A preliminary correspondence will have made it possible for the teacher to meet anyone she is likely to see on the class visit. This early meeting will be valuable in establishing a relationship, and later, with the class, a relaxed atmosphere is likely to prevail from the beginning.

Every teacher will have a different purpose for an excursion, and what this is needs to be defined for the people who are hosts for the day. A tactful approach needs to be made, but it is important that certain matters are made quite clear. The age of the children, the extent of their knowledge in the subject, and the size of the party are all relevant factors. Often the kind of questions that children are likely to ask can be anticipated, and where facts and figures are needed the farmer or the factory manager will appreciate advance notice. Often talks contain too much technical data and statistics, and these, if unrelieved, become a bore. The more basic the information provided, the better the children will like it, and the more valuable the visit will be.

It is important that on the preliminary visit, the whole route to be followed is gone over. In this way some idea of distance to be covered can be gained (and the time doubled for a party of children!).

One should look for about half-a-dozen stopping points. The first consideration is that there is something to see at each one. It will probably be that at each place the guide and/or the teacher will wish to say something. It is useful if the adult can stand away from the party for this purpose. This is usually easier said than done, but on a farm visit, the shepherd can retire behind a gate; on a river walk, the bailiff can stand on a bridge; on a factory visit, the foreman can jump up onto a loading gantry. From such positions he can be heard and seen, and so can anything in his hands. There is nothing more irritating or understandable than the mutterings from the back of a tightly packed class not able to see. A loud voice helps out of doors, and so does a forceful personality in a speaker, in commanding the attention of the children. Your host could be someone who is terrified at the prospect before him, and would rather face a Force 6 wind off Iceland than show forty lively ten-year-olds over his trawler. Or he might be an accomplished speaker who has young children of his own. On the preliminary visit you will discover where between these two extremes your host lies.

Suggest that the explanations are kept short, and if there is to be a slightly longer introductory talk, then it should be away from noisy machinery and too many other distractions. Questions need to be included to keep everyone on their toes. However, there is a tendency for the alertness of many to be dulled when in a large group, and so it is important to get across to the host that the exercise should not be thought of as a perambulation around a forest or a factory, with stops for information to be given out. On this visit, it is important that the teacher keeps an eye open to spot other likely activities for the children to engage in.

Notes need to be taken, because the memory is unreliable when so many facts are being received. The teacher should be quite certain that all the features seen on the reconnoitring visit will be available when the class arrive; will the calves still be on the farm? will silage making have finished? A crucial question on a dairy farm visit is whether the farmer will allow forty children into his dairy at milking time? Many won't, and one needs to appreciate that any noise will affect the milk yield, to understand and accept such a refusal. Some firms are unwilling to accept children who are below a minimum age, because of the dangers of moving machinery and the ways in which switches and levers seem to invite the attention of small hands; newspaper printing works usually insist upon only older children in a visiting party.

In some museums, because of a shortage of staff, one or more galleries are closed on alternate days; the re-arrangement of exhibits may also close a gallery for a period of time. Some smaller museums have limited opening hours, and in some cases take a day's closure during the week so that they can open to the public on a Sunday. A lifeboat may have to be taken out of service for annual overhaul, and the same could apply to a lighthouse. A church or cathedral may be conducting a special service on a particular weekday, which might not be the same as the day of the preparatory visit. Such details need to be checked to avoid disappointment.

The question of the size of party needs to be considered. Usually it is too large, but it is often economically necessary to take out a whole class when a coach is being hired. Where more than one class is involved in the excursion (and there would need to be a very good case made for such a proposition) different activities need to be suggested for each group. At least two teachers are needed with each class on educational excursions. More help would improve the situation, but in many schools it is problem enough to get one additional teacher relieved of her class responsibilities, and to expect more would throw an unduly heavy burden on colleagues. Student help is available during school practice time, and in these days of increased parent-teacher co-operation some of the children's mothers may be available and, when tactfully invited, can prove to be invaluable, especially when domestic chores are involved, and being responsible for a small group in a museum gallery while another teacher is working with another party elsewhere in the same room. Wherever possible, group work should be arranged, and if the groups are as few as two, then alternative work can be planned with a changeover half-way through. Occasionally an organisation will insist upon a certain pupil-teacher ratio, e.g. Hampton Court requires one teacher to be with each fifteen pupils. When infants are involved in visits, authorities insist on greater supervision and such conditions need to be checked before proceeding far with the planning.

Where space is restricted, for example, in a small town bakery or a studio pottery, it is imperative to realise that only small parties can be accommodated. Where such a place is within easy reach of school, it is often possible to arrange to shuttle groups of children to and fro by public transport. The project teacher (for want of a better term) can take the first group into the blacksmith's shop, and after some pre-arranged interval of time, the ancillary teacher brings along the second group and returns with the first group to commence follow-up work at school. Where even smaller groups are envisaged, then it is possible to start the process during the latter half of lunchtime, while playground supervision is in force, and arrange for at least one group to be back and in school at afternoon playtime, so that once again a responsible person is looking after them. On certain occasions it is possible to transport groups by private car to some venue. Some insurance companies provide cover for teachers who convey pupils in this way. It would be as well to clear such activity both with the authority and the insurance company. While on the subject, a form of insurance ought to be taken out on any long journey. Most authorities insist upon this safeguard.

While half-a-dozen may be enough in a studio watching some pottery throwing, to make sure they don't knock over any glazed ware or touch the side of a hot kiln, there are many situations, a milk bottling plant for instance, which can accommodate a large group comfortably.

Some museums welcome children more than others. It may well be that some have had unfortunate experiences with ill-disciplined (but more likely ill-prepared) classes, and some of the attendants have an unfortunate habit of insisting that the children stay together as one group. It should be possible for older juniors and all secondary children to walk around in pairs or small groups. Where this is not encouraged by the museum authorities, the leader should take the majority of the party onto the next gallery, while the other member of staff stays with the remainder, who may be slower (or more industrious) than their companions or have been given a more difficult task. Certainly there is little to be gained from moving around in close formation either in or out of a museum, nor of course from running about wildly shouting and being a nuisance to everyone. Many museums with sound educational ideas, but possibly with some thoughts on self-defence, have devised worksheets; some of a very general nature, and others on specific topics, and designed for different age groups. Particularly interesting are the comprehensive sheets from the London Museum; the attractive worksheets from the Geffrye Museum in Shoreditch, and the inspired Nature Trails in the Natural History Museum, South Kensington. We advocate the use of worksheets, and suggest that these should be prepared for the particular class carrying out the fieldwork of a specific project. In Appendix 4, examples are given of the kind of sheet designed to meet certain situations and they may suggest guidelines for others to use when preparing their own. The provision of worksheets prevents the visit being merely one in which the party follows another person who is talking.

Since the ultimate purpose of the visit will be to bring back a report of some kind, the teacher will know what she wishes the class to find out, and so will prepare the worksheet accordingly. The questions should encourage the children to think and not simply record obvious information, although for very young children such work will need to be at a very simple level. But even for these of course the aim should be to encourage them to look and listen carefully. To bring variety into the work, such activities as counting, searching, assessing, sketching, collecting, taking rubbings, etc., should be included where possible. Simple base maps and plans should be included where relevant, and on these some information needs to be given so that the child can locate himself. Once he has done this he can be invited to record information in symbol or written form.

Enough space needs to be left beside each question so that an adequate answer can be written. Where a sketch is requested, then there ought to be somewhere to put it. A supply of spare lined and unlined paper needs to be included in the worksheet.

Each child should have a workboard. This can be made for about 10p from a piece of hardboard cut rather larger than a foolscap sheet, and a bulldog clip. The worksheets and papers can be clipped to the smooth side of the board, other papers – guide sheets, maps and postcards – can go on the other. Not only will the sheets stand up to the day's wear and tear better by using the board, but a much more legible set of observations will result. In addition children may wish to carry and use such things as I-Spy books where they closely relate to the theme, and also purchase publications especially written for them, e.g. *A Children's Guide to Norwich Cathedral*, *Let's Explore Saint Alban's Abbey*, and *What Is Stonehenge ? A Junior Guide*. These and many other guidebooks are useful for the teacher to collect and use in making her own plans, for example, the guide leaflets *The Church of St Peter the Apostle in Thanet* and *A Walk Around the Cathedral of Llandaff* would be valuable lines on which to base a visit to a church. London Passenger Transport Board issue leaflets from time to time – a random selection of titles is *Shakespeare's London*, *Nash's London*, *A Day in*

Guildford, *A Day in Epping Forest*, *Opera and Oranges* and *Windmills*.
The petroleum companies issue literature designed to encourage
the motorist to get out and about on a particular brand, and
educate himself. Esso dealt with Cornwall in their Tiger Trail No. 1
series, and Shell produced some curious and surprise items for each
county every month.

Other equipment may be needed on the excursion. Spare pencils
and duplicated sheets should be included for those who regularly
mislay them! For a visit to a pond or river – nets, sieves, collecting
jars and wellington boots will be needed; for a church visit, wax
crayons and detail paper for brass rubbing (providing permission
to rub has been requested in advance); for a woodland visit,
collecting boxes and polythene bags, measuring tapes and
compasses and so on. Identification books will be needed, and
probably much more. A list of the special items should be kept,
and the names of the volunteers who may quite happily carry them
on the outward journey but need reminding that they have to be
brought home again.

Field sketches and architectural drawings are important to introduce
into an excursion where possible, not only because this means a
more varied day, but as a way of recording they are invaluable.
Often they have advantages over a camera, because the artist can be
selective and annotate his drawing, and make it to any desired scale.
So sketching blocks should be carried on the visit. Needless to say,
cameras should be encouraged, and the children persuaded to use
them for much more than a hilarious picture of their friends eating
ice-cream. The offer of a prize for the best photograph or set of
pictures illustrating the themes of 'A Village' or 'A Castle' is
sufficient inducement. If a series of visits is being made to the same
place, to watch the progress of a new housing estate, or an
archaeological site, to see the various stages in the dig, or a piece
of derelict land which the class are clearing and adopting as a forest
plot, then a field diary would be a useful way of recording progress,
supplemented by the use of camera and portable tape-recorder –
both operated by groups of children.

Obviously not all children will be able to carry out all the activities, nor would it be desirable. Since most children will be accustomed to working in groups within the classroom situation, it should be possible for them to do without a rigid class formation outside. Various tasks need to be thought out for half-a-dozen groups, as well as any activities in which they will all engage. For young children a whole day may be exhausting, and young juniors will need a change of activity during the day if weariness and boredom are not going to set in. Certainly all the work should be pitched at the right level, so that the children will find it demanding but within their capacity and therefore satisfying. Since the occasion should be regarded as a pleasant social one, a certain degree of choice should be given as to working companions, but the point needs to be made that 'working' is the operative word. Where a teacher has had experience of a particular group of children who are rather work-shy, gravitating together, then some degree of direction will be imperative. There is no point in anyone coming along just for the ride. The pairing of the less able with an average or above average pupil is a good idea, and where groups are formed everyone can be found a job – as scribe, equipment officer or leader.

The journey itself can provide a stimulating opportunity for work. On a very long one, a stop can be arranged for refreshment where there is something of historical or geographical interest – associated as closely as possible with the theme of the project. The route itself – checked carefully with the coach company beforehand – can follow the line of a river or a road used by an advancing army centuries ago or a particular geological formation with its unique type of vegetation. Once again *I-Spy On a Rail Journey* or *On a Car Journey* can be used or a personal quest arranged by the teacher who has gone over the route beforehand. Recognition of breeds of cow and growing cereals is not impossible even at 30 m.p.h. There are some games and other activities which will do more than pass the time, and many of these are listed in *Fun on Wheels* by Dave Garroway and Courtenay Edwards (Muller) and *Games to Play in the Car* by Michael Harwood (Rapp and Whiting). A log of the journey can also be kept, and the artistic humorists in the party can be invited to prepare a series of cartoons of incidents on the way there and back. A little light relief never comes amiss, but you may feel that the choral singing of the latest pop songs might be a little undignified for a school outing!

It is as well to check the departure times, routes and destination with the coach-hire firm, on the day previous to the outing. Usually drivers are most co-operative, but where they have been inadequately briefed by their employers, problems can arise which can affect the success of the day. A road which the teacher negotiated in a minicar may be quite unsuitable for a forty-one-seat coach – so it will be as well if the route is checked with the driver before departure. We have had experience of one driver who was unable to find his way in a different part of London, causing the cancellation of part of the work, and another who took a party to Crockham Hill instead of Crockenhill with the subsequent correction affecting a whole morning's activities.

Tuesdays, Wednesdays and Thursdays have advantages as excursion days particularly, because they allow in the working week a day before for preparation, and a day after for follow-up. Mondays would mean stale bread for sandwiches, but often that is a day when the coach company can quote a cheaper rate, especially in the summer, when so much fieldwork will be envisaged. Remember, however, that the shorter days of spring and autumn often provide some of the best weather. The briefing of the class should be as close to the excursion as possible, preferably the afternoon before. The children will need to be taken through the programme. The worksheet should be issued at this time, so that the party will be able to see and hear how the day has been planned. It may be possible for one of the hosts to join the class for this session, and in the more disciplined situation, with fewer distractions in it, explain what the children will see. Alternatively the teacher may be able to show some slides or even an 8-mm film taken on the preparatory visit. Such visual aids can be used to get them to look at buildings in a critical way, looking for clues to age, style of architecture, use of materials, weathering and so on. By showing two pictures consecutively, the idea of causal relationships can be discussed, so that on the visit they will be on the alert for similar situations.

Part of the craft work might well have been the production of a model of the place to be visited, and this can be valuable because of its three-dimensional nature in giving the children some idea of the feel and shape of the land. Sometimes a commercial film or filmstrip has been made showing that region or building which is on the itinerary, and arrangements should be made to hire or purchase such an aid. A filmstrip on the *Medway River* by Educational Productions, and a film *Norwich, a Fine City* by the Norwich Union Insurance Company, are two such aids which we have used for briefing sessions.

Certain other matters will need to be brought out on this occasion. A place to have lunch will have been noted by the teacher on the preliminary visit (along with suitable toilet facilities). Some children need reminding that they are only going for one day and so will only need one meal. The time when everyone will eat should be announced, so that surreptitious eating of apples and crisps on the outward journey can be avoided. In some cases it is easier and safer for the children to purchase drinks on arrival, in their break period. Where the place being visited is far away from a refreshment stall, drink can be carried in a polythene container and dispensed in paper cups.

There is danger in many situations. If one only considered these, then no outside visit would ever take place. However, it is better to be on the alert for these. On the farm there is a lot of machinery; on the dockside there are bollards and swinging jibs; on a canal or riverside there may be a slippery path; in an ancient monument there may be dangerous masonry. A timely warning should do much to prevent accidents. In country areas, there may only be a narrow footpath or none at all, and with children intent upon some activity, and motorists unaware that a school party is around the corner, some care needs to be given to movement. Single file will be essential and facing the on-coming traffic the procedure to adopt.

There needs to be a code of behaviour clearly laid down for the party. Children need to have impressed upon them that they must respect other people's property and privacy. There is a way of behaving inside a church and a museum, which should be quite obvious to everyone. There needs to be instruction on what should and what should not be collected, and the quantity of it. The teacher should make a list of all the points she intends to raise, with the final one inviting 'Any questions ?' Many of the queries are personal in nature, but often there is a fundamental matter which could affect everyone. The accompanying teacher should be at the preparatory session, so that she also knows the order of procedure. Not being quite so involved, she may be able to bring up matters of general interest, because of greater experience, familiarity with the venue, or theme.

The time of departure – especially if it is before the normal school hours – needs to be impressed upon the class. An extract register needs making out, and group lists for each of the accompanying adults. Where the visits are to crowded places, for instance, to the Zoo or Tower of London, frequent roll calls need to be taken, especially when the children are working in the free way suggested. It is not unknown for children to be left behind – without the knowledge of the teacher !

Some coach-hire firms do not carry a first-aid kit and one should be available for minor ailments. Long journeys and jerky passages through busy towns soon find out the poor travellers, and for these a polythene bucket, polythene bags, paper tissues, a sponge and a pile of newspapers are a good insurance.

This chapter may in parts have seemed unduly cautious, but problems do arise. One should always hope for the best but prepare for the worst, and the points have all been made so that the excursion will be one of the most memorable occasions of the project for the best of reasons ! It is very cheering after a day, when it rained hard and there was no cover, half-a-dozen kids were sick, someone cut their foot on the beach, another fell in the sea and was soaked, when they all turn up the following day and say it was smashing.

If the teacher has any strength left after the visit, the worksheets should be gone through to see what has been gained from the excursion. The next day these should be issued again to the children and a discussion held on the day's activities. Some special way of collating all the facts and impressions needs to be thought out beforehand.

Various suggestions on how these can be carried out and used are given in the sections on Creative Aspects of Projects and The Presentation of a Project. Certainly the excursion is going to provide the greatest stimulus of the project, and one should expect a maximum return from it if all the work which has gone into it is going to be worth while.

BIBLIOGRAPHY

Archer, J. E. & Dalton, T. H.: *Fieldwork in Geography* (Batsford).

Barnard, H. C.: *Observational Geography and Regional Study* (Le Play Society).

Beardsmore, G.: *Going Into the Country* (Phoenix).

Bennet, D. P. & Humphries, D. A.: *Introduction to Field Biology* (Arnold).

Briault, E. W. H. & Shave, D. W.: *Geography In and Out of School* (Harrap).

Bryant, M. E.: *The Museum and School* (Historical Association).

Casson, Hugh: *Museums* (National Benzole).

Chorley, R. J. & Hagget, P.: *Frontiers in Geography Teaching* (Methuen).

Coleman, A. & Maggs, K. R. A.: *Land Use Survey Handbook* (University of London, Kings College, Strand, London WC2).

Copley, Gordon: *Going Into the Past* (Phoenix).

Department of Education and Science: *Geography and Education; Schools and the Countryside* (HMSO).

Dilke, M. S.: *Field Studies in School*, Vol. 1 (Rivington).

Doncaster, Islay: *Discovering Man's Habitat* (National Froebel Foundation).

Douch, Robert: *Local History and the Teacher* (Routledge & Kegan Paul).

Finberg, H. P. R. & Skipp, V. H. T.: *Local History Objectives and Pursuit* (David and Charles).

Graham, V. E.: *Activities for Young Naturalists* (Methuen).

Hammersley, A. *et al.*: *Approaches to Environmental Studies* (Blandford).

Harrison, Molly: *Learning Out of School* (Ward Lock); *Changing Museums* (Longman).

Himus, G. W. & Sweeting, G. S.: *Elements of Field Geology* (University Tutorial Press).

Hopkins, M. F. S.: *Learning Through the Environment* (Longman).

Hoskins, W. H.: *Local History in England* (Longman).

Hutchings, G. E.: *Landscape Drawing* (Methuen).

Layton, E. & White, J. B.: *The School Looks Around* (Longman).

Nicholson, E. M.: *Science Out of Doors* (Longman).

Palmer, J.: *Going to Museums* (Phoenix).

Philips, H. & McInnes, F.: *Exploration in the Junior School* (ULP).

Pluckrose, Henry: *Let's Use the Locality* (Mills & Boon).

Sankey, John: *A Guide to Field Biology* (Longman).

Sauvain, P. A.: *A Geographical Field Study Companion* (Hulton).

Simpson, C. A.: *Making Local Surveys —An Eye for Country* (Pitman).

Trent, C.: *Exploring the Rocks* (Phoenix).

Unesco Source Book for Geography Teachers (Longman).

Waters, Derek: *Creative Work with Found Materials* (Mills & Boon).

Watson, Geoffrey: *A Junior Naturalist's Handbook* (Black).

Wheeler, K. S. & Harding, M.: *Geographical Field Work* (Blond).

White, Anne: *Visiting Museums* (Faber).

Youth Hostels Association: *Youth Hostels for Field Studies.*

Series and Annuals

Discovering Books: *The Gloucester Road, Stained Glass, English Fairs, Canals* (Shire Publications).

Discovering Series: *Rivers, Roads and Bridges, Castles* (ULP).

Finding Out About Series: *Railways, Castles, Farming* (ULP).

Get to Know Series: *Inland Waterways, Farms, Village Survey, Country Town Survey, British Railways* (Methuen).

Hamlyn All-Colour Paperbacks: *Natural History Collecting, Trains, Architecture* (Hamlyn).

Historic Houses and Castles: annual (Index Publications).

How to Explore Series: *A Town, Village* (ESA).

I-Spy Series: *At the Seaside, On the Road, Sights of London, Trees* (Dickens Press).

I-Spy Superbooks: *At the Zoo, Archaeology, On a Train Journey* (Dickens Press).

Looking and Finding Series: *On a Journey by Road, On a Railway Journey* (ESA).

Museums and Galleries: annual (Index Publications).

National Trust Publications, including the National Trust Atlas.

Observer Books: *Pond Life, Sea and Seashore, Wild Flowers* (Warne).

Puffin Picture Books: *Seashore Life, Pond Life, Churches and Cathedrals* (Penguin).

Shell Guides: *County Guides* (Faber & Faber); *Nature Book, Country Book* (Phoenix); *Country Alphabet* (Michael Joseph).

Treasures Series: *Country Treasures, Seaside Treasures* (Mills & Boon).

What Can You Find? Series: *In a Wood, Along a River Bank* (ESA).

WORKSHEETS

The questions and directions on a worksheet should be so planned that the children are encouraged to use their eyes to observe buildings and objects, and not only the labels which are attached to them. Sometimes it is a good plan to ask a question which will require an interpretation of a label, which can only be achieved by the careful examination of the specimen or picture.

Wherever possible questions should be phrased to make use of background knowledge — for instance, architectural features, breeds of sheep or species of trees.

Where the curator of a museum, the vicar of a church, or a guide on a ship of historical interest, has been invited to give a talk, he should be sent a copy of the worksheet. He may then include in his description special references to the project, without necessarily providing all the answers. This is valuable especially when the lecturette is something of a set piece — delivered to all ages, creeds and nationalities irrespectively!

One of the chief aims of the worksheet is to act as a summary of observations on which later classroom work can be based. The invitation to draw some of the answers makes even greater demands on the pupil than a written answer, because of the need to observe more carefully.

Some organisations — for instance, the National Gallery and Queen's House at Greenwich — have portable sound guides which can be hired to inform a very small group. In Trafalgar Square and the London Zoo there are fixed tape-recorders which provide short commentaries which describe what the subscriber can see. Where these aids exist in places visited, worksheet questions and suggestions could be prepared on parts of their commentaries.

Teachers with a particular interest in the use of the tape-recorder can employ this method to prepare their own sound guides to places to be visited. With an accompanying ground plan, it is possible to prepare a cassette tape to guide a small group around an abbey ruin. Questions can be interpolated. With only minimum instruction young children can learn how to stop the machine and rewind it. An even more imaginative tape can be planned, which tries to recreate the scene the children are seeing —bells, plainsong, a reading in Middle English, and some dramatisation can bring alive a visit to a medieval abbey as suggested above. See Appendix 4 for specimen worksheets.

5. THE CREATIVE ASPECTS OF PROJECTS

Plate 5 Music making is an interesting aspect to include in every project. Fortunate are the schools where a spare classroom or space can be found for this activity.

Since we are seeking the active involvement of all the children within the project, rather than a passive reception of information and ideas, there need to be many opportunities for the children to be creative. Elsewhere in the book, there are references and suggestions concerning this aspect of the work, but we felt it important that many of the ideas expressed and implied should be brought together in one chapter.

As fluency in reading develops, and vocabulary, ideas and experience expand, written expression will play an increasingly larger role in the project. Too frequently this is taken as the opportunity to limit, if not prohibit, conversation. Inevitably discussion will arise between children at work, and as the teacher moves around the room, she needs to do all she can to encourage and develop this oral work. By interjecting questions, posing additional problems, introducing some new thought, further talk between the members of the group will be stimulated. Individuals and groups working together should be encouraged to talk about their work. Any visitors coming into the room can be invited to discuss the project with individuals and groups. The very act of talking, explaining and discussing a piece of work usually clarifies it in the mind of the speaker (and we hope in the mind of the listener). The teacher needs to be particularly careful not to direct the conversation too much (and this is not as easy as it sounds). To pretend to misunderstand is one subterfuge which can encourage a child to look for another path of explanation. This should not be done too frequently in case the class come to the wrong conclusion! The questions need to be framed in such a way that 'Yes' and 'No' are almost impossible answers. The more open-ended the query can be, the greater will be the child's search for words of explanation and description.

There are plenty of opportunities for writing during a project. Factual writing will form a considerable part with answers to workcards, writing up of experiments, follow-up work after excursions, and the preparation of various kinds of letters – requests, thank-yous and so on.

Equally important is the creative writing stimulated by some project situation: the handling of some historical artefact – an antler pick in a tunnel forty feet underground in Grimes Graves in Norfolk;

the watching of a merlin swooping down on the lure at the Falconry at Newent in Gloucestershire; listening to the roar of the sea on the pebbles of Chesil Beach in Dorset; the watching of a writhing mass of crawfish in the seawater tanks at Porthleven in Cornwall; going through a lock on the Grand Union Canal.

Many situations will be less dramatic than these, and rightly so. The accidental or contrived occasions need to produce responses at different levels, unless we are to develop a group that fully expect things to be made more interesting for them, rather than having to take any trouble themselves.

Most children, especially those whose experience has hitherto been limited, will need discussion to bring words to the surface and encourage vivid forms of expression. With the very youngest children the teacher can list words and phrases which have been suggested. From these, the children can select those which meet their needs. Primarily the aim of such a collection of words evoked by an experience is to involve everyone's senses and imagination so that they can translate the visual and aural experience into words. This is one of the most difficult tasks we require of children, and so frequent opportunities should be taken to practise it.

Where possible a small group should be gathered together for such a discussion. Quite a few children are more forthcoming in a small gathering, and in any case a child opting out can quickly be noticed and encouraged to make a contribution. In the general discussion before writing, the teacher will need to work hard stimulating and guiding the speakers. A positive approach is required, but the aim must always be that the work remains clearly the children's own. They must achieve the end product and not have it determined entirely by the teacher.

As well as writing in story form, some children will prefer to set down their ideas as poems. Here the words and their rhythmic pattern are more important than rhyming. Where a child is obliged to follow a set pattern of poetry-writing, the framework may stifle the free and creative use of words.

When this kind of writing is first invited, many of the children may need help in the setting out. The suggestion that they read their poem aloud is sufficient to indicate the rhythm and pattern which is natural to that piece of work. The display of some good examples of the class poems with attractive embellishments, such as drawings or patterns, can command immediate attention. The reading aloud of some of the poems by the writers is another way to suggest interesting ways of composing. The way in which an onomatopœic word, or an alliterative phrase or a repeated line, gives some particular interest and distinction to a piece of writing may need pointing out at first – with the comment added that these forms fitted a particular poem.

It is often difficult for a child to maintain a consistent style throughout a poem. In such cases an extract can be used or the child can be persuaded to look again at a particular passage. If this is felt to be exercising too much control, then a section of the child's work can be exhibited. At various stages in the project, collections of stories and poems can be made, and at the end a typewritten and duplicate booklet can be prepared. Such anthologies are eagerly read by the children and make an interesting form of project record for the school to keep.

The spoken anthology is another variation which can be introduced for such occasions as a school assembly. Emphasis and variety will be increased by the use of different numbers of speakers, and by contrasting girls' and boys' voices. Further interest will come from the introduction of other sounds – clapping of hands and thighs, snapping of fingers, and the stamping of feet. A conductor will be required to regulate the time and volume of sound, to bring in and fade out groups. The use of instruments is the natural extension of this process.

A suitably equipped music corner needs to be built up for use by groups of children. There needs to be a generous supply of percussion instruments which will enable children to experiment widely with sound and rhythm. Some instruments can be made or improvised in class, for example, wood blocks, shakers, bottles containing various quantities of water. (See reference to Lively Craft Cards, p. 77.) These home-made devices should be adequately supplemented with tambourines, drums, xylophones, glockenspiels and chime bars. Only good-quality instruments should be purchased as only those capable of making a good sound will produce satisfactory creative music when used by children. Since the quality will bear a direct relationship to the materials used and the standard of workmanship applied in their production, such instruments are likely to be expensive, but they will represent a good investment.

Children enjoy developing their own tunes, but it is better to restrict their earliest efforts to a few notes. The choice of notes C, D, E, G and A constitute the pentatonic scale.

By using this scale, more than one melodic instrument can be introduced into the group and played simultaneously without discord – a situation which has much to commend it.

An introduction to musical form will help the individual child to produce longer tunes or bring together a number of group melodies or rhythms into a class composition.

The most useful form is the rondo, e.g. ABACADA, where
    A might be rhythmic handclapping, fingers snapping, and slapping;
    B rhythmic speaking of a poem or series of phrases;
    A repeat of rhythmic pattern;
    C melody on tuned percussion;
    A rhythmic pattern;
    D different melody on tuned percussion;
    A final repeat of rhythmic pattern.

Work of this kind has been extensively developed by Carl Orff. There are records giving examples of this method, and many local authorities have organised in-service courses for teachers who wished to introduce this exciting form of creative activity into their classroom.

A railway journey, with a constantly changing scene outside, the regular rhythm of the wheels, and diesel siren, is a situation which can be developed in this way. An incident at sea with the wave movement, the sound of the wind rising and falling, sounds of seagulls and ships' hooters, and the shouts from the wheel-house, is an even more dramatic situation to explore by this method.

Individual compositions can be invited to illustrate some aspect of a story or theme, and these can be put together to make an opera or oratorio or perhaps more modestly a programme of songs about Harvest, for instance. The radio ballads of Ewan McColl and Peggy Seegar, for instance, *Singing The Fishing* and *Driver Axon*, illustrate how songs, interviews and sound effects can be linked in a narrative form which is effective and different. A dramatic sequence of events seems to suit this form of expression, and a short journey on a canal travelled by a school party could be illustrated in this way. The interviews with people met on the voyage would probably include some reminiscences which could provide exciting incidents to write about and set to music.

Dylan Thomas in his revealing look at his home town of Laugharne, in *Under Milk Wood*, suggests the way in which a portrait of a village can be built up by marrying together narrative, interviews, descriptions in prose and verse, and sound effects to link one with the other.

Nor should one ignore the rich collection of songs which can be used with imagination. Thus the story of the 1745 rebellion could be told chronologically by making a selection of the romantic songs and ballads which grew up around the person of Bonnie Prince Charlie. The projection of slides showing places and people connected with the adventure would admirably complement the music. Tape-recorded sounds of gun and rifle fire, marching feet and galloping horses, all help to bring such scenes alive. The final touch is to introduce a piper, not so difficult to achieve even well south of the border.

This also serves to remind one that the piano is not the only instrument to accompany singing, nor is it as appropriate as some. In the case of the canal ballad mentioned earlier, the plaintive note of the melodeon would conjure up the waterside scene much more effectively than any other instrument.

Where movement work is included as part of the project, some of the compositions can be developed with this kind of interpretation in mind. The movement of animals, varying from the slow ponderous steps of the elephant to the graceful freeflowing action of a watersprite, can be suggested by music if the instruments, volume of sound and tempo are thought about. There are a number of records available which can be used to illustrate the kind of music required or to provide the inspiration for movement work. The BBC Schools programme 'Music, Movement and Mime' is splendid for the inexperienced teacher to use (or the one whose creative energies are being used on the many other aspects of the project).

The story *Oliver!* may be selected to fit in with a study of the Victorians, and while a straight dramatic performance of the tale would be quite acceptable, the music composed by Lionel Bart is difficult to exclude. As classic after classic attracts the attention of the composer, teachers may be able to include more and more of the productions of these stories where they add another dimension to the project. This is by no means suggesting the use of scripted plays. There is scope for improvisation and development of character and episode when the children have been told the story.

As many opportunities as possible should be taken to dramatise stories written by the children. They should have time to discuss, in small groups, how they think the play should develop, with the teacher providing encouragement and indicating how more could be made of an entrance or a speech. Whenever possible, everyone should be involved in some capacity and every effort made to change the leading players in each production. Often the use of a most able child as a supporting character can help to boost the confidence of a less experienced child. Often the dramatic activities will be for home consumption only – the purists will argue that to provide an audience is too inhibiting for young actors. However, children enjoy giving performances to their friends and parents, and part of the final presentation of a project through a play is usually most effective, and worth the extra rehearsal time needed to get the whole thing up to concert pitch. But this activity must remain enjoyable for everyone taking part, so great efforts need to be made to avoid over-rehearsing. Loud clear speech is required, and a good dramatic story with plenty of parts and action.

There is an eloquence in a picture or model which often far exceeds that which could be described in words, yet seldom is such an idea as this paid more than lip service. Yet sometimes the most expressive way to present an impression is by non-verbal means. Within a project there is an important place for sketching in and out of doors, from the small Roman coin in the museum at Verulamium, to the large panoramic view of Swanage Bay from the top of Ballard Down, and for this charcoal, pencil or a felt-tip pen can be employed, preferably on a sketching block. Similarly crayon, water colour, and acrylic paints should all be used in the classroom. The teacher needs to keep a conscious eye on all art work to ensure that various new skills are learnt and developed and new materials explored. One of the great dangers within any project, and a frequent charge levelled at it, is that full opportunities are not taken to develop artistic skills.

As well as individual pictures, group work should be introduced frequently. Such friezes and collages may be used to provide atmosphere in the classroom. As soon as a picture appears to have become part of the wall, it should be removed – possibly to another part of the classroom, where with just a few additions it can make yet another impact. It can be displayed in the school hall or corridor or library again, for a short period of time. If it is going to be required for the final presentation, then it needs to be carefully rolled up, with a newspaper wrapping, and stored safely somewhere. It is surprising how things *can* be stored in the most crowded schools. Hooks from the ceiling can be used to provide a support for a large picture, and the staffroom carpet can be lifted to provide a very safe place for storage.

For most projects there will be little or no dividing line between art and craft, because so many of the things done make use of techniques which might be thought of as belonging to different disciplines. For three-dimensional work there will be plenty of enthusiasm and the main requirement will be an abundance and variety of materials. Some of these will be the traditional craft materials – paper, card, adhesives, cane and raffia. Supplies of chicken wire, plaster of Paris, Sundeala boards, and lengths of timber will be needed, and these can be bought from local suppliers. A junkbox is another valuable reservoir of materials such as feathers, cones, matchboxes and polythene bottles. These cost nothing but are often the most valuable items to use.

There are some projects ('The Sea' for instance) in which a traditional craft such as net-making or rope-laying can be included; spinning, dyeing and weaving would quite naturally be included in a project on Wales. However, even these crafts are far removed from the days of children producing forty identical articles. Individuals and groups will choose to produce a model which will illustrate some aspect of the project. Their own drawings, or pictures from some source of reference, will be consulted. Materials will be tried out, selected or rejected. Adhesives will be chosen to suit the materials to be used. Care will have to be taken with the final surface treatment and the inclusion of detail, because all the groundwork which has gone into the production of the model will be so much waste, if the finish is not satisfactory. Just because the material used may come under the heading of junk it does not mean there are no standards to apply. There is no excuse for scrappy, untidy, unrecognisable models – or a room which looks as though a bomb has exploded in it. Nor is there a place for the model which is quite evidently teacher's effort, produced merely for Open Night!

In a team-teaching situation it may become the responsibility of one teacher to supervise the craft work. But where one person is carrying out a topic, a colleague on the staff might be persuaded to give a hand in this department (as others might be asked to assist with music and drama if these are areas where the teacher lacks confidence).

Models take up a lot of space, and so the size of them is an important consideration. The larger ones might well be left until the end of the project, but often children do not object to doing the more formal aspects of their work around the model of Vesuvius or underneath the hanging banners of a Hong Kong street scene – in fact, they usually enjoy it.

Tops of cupboards, or spare rooms (if they exist), can be used to store models. Landscape scenes prepared on large baseboards can often be stored on their ends. Where a classroom is very short of space, a model created on the wall or display panel of the dairy farm or the estate will offer quite an unusual viewpoint. Where space is at even greater premium, window sills can be used and often a low relief model can be created to make the best use of such areas; a canal, because of its straightness and narrowness, lends itself to this treatment; it can, to a depth of about ten inches, go around more than one wall and with the use of a painted backcloth provide a variety of features, including locks, viaducts, tunnels, etc. If there is ever an intention to move the model out of the classroom, consider the size of board and the scale of the model at the planning stage. One of the authors will not be caught again on this point!

Cardboard boxes can be used to store completed models which have had a period of display. They need to be carefully labelled so that they will escape the attention of over-zealous cleaners or 'magpies' from other classes.

Craft work can be the most time-consuming part of a project. The smaller the group working on a large model the better, and each child should have an area of responsibility for part of the production, with a leader ready to sort out any demarcation-line disputes, and to generally chivvy along his team.

The results of this aspect of creative work will play a very important part in final presentation of the project, because of its obvious visual appeal. So this work will need just as much careful planning as any other aspect of the project.

Very often the teacher planning a project finds that mathematical and scientific work is difficult to integrate. It is important to avoid stretching the boundaries of the scheme too far to include everything, but careful consideration needs to be given to all such correlations rather than rejecting them out of hand. To take an obvious example, in a project on shops and markets, the use of money could hardly be avoided; in a theme on milk, liquid measure would be an obvious concept to include; in a river study, there are many experiments involving the properties of water, in which some work on hydrostatics could be adapted to suit the age and experience of the children, and the particular requirements of the project.

No one is expecting the class to make any new dramatic discoveries, but all this work will be new to them, and as such will interest and excite them. They will learn something of elementary scientific method. The job of the teacher is to indicate the methods of working, probably through a workcard, without telling them the results they are likely to achieve. If there is any force in the argument that children will work more earnestly when they see the point of an exercise, the opportunities need to be frequently sought in which they can use the basic skills learnt in mathematics.

Because there are observable happenings in scientific experiments, the child is interested. It is necessary to help him to become clear about what he has done and seen, to ask him to describe the experiment, and what conclusions he has come to, as a result of it. In the BBC TV series 'Science Fair', there have been some admirable activities carried on, inside laboratories and outside, and the way in which the teams have reacted to the searching questions and comment of the experts has been most praiseworthy.

The keeping of weather records in a local study, the ways of recording statistical information in various graphical ways, aspects of scale drawing, and so on, are examples of the basic skills which will need to be introduced where they can be employed within a particular project, in various forms of problem solving.

The measure of the success of the actual work accomplished during a project is in the amount of creative work the children have been encouraged to carry out. Their urge to do this will be directly related to the amount of stimulation they have received, and what work the teacher does to provide the inspiration will be repaid many times.

BIBLIOGRAPHY
Marshall, S.: *An Experiment in Education* (Cambridge University Press).

Creative writing
Druce, Robert: *The Eye of Innocence* (Brockhampton).
Lane, S. M. & Kemp, M.: *An Approach to Creative Writing in the Primary School* (Blackie).
Maybury, Barry: *Creative Writing for Juniors* (Batsford).
Pym, Dora: *Free Writing* (University of London Press).
West Riding County Council: *The Excitement of Writing* (Chatto & Windus).

Drama and dance
Bruce, V.: *Dance and Drama in Education* (Pergamon).
Morgan, Diana: *Living Speech in the Primary School* (ULP).
Pemberton-Billing, R. N. & Clegg, J. D.: *Teaching Drama* (ULP).
Russel, J.: *Creative Dance in the Primary School* (Macdonald & Evans).
Slade, Peter: *Child Drama* (ULP).
Walker, Brenda: *Teaching Creative Drama* (Batsford).
Way, Brian: *Development Through Drama* (Longman).
Woodman, H.: *The Drama Tape Book* (Focal Press).

Music and film

Beal, J. D.: *How to Make Films at School* (Focal Press).
British Standards Institute: *Percussion Instruments:* BS 3499 Part 1.
Gray, V. & Percival, R.: *Music, Movement and Mime* (OUP).
HMSO: *Music in Schools:* Education Pamphlet No. 27.
Roberts, R.: *Musical Instruments Made to be Played* (Dryad).
Thackray, R. M.: *Creative Music in Education* (Novello).
Williams, Peter: *Making Musical Instruments:* Lively Craft Cards Set 2
    (Mills & Boon).

Science

ATCDE: *Science in the Primary School* (John Murray).
Craddy, Gwen: *Topics in Mathematics* (Batsford).
Nuffield Junior Science: *Mammals in Classrooms* (Collins); *Science and
    History* (Collins); *Teacher's Guide* (Collins).
Nuffield Mathematics: *Checking Up* (John Murray); *Environmental
    Geometry* (John Murray); *Weaving Guides* (John Murray &
    Chambers).
Waters, Derek: *Milk and Maths* (National Milk Publicity Council).

Art and craft

Alexander, Eugenie: *Fabric Pictures* (Mills & Boon).
Andrew, Laye: *Creative Rubbings* (Batsford).
d'Arbeloff, Natalie & Yates, Jack: *Creating in Collage* (Studio Vista).
Arundell, Jan: *Exploring Sculpture* (Mills & Boon).
Aspen, George: *Modelmaking in Paper, Board and Metal* (Studio
    Vista).
Benbow, Mary, Dunlop, Edith & Lucking, Joyce: *Guys and Dolls*
    (Harrap).
Crofton, K. & Denty, M.: *Creative Work in the Junior School* (ESA).
Gettings, F.: *You Are an Artist* (Hamlyn).
Grater, Michael: *Make It in Paper*; *One Piece of Paper*; *Paper Faces*;
    Paper People; *Paper Play* (Mills & Boon).
Green, Peter: *Introducing Surface Painting* (Batsford).
Hartung, Rolph: *Creative Textile Craft* (Batsford).

Honda, Isa: *How to Make Origami* (Museum Press).

Johnson, Pauline: *Creating with Paper* (Kaye).

Lldstone, John: *Building with Cardboard* (Van Nostrand Reinhold).

Maile, Anne: *Tie and Dye as a Present-Day Craft* (Mills & Boon); *Tie and Dye Made Easy* (Mills & Boon).

Moorey, Anne & Christopher: *Making Mobiles* (Studio Vista).

Pluckrose, Henry: *Let's Make Pictures* (Mills & Boon); *Let's Work Large* (Mills & Boon); *Creative Arts and Crafts* (Batsford); *Creative Art and Craft* (Oldbourne).

Robinson, Stuart & Patricia: *Exploring Fabric Printing* (Mills & Boon).

Rottger, Ernst: *Creative Wood Craft* (Batsford); *Creative Clay Craft* (Batsford); *Creative Paper Craft* (Batsford).

Seyd, Mary: *Designing with String* (Batsford).

Slade, Richard: *Masks and How to Make Them* (Faber).

Tritton, Gottfried: *Art Techniques for Children* (Batsford).

Viola, W.: *Child Art* (ULP).

Waters, Derek: *Creative Work with Found Materials* (Mills & Boon).

Weiss, Harvey: *The Young Sculptor* (Kaye); *The Young Print Maker* (Kaye).

Williams, Peter: *Using Waste Materials:* Lively Craft Cards Set 1 (Mills & Boon).

Zanker, Francis: *Foundations of Design in Wood* (Dryad).

6. THE PRESENTATION OF A PROJECT

As the project proceeds, the children will complete pieces of work. Some of this will be written work in notebooks and files, but pictures and models will be included in the regular output. However limited this might be, the display area within the classroom should be fully utilised. This means more than filling all available wall space with pictures. Rather it should be an opportunity to select and mount material (of all kinds) in an attractive way, to illustrate some feature of the project.

Some schools make a feature of displaying the work of classes in the hall, foyer, library and corridor, and children feel a great sense of pride in seeing their work thus exhibited. Where children's assemblies are a regular feature of the school worship, some work that the class has done can be shown and used when it is their turn to lead the school in this activity.

However, we can regard these events as relatively minor even if valuable aspects of the project, certainly when we compare them with the final presentation of the story. This must be a fitting climax to the whole venture. In the initial planning, this final act must come into the thinking and a decision made on the date of the event and the form likely to be adopted.

Teachers working in this way, who think themselves progressive, are often surprised when it is suggested that their work is becoming stereotyped. It is important that variations in approach should be adopted in different projects, and so should the particular way of presenting it at the end of the study.

Although we are improving in this respect, the British seem to take a perverse pride in letting things speak for themselves. Certainly in many exhibitions, shop windows, school displays, there is a complete lack of visual imagination and enterprise in presentation. It is appreciated that a school does not have £5000 that an exhibitor at Earls Court might use in selling his wares, but nevertheless some care, and a little money too, might be employed in showing the results of a term's endeavours.

A number of suggestions are given in this chapter which indicate some of the ways in which the story of the project can be communicated to others.

The teacher needs to know exactly what has been produced during the project. While this may seem to be an obvious statement, it is quite easy to overlook some work completed in the early weeks and stored away. When the date for exhibition approaches, this is announced to the class. Working towards a deadline is a valuable spur, and gives the final fillip to the project. Individuals, groups and the class will need to get their particular contribution into a condition in which its message can be understood, and its association with the other features of the display can be seen quite clearly.

This means that a process of selection has to be carried out. Some work may need repairing, remounting and even rewriting. Time plays havoc with materials, however well they are stored, and this will apply particularly to the three-dimensional items. While they do not necessarily represent the greatest effort, these models do attract a great deal of attention when displayed, and so a coat of paint may be required, and some attention given to the fragile features which may have suffered.

A decision, and probably an early one, will be needed on the place to have the exhibition. It may have to be in the classroom. Some schools are fortunate in having a spare room available, and it may be possible to persuade the teacher of a small class to move in with another one for the short period of an exhibition. The hall, being a larger space than the classroom, is an attractive proposition, but such factors as the needs of the meals service and evening use of the building may have to be considered. Assembly times can be altered, hall periods for other classes cancelled, and so on, as long as early enough notice is given.

While a few schools are able to afford to buy, and have space to store, display stands and boards, most of them are able to make requests to their local authority to borrow some. Once again, early notice will avoid disappointment, especially when the chosen date is near the end of a term, when many schools are exhibiting.

A plan for the exhibition is necessary. This should be prepared on squared paper, and a scale adopted. The position of doors, lights and any other features likely to affect the appearance of the display must be noted. The proposed layout of tables, benches and other display units should then be added. The arrangement of display boards can help to give a shape and coherence to the theme. They can suggest a route to follow; they can form small bays in which particular facets of the project can be arranged; they can form a horseshoe shape and the backcloth for some dramatic presentation; they can divide up a project into parts; they can prevent an all-through look at the exhibition, and so provide a series of surprise views; they enable some material to be exhibited from one side only.

The teacher needs to be as practical as possible in planning an exhibition, to be able to work quickly and modify in an instant when this proves to be necessary.

About six feet needs to be left in front of a board – and even more when a practical demonstration is being given. This will ensure that many more can see the processes, and traffic flow is not impeded.

On the other hand, avoid having very large empty spaces. If these are likely to arise, choose a smaller room to mount the display or arrange it in one part, or where some dramatic presentation is planned, leave an area for the performance.

If there is too much material for the main centre chosen for exhibition, a number of decisions are possible. Only a selection of the work is shown, and one criterion could be that all the material is on show for the first time. Where an exhibition is open for a few days, then certain aspects could be changed at some convenient time. Some particular aspect could be contained in a smaller area, for instance in the library or an adjacent classroom. Some part, carefully chosen for its eye-catching appeal, can be used either at the entrance to the hall or to the school to set the scene.

Yet another aspect of the space problem affects some schools where certain rigid factors apply. Where the only hall serves as the dining centre, then it may be possible to arrange for the exhibition to occupy the perimeter of the hall, and have an arrangement whereby the dining tables serve as the display space, for models and workbooks. The exhibits will have to be stacked elsewhere when meals are being eaten, and the exhibition is closed temporarily.

When arrangements have been made about the hall or classroom space to be used, select a team to arrange the furniture. Adult help may be needed to lift and erect some types of stand. Tables, drama blocks and PE benches are now put into position. Most boards and display tops will need some form of clean covering. This may be paper of various types, including wallpaper. Materials of other kinds can be used, and most of these, especially fabrics, can be reclaimed after use. Some careful thought should be given to the colour, texture and pattern if any, so that the background does not dominate but adds something to the display.

When the organisation of the display has been worked out, particular areas should be handed over to groups of children who will arrange them. Backgrounds need to be put in position first and very critical attention needs to be given on the first tour of the developing exhibition to make sure that a high standard of mounting is achieved; where it is not, then the deficiency is pointed out and a change made (of arrangers if necessary!).

People come to see things, and so models will attract a great deal of attention. They should be displayed to their best advantage. Height, aspect and light should be considered in the siting of these exhibits. Where a model is not an all-round one, the rear should be camouflaged, if it is not possible to put it against a wall or display stand. Where books and written work are on display, they are probably going to take up a lot of space. Some overlapping can be attempted, with selected pages on show – but exhibitors should remember that visitors are unlikely to stop and read large tracts.

Most people, in fact, are only prepared to read short captions, and the labelling of pictures and models should be limited to these. Bold simple lettering should be employed, with the size chosen to suit the dimensions of the model, picture, or aspect of the display.

Felt-tip pens can be used – but where perfection is sought after, and time is available, stencils or transfer letters can be employed. Wherever possible this work should be carried out by children. But they do need practice, and only the best should be accepted. Until such time as a high standard can be achieved, it is better if the teacher does the labelling of the major items, and the children are made responsible for smaller captions.

Some visitors to exhibitions seem to take a delight in travelling in the wrong direction. Where the class are anxious that displays are seen in a particular order, a system of arrows should be arranged. Some care should be taken with these, and an attempt made to make them interesting either in shape or colour – all the time remembering that the aim is to direct people in a particular way.

It may be interesting to try to devise a symbol to appear in various places in the exhibition, on the programme, and on the letter of invitation. For a seashore project, a periwinkle shell might be adopted; for an animal study, a panda face; on a fire theme, a flickering flame and so on.

A school may have one or more spotlights for use in dramatic activities. Parts of the exhibition can be lit with these, for special effect. Colour filters can be introduced in front of spotlights, where a particular hue is required. Teachers with a particular bent may wish to experiment with special lighting effects – flickering, occulting, etc.

The use of sound adds another dimension to an exhibition. Records chosen because a musical composition is relevant can be played in the background. Special tapes can be prepared when effects are required in one part of the display. A long length of tape, say two yards, is prepared where there is a repetitive sound to be recorded. This is placed in position on the tape-recorder, and the slack taken up and placed around a spool which can turn freely, and so allow the tape to move in a continuous track. Some plainsong is appropriate to a study of the monasteries; the sound of the sea on a project on ships; birdsong for a woodland study; shouts, screams, bangs and wallops for a theme which features a battle.

An exhibition will come alive when the children involved act as guides. Where possible they should all be recruited for this work, but it may be necessary to prepare a rota of duty. Their stations should ideally be where their work is on show. Visitors should be encouraged to ask questions of the guides and attendants, and it is interesting how the confidence of the groups increases as more and more visitors arrive and ask searchingly about certain aspects of the exhibits.

Often it will be possible to costume the attendants and make them a colourful part of the exhibition. Milkmaids in traditional costume provide a kind of authenticity to a Dairy Show; coloured blankets and head-dresses of feathers worn by children during an Indian theme increase the interest. Add to this a live demonstration of some activity, and the level of interest increases even more.
A number of girls in medieval costume, spinning and weaving, will attract a lot of attention; two boys in leather aprons working at a cardboard forge and anvil can simulate a blacksmith's shop for a village project. Visitors can be invited to taste foodstuffs which the

children have made – bread, butter, cream cheese, jam. In some projects where science is an integral part, some experiments can be demonstrated, and in certain cases the visitors can become involved in these too.

Where the room being used is a large one, some parts of it can be given over to specialised activities. A mini-studio can be prepared in a corner, and there a series of slides can be shown by children who will add a commentary. Similarly some tape-recorded features can be played back to small groups of visitors. Interviews, recorded sound effects, a number of poems written during the project and so on can be relayed in this fashion.

In the same way that maximum benefit from a visit to an outside place of interest was assured by the preparation of a questionnaire and worksheet, a quiz can be prepared for use by visitors at the exhibition. By using these, the young visitor must look more carefully at the display, and talk to the attendants. Prizes can be provided for those who produce the most interesting answers.

There are numerous other ways to illustrate aspects of the project which complement the static type of exhibition. A talk can be given by a group leader on some aspect of the study. His team can support him by holding up pictures or specimens, or pointing out features of a model as he explains it. A small studio set can be built for this type of presentation. Further developments of this method would be the introduction of tape-recordings, slides and the use of an episcope and overhead projector.

A series of tableaux can be built up as a narrator provides background details; for instance, certain incidents from the History of America could be chosen. Where a number of classes have worked together, a pageant of history could be attempted with a number of main characters and supporters who may need to engage in quick costume changes as the events unfold. A playground presentation of this activity could be considered, with a hired Tannoy system for commentary.

86

Puppetry is another method by which a story can be told. Glove puppets are easier to control, but simple cut-outs can be used for shadow puppet plays.

Mime, movement and straight dramatic methods can be employed to tell a particular part of the project story. The idea of the television series 'This Is Your Life' can be employed where a character, in a historical project, can be put in the centre of the stage and his life re-created before his and the audience's eyes. At the end of the 'programme' a written and illustrated book is produced which also tells the story.

A concert of songs can be prepared around the theme and mimed situations performed during the singing, or between items – for example, the songs of the Negro slaves of America describing the suffering and hopelessness of their situation.

By ringing the changes in the form of presentation, seeking for ideas appropriate to the theme, the visitors will be assured of an interesting and new experience, while for the class involved, a new series of techniques of communication will have been explored.

Anyone who has helped in the project should be invited to the presentation. Other distinguished visitors should be asked to come, and their presence will enhance the occasion for the class. Parents come within this category, and since it is a school event quite different from the open evening, it is hoped that many will come to see the combined efforts of the whole group. Some of the parents may have become involved in the project in various ways, and a good attendance can usually be assured, especially if it is an evening event.

Photographs of the exhibition form a valuable record of the project along with a set of notes and appraisal. After the display, there is no room for sentimentality. Children will usually want to take their work files home and some of their paintings. Some of the more manageable of the models are taken home, where it is known that there is an indulgent mother. The rest of the material must go.

It is surprising how rapidly the whole exhibition can be dispersed. Probably the end of term follows a day or two later. Time for one last quiz, and a discussion about the next theme to be followed. What will it be? The teacher will need to know, because the preparation and planning will have to start straight away if it is going to be a success.

BIBLIOGRAPHY

Black, Mischa, Ed.: *Exhibition Design* (Architectural Press).

Corbin, T. J.: *Display in Schools* (Pergamon).

Leggatt, R.: *Showing Off* (Visual Education Book Service).

Mills, V.: *Making Posters* (Studio Vista).

Muscutt, H. C.: *Display Technique* (Mills & Boon).

National Council of Social Services: *Local History Exhibitions.*

Plowman, A. & Pearson, V.: *Display Technique* (Blandford).

Plowman, A. & Matthews, K. C.: *Animated Display* (Blandford).

PART II

GUIDELINES FOR PROJECTS

INTRODUCTION

This part of the book suggests guidelines to twenty-one projects. These vary in 'weight', and because of this we hope that topics will be found to meet all kinds of needs. For all of them we have provided a framework in which will be found sources of information and inspiration, and the directions in which the creative responses to these stimuli might take. Poetry, music and story suggestions have been included in the greatest quantity possible, not only so that a choice is available but also to underline the importance of this material in enlarging experience and awareness, as well as a possible secondary use in providing further information. We do not want to suggest in any way that the success of a project can be merely equated to the number of facts acquired.

Too frequently, the results of projects are a series of notebooks which represent little more than the re-writing of large chunks of uninteresting, out-of-date, second-hand information. Rather we would see that the children have several sources to refer to, plus the opportunity to observe the evidence out of doors, and meet with people knowledgeable in the field in which they are interested. In this way they will learn the excitement of some individual research or group enterprise, and whether it be the library, the local spoil heap, or the ruin of a castle, they will feel the real pleasure of exploration. The excitement of this personal interest through active participation is one of the fundamental aims of project work as we see it.

I think we frequently undervalue children's endurance and understanding, and so some of the projects have been suggested because they can be taken over a longish period of time, and in some depth.

90

To avoid too much repetition, techniques suggested for one idea have not been used for another, and so the reader may find a treatment appropriate to a modelling idea, under another project. Similarly what is suggested under 'Drama and Movement' may appeal more to some people as an idea for a large picture, and so on.

In some cases it might be useful to take one project framework as a pattern for another. For example, using 'Trafalgar' tactics as it were for 'Waterloo'; or casting 'Sir Walter Raleigh' in the mould of 'Captain Cook'. Where a reader has a special interest, perhaps a single suggestion may spark off several ideas in his mind. For instance, Dickens enthusiasts may know of many more 'River' ideas than the one suggested under that topic. In Chapter 5 of the *Old Curiosity Shop* there begins the section 'It was flood tide . . .' Chapter 50 of *Oliver Twist* starts with 'Near to that part of the Thames . . ', and so on. We would like to suggest that the reader keeps the references up to date as new material is produced or old sources are discovered for the first time.

Frequently the outlines can be joined together to make a larger study; milk, bread, fruit and vegetables could form the nucleus for a project on food and nutrition. Alternatively various ingredients could be taken from a number of projects and a completely new 'cake' prepared.

From an excursion, the watching of a film together and so on, various kinds of work will commence and develop because of the interest engendered by the experience. Under the heading 'Written work' with which we have introduced 'Creative activities' several suggestions are given. As they appear, they smack very much of the old idea of titles for the blackboard during the period labelled 'Composition'. Where these ideas are used or modified to suit the local situation, they will need to be carefully introduced, talked over, and the class or group stimulated to write. Otherwise to provide only the titles and the instruction to write two pages – at least – will only get a certain kind of result, and that from those keen to please the teacher or avoid trouble. The same can be said of all such creative activities.

Lists of poetry anthologies and addresses of suppliers of visual aids are provided at the end of the book, as appendices. A selected bibliography of books to stimulate work in art and craft appears at the end of Chapter 5 of Part I – The Creative Aspects of Projects (pages 77–8).

MILK

There are very many exciting projects that can be developed with children. We hope that we have included several of these in this book, but there are others – and we know that we have included some of these too – which we might describe as the bread-and-butter type! In fact these two projects – Bread and Milk – appear now. Although these cannot be called novelties, we include them because they are useful, modest topics on which to start with a class. However, we do expect them to be interesting and valuable both to the class and the teacher. For both, they will provide a training ground, and after such experience (with an almost built-in guarantee of success) one of the more ambitious kinds of projects, with many more personal opportunities for the children, can be embarked upon.

Special aspects

This project can certainly be claimed to be one from which the child begins with a familiar object – the bottle of milk. It is a project admirably suited to the needs and interests of young children. There are numerous opportunities for visits in this project, including one to a farm. If this is well prepared, the project will move towards the 'exciting' class. Extensions are possible – butter-, cream- and cheese-making, and studies of the great dairy exporting countries – New Zealand and Denmark. Like bread, this theme presents situations where the manufacture of various products can be included for group study.

The subject of nutrition is increasingly felt to be one of considerable importance. The concern shown by medical authorities about the question of obesity among children is one reason for this. Another is the need to educate the future parents about the planning and preparation of well-balanced meals for their families. Such education can start at a much earlier age than has been thought hitherto. The National Dairy Council, who have produced a large number of aids to support learning at different levels, have recently issued a manual of suggestions for teachers of children in the primary age range on nutrition (*Learning About Food* – Derek Waters).

94

Within the larger framework of a project on food and nutrition, children could exercise some choice in their studies. In such a study, milk could be one of the options, and occupy a group of six to eight children for a period of half a term.

Plate 7 A small group can investigate the work of the local roundsman.

INSPIRATION AND INFORMATION
Reference books
The Farm; *Grassland*; *Cows and Milk*; *Arable Crops*: Young Farmer's Club Booklets (Evans Brothers).

Clair, Colin: *The Things We Need — Milk* (Gawthorn).

The United Kingdom Dairy Industry: (UK Dairy Association).

Here is a list of books and booklets published by the National Dairy Council:

The Cows that Give Us Milk
How We Get Our Milk
What We Get From Milk
Let's Find Out About Dairy Cows
Let's Find Out About Milk
Let's Find Out About Butter, Cream and Cheese
How Peter and Peggy Found Out About Milk
Dan Dawson Reporting on the Dairy Industry

The above booklets are free.

Churns and Cheese (5p)
A Handbook of Dairy Foods (25p)

Obourn, E. S.: *Science in Everyday Life* (Van Nostrand Reinhold).
The Class and the Cow and *Milk and Maths* are written for the teacher.

Stories

Gallico, Paul: *Ludmilla* (Penguin & Michael Joseph).
Krasilovsky, P.: *The Cow Who Fell in the Canal* (Worlds Work).
Tickell, Jerrard: *Appointment with Venus* (ULP).

Poetry

Frost, Robert: *The Cow in Apple Time.*
MacCaig, Norman: *Fetching Cows.*
Massingham, Harold: *Cow.*
Reeves, James: *Cows.*
Roethke, Theodore: *The Cow.*
Stevenson, R. L.: *The Cow.*
And this riddle: Four stiff hangers.
Four down hangers.
Two crooked crooks
And a ding dong.

Films

Channel Islands Milk Production (Rank Film Library).
The Cream of Good Milk (Rank Film Library).
The Dairy Farmer (Boulton Hawker Films).
Devon Dairy Farming (Rank Film Library).
Milk (Boulton Hawker and NCAVAE).
Milkman's Progress (United Dairies).
Milky Way (United Dairies).
£1,000,000-a-Day (National Dairy Council).
Modern Dairy (BIF).
The Daily Round (Rank Film Library).
The Great Milk Bottle Mystery (Home Counties Dairies Ltd).
Untouched by Hand (Express Dairy Co Ltd).
Aluminium Dairy Closures (Fords Finsbury Ltd).
Tetra Instructional Film (Tetra Pak (London) Ltd).
Butter (United Dairies).
Buttermaking (BIF).
Cheddar Cheese (United Dairies).
Cheese from Milk (BIF).
Condensed Milk (United Dairies).
Cottage Cheese (Express Dairy Co).
Meet English Cheeses (National Dairy Council).
Modern Cheese Making (Co-operative Wholesale Society).
Meet Miss Muffet (Co-operative Wholesale Society).
Mousetrap Is Out (National Dairy Council).
Taste the Cream (Cadbury Brothers).
The Young Herdsman (Foundation Film Library).
The Cow (Gateway Film).

Filmstrips

Milk (two parts – *On the Farm*; *Your Bottle of Milk*) (Educational Productions).
Milk (Common Ground from Foundation Film Library).
The Miracle of Your Morning Milk (National Dairy Council).
The Story of Milk (Camera Talks).
Bread and Butter (Pitman from Foundation Film Library).

Butter from Milk (BIF).
Cheese from Milk (BIF).
Cheese — Its Story Down the Ages (Unicorn Head).
English Country Cheeses (National Dairy Council).
Milk, Butter and Cheese (Common Ground from Foundation Film
   Library).
The Story of Butter (Foundation Film Library).
The Cow (Educational Productions).
Dairy Farming (Common Ground).
A Dairy Farm in New Zealand (Foundation Film Library).

Film loops
Composition of Milk ; Processing of Milk (National Dairy Council).

Charts
All at nominal prices, with teachers' notes from the National Dairy
Council.
Milk Through the Ages.
The Story of Cheese.
How Cream and Butter Are Made.
Milk Production.
Milk Distribution.
History of Milk.
Butter and Cream Production.
British Dairy Cows.
How Cows Make Milk.
How Butter Is Made (Butter Information Council from Educational
   Productions).
How Cheese Is Made (Dutch Dairy Bureau from Educational
   Productions).
Cow (Educational Productions Ltd).

Wallet of documents: Jackdaw 79 — *Dairy Farming* (Jonathan Cape).

Farm adoption schemes can be purchased from the Association of
Agriculture, 78 Buckingham Gate, London SW1. Folders giving

information about dairy, arable and mixed farms are available in this country, Canada and New Zealand.

Ask the milk roundsman, dairy manager and dairy farmer to visit the class — preferably before the class goes out of school to meet them.

Useful addresses
National Dairy Council, National Dairy Centre: 5 John Princes Street, London W1M 0AP.
For teachers and students working in the following areas, these addresses will be more appropriate:
Scotland: Scottish Milk Publicity Council Ltd: 41 St Vincent Place, Glasgow, C1.
   Aberdeen and District Milk Publicity Council: Twin Spires, Bucksburn, Aberdeen.
   North of Scotland Milk Marketing Board: Claymore House, 29 Ardconnel Terrace, Inverness.
Northern Ireland: Northern Ireland Milk Publicity Council: 7 Donegal Square West, Belfast, N. Ireland.
English County Cheese Council: John Princes Street, London W1M 0AP.
Butter Information Council: Salisbury House, London Wall, London EC2.
Unigate Ltd, PR Dept: Superity House, Western Avenue, London W3.
Cadbury Brothers Ltd, Schools Dept: Bournville, Birmingham.
The Dutch Dairy Bureau: The Dutch House, 307-308 High Holborn, London WC1.
New Zealand Dairy Board: St Olaf's House, Tooley Street, London SE1.

Excursions
Visit the local bottling depot. Most dairies are very willing to provide a tour of their plant, including the laboratory.

Arrange an excursion to a dairy farm. Since the milk yield of the cow can be affected by undue noise, some assurance will be needed by the farmer that the party will be very quiet while in the milking shed.

Look up the telephone number of the local National Farmer's Union representative to ask about farm visits. Winter visits, with appropriate clothing worn, are just as interesting as those made in summer. Where there is a butter- or cheese-making plant in the area, this too makes an interesting visit.

At a much more local level, the manageress at the dairy and the milk roundsman may be willing to be interviewed.

Zoos which have children's sections (London (Regent's Park), Crystal Palace, Battersea, Whipsnade, Edinburgh) have calves and sometimes milking cows.

At certain seasons, the London Parks Department send their animals on tour, bringing them obviously much closer to some schools. We were fortunate in being able to invite the zoo to stay in the school grounds for a week. The value of this experience for an urban school was tremendous.

Local county agricultural shows and national events like the Dairy Show at Olympia are important experiences for children to have and very relevant to this topic.

CREATIVE ACTIVITIES
Written work
You are a farm apprentice and since you attend agricultural college on day release you need to keep a diary of your work. Produce one giving details of this week's happenings on Oak Tree Farm.

The farmer has gone to the agricultural show for the day, leaving you in charge. The milking machine gives up and you are obliged to start milking by hand. Describe your morning in the milking parlour.

Make up a new nursery rhyme in the style of *Little Miss Muffet* but include a mention of yoghourt, and a different creature which frightened the girl — or boy.

Invent some suitable names for your dairy herd and write down these names in a rhythmical form. Use percussion instruments to emphasise the rhythm you have worked out.

Write and tell your town cousin about the arrival of a new calf on the farm.

You find yourself in a bottling depot — at night. As you wander around, you keep knocking on switches and falling over crates. Write a narrative poem about this night of nights.

Drama and movement
Talk about the events which would occur if the herd of cows got out on the road and then act out the possibilities.

On market day, a rather lively calf escapes from the sale ring and runs into the town. Let everyone choose parts of auctioneer, drovers, farmers, policemen, stall holders, shoppers, shopkeepers, including the owner of a china shop, and perform the sequence of events.

Select suitable music and perform the story of milk production and distribution.

In small groups, one acting as the roundsman and the others as householders, deliver the milk, pass the time of day, settle the accounts, and provide any other commodities you carry.

Dramatise the efforts of the farmer's son who goes to market to sell the cow, and ends up exchanging it, and the resulting 'things', for others until he returns home with . . .

Mathematical and scientific assignments

By arrangement, follow the milk roundsman and map his route. Ask for details of the type, quantity and price of the milk he delivers. Where there are two or more dairies in the same area, replot the findings onto a map, and the statistical information on a graph.

Find out about milk distribution in your school – quantities, delivery times and so on. When this is recorded in graphical form, produce a questionnaire which will invite some careful analysis and thought. For example, which class drank most milk? How many classes drank over one gallon of milk in the week? Why was the consumption down on Friday in Class 4P?

At the dairy depot, the pasteurisation details should be asked for and the quantities of milk coming in and out. On the farm ask about the daily yields of cows, and the amount of food each one receives. The variation between the milk yields of the various breeds can also be investigated. The breeding programme of the dairy farmer will reveal how he arranges to have his cows deliver calves at intervals to produce a continuous supply of milk.

Invent a milk game, in which four roundsmen have to dispose of their supplies as rapidly as possible. Details of such a game, and other ideas, are given in the booklet *Milk and Maths*, from the National Dairy Council.

Young children will enjoy creating a Dairy Shop within their classroom, and the opportunity to buy and sell the products there.

In the National Dairy Council booklet, *Science in Everyday Life*, there are experiments which the children can carry out. The co-operation of a secondary school might be engaged when trying some of the more advanced exercises.

The nutritional value of milk can be investigated during such a project and some comparison made with other foodstuffs. (Many of the publications and other aids listed above will assist the children to discover the composition of various dairy foods.) During such a study as this the fact that Vitamin C is deficient will emerge, and discussion can take place on this important vitamin, and what alternative sources there are for it.

Similarly it will be learnt that milk is particularly important as a source of riboflavine, a link by which the body obtains energy from food. Since this vitamin is destroyed by sunlight (and even daylight) children can be taught the reason for bringing in milk from the doorstep as soon as possible. In the same way, the reason for rinsing out a milk bottle in cold water first can be pointed out, since hot water would start off a chemical change in the protein content of the milk — a fact easily demonstrated.

Art

Make a long frieze of the cows coming across the fields towards the milking parlour — a group activity.

Refer to a reference book and create a picture of a milkmaid carrying a yoke and milking pails while her friend is milking a cow.

There has been a road accident and the milk tanker has spilled its load all over the road. Make a lino cut of this scene.

Make a fabric collage picture of a field of cows of different breeds.

Ask each member of the class to produce an item for the 'Story of Our Daily Milk' picture.

Craft

Make a model of a dairy farm. On a base board, create fields, using dyed sawdust for grass and other crops, foam rubber for hedges and so on. Make the farm buildings from empty cartons. Use model cows to complete the scene. Try to model the farm visited.

Build a large milking parlour with cut open roof to show the cow stalls below and the milking machinery. Milk straws can be used as pipes, and the aluminium tops from milk bottles to simulate the metal parts. Simple cut-out figures of the dairyman and the cows should be added.

Use a spare table or build a strong armature to build a life-size model cow. The neck can be made from stout cardboard tacked onto the body, while the head can be made from manilla or chicken wire, which is later covered with papier mâché. Large sheets of card are used to represent the flanks, with pads of newspaper to soften the corners. A rope covered with material will suffice as a tail, and the udder can be made from one slung piece of material to which four fingers of an old glove have been sewn.

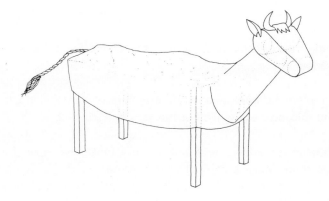

Fig. 1 An old table can serve as the framework for a model cow.

Butter-making
This is a simple operation. Each child might be persuaded to allow her share of the cream to be poured off carefully into a jar with a close-fitting lid. Shaking of butter is done by turns until the globules of butter are formed. Pouring through a sieve removes the buttermilk. Clean pieces of wood can be used to pat the butter into shape. Attractive butter moulds are available to create interesting shapes, and some of the children might have these (salt can be added to taste).

104

Fig. 2 Moulds can be bought to embellish the butter production by the class. Rotary and flat moulds can be found with a variety of traditional designs.

Cheese-making
Heat two pints of milk to a temperature of 100°F (38°C). Add three teaspoonfuls of junket rennet or half a teaspoon of cheese-making rennet. When the junket has formed, strain through a sieve and then allow to dry. Press the curds into a mould.

A small cheese and soft drink party might be a fitting end to a project such as this. Special syrups can be bought from the grocer to flavour milk shakes.

Further developments
This project could occupy half a term in a year's study of farming. The cooking aspects – using milk, butter and cheese – have great possibilities. Develop your own dairy festival for the month of June.

BREAD

A loaf of bread is taken very much for granted, yet it is an important item in our daily diet. Because of this, bread appears to be an ordinary subject and so not very exciting. However, it usually lends itself to most successful projects. It is suitable for younger age groups in the primary school, but older children will understand more of the technical aspects of a modern bakery. The history of breadmaking and milling, yesterday and today, the development of farming and distribution of the grain-growing areas in the world are all important aspects which can be covered.

Special aspects

This project is one which can be taken as a single subject or as part of a larger project on food or family. The practical aspects of breadmaking are a popular aspect of the study.

INFORMATION AND INSPIRATION
Reference

Bradbourne, E. S.: *Bread* (Schofield & Sims).

Carey, D.: *How It Works: Farm Machinery* (Wills & Hepworth).

Chetwood, D.: *Breadmaking Is Child's Play.*

Clair, C.: *Bread* (Burns & Gawthorne).

Deverson, H. J.: *The Story of Bread* (Puffin).

Fisher, Patty: *Let's Cook with Yeast* (Mills & Boon).

Gregory, O. B.: *Bread* (Wheaton).

Hinds, H.: *Floury Fingers* (Faber & Faber).

Hugget, Frank: *Farming* (Black).

Hughes, M. E.: *The Importance of Bread* (set of workcards – Rupert Hart-Davis).

Jenkin, J. I.: *Let's Make Gingerbread Boys* (set of four books – Longman).

King, Charles: *The Story Behind a Loaf of Bread* (Cassell).

Lee, N. E.: *Harvests and Harvesting Through the Ages* (CUP).

Manning, S. H.: *Bread* (Blackwell).

Perry, G. A.: *The Farmer's Crops* (Blandford).

Petersham, M. & M.: *The Story Book of Wheat* (Wells, Gardner, Darton & Co).

Scheib, I.: *The First Book of Food* (Ward).
Shannon, T.: *About Food and Where It Comes From* (Muller)
Warburton, C.: *Study Book of Farming* (Bodley Head).

Plate 8 A project on bread could stimulate the making of bread in the classroom.
(Photo by courtesy of Henry Grant)

Stories

Carruth, J.: *Hansel and Gretel* (retold) (Odhams).
Elishen, E. & Garfield, J.: *The God Beneath the Sea* (Longman).
Grimm & Humperdinck: *Hansel and Gretel* (Ward).
Guerber, H. A.: *Myths of Greece and Rome* – The Story of Demeter
    (Harrap).
Southgate, Vera: *The Gingerbread Boy* (Wills & Hepworth).

Biblical references

Joseph in Egypt: Genesis 41.

Ruth: Ruth.

Feast of the Passover: Exodus 12: 34–39.

Parable of the Leaven: Matthew 13: 33.

Feeding of the Five Thousand: John 6.

The Road to Emmaus: Luke 24: 28–35.

Poems

Fisher, K.: *Story of the Corn.*

Give Us This Day.

> Back of the loaf is the snowy flour.
> And back of the flour the mill.
> And back of the mill is the wheat and the shower.
> And the sun and the Father's Will.
>   Anon.

Music

Humperdinck: *Hansel and Gretel*: Story and Songs (Walt Disney Prod.
LLP 317).

Songs

There Was a Jolly Miller.

The Miller of Dee.

Films

Harvest Time (BIF).

Cereal Story (ICI).

Corn Harvest (Boulton-Hawker).

Speed the Plough (Shell Mex Ltd).

Good as Gold (Hovis Ltd).

Filmstrips

Seedtime and Harvest (Marian Ray).

Booklets
The Good Oat (Quaker Oats Ltd)
Wheat (Nabisco Foods Ltd).
The Story of a Bag of Flour (McDougalls Food).
The Grains Are Great Foods (Kellogg Co of Great Britain).
Looking at Wheat (Hovis Services).

Charts
The Wheat Plant (Educational Productions Ltd, Apha House, East
  Ardsley, Wakefield, Yorks).
How Self-Raising Flour Is Made (McDougalls Food Ltd).
Bread Making C1021 (Educational Productions Ltd).

Association of Agriculture
Farm Studies: No. 3. *An Arable and Stock Farm in the Scottish
  Borders.*
  No. 7. *An Arable Farm in North Norfolk.*
  No. 15. *A Grain Farm on the Portage Plains of Manitoba.*

Useful addresses
Association of Agriculture: 78 Buckingham Gate, London SW1.
Brown and Polson Ltd: 125 Strand, London WC2.
Canadian Wheat Board: 1 North Court, Great Peter Street, London
  SW1.
Flour Advisory Bureau Ltd: 21 Arlington Street, London SE1.
Ford Motor Co Ltd: Dagenham, Essex.
Hovis Ltd: 154 Grosvenor Road, London SW1.
International Harvester Co Ltd: 259 City Road, London EC1.
Kellogg Co Ltd: Stretford, Manchester.
Massey-Ferguson (UK) Ltd: Banner Lane, Coventry, Warwks.
McDougalls Ltd: Wheatsheaf Mills, London E14.
McVitie and Price Ltd: Harlesden, London NW10.
Ministry of Agriculture, Fisheries and Food: Whitehall Place, London
  SW1.
Nabisco Foods Ltd: Welwyn Garden City, Herts.

National Federation of Young Farmers' Clubs: 55 Gower Street,
London WC1.
Protein Bread Advisory Service: 109 New Bond Street, London W1.
Quaker Oats Ltd: Southall, Middlesex.
Rank, Hovis, McDougall Ltd: Millocrat House, Eastcheap, London EC3.
Weetabix Ltd: Weetabix Mills, Burton Latimer, Kettering,
Northamptonshire.

Excursions
Visit a farm where wheat is grown.

Visit a windmill, a watermill, a bakery.

Agriculture section of the Science Museum; windmill section in the
Science Museum.

Windmills in the London area: Blenheim Gardens, Brixton; Smock-mill
at St Mary's Lane, Upminster; Tower Mill at John Ruskin Grammar
School, Upper Shirley Road, Croydon.

CREATIVE ACTIVITIES
Imagine you are a Neolithic woman who discovers that there are grains
which can be ground to flour and flour made into bread. Describe your
experiences.

Find out about the bread which the Romans made, then imagine you
are a Roman baker. Describe one day in your life.

Write a poem about a windmill and set it to music.

Find out about the medieval three-field system of farming and the task
of the miller.

Use flat stones to grind cereals into flour.

Drama and movement

Portray in movement and mime the work of the farmer: sowing, ploughing, harvesting the corn.

Act the story of the Feeding of the Five Thousand.

Tell the story of Demeter the corn goddess in movement.

Act the story of Hansel and Gretel.

Act a play about a medieval miller who cheated his customers by stealing their corn.

Act the story of the two ears of wheat collected by a boy, to be grown and harvested year after year until enough is grown to be made into flour and a special purchase made.

Act the story of Ruth and Boaz.

Tell the story of the Sower. Use the words from the New Testament (Matthew 13: 3; Mark 4: 3; Luke 8: 5). Mime the action of the story and provide a background of musical sounds.

Mathematical and scientific activities

Grow a cereal seed in a jam jar, trying different seeds. Put the seed in the jar with wet blotting paper holding it to the side of the jar. Mark the jar with a scale in quarter inches or centimetres so that the growth can be noted.

Find out what yeast is and watch what happens when a piece is placed on a dish for a week.

Keep a daily diary to show how much bread your family eats. Get your friends to do the same and then make a graph to show your findings.

Make a circular chart showing the activities of the wheat farmer's year.

112

Find out how windmills work.

Find out what vitamins are. What vitamins are there in bread?

Find out about rotation of crops.

Try some experiments of growing fungus on bread, and find out about the discoveries which Sir Alexander Fleming made.

Art
Paint a picture of a baker putting the loaves in the oven.

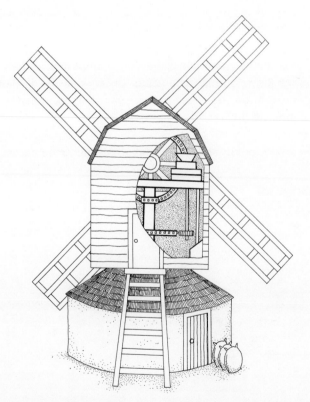

Fig. 3 A model mill. With a little bit of ingenuity, the sails can be made to turn the wheels inside.

Make a large group picture of a baker's shop. On a background of shelves arrange each child's contribution of a loaf. Remember there are many different shaped loaves.

Paint a picture of a post mill on a hill.

Paint or crayon a picture of harvest time on the farm.

Paint a frieze showing a medieval baker being punished for cheating his customers.

Craft
Make a model of a smock-mill cut open to show the stones and hoppers.

Make a large group model, displayed on a large map of Canada, which would show: combine harvester on a wheat field, elevators, trains, grain store on the Great Lakes, grain barges, transfer to ocean-going freighter at Quebec.

Find a recipe for bread and try to make it either at home or in school.

Other activities
The whole project can be linked with the harvest festival. The class could make their own loaves to present at the festival.

FRUIT & VEGETABLES

Fruit and vegetables hold many possibilities for study in primary schools. The topic can be taken very broadly to include fruits of trees and plants throughout the world, and such specialised studies as sweetmaking or winemaking.

Farming can be used as a basis for the topic as a whole, particularly if a fruit farm or market garden can be visited.

Special aspects
This subject is one which is rich in resources from the commercial world with such aids as information booklets and charts. The children can write for many of them, although it is advisable for the teacher to write a covering letter. This gives the opportunity for children to learn how to write letters correctly. Within this project there is scope for the individual child to pursue a personal study of some individual product.

INSPIRATION AND INFORMATION
Reference books
Alnwick, H.: *Our Food and Our Clothes* (Harrap).
Baker, E. M.: *African Fruits* (ULP).
Brett, R. E.: *Man and Plantations* (Hamish Hamilton).
Brooks, K. & Duchesne, J.: *Man Grows Fruit* (Hamish Hamilton).
Claire, C.: *Fruit* (Bruce Gawthorn).
Davidson, H. C.: *The Year's Vegetables* (Warne).
Gregory, O. B.: *Cocoa and Chocolate* (Wheaton).
Jackson, A.: People of the World: *Fruit and Wine Growing in S. Africa* (OUP).
Kirtley, M. E.: *Fruits of the Field and Forest* (Warne).
Noyle, G.: *Fruits and Drinks from Far and Near* (Macmillan).
Pearce, F. G. & Johnson, M.: *The Coconut Lands of Southern India* (OUP).
Perry, G. A.: *The Farmer's Crops* (Blandford).
Philips, E.: Question Time Series: *Coconut; Banana* (Macmillan).
Redmayne, P. & Insull, T.: *Cocoa and Chocolate* (OUP).
Scheib, I.: *The First Book of Food* (Ward).
Selsam, M. E.: *Plants We Eat* (Chatto & Windus).
Waugh, M.: People of Britain: *Fruit and Hop Growing in Kent* (OUP).

Plate 9 A variety of scrap materials brought together to make a model of a hopfield. (Photo by courtesy of Henry Grant)

Stories

Return from the Promised Land: Numbers 13.
Labourers in the Vineyard: Matthew 20.
Wicked Husbandmen: Matthew 21.

Onion Johnny.
The Nutcracker: Warren Chappell (Ward).
The Apple-Stone: N. S. Gray (Dobson).

Poems

Anon.: *Apples.*
Church, Richard: *The Dandelion.*
de la Mare, Walter: *Bunches of Grapes.*
Ember, Brook: *The Witch's House.*
Field, Eugene: *The Sugar-Plum Tree.*
Graves, Robert: *Wild Strawberries.*
Lee, Laurie: *Apples.*
Nesbit, E.: *Baby Seed Song.*
Rosetti, C.: *Goblin Market.*

Music

Eric Coates: *London Suite* (Covent Garden).
Tchaikovsky: *The Nutcracker Suite.*

Songs

Strawberry Fair. Cherry Ripe. Street Cries from 'Oliver!'

Films

Story of Bananas (Boulton-Hawker).
Jamaican Harvest (Rank).
Grape Harvest (Rank).
Sugar as Energy (Sound Services).
Fruitlands of Kent (Rank).
Hoplands of Kent (Rank).
Table Grapes (BIF).
Oranges (S. Africa) (BIF).
Concentrated Sunshine – Sultanas (Australian News and Information
    Bureau).
Grape Fruit (Rank).
Cocoa Highlife (Cadbury's Schools Dept).
Every Day Except Christmas (Covent Garden – Sound Services).
The Harvest Is Yours (Sound Services).
The Cape of Good Fruit (Sound Services).
The Good Things of Life (Smedley's Film Dept).

Filmstrips

Cocoa and Chocolate (Unicorn Head, EFVA).
The Ghana Cocoa Farmer (Educational Productions, EFVA).
The Groundnut (Unicorn Head).
The Coconut (Unicorn Head).
The Story of the Banana (Unicorn Head).
Coffee (Unicorn Head).
Sugar (Common Ground).

Charts

Fruits and Berries 1 (EP BC1).
Fruits and Berries 2 (EP BCP2).
Nuts (EP BC6).
Apple Growing in New Zealand (EP C618).
Banana Growing in Jamaica (EP C1001).
Deciduous Fruit Growing in South Africa (EP 10003).
Orange Growing in South Africa (EP C554).
Peach Growing in California (EP C990).
Pineapples (EP C556).
How Potatoes Are Grown (EP C937).
Potatoes – Ways of Cooking (EP C855).
Life and Work on the Fruit Farm (Classroom Educational Co).
Sources of Sugar (British Sugar Corporation).
Sugar Beet Growing (British Sugar Corporation).
A Sugar Cane Plantation (British Sugar Corporation).
Cape Fruit (EP).
Cocoa Farming (Cadbury's Schools Dept).
Chocolate Making (Cadbury's Schools Dept).
Jaffa Oranges and Grapefruit (EP).
New Zealand Apples (EP).

Workcard material

Trailblazers – *Markets* (Hamish Hamilton).

Useful addresses

Booklets, charts and information are available from the following:
Australia House: ('Project' booklet), Strand, London WC2.
Australian Dried Fruit Board: Imperial House, Kingsway, London WC2.

Bassett Geo. & Co. Ltd: Beulah Road, Sheffield 6.
British Sugar Bureau: 140 Park Lane, London W1.
British Sugar Corporation: 134 Piccadilly, London W1.
Cadbury Bros Ltd: Bournville, Birmingham.
California Raisin Advisory Bureau: c/o British Trades Alphabet, East
    Ardsley, Yorkshire.
Callard & Bowser Ltd: Western Avenue, London W3.
Campbells Soups Ltd: Dept BTA, King's Lynn, Norfolk.
Citrus Marketing Board of Israel: ('Jaffa' booklet) W. S. Caines Ltd,
    Andover House, 193/195 Balaam Street, The Broadway, London E13
Coffee Promotion Council: 10 Eastcheap, London EC3.
Commonwealth Institute: (Commodity booklets – *1. Oranges and Other
    Citrus Fruits*; *3. The Coconut*; *6. Cocoa*; *11. Coffee*;
    13. Groundnuts; *14. Palm Oil Products*) Kensington High Street,
    London W8.
Covent Garden Market: London WC2.
Fyffes Group Ltd: 15 Stratton Street, London W1
Heinz H. J. & Co Ltd: 195 Great Portland Street, London W1.
National Federation of Young Farmers' Clubs: (*Fruit Farming 21*)
    YFC Centre, National Agriculture Centre, Kenilworth,
    Warwks CV8 2LG.
Nestle Co Ltd: St George's House, Park Lane, Croydon.
New Zealand Apple and Pear Marketing Board: 125 Strand,
    London WC2.
Potato Marketing Board: 50 Hans Crescent, London SW1.
Robertson, James & Sons Ltd: 104 Park Street, London W1.
Rowntree & Co Ltd: The Cocoa Works, York.
Smedley's Ltd: Godstone Road, Whyteleafe, Surrey.
South African Co-operative Citrus Exchange: Outspan House,
    Berkhamstead, Herts.
South African Deciduous Fruit Board: Safmark International Ltd,
    7 Staple Inn, London WC1.
South African Wine Farmers' Association: 22 Great Tower Street,
    London EC3.
Southern Postal and Duplicating Services: (*Apple Time in New
    Zealand*) 63 Old Town, London SW4.
Tate & Lyle Ltd: 21 Mincing Lane, London EC3.
Unilever Information Division: Unilever House, Blackfriars, London EC4.

Excursions

Visit to a fruit farm.   Visit a market garden.

Visit to a jam factory.   Kew Gardens.

Local markets.

Visit to the local park and woods, to gather wild fruit (an important feature of the visit should be the recognition of poisonous fruit and guidance regarding eating of fruit from the hedgerow, e.g. washing before eating, in case they have been sprayed). In certain areas, for instance Kent, Hampshire and Worcestershire, hops are grown. Arrange a visit to see the harvesting of this crop.

CREATIVE ACTIVITIES

Imagine you are a fruit farmer taking your fruit to market. Describe your activities from loading your van to your return with an empty van.

Write a poem about your favourite fruit.

Write a poem about seeds. Think about the words you use; try to describe the appearance and movement of windblown seeds.

Write a story about a boy who used a trail of orange pips to get himself out of difficulties.

Describe a market on a busy morning.

Write a story about some children who eat the fruit of a magic tree.

Create in sound the scene of a market, with street sellers' cries and other background sounds.

Drama and movement

Explore the movements of the different kinds of seed dispersal, e.g. 'aeroplanes', 'parachutes', 'poppers'.

121

Act the story of the Goblin Market.

Use the music of Till Eulenspiegel (R. Strauss) and perform the story of the boy who is pursued through the market overturning stalls.

Use the story The Wheel on the School by M. de Jong (Penguin) at the point where the twins attempt to enter the orchard.

Act the story of Jack and the Beanstalk.

Play Oranges and Lemons.

Use Prokofiev's ballet Love of Three Oranges and perform the story.

Imagine the events which would arise in a village if the prize marrow wouldn't stop growing. Discuss and then act the story.

Mathematical and scientific aspects
Find out how seeds are dispersed — by animals, winds and water.

Find out about types of dry seeds — dehiscent, e.g. gorse, poppy; indehiscent, e.g. sycamore, hazel — and fleshy fruits, e.g. tomatoes, marrow, plums and pears. Make a collection of as many as possible.

Make a farming calendar for a fruit farm and market garden.

Find out which areas are most suitable for fruit growing, giving the reasons why.

Discover the reasons for pruning trees.

Collect different kinds of fruits and try to count or estimate the number of seeds in each fruit. Make a block graph to show which plant has the most seeds.

Make a survey of prices of various fruit and vegetable prices in the local market. Show your results in the form of a graph.

Grow seeds and compare their growth.

Make a display of poisonous fruits and invite every class to see it.

Art
Paint a still-life group of fruit and vegetables.

Make a collage picture of a market scene with a fruit and vegetable stall in the foreground and the barrow boy.

Draw or paint a magnified close-up picture of a seed case, e.g. thistle or clematis.

Use root vegetables for printing – potatoes, carrots.

Make a fruit stall. This could be used for mathematics in the classroom.

Paint a picture of an apple harvest.

Use fruit shapes to make a pattern or design.

Paint or make in fabrics a picture of the banana harvest.

Craft
Make a model of a fruit farm.

Make a large cornucopia of cane and papier mâché. Use as a centrepiece for a harvest festival display.

Make jam from harvested fruit.

Model a hop field and oast houses.

Other activities
Harvest festival. This could be arranged around the theme of fruit and vegetables, displaying the produce on market stalls.

TREES &
WOODLANDS

On visits to the country, in many parts of the British Isles, one might be excused for imagining the countryside to be well wooded. Many of the trees we see grow in the hedgerow, and generally speaking they are trees which are indigenous or have become naturalised. Most of them are broadleaved species – oak, elm, ash and horse-chestnut – and the sight of them, especially in the height of summer, provides us with a landscape artist's impression. Trees are indeed aesthetically important to us, which is the reason why, in cities and towns, municipal parks are planted with ornamental and exotic varieties as well as traditional types of British tree. The existence of quite varied stands of trees in parks makes this topic a most appropriate one for the urban school.

In addition, of course, trees are one of our most valuable natural resources. In little more than a thousand years, this country has used and misused its timber resources and found itself near bankruptcy as far as this commodity is concerned. A sea blockade during the First World War was a sharp reminder of the need for some re-planning on a national scale to support the efforts of many private landowners. So in 1919 the Forestry Commission was set up to perform a salvage operation, and in spite of a further set-back during the Second World War, remarkable progress has been made. Two-and-a-quarter million acres are owned by the nation and already over half this area is planted up. Every year some 100 million trees are transplanted into the forests up and down the country towards the target of 10 per cent coverage of our islands.

In spite of this effort, only 10 per cent of our timber needs come from homeland forests, the rest having to be imported along with other such valuable products as oil. Because we need a lot of softwood, it is sound economics to grow spruces, firs and pines. When first planted, there was much criticism of the straggly nature of the young seedling trees, all in well-ordered rows on land which was bare before. Now that the forests have established themselves and thinning has been carried out, the criticism has lessened. By the planting of ornamental trees along the edge of rides and roadways, the provision of woodland trails, picnic areas, and even trailside museums, the Commission have recognised their responsibilities in the provision of recreation facilities and amenities. The response, especially from schools, has been most encouraging.

Special aspects

Because this topic can be illustrated by local visits, even by the youngest children in the school, it is a popular one. The seasonal changes affecting all trees, including conifers, make this an appropriate topic for a twelve-month study, providing a varied programme can be planned to sustain interest. Otherwise a term or a half-term would be appropriate – spring and particularly autumn with leaf fall and seed dispersal providing opportunities for the collection of material. In fact, a visit to a forest or a well-wooded park can be made at any season and will be found to be rewarding.

Plate 9a Within this project there are many opportunities for mathematical applications. Here the girl measures the girth of the tree while the boy determines the diameter.

INFORMATION AND INSPIRATION

Reference books

Allen, Gwen & Denslow, Joan: *Trees* (OUP).

Badmin, S. R.: *Trees in Britain* (Penguin).

Badmin, S. R. & Colvin, B.: *Trees for Town and Country* (Lund Humphries).

Barth, G.: *Woodland Life* (Blandford).

Brooks, Anita: *The Picture Book of Timber* (Weidenfeld & Nicolson).

Chapman, D. H.: *The Seasons and the Woodman* (CUP).

Edlin, H. L.: *Forestry* – Young Farmers' Club Booklet (Evans); *Trees, Woods and Man* (Collins); *British Woodland Trees* (Batsford); *Woodland Crafts in Britain* (Batsford).

Finch, Irene: *Autumn Trees* (Longman).

Ford, V. E.: *Woodland Field Work* (Murray).

Forestry Commission Bulletin 14 (HMSO).

Gallus, G. C.: *Wonderful World of Trees* (Harrap).

Grigson, G.: *Shell Guide to Trees and Shrubs* (Dent).

Hadfield, Miles: *Discovering England's Trees* (Shire).

Hornby, John: *Forestry in Britain* (Macmillan).

Hutchinson, M.: *In a Wood* (ESA).

Jay, B. A.: *Timber* (ESA).

Jenkins, Alan: *A Wealth of Trees* (Methuen).

Lewer, Ivor: *Let's Look at Forestry* (Warne).

Neal, E. G.: *Woodland Ecology* (Heinemann).

Robbie, T. A.: *Teach Yourself Forestry* (EUP).

Vedel, H. & Lange, J.: *Trees and Bushes in Wood and Hedgerow* (Methuen).

Vesey-Fitzgerald, Brian: *Trees* (Ladybird).

Waters, Derek: *Forestry* (Pergamon).

Wolff, Leslie: *Science and the Forester* (Bell).

Applications can be made to the Information Officer, Forestry Commission, 25 Savile Row, London W1, for copies of various pamphlets: *Forestry and the Town School, Starting a School Forest, Forestry in Britain, Forestry in Wales, Forestry in Scotland*, film and book lists.

Stories

Andersen, Hans: *The Fir Tree*.
Grahame, Kenneth: *Wind in the Willows* (Methuen).
Heyerdahl, Thor: *The Kon-Tiki Expedition* — Chapter III (Allen & Unwin).
Jenkins, Alan C.: *A Ship for Nelson* (Hamish Hamilton).
Marryat, F.: *Children of the New Forest* (Blackie & Pan).
Scott, Sir Walter: *Ivanhoe* (for the description of English woodlands) and *The Lady of the Lake* (for the description of West Highland woodlands).
Seton, Anya: *The Two Young Savages* (Hodder & Stoughton).
Williams, J. H.: *Elephant Bill* — for Chapters II and IV particularly (Hart-Davis & Penguin).
The Legend of the Glastonbury Thorn.

Some biblical references

Behold the Assyrian was a cedar in Lebanon (comparing a great nation to a mighty tree): Ezekiel 21; 3–9.
The carpenter stretcheth out his rule (the usefulness of timber): Isaiah 44; 13–16.
Elijah and the Juniper Tree: I Kings 19; 4–5.
The Rod of Aaron: Numbers 17.
Blessed is the man that walketh not (comparing a man to a flourishing tree): Psalm 1; 1–3.

The Spanish Prayer of the Tree

You who pass by and would raise your hand against me
Hearken ere you harm me.
I am the heat of your hearth on the cold Winter night,
The friendly shade screening you from the Summer sun.
And my fruits are refreshing draughts quenching your thirst,
    as you journey on.
I am the beam that holds your house, the board of your table,
    the bed on which you lie.
The timber that builds your boat.
I am the handle of your hoe, the door of your homestead,
    the wood of your cradle.
The shell of your last resting place.

I am the gift of God and the friend of man.
You who pass by, listen to my prayer.
Harm Me Not.

Music
Kendell, Iain & Allin, Steuart: *The Tree.*
Macdowell, Edward: *Ten Woodland Sketches for Piano.*
Mendelssohn, Felix: *Midsummer Night's Dream.*
Resphigi, O.: *Pines of Rome.*
Sibelius, Jan: *Tapiola* (Domain of Forest God – Tapio).
Smetana, F.: *Woods and Fields.*
Wagner, R.: *Forest Murmurings* (from *Siegfried*).

Songs
The Walnut Tree (Roger Fiske).
The Holly and the Ivy.
The Holly.
Green Grow the Leaves.
Hearts of Oak.
The Trees of England.
Song of the Lumbermen.
The Holly Bears a Berry.
Heigh-ho to the Greenwood.

Films
A Growing Concern – Parts I and II (Scottish Film Library).
Forest Heritage (Central Film Library).
Culbin Story (Central Film Library).
A Tree Is Planted (Central Film Library).
Twilight Forest (Unilever Film Library).
Among The Hardwoods (Australian News and Information Bureau).
Tropical Lumbering (Scottish Central Film Library).
Life in a Forest (Educational Foundation).
The Woodlands (Educational Foundation).
Green Gold (United Nations Information Centre).

Forestry (Central Film Library).
The Spruce Bog (Central Film Library).
Journey Into Spring (British Transport Commission).
From Bogland to Forest (Ford).
Transplanting Large Trees (National Coal Board).
Mill by the Medway (Reed Paper Co).
School Forestry (Forestry Commission).

Filmstrips
Growing a Forest (Unicorn Head).
Uses of Timber and *More Uses of Timber* (Educational Productions).
From Tree to Paper (Hulton Press).
Trees and Woodlands (Common Ground).
Life in a Wood (Common Ground).
The Forester (Educational Productions).
The Woodlands (Educational Productions).
Badger (Common Ground).
Hedgehogs and Squirrels (Common Ground).
Woodland Plants (Common Ground).
British Woodland Birds (Educational Productions).
Studies of Common Trees: Parts I and II (Common Ground).
Coniferous Trees (Educational Productions).

Wallcharts
Wood Technology (Educational Productions Ltd).
British Trees: Summer and Winter Identification (Educational
    Productions).
Canadian Timber (Council for Education in World Citizenship).
Picture Sets (Forestry Commission).
Trees of Britain: 1 and 2 (National Savings Posters, HMSO).
Trailblazers — *Forests* (Hamish Hamilton).
Charts — *Birds of the Woodlands, 1–11; Squirrel; Fox; Deer; Rubber*
    (Educational Productions).
Trees and Working with Wood (Schools Council material from
    Bristol University).

Excursions

A series of visits to local parks and woodlands. Permission will be needed for private woodlands.

Visit to a State Forest. Apply to local conservator – address on Forestry Commission pamphlets and telephone directory. A number of forests now have nature trails. Current lists from Council for Nature, Zoological Gardens, Regent's Park, London NW1, and British Tourist Authority, 64 St James's Street, London SW1.

Visit to a tree nursery.

Visit to an arboretum, e.g. Kew Gardens, London; Bedgebury Pinetum, near Tunbridge Wells; Westonbirt Arboretum, near Gloucester.

Museum visits can include No. 4 House, Kew Gardens; Birmingham City Museum which now houses the Pinto Collection; the Natural History Museum where there is an inside Woodland Trail; Buckler's Hard Museum in Hampshire where the Wooden Walls were built.

See *The Shell Nature Lovers' Atlas* (Michael Joseph & Ebury Press) for other local suggestions.

Visit the Commonwealth Institute in Kensington to study timber resources and uses in a variety of countries.

Visit craftsmen shops, e.g. wheelwright in the Science Museum, South Kensington; chair bodger in Castle Hill House, High Wycombe; bow and arrow maker in Edwinstowe in the heart of Sherwood (by appointment only). Write to the Rural Industries Bureau, 35 Camp Road, Wimbledon, London SW19, for addresses of craftsmen in wood.

Docks where timber is unloaded. Timber yards. Furniture manufacturers. Paper makers.

A considerable acreage of woodland in this country is privately owned. Requests in writing might be made to the owners or their agents for permission to enter the woodland and carry out a particular piece of work. The Royal Forestry Society of England and Wales, 102 High Street, Tring, Herts, might be approached for help in this matter. Their quarterly Journal contains interesting articles of general interest and, from time to time, features about the studies of trees and woodlands by children. Off-prints of the latter are sometimes available.

CREATIVE ACTIVITIES
Written work
Write a story about your school or home in which each article or part of the building made of wood disappears.

As part of an adventure course, you have to camp for a weekend in a woodland area. Write about your experiences.

Write a poem about the felling of an old oak tree which has become a traffic hazard.

Write a poem about the birds and other animals which live in the forest.

Walk through woods, in winter, autumn, on a clear day, windy day, etc., and write a poem about it.

Drama and movement
Act the story of Noah and the Ark (Genesis 6, 7, 8 and 9). (Refer to Miracle Plays, e.g. Chester.)

Act the story of Joseph of Arimathea.

Use the ballads about Robin Hood to build up a series of Sherwood Plays.

Act woodland scene from *A Midsummer Night's Dream.*

Build up a story of a magic forest with wood nymphs for a dance sequence.

Mime the felling of a tree, with sound effects of axes, saws, donkey engine and final crash, Try the human voice for all the effects, not forgetting 'Timber!'

Mathematical and scientific assignments
Seeds brought into the classroom, put into groups – wind-dispersed, animal-dispersed, water-dispersed.

Test germination rate of seeds, e.g. sycamore. Soak 100 seeds for twenty-four hours. Lay out on a ten-inch square piece of blotting paper. Keep this moist for two weeks and count the number of seedlings which have sprouted.

Fig. 4 Tree seeds can be germinated in plant pots to observe early growth.

Plant seedling trees in pots or school grounds, if any. Give full details on labels and in record book. Further attention when required, e.g. water, light, more space.

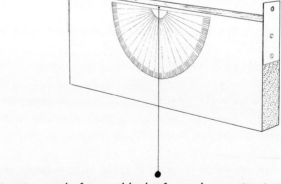

Fig. 5 A simple clinometer made from a block of wood, a protractor, plumb line and two metal plates. Angular measurements of tree heights can be carried out with this instrument.

133

Measurement of trees. Use a variety of methods to find the heights of trees – by shadow stick, by stepping-up method, by distance and angle measurement using instruments made in craftwork.

Measure girth of tree with tape at chest height (as the forester does).

Measure the diameter of trees using home-made callipers.

Measure the tree spread. Use a compass for direction and a tape to measure the distance of outermost branch from the trunk of tree along eight cardinal compass directions.

Other outside activities
Collect twigs, leaves, leaf skeletons, fruits and seeds, fungus, fallen branches.

Make plaster casts of animal tracks (including dogs and cats, birds if in city park).

Carry out tree survey of park after considerable recognition and mapping practice.

Keep a month-by-month record of changes in particular trees – adopted by members of class.

Carry out tree sketches in winter and summer for work later in art.

Carry out study of a tree stump, a tree nursery, woodland, a coppice.

Make a collection of articles which are traditionally made from particular species of wood, e.g. the cartwheel with its hub of elm, spokes of oak and felloes of ash, chessmen and rulers made of box.

Part of the study initiated in class, with material brought into school, and later with work in the field, will be the gradual and systematic build-up of knowledge of the recognition features of the trees common to the area. Leaves, seed forms, tree shape, winter buds, flowers and bark are the main features to concentrate upon. Usually more than one is present and this is a great help at the beginning, but as such a project proceeds, the features can be taken in isolation to test achievement. By beginning with well-known trees like the oak, horse-chestnut, ash and Scots pine, a large repertoire can be quickly built up. Well-tried techniques such as flash cards and snap, as well as the use of filmstrips and other picture material, will all speed up the process.

Art

Make pictures using crayon or paint showing an old neglected forest; a young national forest of coniferous trees; a tree-felling scene in Canada; in Britain; a tree fallen across a road after a gale; an old and decaying tree-stump with animal and plant life; a Red Indian encampment in a forest clearing of tall trees.

Make pen and ink sketches of particular species of trees with insets of leaf and seed shapes for recognition.

Use scraper-board technique to make studies of animals of the woodland scene.

Use leaves for spatter prints and stencils; use leaves for scribble prints; use leaves for printing — ink rolled onto underside of leaves for off-printing.

Make a collection of bark rubbings. In addition to wax crayons and cobbler's wax, use candle for wax-resist treatment afterwards.

Make 'stained-glass' picture of the Tree of Jesse.

Craft

Models: forest scene from Canada, showing logging camp, aerial ropeway for logs to frozen river.
Forest fire beside railway, with steam train, fire towers, etc.
Dock scene with timber being transhipped.
Furniture factory.
A model house with furniture.
A charcoal burner's hut and fire.

Instruments for mensuration: callipers; tapes; clinometer.

Make a wall hanging with trees as a theme: leaves; tree shapes; tracery of branches; conifers. Use appliqué and embroidery techniques.

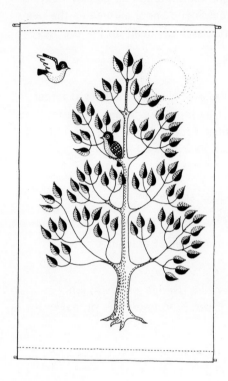

Fig. 6 A tree banner. Several children can collaborate in this appliqué exercise.

Further developments
Studies of paper, rubber, rayon.

Adopt a forest plot (details from the Forestry Commission).

The Village

It is important that children in our primary and middle schools
have the opportunity to study their environment. Often local studies
are made and it can be most valuable for the same children to
make a comparative study of another community. For children in
the town or city, village life will provide the contrast and a compact
unit for survey work. The choice of village is important; it needs to
be near enough to the school for several visits to be made. For
instance, we were able to study the village of Eynsford sixteen miles
away in Kent, where there is a Saxon ford, Norman castle,
Elizabethan and Georgian houses, an interesting parish church,
the River Darent and, near enough to be included in the study,
Lullingstone Roman Villa.

Special aspects

For this topic visits are essential and at least one of the visits needs
to be arranged at the beginning of the topic. This first visit can take
the form of a survey of all the facilities of the village, which will
provide an accurate reference book for further work. After this the
children can work in more detail on various aspects of the village
and plan their work for the next visit. The use of the tape-recorder
on these visits can lead to preparation of a portrait of the village
in sound.

INFORMATION AND INSPIRATION
Books
Allen, A.: *The Story of the Village* (Faber).
Badmin, S. R.: *Village and Town* (Puffin).
Beresford, M. W.: *History on the Ground* (Lutterworth).
Boog-Watson, E. & Carruthers, J. I.: *Country Life Through the Ages*
    (Allen & Unwin).
Bracey, H. E.: *Village Survey* (Get to Know Series – Methuen).
Carey, K. R.: *A Changing Village* (Longman).
Copplestone, T.: *Architecture* (Paul Hamlyn).
Cundall, L.: *The Home District* (Evans).
Daffern, T. G.: *A Guide for Citizens* (Blackwell).
Dalzell, W. R.: *Architecture* (Paul Hamlyn).

Plate 10 A study of a blacksmith's forge can form part of a project on the Village or Fire.
(Photo by courtesy of Pace Ltd)

Davis, D.: *History of Shopping* (Routledge & Kegan Paul).

Deverson, H. J.: *The Map that Came to Life* (OUP).

Duggan, A.: *Look at Churches* (Hamish Hamilton).

Finberg, J.: *Exploring Villages* (Routledge & Kegan Paul).

Fry, L.: *British Railways* (Get to Know Series – Methuen); *Post and Telegraph* (Get to Know Series – Methuen); *Castles* (ESA).

Hellings, M.: *Studying the History of a Village* (Encyclopaedia Britannica).

Hood, P.: *About Maps* (Penguin).

Huggett, R.: *Shops* (Batsford).

Jennings, P.: *The Living Village* (Hodder & Stoughton).

Jones, L.: *Observer Book of Old English Churches* (Warne).

Leacroft, H. & R.: *Early Architecture in Britain* (Methuen); *Churches and Cathedrals* (Puffin).

Lindley, K. A.: *Churches* (ESA).

Martin, E. W.: *Book of the Village* (Phoenix).

Morris, J. A.: *A Junior Sketch Map Economic History of Britain* (Harrap).

Osmond, E.: *Villages* (Batsford); *A Valley Grows Up* (OUP).

Redmayne, P.: *How We House Ourselves* (Philip).

Reeves, M. E.: *The Medieval Village* (Longman).

Rose, W.: *The Village Carpenter* (OUP).

Sellman, R. R.: *English Churches* (Methuen).

Semake, E. E. & Hellberg, R.: *Shops and Stores Today* (Batsford).

Sharp, T.: *The Anatomy of the Village* (Penguin).

Shillito, G. H.: *A Village* (ESA).

Tate, W. E.: *The English Village* (Gollancz).

Thornhill, P.: *Houses and Flats* (Get to Know Series – Methuen); *The Parish Church* (Get to Know Series – Methuen); *Roads and Streets* (Get to Know Series – Methuen).

Tomalin, M.: *Shops and Markets* (Get to Know Series – Methuen); *Water Supply* (Get to Know Series – Methuen).

Vale, E.: *Churches* (Batsford).

West, J.: *Village Records* (Macmillan).

Wilkins, F.: *Markets and Shops* (Blackie); *Laxton* (HMSO).

Williams, V. M.: *Sociology of an English Village* (Routledge & Kegan Paul); *A West Country Village* (Routledge & Kegan Paul).

Stories

Burton, H.: *The Great Gale* (OUP).
Edwards, R.: *The Bypass* (Burke).
De Jong, Meindert: *The Wheel on the School* (Butterworth).
Faulkner, J.: *Moonfleet* (Puffin).
Robertson, W.: *Village by the Stones* (Phoenix).
Sayers, D.: *The Nine Tailors* (New English Library).
Thomas, D.: *Under Milk Wood* (Dent).
Von der Loeff, A.: *They're Drowning Our Village* (ULP).

Poems

Betjeman, John: *The Dear Old Village; The Village Inn.*
Brooke, Rupert: *The Old Vicarage, Grantchester.*
Goldsmith, Oliver: *The Deserted Village.*
Street, Pamela: *The Village Shop.*

Music

Beethoven, L. van: *Pastoral Symphony.*
Delius, F.: *A Village Romeo and Juliet.*
Weiss, W. H.: *The Village Blacksmith* (Longfellow's poem).

Films

The Beginnings of History (Crown Film Unit).
Medieval Village (Rank).
Medieval Castles (Rank).
Your Inheritance (Selwyn Films Ltd).
The Village Blacksmith (BIF).
The Village Bakery (EGS).
The Village Potter (EFVA).
Birds of the River (EFVA).
Mathematics and the Village (three films from Rank).

Filmstrips

The Parish Church (Vista Concord Productions Ltd).

The Castle (Vista Concord Productions Ltd).
The Parish Church (EP).
The English Parish Church (BT).
The Parish Church (Hulton).
The Parish Church (GB).
How Country Folk Get Their Water (Trident).
The Village (CG).
The Medieval Manor (EP).
Piers the Villein (UH).

Charts
Churches – set of fourteen (Wheaton's Architectural Charts).
Houses – set of ten (Wheaton's Architectural Charts).

Excursions
Visit to the village to be studied with a survey carried out.

Abergavenny and District Museum (Rural Crafts); Ashwell Village Museum, Herts; English Rural Life Museum, Reading, Berks.

CREATIVE ACTIVITIES
Find out all that you can about the name of your village. Then write a story about how it was named.

In a small village, the shopkeeper often knows the local news. Write an entry for her diary telling of some of the happenings in the village.

Find out about the parish church, then produce an illustrated guide book which includes architectural details, and any interesting stories about the church.

Look out for interesting names for cottages you may be able to write a story about, e.g. Toll-gate Cottage – a story about the people who used the toll road; the forge, the manse.

142

If there is a blacksmith at work in your village, watch him and then write a poem about this work. Set the poem to music afterwards, or add rhythmic clank of hammer on the anvil.

If there are special fairs or customs associated with your village, describe one of these events.

Imagine you lived in the village in medieval times and describe your life as a villein.

Drama and movement
Create a scene of the village celebrating some special event, e.g. fair on the village green.

Explore in movement the activities on a farm, both of people and machines.

If fairly detailed accounts of village history are available, produce a pageant of the history of the village.

Learn some country dances which are typical of the dancing of the county in which your village is situated.

From the information available on the village of Laxton in the HMSO pamphlet and the film *Medieval Village*, create a play about a family in this village in the Middle Ages who break one of the rules of the Manor, and the consequences of not agreeing to pay the fine imposed.

Mathematical and scientific aspects
Take a traffic count along the main roads in your village. Produce graphs to show the number of vehicles passing the checkpoints at different times of the day.

Carry out a traffic survey of different types of vehicles passing through the village.

If any of the village shops deliver to customers, find out the distances travelled, and plot on a large-scale map or on a graph.

Use bus and train time-tables to find the quickest way to travel to the nearest large town at different times of the day.

Measure your parish church and draw a scale plan of it.

Find out about gradients. If there are hills in your village, try to measure the gradient.

Try to make a sketch map of your village. If it is very small, measure carefully with trundle wheel and draw it to scale.

If there is a stream or village pond, discover what creatures live in it. Prepare a profile drawing with inhabitants shown.

Make a survey of trees growing in the village. Find out which ones have been specially planted and why, and which ones are apparently self-sown. (In Eynsford Village there is a line of trees, the initial letters of which read – Be Wise, My Son. Appropriately the grove runs along the boundary of the school.)

Find out about the village school, and the number of children. If good relationships are established, graphs and charts can be made to record the distances travelled by the children from home to school, as well as other personal information (a counter-invitation to visit your school can be usefully extended here).

Conduct a survey of groups of people in the village, e.g. pensioners, underschool age, schoolchildren, housewives, shopkeepers, farm employees and tradesmen.

Art
This topic gives an ideal opportunity for charcoal and pencil sketches of interesting parts of your village.

A lino cut of an important building in the village – the church – can be made and used for printing. This print could be used for all the booklets about the village produced by the class.

Fig. 7 Book illustrations can be the starting point for a lino cut.

Make a large group fabric collage picture of the villagers celebrating some special occasion, e.g. May Festival, a wedding or Harvest Festival.

Use wax crayons to portray a blacksmith at work.

Paint a series of portraits of people who would have lived in your village in medieval times (provide tools and other trade materials).

Craft
Make a scale model of your village with plaster of Paris on a wire base (or papier mâché). The contour lines can be marked on the base board and balsa-wood posts of scaled height fixed along each line. Newspaper can be used to fill the gaps, and then plaster and bandage technique can be used to produce the required surface. Small blocks of balsa wood can be used to represent the houses and buildings. (See *Making a Miniature Village* by Guy R. Williams, Faber.)

Make a model of the parish church using folded cartridge paper. The nave, chancel, tower transepts and porches are better made separately and then fixed together. Windows and doors can be drawn on by felt pen.

If there is a castle in your village, a model could be made either in its present state or as it was in the past.

Make models of the various types of houses found in your village, e.g. Tudor, Victorian, Georgian. (See a useful series of books, *People and Their Homes*, Books 7, 8, 9, 10, 11 and 12 by H. T. Sutton and G. Lewis, published by Cassell.)

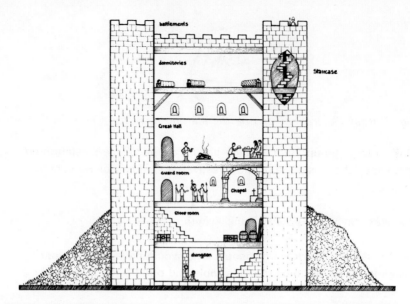

Fig. 8 A model castle can be built with one wall open, showing the various activities within.

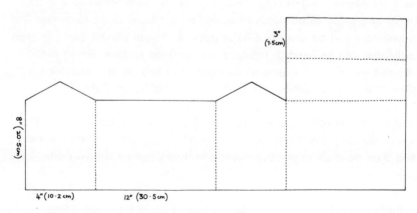

Fig. 9 The layout of a simple building unit.

Where crafts persist or existed in the past in the village being studied, invite groups to learn how to do them, e.g. baking, milling, basketry, pottery, thatching.

146

THE
CITY

This unit of settlement usually represents the ultimate in human development and, as such, can display to a class studying it the great diversity of human activity and organisation, and also represent a unique example of close human co-operation.

Every county has one or more cities, and so a study such as this is feasible for almost every school. Some schools far distant from the capital might choose to base themselves in London for a week or a fortnight to provide themselves with a unique opportunity to study a city from the inside as it were. Help with the planning of such an enterprise can be got from the School Journey Association, 23 Southampton Place, London WC1.

Some schools may prefer to seek within their county (or even in a neighbouring county) a city which can offer a variety such as suggested, and which will include close links with historical events, writers, poets and so on. Certain large towns and even cities might be lacking in so many features that the study of them might have to proceed along a narrower spectrum than is desirable. Often such places have much to offer, but a great deal of research would be necessary to assemble background information before the work with the class can begin.

Greenwich, Eltham and Woolwich have many associations with the past and much to show the present-day investigator. Nevertheless, the number of books of a suitable nature which I can put into young hands is severely limited. However, over ten years, we have gathered together three files of local guidebooks, church histories, leaflets and newspaper cuttings, so that information can be referred to, in order to complement direct observations. One unusual piece of evidence available to us in the *Woolwich Story* by E. E. Jefferson (Woolwich Antiquarian Society) is a chapter on our estate. This gives the reactions to their new situation which the Boxgrove children of ten years ago recorded for posterity.

While on a school journey, we studied Winchester, and this is given as the example of a city study. Some of the situations and activities suggested are unique to that city, but many will have general application to other places. We have introduced a village study in

Plate 11 A model inspired by a visit to the Abbey of St Cross. The rather enthusiastic response of one of the brethren is the sort of reaction one hopes to see during a project.

this book, but the intermediate stage, the town, is an important one too, and so references have been included which would be useful in the study of this smaller community. Once again in the adoption of a town for close study, many more opportunities are available if some care is taken in the initial selection, even if this means travelling a greater distance for the fieldwork.

Special aspects

Where one is in a city school, or nearby, then many field trips should be possible; concentrating day visits on such features as the cathedral, the castle, museums and so on. Because the commercial and business interests will be large – newspapers, factories, workshops – requests for permission are likely to be favourably received, because such organisations will be geared to receiving and entertaining questing youngsters.

Because of the great wealth of material available in many cities there should be many options open for the children to choose from. A school may wish to make a comprehensive study of a city; each class could adopt particular features or historical eras, and after an agreed period of time the results of the individual researches could be combined in a large exhibition or pageant. An even larger 'picture' of a city could be achieved by combining the work of several schools who had agreed to take part in a joint enterprise.

To look particularly at Winchester for a moment, there are some features which make it a valuable place for study. Apart from the beautiful cathedral, there is a 'working' abbey nearby; pilgrims began their long journey to Canterbury from here; amongst the museums are those featuring the histories of the Royal Hampshire Regiment and the Royal Greenjackets – a situation of immediate appeal to boys.

INFORMATION AND INSPIRATION
Books
The City Librarian can be asked to provide a list, and for Winchester these were recommended, and available for consultation in the Reference Department.

Atkinson: *Elizabethan Winchester*, 1963.
Ball: *An Historical Account of Winchester, 1819*
Biddle: *Winchester: Two Thousand Years of History*; *City of Winchester official guide*, 1969.
Goulder: *Winchester Pilgrimage* pamphlets, No. 7.
Milner: *History of Winchester, 1798.*
Northeast: *With an Artist in Winchester*, 1961.
Vesey-Fitzgerald: *Winchester*, 1953.
Victoria County History of Hampshire, Vol. 5, 1900–12.
Woodward: *History of Winchester,* 1889.
Wymer: *The Story of Winchester.*

The City Corporation Publicity Department issues leaflets giving concise information with street plans. Various topical events are advertised, and party rates are usually available for parties of schoolchildren. Guidebooks, postcards, transparencies are available at the Cathedral and information available at other places in the city.

Various guides to the county or geographical region in which the city lies, are also useful to consult: *Pitkin's Guide to Winchester*; *St Cross Hospital Official Guide*: *The New Forest*, etc.

Bell, Gerard: *What Happens when a By-Pass Is Built* (Oliver & Boyd).

Blishen, Edward: *Town Survey*, Books 1–3 (Blond Educational).

Boon, Gordon: *Town Look*, Books 1 and 2 (Pergamon).

Bull, G. B. G.: *A Town Study Companion* (Hulton).

Daffern, T. G.: *A Guide for Citizens* (Blackwell).

Dance, E. H.: *Living in Towns* (Longman).

Duckett, Eleanor: *Alfred the Great and His England* (Collins).

Edwards, R. P. A.: *The By-Pass*; *The New Town* (Burke).

Grove, Jane: *A Town* (ESA).

Hammersley, Alan: *Towns and Town Life* (Blandford).

Lancaster, Osbert: *Draynefleet Revealed* (Murray).

Leacroft, H. & R.: *Churches and Cathedrals* (Puffin).

Lindley, Kenneth: *Town Life and People* (Phoenix).

Mary, John: *Living in Cities* (Longman).

Morris, R. W.: *Town Life Through the Ages* (Allen and Unwin).

Osmond, E.: *Towns* (Batsford).

Rowland, K.: *The Shape of Towns* (Ginn).

See the books suggested at the end of the chapter 'Resources for Learning Outside the School', on page 61 in the first part of the book.

Stories

Baker, George: *Golden Dragon* (about King Alfred the Great) (Lutterworth).

Green, Roger L.: *King Arthur and the Knights of the Round Table* (Penguin).

Hodges, Walter: *The Marsh King* (Penguin); *The Namesake* (about King Alfred) (Bell).

Oman, Carola: *Alfred, King of the English* (Dent).

Sutcliffe, Rosemary: *The Witch's Brat* (Oxford).

Trease, Geoffrey: *Mist Over Athelney* (Macmillan).

Treece, Henry: *Great Captains* (an example of an Arthurian story) (Bodley Head).

In such a study of a particular place, stories can usually be found to illustrate a specific period. For example:
Child, William: *In the Wake of Rebellion* (which tells of Judge Jeffreys) (Warne).
Power, Rhoda: *Redcap Runs Away* (about medieval town life) (Puffin).

Poems
Arlott, John: *A Little Guide to Winchester.*
Browning, Robert: *Up at the Villa — Down in the City.*
Gill, D. M.: *Come Let Us Remake the Joys of Town.*
Masefield, John: *Wanderings — The Town.*
Muir, Edwin: *Good Town.*

Music
Coates, Eric: *London Suite.*
Copland, Aaron: *Music for a Great City*; *Quiet City.*

Songs
Strawberry Fair.
Up and Down the City Road.

Music in Action — The City by William Bulman (Rupert Hart-Davis) is a useful book with many suggestions on the creative work that can be developed on this subject.

Filmstrips
Police Constable (Common Ground).
The Policeman (Rank).
The Dustman (Common Ground).
The Sewerman (Rank).
The Town (Rank).
The City (Rank).
Local Government (Rank).
The Medieval City (Vista Concord Productions Ltd).

Films
Your Local Council (Rank).
The City (six films) (BFI).

Other aids

Set of twenty wallcharts — *You and Your Town* (Educational
Productions).

CREATIVE WORK
Written work

Write a story about your day as a city road sweeper. Include in your
account a description of your usual routine and then tell us about a
most interesting find . . .

Read *The Ice-Cart* by Wilfred Wilson Gibson which begins 'Perched on
my city-office stool . . .' Write a poem from the same viewpoint —
but instead of a hot day on which the poet saw an iceman at work,
deal with a very cold day, or a windy one, and the daydreams you had.

At the corner of a street make a note of the various vehicles which
pass by, and note anything particular about them — especially their
sound. On return to the classroom, compose a series of short poems
about the city street, and add music composed on percussion
instruments, which portray each type of transport.

Paint a picture of a bus queue for some half-a-dozen people. Prepare a
dialogue between changing pairs in the group. Tape-record this with
the sounds of traffic in the background (this could be done with a
second tape-recorder playing traffic noise). Play the recording beside
the picture.

Write a story about the search for a young child missing in the city.

Describe the contents of an antique shop you have been allowed to
explore, concentrating on certain items which intrigue you.

Write a newspaper report of a big parade through the city streets, and
include a special service in the cathedral. Remember that the readers
of the newspaper like to read all about costumes, clothes and the
names and positions of the important people involved.

Write a song about the weekly market in a city square, in which various stall holders shout their wares, and animals and machines of various sizes and kinds make appropriate noises.

Write a documentary play about Cardinal Beaufort, 1404–47. Refer to *Henry Beaufort, Bishop, Chancellor, Cardinal* by L. B. Radford (Pitman).

Drama and movement
Prepare a play called 'Morning in the City' in which various tradesmen and public servants go about their business in a city street. Provide sound effects.

Discuss the story of King Alfred and prepare a pageant of his life story.

Enact the story of St Swithun and the attempts of the monks to re-bury him. (See 'Festival of St. Swithun' in *A Book of Festivals*.)

In the City Hall, there is a representation of the Round Table. Select various stories from Arthurian legends and act them.

On top of St Catherine's Hill outside the city is an Ancient British camp. Develop a play in which the daily routine is demonstrated, only to be shattered by the attack of an enemy.

Research into the story of St Catherine and perform her story for an assembly.

St Giles Fair was an important fair in the Middle Ages. In costume, and with props, re-create the scene of bustle, and excitement. If the sideshows and events could be well prepared, then the whole school could become involved (see 'May Fair' in *A Book of Celebrations* published by Mills & Boon).

Prepare a drama sequence of the monk's day as at St Cross. Boys can dress and act as monks, and the girls take the part of wayfarers who ask for the dole (still provided today) for the sick and needy of the city.

154

Judge Jeffreys presided at the Bloody Assizes in Winchester in 1685. Portray the story of one prisoner, captured, brought to trial and sentenced.

Prepare a Festival of Winchester, including the personalities mentioned above, and William the Conqueror, Sir Walter Raleigh, William of Wykeham, Bishop Henry de Blois, Jane Austen, Sir Christopher Wren, all appearing in short sketches, linked by some prepared music. Possible backcloth of a series of pictures of the city — exteriors and interiors, e.g. slides purchased or taken in the city, or from pictures prepared by the class.

Mathematical and scientific assignments
Izaak Walton fished in the River Itchen. Make up a fisherman's guide to this river with details of the fish which live there, how stock is kept up, who owns the rights, seasons and so on.

It was from Winchester that William the Conqueror began the compilation of the Domesday Book. Plan a similar venture around the city with the co-operation of landowners.

July 15th is St Swithun's Day. Investigate the truth of the legend by asking for access to local newspapers and weather records. Begin weather recording at school over a period of time, at least a term. Record at the same time each day maximum and minimum temperature, amount of rainfall, wind direction and strength, estimate of cloud cover and visibility, air pressure and tendency, wet and dry bulb temperature. All of this will depend upon whether the correct instruments are available. The purchase of these, and the housing of some of them in a Stevenson Screen, will provide opportunity for sustained work not only for the class working on this project, but others in the school too (*Working With Weather* from Bailey Brothers & Swinfen, and the *Ladybird Book of Weather* from Wills & Hepworth, are useful books for beginners).

In the Westgate Museum there is a civic collection of standard weights and measures. Make this a starting point for an historical study of measurement, and prepare a group study of the subject.

Carry out a shopping survey in the city. Allocate streets, roads and squares and groups within the class and establish a colour code for each type of shop: white for food; green for public services and utilities; red for furniture. Plot the findings on a master sheet on your return.

Art

Divide the class into small groups and invite them to prepare a series of pictures showing how Winchester has developed and changed over the centuries. See *A Valley Grows Up* by Edward Osmond (OUP).

Make a series of portraits of the famous people who have been connected with the city (charcoal sketches; acrylic paints used like oils; wax crayons).

Make a series of drawings of interesting features of the city – God Begot House; the City Cross; the Westgate; the old City Mill.

In late Saxon times Winchester was the home of the finest school of calligraphy and manuscript illumination. Make this a starting point for handwriting work and decorated letter forms.

Make a fabric collage of the Emerald City from *The Wizard of Oz*.

Models

Make a model in clay or other modelling medium of King Alfred.

On a large base board draw out the city plan and in cardboard make up a series of models of important buildings. Where time permits, houses and shops in the city's main street can be added to the scene. Use this as a briefing model or as a centrepiece for an exhibition of work. In a classroom where space is at a premium, stick the models on a large display board and produce a different type of bird's-eye view.

156

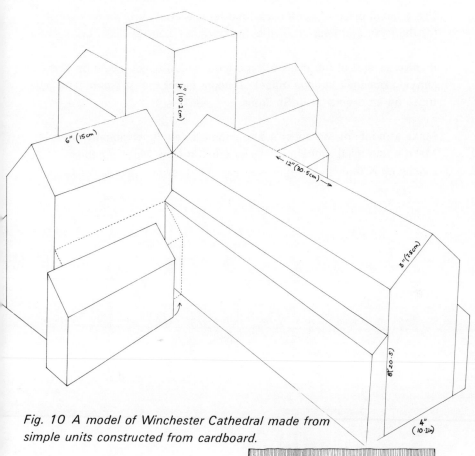

Fig. 10 A model of Winchester Cathedral made from simple units constructed from cardboard.

6" (15cm)

4" (10.2cm)

12" (30.5cm)

3" (7.5cm)

8" (20.5)

4" (10.2cm)

Fig. 11 The city crest of Winchester. The details can be made from cardboard or a modelling medium such as New Clay.

157

Use a small piece of cardboard tube for the body, a table tennis ball for the head and hessian of the appropriate colour to make up a monk.

Involve several of the class to produce a group which could be shown carrying out their various offices. Prepare larger monks' garbs and use these on an excursion to St Cross.

Make a model of the abbey using simple three-dimensional shapes. Make a low relief model of the city crest in clay. Make a papier-mâché copy from this mould (see Fig. 11, previous page).

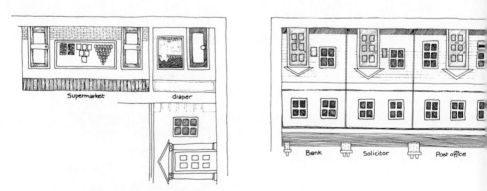

Fig. 12 A field-sketch layout of a city street.

The dawn of history

Children have a natural curiosity about their origin, and as they grow older this extends to an interest in the beginning of the world, and how man and other forms of life developed. Time is a very abstract concept and most teachers would agree that infant and junior children have no real understanding of the size of a thousand years, let alone one million (have we, I wonder ?), and so the subject treatment at this level is often referred to as patch history. By adopting such a method, the period or topic covered is dealt with in some depth, and as well as a knowledge of the Vikings or the Middle Ages, certain other general principles will be learnt which appertain to other periods. It is important that the particular study made by the child appears on his record card. In this way, it is to be hoped that he would not have to do two Norman topics.

The world of prehistoric monsters is a fascinating one, and this interest extends to infants too, who may be having trouble with such words as 'See The Boats', yet can often let such tongue-twisters as 'Tyrannosaurus Rex' roll off their tongues.

Special aspects
Some measure of the continuous and developing interest in this subject has been the almost unbroken run of a series of schools broadcasts for some twenty or so years. Formerly called 'How Things Began', the current radio series is called simply 'Man'. This particular section might therefore be read as an example of a project which is built around a series of broadcasts. But of course, as with all such resource material brought into the classroom, preparation and follow-up work are essential if the programme is going to have any value.

Most theologians today would agree that the Creation story should be treated as a myth, and a very remarkable one. What is so interesting is that the order of events seems so closely to parallel the sequence as suggested by the scientists. Children will enjoy hearing this story from the Bible and similar accounts from other cultures.

Geology and archaeology are both possible sub-projects within this theme, with the inclusion of fieldwork an important aspect of the study, especially on school journeys.

A study of the Bushmen of South Africa makes an interesting comparative piece of work for a group to follow.

Young children particularly have difficulty coping with the concept of time, and the building up of a well-illustrated time chart as the project proceeds will go a long way to eliminate many of the misconceptions which arise, e.g. that the dinosaurs and man were on the earth simultaneously. Some care may need to be taken when using some illustrated books where a degree of artist's licence has been used – in this project, and in fact any other.

INFORMATION AND INSPIRATION
Books
Ager, D. V.: *Introducing Geology* (Faber).
Atkinson, R. J. C.: *Stonehenge* (Hamilton); *Silbury Hill* (BBC).
Bowood, R. & Lampitt, R.: *Our Land in the Making*, Book 1 (Wills & Hepworth).
Carrington, R.: *The Early Days of Man* (Chatto & Windus).
Copley, G. J.: *Going Into the Past* (Phoenix House and Penguin).
Cox, B.: *Prehistoric Animals* (Hamlyn).
Green, G. & Sorrel, A.: *Prehistoric Britain* (Lutterworth Press).
Hanson, H. O.: *I Built a Stone Age House* (Phoenix).
Harland, W. B.: *The Earth: Rocks, Minerals and Fossils* (Studio Vista).
House, F. Clark: *Early Man* (Time-Life).
Hume, E. G.: *Days Before History* (Blackie).
Jessup, R.: *The Wonderful World of Archaeology* (Macdonald).
Kirkaldy, J. F.: *Fossils in Colour*; *Minerals and Rocks in Colour* (Blandford).
Lloyd, Noel & Palmer, Geoffrey: *Quest for Prehistory* (Dobson).
Milburn, D.: *A First Book of Geology* (Blackwell).
Ministry of Public Buildings and Works: *What Is Stonehenge?*
Napier, John: *The Origins of Man* (Bodley Head).
Oakley, K. P.: *Man the Tool Maker* (British Museum, Natural History).

161

Ordnance Survey: *Field Archaeology: Some Notes for Beginners* (HMSO).

Peach, L. Du G.: *Stone Age Man in Britain* (Wills & Hepworth).

Place, R.: *Down to Earth; Britain Before History* (Barrie & Rockliffe).

Quennell, C. H. B. & M.: *Everyday Life in Prehistoric Times* (Batsford).

Shepherd, W.: *Archaeology* (Young Scientist) (Weidenfeld and Nicolson).

Swinton, W. E.: *Digging for Dinosaurs* (Bodley Head); *The Dinosaurs* (Allen & Unwin); *Fossil Amphibians and Reptiles* (British Museum, Natural History).

Titterton, A. F.: *Britain Before the Romans* (Ginn).

White, A.: *Story of Our Rocks and Minerals* (Wills & Hepworth).

Wood, E. S.: *Field Guide to Archaeology* (Collins).

Zim, H. S. & Shaffer, P. R.: *Rocks and Minerals* (Hamlyn).

Stories

Capon, Paul: *Warrior's Moon* (Hodder & Stoughton).

Cornwell, L.: *Hunter's Half Moon* (John Baker).

Doyle, Conan: *The Lost World* (Murray).

Horler, H.: *Kell of the Ancient River* (Harrap).

King, Clive: *Stig of the Dump* (Puffin).

Kipling, Rudyard: *Just So Stories* (Macmillan) (for such stories as *How the First Letter Was Made*; *The Cat that Walked by Himself*; *How the Alphabet Was Made*).

Marshall, James Vance: *Walkabout* (Penguin).

Perkins, L.: *The Cave Twins* (Cape).

Reason, J.: *Bran, Bronze-Smith* (Dent).

Schmeltzer, Kurt: *The Axe of Bronze* (Constable).

Smith, V.: *Moon in the River* (Longman).

Sutcliffe, Rosemary: *Warrior Scarlet* (Oxford).

Tolkien, J. R. R.: *Farmer Giles of Ham* (Allen & Unwin).

Treece, H.: *Man of the Hills*; *Golden Strangers* (Bodley Head).

Films

Building a Bronze Age House (Plymouth).

The Beginning of History (EFVA).

Primitive Iron Smelting (EFVA).
Stone Age Tools (Burroughs Welcome).
Stone Age — two films (Crown Film Unit).
Bronze Age — two films (Crown Film Unit).
Iron Age — one film (Crown Film Unit).
Paleolithic Man (Gateway).
Stonehenge (Gateway).

Filmstrips
People Before History (Educational Productions)
People Before History (Common Ground).
How Man Began (Educational Productions).
Living Before History, 1. *Cave Men and Hunters*; 2. *Farmers and Craftsmen* (Common Ground).
Hunters of the Stone Age; *Farmers of the New Stone Age*; *The Bronze Age*; *The Iron Age* (Unicorn Head).
Palaeolithic Hunters and Foodgatherers; *The New Stone Age*; *The First Metal Workers*; *The Iron Age* (Dansk Brandfilm — from Educational Productions).
8-mm Cassettes: *Prehistoric Man in Europe* — (a) Old and Middle Stone Age; (b) Late Stone Age (Macmillan).

Other aids
A series of broadcasts, 'Man', BBC, with pupils' and teachers' pamphlets.
The Beginning of History (Ministry of Education Visual Unit).
Ancient Britain, two Ordnance Survey maps (HMSO).
London University, Institute of Archaeology — useful organisation for teachers to join.
Archaeological News Letter (from 60 Frederick Street, Gray's Inn Road, London, WC1), for details of digs and current discoveries.

Excursions
Many museums, national and local, have material which would illustrate this topic — rocks, fossils, artefacts, jewellery.

Natural History Museum, South Kensington, for Fossil Gallery.

Crystal Palace Park, SE London, to see life-size concrete reconstructions of prehistoric monsters.

Quarries, seashore, cuttings, etc., to see rocks, minerals and fossils.

Prehistoric remains in various parts of the country. Many of these are in the care of the Ministry of Public Buildings and Works and so, if prior application is made, free passes can be issued. For example, Grimes Graves, Norfolk; Stonehenge; Avebury; Silbury Hill; Kennet Long Barrow; Wookey Hole.

Arrange a visit to see potters and weavers at work, and note those tools and implements which are similar to those used by early man.

In the Norfolk area, try to visit the flint knappers at Brandon.

In Kew Gardens, in No. 1 Museum there are a number of show cases for which the staff have prepared quiz sheets, e.g. 'The Origins of Plant Cultivation', 'Crop Plants and Centres of Origin', and an intriguing one on 'Arrow Poisons'.

CREATIVE ACTIVITIES
Written work
You are helping with a dig on the top of the Herefordshire Beacon in the Malvern Hills. You are camping with the party. Write about a dream you had after you had discovered a piece of bronze jewellery.

You are a cave dweller. Tell of the day in your life when the rest of the family went out hunting, leaving you to guard the animals.

You witness a struggle between two great monsters — a stegosaurus and a triceratops. Describe the conflict — in words, pictures and models.

You have gone to Cheddar, to visit one of the famous caves — Cox's or Gough's. Write a poem in which you describe the stalactites and stalagmites, pools and other strange and beautiful sights.

164

Try to invent a primitive language with very few sounds — and words for animals, enemy, food, fire and so on. Use a sign language to record this.

Write a technical account of the making of a stone axe.

Drama and movement work
Act the preparation for the trapping of a wild animal for food. Include dance, sacrifices and painting.

Mime the action of the fisherman telling a landsman how he catches his food, and vice versa.

Tell the story of an attack on a village, and what happens to the vanquished and their possessions.

Other outside activities
Where permission can be obtained, try to make up houses of the different ages of wood, leaves, etc. The lighting of a fire makes a challenging exercise. (Old fur coats might be pressed into service as costumes.)

Mathematical and scientific assignments
Work out a simple way of counting (help from books on the way that shepherds still count today: *How Things Began — Arithmetic* by E. R. Boyce published by Macmillan).

Determine ways in which primitive man, cooked, captured prey, warmed himself, and preserved food.

With help from books and museum visits, learn how scientists are able to date the past.

Art

Alan Sorrell has produced some remarkable reconstructions of many historical buildings. After a visit to a prehistoric site, try to draw a picture in which buildings, people and livestock are present.

Make a large cave painting of a deer. Try scratching this into a layer of wax crayon heavily applied to a piece of paper. Soot was used for colouring work and this can be collected on a saucer, carefully held above a candle flame. Mix with vaseline or other greasy substance.

Make a long frieze of the various kinds of prehistoric animal. Group them in order of size or into plant-eating and flesh-eating animals.

Collect large, round, smooth stones and decorate these with paints in simple patterns. The early hunters used these. Were they signs or counters for a game?

Fig. 13 Painted stones.

Draw a large outline of a prehistoric monster. Using a strong adhesive (Gluak), stick sections of egg boxes onto the monster to give a scaly appearance. After it is dry, cut out the shape and remount on a large frieze already prepared with hunters, landscape, etc.

(See *The Possible Worlds of Fernando Krahn* (Cape) for a very light-hearted look at the terrifying world of prehistory.)

Craft

Refer to various county guides to find out where there have been archaeological finds, and ask permission to search for stones which may have been used in tools and weapons. Look at books and in museums to see the shape of these, and from the seashore or riverside look for similar shapes. With wooden hafts, try to re-create an armoury of Stone Age weapons.

Construct a cave in the classroom. This is best done across a corner of the room, with lengths of timber to support the roof. A stockroom cupboard or an awkward space in the classroom would be just the location. Very large sheets of brown paper can be joined, and folded, and pinned to wall and ceiling and chairs, and other furniture fixed behind. Pieces of muslin dipped in plaster of Paris can be draped over the top of a series of boxes fastened together to produce columns for the cave. Polystyrene pieces can often be had just for the asking from radio and other dealers. These, sprayed in various colours, can be arranged inside the cave. A wall painting, a 'fire' of sticks, some bones and children in costume will complete the scene.

Prepare a wire armature, stapled to a wooden block, to create a small prehistoric monster. Cover the wire with newspaper and then cover with papier mâché.

Fig. 14 The wire armature prepared for a prehistoric monster model.

Fig. 15 Details of head after addition of papier mâché.

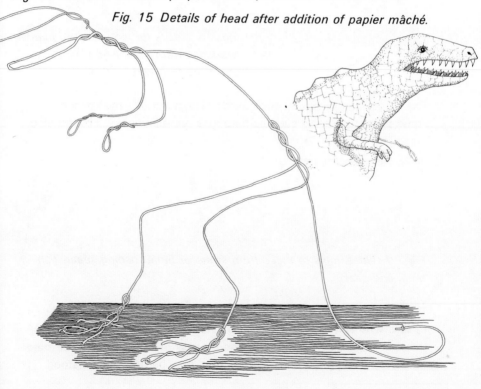

Make a large monster with chicken-wire shapes for torso, legs and head. Cover with muslin and plaster of Paris. Embellish with egg-carton material and then paint. An old table can be used as the basis for a model, but efforts should be made to relieve the 'stiffness' by having the tail and neck and head curve away from the longitudinal axis.

Use clay to make up shapes for the preparation of necklaces. Make holes in the beads for threading after they have dried and been decorated. Biscuit firing in a kiln will ensure some permanence in the model.

Fig. 16 Beads for a Stone Age maiden. Modelled from modelling clay and fixed to a wire necklace.

Use a modelling medium such as Newclay to create the shapes of some prehistoric tools such as harpoons and fish-hooks. Fix and bind these into wooden hafts.

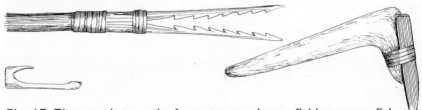

Fig. 17 Three tools to make from stone or bone: fishing spear, fish hook and adze.

The building of a Stone Age home would be an interesting project for a class with some open space available. Dressed in suitable costume they could go through the day. The process of cooking might be tried under supervision, so that the problems may be better understood.

Previously cleaned vegetables can be wrapped in a covering of leaves (with sharp twigs holding them in place). A fire of hot ashes should be prepared and the food placed on it for about an hour. With care the vegetables should be removed and unwrapped for examination. It would be advisable to terminate the experiment there because of the risks to stomachs more attuned to the food of the twentieth century. (Other ideas to be tried out in a similar experimental way can be found in *The French at Table* by Raymond Oliver, published by Michael Joseph.)

Dig up some clay from the ground (as far down as possible to avoid impurities), fashion simple vessels and leave in the sun to dry. Rub inside and out with a pebble to 'glaze'. Place into the hot ash of a fire and keep there for as long as possible.

With permission from a farmer collect thin twigs from hazel, rowan or willow hedges. Attempt to make a simple basket shape. Lay four stakes across four in the form of a cross and weave a long pliable willow under and over each four twigs of the base. After a few rounds, open the crossed twigs to make eight sets of two; after more weaving open to make sixteen separate rods. Trim off the excess lengths of willow when a diameter of a foot has been reached. Another eight new rods should now be pushed alongside the cut-off lengths and forced into an upright position.

Where the rods have dried out they should be soaked in water for an hour or so before weaving. More pliable rods should be used for the weaving, or up-setting as it is called, and only a simple in and out stroke should be used to begin with. The basket should now continue up as far as possible. Considerable strength is needed to work willow and hazel, and experience with ordinary cane will be invaluable before trying it. New wands of willow will have to be introduced frequently, laying these on top of the rod about to run out. The plaiting of a border is rather elaborate, and the child should be asked to bend over all the uprights and pass them under the last weaving stroke and pull them tight. (A fuller treatment can be found in *Willow Basket-Work* by A. G. Knock, Dryad Press.)

Spinning, dyeing and weaving work can also be introduced in this project.

Life in Tudor England

The Tudor monarchs each had a vital part to play in the growth of England. Their interest in entertainment encouraged the development of the theatre and music. England at this time was lively and colourful, the simple life of the ordinary peasant contrasting with the gay life and beautiful homes of the rich. However, there were the festive occasions, May Day revels and annual fairs, which were enjoyed by all. It was a time of great sea battles and sailors exploring the seas of the world, discovering countries which in time would become part of the British Empire.

There are many aspects of this part of English history which excite and interest children and this encourages them to make a detailed study of this period.

Special aspects
This topic might well be approached through a local village which has a good number of Tudor dwellings or by the creation of an imaginary Tudor village. The class could divide into families each of which would take a particular trade or position in the village, and many creative activities could be based on these family units.

Another approach to the study of the Tudors is through one particular family. For instance, the Petre family which lived in Ingatestone Hall in Essex is an excellent example as there is so much archive material available on which to base the study.

INFORMATION AND INSPIRATION
Books
Allen, J.: *An Elizabethan Actor* (Oxford).
Ault, S. & Workmam, B.: *Tudors and Stuarts* (Blackie).
Bindoff, S. T.: *Tudor England* (Penguin).
Black, J. B.: *The Reign of Elizabeth* (OUP).
Boog-Watson, E. J.: *An Elizabethan Sailor* (Oxford).
Brooke, I.: *English Costume in the Age of Elizabeth* (Black).
Brown, I.: *Shakespeare* (Nelson).

Burgess, C. V.: *Discovering the Theatre* (ULP).

Burton, H. M.: *Shakespeare and His Plays* (Methuen).

Cunnington, P.: *Costume* (Black).

Donahue, P.: *Plymouth Ho!* (Longman).

Doncaster, I.: *Elizabethan and Jacobean Home Life* (Longman).

Emmison, F. G.: *Tudor Secretary: Sir William Petre* (Longman).

Essex County Record Office: *Elizabethan Essex: Chelmsford; Introduction to Ingatestone Hall* (Essex County Council).

Henderson, A.: *The Family House* (Phoenix).

Hodges, C. W.: *Shakespeare's Theatre* (OUP).

Kennett, J.: *With Powder, Shot and Sword* (Blackie).

Kyle, E.: *Queen of Scots* (Nelson).

Macower, F.: *A Sixteenth Century Clothworker* (Oxford).

Magnus, P.: *Sir Walter Raleigh* (Collins).

Mattingly, G.: *The Defeat of the Spanish Armada* (Penguin).

Neale, J. E.: *Queen Elizabeth* (Penguin).

Nicolai, C. L. R.: *Shakespeare's England* (Bruce & Gawthorn).

Peach, L. du Garde: *Sir Walter Raleigh; The Story of the First Queen Elizabeth* (Wills & Hepworth).

Reece, M. M.: *William Shakespeare* (E. Arnold).

Reeves, M. E.: *Elizabethan Court; Elizabethan Citizen* (Longman).

Richardson, H.: *An Elizabethan Lady of the Manor* (Oxford).

Richmond, B.: *A Band of Beggars and Rogues* (Oxford).

Robinson, G.: *Elizabethan Ship* (Longman).

Titley, Paul: *Tudors and Stuarts* (Look and Remember Series) (Allman).

Unstead, R. J.: *Tudors and Stuarts; A History of Houses; Travel by Road; People in History* 3 (Black).

Welchman, C.: *A London Apprentice* (Oxford).

Williamson, J. A.: *Sir Francis Drake* (Collins).

Stories

Baines, Reed M.: *The Gate House* (Arnold).

Bell, D.: *Drake Was My Captain* (Warne).

'Bryher': *Player's Boy* (Hodder & Stoughton).

Chute, M.: *The Wonderful Winter* (Dent).

Dallow, M.: *Heir of Charlcote* (Puffin).

Daniell, D. S.: *The Boy They Made King* (Cape).

Davey, C.: *The Monk who Shook the World* (Lutterworth).

Dawlish, P.: *Aztec Gold* (OUP); *He Went with Drake* (Harrap).

Fidler, K.: *Tales of the West Country* (Lutterworth).

Hall, M. K.: *Sturdy Rogue* (Nelson).

Harnett, C.: *The Woolpack*; *Stars of Fortune* (Methuen).

Kingsley, C.: *Westward Ho!* (Everyman).

Kirtland, G. B.: *One Day in Elizabethan England* (Macmillan).

Knight, F.: *Remember Vera Cruz!* (Macdonald).

Lamb, C. & M.: *Tales from Shakespeare* (Longman).

Lane, J.: *The Escape of the Queen* (Evans).

Lewis, C. Day: *Dick Willoughby* (Blackwell).

McGraw, E. J.: *The Golden Goblet* (Penguin).

Oliver, J.: *Queen Most Fair* (Atlantic Book Co).

Ross, S.: *A Masque of Traitors* (Hodder & Stoughton).

Rush, P.: *My Brother Lambert*; *London's Wonderful Bridge* (Harrap).

Sutcliff, R.: *Queen Elizabeth Story*; *Brother Dusty Feet*; *The Armourer's House* (OUP).

Sutton, S.: *Queen's Champion* (E. Arnold).

Trease, G.: *Cue for Treason* (Penguin).

Treece, H.: *Wickham of the Armada* (Hulton).

Upson, D. B.: *Elizabethan Adventure*; *They Lived on London Bridge* (Hutchinson).

Wibberley, L.: *The King's Beard* (Faber).

Wood, A. S.: *Beat the Drum* (Hodder).

Poems

Barnefield, Richard: *The Nightingale*.

Campion, Thomas: *Cherry Ripe*; *Jack and Joan they think no ill.*

Daniel, S.: *Care-Charmer Sleep*.

Dekker, Thomas: *Golden Slumbers*; *Art thou poor.*

Herbert, G.: *The Gifts of God.*

Herrick, R.: *Counsel to Girls*; *The Poetry of Dress*; *To Daffodils.*

Heywood, Thomas: *Pack clouds away.*

Howard, Henry (Earl of Surrey): *Description of Spring.*

Jonson, Ben: *The Noble Nature*; *Witches Charm*; *Hymn to Diana.*

Nash, T.: *Spring.*

Shakespeare, W.: Over hill, over dale (*A Midsummer Night's Dream*, Act II, Scene I); I know a bank (*A Midsummer Night's Dream*, Act II, Scene II); The Three Witches (*Macbeth*, Act IV, Scene I). See 'Music' for other poems.

Sidney, Sir Philip: *A Ditty.*

Spenser, E.: *The Butterfly in the Garden*; *Cygmis*; *Una and the Lion*; *Prothalamion.*

Tennyson, A.: *The Revenge.*

Wyatt, Sir T.: *The Lover's Appeal.*

Music

Bull, John & Farnaby, Giles: Quartet for Recorders: *Two Tudor Self-Portraits* (Faber).

Byrd, William: *The Queenes Alman* and *Galliard* (Faber).

Songs

Arne, T. A.: *When daisies pied*; *Where the bee sucks*; *Blow, blow thou winter wind.*

Armstrong, Gibbs. G.: *You spotted snakes.*

Anon: *Have you seen but the white lily grow.*

Campion, T.: *There is a garden.*

Dowland: *Come again, sweet love.*

Dunhill, T.: *Full Fathom Five.*

Dyson, G.: *When icicles hang by the wall.*

German, E.: *O peaceful England.*

Morley, T.: *It was a lover and his lass.*

Purcell, H.: *Come unto these yellow sands*; *Hark the echoing air*; *Nymphs and Shepherds.*

Schubert, F.: *Who is Sylvia?*

Traditional: *Greensleeves*; *Cherry Ripe*; *Drink to me only.*

Music for dancing

Country dances: *Sedany* or *Dargason*; *Sellengers Round.*

Music for listening

Berlioz, H.: *Romeo et Juliette*, Op. 17 (Decca LD 6098).

Elgar, E.: *Falstaff*, Op. 68 (Decca LXT 2940).

Mendelssohn, F.: *A Midsummer Night's Dream*.

Music from Hampton Court: *Tudor Music of Henry VIII*
(HMV HQS 1141).

Tchaikovsky, P.: *Hamlet* (Decca ACL 10); *Romeo and Juliet*
(Decca ACL 11).

Williams, V.: *Greensleeves* (Nixa NLP 905); *Elizabethan Top 20*
(EMI).

Films

Sir Francis Drake (Plymouth).

Sir Francis Drake (GB).

Elizabethan England (Gateway).

The England of Elizabeth (British Transport Co).

William Shakespeare (Rank).

Introducing Shakespeare (Plymouth).

Henry V Elizabethan Stage Extract (Rank).

Filmstrips

Tudor London (Common Ground).

Under Tudor Kings (Educational Productions).

Henry VIII (Common Ground).

Queen Elizabeth I (Common Ground).

Tudor Life (Common Ground).

Thomas the Apprentice (Hulton).

Elizabeth (Visual Productions).

Drake (Visual Productions).

North-East Passage (Visual Productions).

North-West Passage (Visual Productions).

Sir Walter Raleigh (Visual Productions).

The Revenge (Visual Productions).

The Evolution of the English Home, Part 4 (Common Ground).

Other aids

Jackdaw Publications (Cape Ltd):

No. 5. The Armada.

No. 9. Young Shakespeare.

No. 25. Henry VIII and the Dissolution of the Monasteries.

No. 53. Queen Elizabeth I.

Macmillan History Pictures.

Record: Makers of History: *Elizabeth I Queen of England* (HMV).

Picture postcards from National Portrait Gallery.

Excursions

Cambridge: Sawston Hall, Cambridge.

Cheshire: Adlington Hall, Macclesfield.

Cheshire: Churche's Mansion, Nantwich; Little Moreton Hall,
Congleton; Lyme Park, Disley.

Cornwall: Godolphin House, Helston.

Cumberland: Naworth Castle, Brampton.

Derbyshire: Hardwick Hall, Chesterfield.

Devonshire: Elizabethan House, Plymouth; Buckland Abbey, Tavistock;
Cadhay, Ottery St Mary; Hayes Barton, Budleigh Salterton.

Essex: Gosfield Hall, Gosfield; Paycockes, Coggeshall.

Hampshire: Breamore House, Breamore.

Hertfordshire: Hatfield House, Hatfield.

Kent: Boughton Monchelsea Place, Maidstone; Knole House,
Sevenoaks; Penshurst Place, near Tunbridge Wells.

Lancashire: Platt Hall (costume), Manchester; Speke Hall, Liverpool.

London: Geffrye Museum, London.

Lincolnshire: Doddington Hall, Doddington.

Middlesex: Hampton Court Palace, Hampton Court.

Norfolk: East Barsham Manor, East Barsham; The Elizabethan
Museum, Great Yarmouth.

Shropshire: Hodnet Hall, near Market Drayton.

Somerset: Montacute House, near Yeovil.

Surrey: Loseley House, Guildford.

Sussex: Danny, Hurstpierpoint; Parham, Pulborough.

Warwickshire: Shakespeare's Birthplace, Anne Hathaway's Cottage,
Hall's Croft, Mary Arden's House, New Place, all in Stratford-on-

Avon. Combine with visit to Memorial Theatre to see Shakespeare play; theatre visit to see Shakespeare play, or performance by another school.

Wiltshire: Avebury Manor, near Marlborough.

Yorkshire: Burton Agnes Hall, Bridlington.

Ben Jonson's comedies are difficult reading for children but wonderful theatre. A chance to see one performed, professionally or by a senior school, should not be missed.

CREATIVE ACTIVITIES
Written work

Write about a visit to a fair in Tudor times.

May Day revels. Imagine you are one of the May Queen's attendants.

Imagine you are in a town or village which is visited by Queen Elizabeth on one of her 'progresses'.

Write a poem in praise of Queen Elizabeth I.

Write a poem about the Armada.

Describe the visit of the players to the village innyard.

Imagine you are a new sailor on board an Elizabethan ship; describe your first few days out of harbour crossing the stormy Bay of Biscay.

Imagine you are one of the crowd watching a royal river procession, and describe this as it passes you.

Imagine you are one of the players at the Globe Theatre, acting with William Shakespeare. Write about a boisterous audience you performed before.

On a visit to a tournament, you are challenged to take a lance in the tilt yard. Make up a ballad about this exciting event. Accompany with the guitar.

Describe Christmas festivities in the Royal Palaces.

Drama and movement
May Day revels.

Tudor fair and market.

Plan and act a play on the life of Sir Francis Drake.

Invent a masque or pageant to entertain Queen Elizabeth I.

Act suitable scenes from Shakespeare's plays, e.g. *Midsummer Night's Dream, Twelfth Night.*

Country dancing.

Mathematical and scientific aspects
Find out about the uses of the astrolabe, backstaff, quadrant and mariners' compass.

Make scale drawings of the plans of ships.

Find out how tonnage was calculated in Tudor times.

Art and craft
Model of a Tudor village.

Make a maypole and either erect it in the classroom and decorate the whole room as a May Day scene with dancers and decorations or erect it outside on a grass area where May Day festivities could be held.

Arrange the room as a Tudor fair, with stalls and entertainments displayed in models and large paintings.

Make models of Tudor homes, e.g. Elizabethan mansion, timber-framed houses.

Model an Elizabethan port.

Make a large model of an Elizabethan ship.

Make a model of an inn with the innyard set out for visiting players.

Model a kitchen scene.

A working model of a ducking stool.

A model of a pillory.

Make armour out of cardboard.

Using chicken wire as a base, make figures of ladies dressed in Tudor costume.

Make a model of the Globe Theatre.

Many of the Tudor hats and shoes can easily be made out of felt.

Make pomanders, with cloves and oranges. Tie a ribbon firmly round an orange, then stick cloves into the orange so that the heads of the cloves touch, then wrap the orange and leave it in a warm dry place.

Make a study of Elizabethan embroidery and produce examples of it. (There are good examples in museums and stately homes.)

Make pot-pourri, by collecting petals and scented leaves, mixing the dried petals with salt, spices and cloves (there is a chapter on this in *Pleasure and Profit*, published by the Women's Institute).

Group paintings or large material pictures of: The Queen Hunting; A Royal River Procession; The Queen's Progress; A Masque; The Armada.

Paint or crayon pictures of: Street Scenes; The Bear Garden; A Tournament; The Theatre; Ships.

Dress teenage dolls in Elizabethan costume to make a court scene.

Make a Tudor court scene in cut-out folded card.

Make some of the weapons used in Tudor times.

Make a medium-size or full-size figure of Queen Elizabeth. Use chicken wire to produce basic shape of body, with large skirt, etc. Cover with papier mâché and paint. Facial details can be made from modelling clay.

Outside activities
The class could plan a May Day festival or a Tudor fair on a grass area or in the playground and invite other classes to join in the festivities, e.g. country dancing, crowning the May Queen.

CAPTAIN COOK

Special anniversaries and centenaries can provide interesting subjects for projects. There are usually special exhibitions, booklets and special films available. During 1969–1970 many events took place to celebrate the bicentenary of Cook's first voyage; amongst these events was a Royal Tour to places visited by Cook. This naturally aroused interest among the children and so a study of the life of Captain Cook was started. The project included studies of the many places which Cook visited on all of his voyages. This project can still remain topical until 1980 when the third voyage bicentenary celebrations will take place.

Special aspects

As this topic is linked together by the life of one man, it lends itself to a documentary-type story of his life. The story can be divided into four sections: his early life and Navy experience and each of the three voyages. Part One: a straightforward narration and a poem about the charting of the St Lawrence River. Part Two: a narration with creative music about the *Endeavour* on the Great Barrier Reef. Part Three: use of the Radio Vision filmstrip of Cook's second voyage with taped commentary by the class. Part Four: a dramatic sequence. Each part could be linked by short scenes on board ship, with shanties sung and composed by the children, accompanied on the accordion.

INSPIRATION AND INFORMATION

Books

Beaglehole, J. C.: *The Journals of Captain James Cook* (CUP).

Belcher, N. H. & Moore, W. G.: *A Family in New Zealand* (Hulton).

Bethers, R.: *Islands of Adventure* (Constable).

Bianchi, L.: *Hawaii in Pictures* (Oak Tree Press).

Bigwood, K. & J.: *New Zealand in Colour* (Thames & Hudson: 2 vols.).

Brindley, A.: *Living in New Zealand* (OUP).

Brown, B.: *People of the Many Islands* (Chatto & Windus).

Burchfield, R. W. & E. M.: *New Zealand* (A. & C. Black).

Burns, Sir A.: *Fiji* (HMSO).

Caldwell, J. C.: *Let's Visit New Zealand* (Burke).

Cochrane, R.: *Houses* (Life in the Pacific) (OUP).

Coggins, J.: *By Star and Compass* (World's Work).

Crocombe, R.: *The Cook Islands* (Wellington, Government Printer).

Crombie, I.: *Fiji* (Longman).

Daniell, D. Scott: *Flight One Australia* (Wills & Hepworth).

Du Garde Peach, L.: *The Story of Captain Cook* (Wills & Hepworth).

Finkel, G.: *James Cook, Royal Navy* (Angus & Robertson).

Finlayson, R. & Smith, J.: *The Maoris of New Zealand* (OUP).

Fraser, C.: *With Captain Cook in New Zealand* (Muller).

Greenhill, Basil: *James Cook* (The Opening of the Pacific) (HMSO).

Hawkins, S.: *Australian Animals and Birds* (Angus & Robertson).

Heyerdahl, T.: *The Kon-Tiki Expedition; Aku-Aku: The Secret of Easter Island* (Allen & Unwin).

Hobley, L. F.: *Exploring the Pacific* (Methuen).

Hornby, J.: *The Beachcombers' Bell* (Macmillan).

Kaula, E. M.: *The First Book of New Zealand* (Ward).

Kennedy, R.: *Farmers of the Pacific Islands; Fishermen of the Pacific Islands* (Wellington Reed).

Knight, Capt. F.: *Stories of Famous Ships* (Oliver & Boyd).

Knight, Frank: *The Young Captain Cook* (Max Parrish).

Lloyd, C.: *Captain Cook* (Faber).

Longley, J.: *New Zealand* (Friday Press).

Maziere, F.: *Tieva — His Life in the Pacific Isles* (Chatto & Windus).

Merrett, J.: *Captain James Cook* (Muller).

Moore, W. G.: *A Family in Samoa* (Hulton).

Moorehead, A.: *The Fatal Impact* (Penguin).

Nyacakalou, L.: *Village Life in Fiji* (Wellington, Government Printer).

Purton, R.: *Captain Cook* (McGraw Hill).

Purton, R. W.: *Man in New Zealand* (Hamish Hamilton).

Reed, A. W.: *How the Maoris Came; How the Maoris Lived; Games the Maoris Played* (Reed, Wellington, distributed by Bailey Bros. & Swinfen).

Reinits, R. & T.: *The Voyages of Captain Cook* (Paul Hamlyn).

Robson, M.: *New Zealand in Pictures* (Oak Tree Press).

Shadbolt, M.: *Shell Guide to New Zealand* (Michael Joseph).

Sperry, A.: *All about Captain Cook* (W. H. Allen).
Villiers, A.: *Captain Cook the Seaman's Seaman* (Puffin).
Ward, R.: *Islands of the South Pacific* (ESA).
Warner, O.: *Captain Cook and the South Pacific* (Cassell).

Stories
Alpero, A.: *Legends of the South Seas* (John Murray).
Arnold, R.: *The Freedom of Ariki* (Angus & Robertson).
Bacon, R. L.: *The Boy and the Taniwha* (Collins).
Godfrey, M.: *South for Gold* (Deutsch).
Hames, Inez: *Folk Tales of the South Pacific* (ULP).
Hodgson, D. & Lawson, P.: *Kuma Was a Maori Girl* (Methuen).
Kamm, J.: *He Sailed with Captain Cook* (Harrap).
Kohlap, G.: *David, Boy of the High Country* (Collins).
Park, R.: *The Ship's Cat*; *Uncle Matt's Mountain* (Macmillan).
Powell, L. C.: *Turi, the Story of a Little Boy* (Angus & Robertson).
Price, W.: *South Seas Adventure* (Jonathan Cape).
Reed, A. W.: *Wonder Tales of Maoriland* (Reed, Wellington).
Swift, J.: *Gulliver's Travels* (Constable Young Books).
Syme, Ronald: *Gipsy Michael* (Hodder & Stoughton).
Westphal, F.: *Tonga Tabu* (Methuen); *John Williams of the South Seas*; *Nott of the South Seas*; *James Chalmers* (The Carey Press).

Poems
August, S.: *I Would Have Songs.*
Coleridge, S.: *The Ancient Mariner.*
Glover, D.: *I Remember.*
Kipling, R.: *Song of the English.*
Sladen, Douglas: *The Flying Mouse.*
Stevenson, R. L.: *Christmas at Sea.*
Tennyson, A.: *Ulysses.*

Music
Captain Cockatoo (BBC).
Sea Shanties (see the North Sea project).

Taboo (VA 160142 – Mono Vogue Records Ltd, 9 Albert Embankment).
Music of Tonga (Viking VP 108).
Sweet Hawaiian Melodies (Fontana SFL 13065 Stereo).
South Pacific.

Films
Royal Tour of Fiji (AB Pathé).
Royal Tour of New Zealand (AB Pathé).
Royal Tonga (BBC TV Enterprises).
Fire Walkers of Fiji (BBC TV Enterprises).
Outer Island of Fiji (BBC TV Enterprises).
Canoes and Coconut Crabs (BBC TV Enterprises).
Sailing to the Cape (GB).
Land Divers of Pentecost (New Hebrides) (BBC TV Enterprises).
Tieva (Polynesian Boy) (Gateway).
The New Zealand Film Library, New Zealand House, Haymarket,
London SW1, issues a catalogue of over 150 films on various
aspects of the country.

Filmstrips
Cook's Second Voyage (BBC Radio Vision).
Captain Cook (CG).
Everyday Life in Samoa (EP).
South Sea Island (CG).
Tonga (HP).
Fiji (Rossite Productions).
Land of the Maoris (Visual Information Service).
Everyday Life in New Zealand (EP).
Life in New Zealand (Common Ground).

Film slides
On loan from New Zealand Film Library.
Introducing New Zealand – seventy-two slides.
Sports and Pastimes in New Zealand – thirty-six slides.

Other aids

Jackdaw Series No. 20: *The Voyages of Captain Cook* (Jonathan Cape).

Leaflets from Commonwealth Institute, and the following from the Central Office of Information: Fiji and Pitcairn Islands fact sheet; Gilbert and Ellice Islands fact sheet; New Hebrides fact sheet; Solomon Islands fact sheet; Papua and New Guinea fact sheet; Western Samoa fact sheet.

Useful addresses

New Zealand House: Haymarket, London SW1, for booklets, leaflets, film lists and loan sets of New Zealand school books.

New Zealand Shipping Company: 138 Leadenhall Street, London EC3.

Australia House: Strand, London WC2, for booklets and leaflets.

Illustrated lecture arranged by the Commonwealth Institute on one of the countries visited by Captain Cook.

Excursions

Natural History Museum in Kensington.

National Maritime Museum in Greenwich.

Commonwealth Institute in Kensington.

Cook Museum in Whitby.

Cook Museum in Middlesbrough.

British Museum in London.

Visit the zoo to see birds and animals of the Pacific.

Visit Clandon Park, Surrey, where a meeting house from New Zealand has been erected.

Kew Gardens and other botanical gardens to see plants from the Pacific.

186

CREATIVE ACTIVITIES

Imagine that you are James Cook. Write an entry for your diary after you have charted the St Lawrence River for James Wolfe.

Imagine you are one of the crew of the *Endeavour*. Describe the reaction of your crew mates to the different food which Captain Cook has provided.

After watching the film *Sailing to the Cape*, write a sea shanty and set it to music.

Describe the scene in New Zealand when Captain Cook first met the Maoris.

Imagine you are Cook being entertained by the friendly people of Tonga; tell of the feast, the dancing and other entertainment.

Using the Carl Orff method, describe in words, poetry and sound the difficulties which the *Endeavour* encountered on the Great Barrier Reef.

Write a poem about the *Resolution* in Antarctica.

Many of the islands which Cook visited have interesting legends. Make a collection of these and re-tell them.

Make up a legend about the Tjatara (a dragon).

Write a poem about the voyage the Maoris made to the Land of the Long White Cloud. Use as many Maori words as you can from reference books.

Mathematical and scientific aspects

Cook's first voyage was primarily to Tahiti to observe the eclipse of the sun by Venus. Find out all you can about eclipses, and the planet Venus.

How did they measure speed in Cook's day, and how is it measured today? What is a knot?

In order to map the coast of New Zealand, Cook would need to take soundings. How is this done?

What is a chronometer? Discover all you can about sextants, quadrants and other aids to navigation.

What is the international date line?

Try to obtain full details of a voyage today from Britain to the South Seas. On the daily news sheets issued on board ship many interesting mathematical details are given, e.g. air and sea temperatures, speed and so on. The following work can result.
(a) Make a line graph of air and sea temperatures throughout the voyage.
(b) Find the average speed in knots.
(c) Make a block graph to show wind force experienced on the voyage.

Cook took an artist with him to record interesting plants and animals. Make careful drawings and find out about the plants and animals which they saw.

Certain aspects of topology can be investigated using loops of string. The Maoris are particularly fond of making cat's cradles and other string patterns (see *Games the Maoris Played* by A W Reed Ltd).

The rhythmic patterns made by the Polynesian pois can also be attempted. The poi is a small ball made from dried grass. If this is not available in quantity then a ball of paper should be prepared about the size of a golf ball. A short string is attached so that the ball can be flicked back to strike the wrist. With experience it is possible to

Fig. 18a A set of pois. Instead of dried grass, paper can be used to make up the shape.

188

attach a poi at either end of the string. The string is held so that the lengths are unequal and one ball is thrown in a clockwise direction and the second one in the opposite direction. By moving the hand up and down it should be possible to keep the pois counter-rotating.

Mu Torere is a popular sand game somewhat reminiscent of Nine Men's Morris, and is played around an eight-pointed star. Each of the players has four white or black stones, placed opposite each other. The outside pebbles are moved first, i.e. pebbles 1, 4, 5 and 8, and the centre of the star is the ninth base (Putahi). Players move in turn, but stones can only be moved to an adjacent star or to the centre if vacant. In the game shown in the diagram, white finally moves into Putahi from number 3 position. Black has no adjacent space to move into and so is blocked, losing the game.

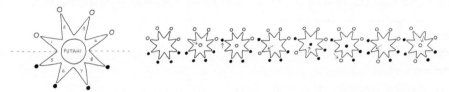

Fig. 18b The game of Mu Torere. The star is drawn out and two sets of four counters are placed in position for the game to start.

Drama and movement
Explore in movement the life of a sailor on board a sailing ship, e.g. turning the capstan, climbing the rigging. Effective group drama can be achieved by miming whilst singing sea shanties.

Plan and act a play about Cook setting up camp in Tahiti at Fort Venus.

Act two contrasting scenes in Hawaii where Cook was acknowledged as a god and then the second time he was killed.

Using the Radio Vision filmstrip of Cook's second voyage, produce a taped script to go with the filmstrip.

Dramatise some of the legends of the Pacific. Tell the story of how Maui caught the Sun, which travelled so fast across the sky that the crops had not time to ripen.

Prepare a festival of the Pacific with songs and dances from the islands that Cook visited. (See 'A Tongan Celebration' from *A Book of Celebrations* published by Mills & Boon.)

Art
Paint a picture of the charting of the St Lawrence River with Cook being watched by the Indians.

Use wax crayons for a picture of the *Endeavour* being loaded with supplies at Deptford.

Use the wax resist method to depict the *Endeavour* in a storm at sea.

Paint a large group picture of the people of Tonga at a feast.

Make a picture of Cook being welcomed in Hawaii using paper, raffia and scrap material.

Paint the scene when Cook lands in New Zealand and meets the Maoris.

Make a series of cut-out Maori heads. With candle trace out the curving tattoo patterns. Paint the head with ebony stain.

Using blue, white and black paint only, depict the *Resolution* in Antarctica.

Make lino cuts of some of the traditional designs of the Pacific Islands. These can be used for printing and decorating folders for various islands which Cook visited.

Make a model of the *Endeavour*.

Fig. 19a Cook's Endeavour.
*A low-relief model of a ship
is usually easier to make
than a full three-dimensional
representation.*

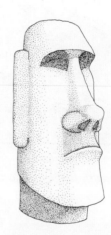

*Fig. 19b An Easter Island figure carved
from a block of salt or plaster of Paris.*

Craft

Use salt blocks or lumps of chalk for carving models of the Easter Island statues.

Make models in wood or card of various types of canoes: long boats, outriggers, or catamarans with sails and high carved prows.

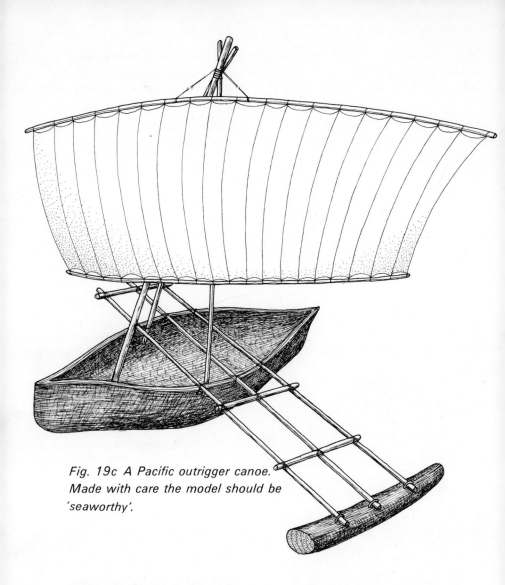

Fig. 19c A Pacific outrigger canoe.
Made with care the model should be
'seaworthy'.

The craft of Tapa (Polynesian). In the native craft, strips of bark and
other material are fixed to a curved surface and a length of material is
laid over it. Dyestuff is rubbed over the surface and this colours the
raised-up pattern. Drying in the sun fixes the natural dyes. In school,
lengths of cardboard or balsa-wood strips can be stuck to lengths of
card. Cloth should then be laid over the relief form and paint or dyes
applied from a sponge.

Make a series of models of the types of homes found on the islands which Cook visited.

Build a pa (Maori village) and surround it with stockade poles. Include large and small whares (houses). Use wood, and thatch with straw. At the end of the large whares put carved boards with curved and whirl patterns. Food store on pole.

Fig. 20a A doorpost from a Maori meeting house. Simulate one of these by adding pieces of card or wood to a strip of hardboard.

Fig. 20b Maori carving from a door lintel or the prow of a canoe. With care, designs like this can be cut from cardboard.

Fig. 20c Plan for a Maori war canoe. Silhouette forms can be prepared in wax crayon and mounted on the window.

From cardboard cut out a series of weapons, clubs, hand-axes and decorated spears. Use strips of wood to strengthen. Decorate with traditional patterns.

Make a diorama model of the *Resolution* in Antarctica with paper-sculpture penguins in the foreground.

Fig. 21a A penguin made from a single piece of card, decorated and folded . . .

Fig. 21b . . . can be placed on ice floes in a diorama showing incidents in Cook's life.

Make kites. Use bark and reeds if possible. Bird shapes are popular, and large kites which need several people to launch them.

Make a Maori throwing stick from a length of one-inch dowel rod. Simple whittling can be attempted on a stick with bark still present, or paint the stick and incise a pattern on it.

Fig. 22 A Maori throwing stick. By whittling or painting and then etching, traditional patterns can be made on a rod or stick.

194

Make a large model of the ostrich-type prehistoric birds of New Zealand, e.g. the Donornis (up to twelve feet high) and the Pachyonis (up to seven feet high) or the larger mammals of Australia like the kangaroo.

A Pakeha is a cape of feathers worn by the Polynesians. A large collection of feathers will be needed for this —from the seashore, field and woodland. A simple cape of hessian can be prepared and the feathers fixed through the weave and held with a stitch or two. If a variety of feathers is available then particular patterns can be created (start at the waist and move upwards to the shoulders).

Where needlework skills are practised, smocking can be introduced to try to reproduce the Maori traditional costume pattern, in which the bodice is decorated using that technique. For the belt, rolled 'beads' of newsprint can be sewn to a strip of canvas (see Canadian craft section on page 302).

Make a set of stilts —a pastime popular with the Maoris.

Shape a dowel rod into a top. Fix a round-headed upholstery tack in the pointed end. Make a whip to spin the top.

Trafalgar

This was a tremendous sea battle – and victory gave Britain mastery of the oceans for the next hundred years. (The next full fleet engagement was the Battle of Jutland in 1916 – see North Sea project.)

Great national feeling was evoked by the events of that conflict, and even a century and a half later, there are few who are not moved by the stirring deeds of 1805.

The dynamic personality of Horatio Nelson was the inspiration for the battle and the victory. His death in the hour of triumph assured him of an even more glorious place in the history of our nation.

Special aspects
This is obviously an exciting event to hear about, and being of comparatively recent times, there are many relics for us to see and handle, including eye-witness accounts by men involved in the battle and providentially preserved by proud relatives.

The hero, who led such a colourful life, has been well served by his biographers. Lady Hamilton is part of the story, and in museums and books there are portraits and references made to her. She will require introduction.

INSPIRATION AND INFORMATION
Books
Bellis, H.: *Admiral Nelson* (McGraw Hill).
Bryant, A.: *Nelson* (Collins).
Burton, H.: *A Seaman at the Time of Trafalgar* (OUP).
Freemantle, Ann: *The Wynne Diaries* (OUP) (especially Freemantle's
    letter to Betsy: 28th October 1805).
Grenfell, R.: *Captain Russell; Nelson the Sailor* (Faber).
Houghton, R.: *True Book about Nelson* (Muller).
Langdon-Davis, J.: *Battle of Trafalgar* (Cape).
Lobban, R. D.: *Nelson's Navy and the French Wars* (ULP).

MacIntyre, D.: *Trafalgar* (Lutterworth).
Oman, Carola: *Nelson* (Hodder & Stoughton).
Peach, L. du Garde: *The Story of Nelson* (Wills & Hepworth).
Pocock, T.: *Nelson and His World* (Thames & Hudson).
Robbins, Ian: *Monday 21st of October 1805* (OUP).
Uden, Grant: *The Fighting Téméraire* (Blackwell).
Warner, Oliver: *Nelson* (Cassell Caravel).

Stories

Austen, Jane: *Persuasion* (for background material on life in the Navy
at the turn of the century).
Burton, Hester: *Castors Away* (OUP).
Forester, C. S.: Hornblower series. Although the author kept his hero
out of the Battle of Trafalgar, the contemporary information and
background detail are relevant. *Hornblower and the Atrophos* is
set in 1805.
Hackforth-Jones, Gilbert: *Hurricane Harbour* (Hodder & Stoughton).
Nelson, C. M.: *He Went with Nelson* (Harrap).

Poems

Graves, Robert: *1805 – Nelson's Funeral.*
Hardy, Thomas: *Night of Trafalgar.*
Newbolt, Sir Henry: *The Fighting Téméraire.*

Music

Nelson and Trafalgar were subjects for a large number of ballads and
songs, e.g. *Bold Nelson Praise* and *Tommy Fought at Trafalgar*. The
singing of these in a programme, along with other traditional songs of
the sea, would form one kind of presentation for this topic.

Filmstrips

The Victory (Visual Publications).
Nelson (Common Ground).

Other aids

The Battle of Trafalgar: Jackdaw No. 1 (Cape).

A.D. 1805: A.D. series of newspapers (Allen & Unwin).

The Times: Thursday Nov. 7th 1805 — No. 6572 (Times Newspapers).

The Fighting Téméraire: reproduction of painting by J. W. M. Turner.

Nelson and H.M.S. Victory at Trafalgar (Sunday Times Wallchart,
     12 Coley Street, London WC99).

Excursions

The *Victory* and the Victory Museum, Dockyard, Portsmouth.

Nelson Museum, Glendower Street, Monmouth.

Nelson Galleries and other sections with contemporary paintings,
models, relics, etc. National Maritime Museum, Greenwich.

Trafalgar Exhibit, Madame Tussauds, Baker Street, London. (There is
an interesting comparison here between the older more static display
and the modern treatment of sound, light and smell in the new
exhibition.)

Buckler's Hard Museum, Hampshire, for models and drawings of the
Wooden Walls of England.

Public Record Office, Chancery Lane, London WC2 (Mondays to
Fridays, 1–4 p.m.). Apply to secretary for sight of Nelson's Log.

Burnham Thorpe for interesting details in the church and reminders of
Nelson's childhood.

Nelson's tomb in St Paul's Cathedral.

Effigy in the undercroft of Westminster Abbey.

CREATIVE ACTIVITIES

Written work

Write a story about your apprenticeship in a shipyard at the beginning of the nineteenth century, when the great sailor came to inspect a new ship for his fleet.

You are a powder monkey on board the *Victory*. Write the story of the engagement at Trafalgar as you heard it in sounds, orders and rumours, as you worked below decks.

After one of the suggested visits, write a poem about Nelson.

Write a ballad about Nelson's life. Include verses which give details of his promotions and record of service: midshipman at twelve; losing an eye in the siege of Calvi in Corsica; losing his right arm during an attack on Santa Cruz in 1797; the battle of St Vincent; Battle of the Nile, 1798; and finally Trafalgar, 1805. You might begin:

> It was in the year of . . .
> That brave Nelson . . .

Write a letter to your wife or mother just before going into battle.

If you learn French at school, write a letter to 'votre mère', telling her of your forthcoming battle with the English.

Drama and movement

Read the story of *Castors Away* and dramatise the story of Tom Henchman.

Use percussion and other instruments to provide sounds of the sea, the wind in the rigging, and act a story of the *Victory* leaving harbour.

Make up a radio play of the Battle of Trafalgar with sound effects and dialogue.

From the reference material suggested, record the various first-person accounts of the battle, and link with a commentary.

Use material from *They Saw It Happen 1689–1897* by T. Charles-Edwards and Brian Richardson (Blackwell) and the Trafalgar section of *The Pick of the Rhubarb* by Antony Jay (Hodder & Stoughton) for additional references.

Other outside activities

Plan a war game in the playground, each child representing a French or British ship. Use formation plans from the Jackdaw folder and re-enact the battle scene. A public-address system can usually be borrowed from a local authority, but a tape-recorder with a good amplifier could be extended from an electrical point nearby. In this way a commentary and instructions could be given. A simple boat shape of cardboard could be constructed and 'worn' by each child with rope braces.

Trafalgar Square was created on a site cleared in 1829 as a memorial to Nelson. A visit to the Square is a London 'must', and after the statue has been admired, there are other activities which can be followed.

The height of the column can be measured (and checked) – using the shadow method, a clinometer, or the Boy Scouts stepping up idea.

Measure the dimensions of the square.

Draw and sketch features of the square, e.g. fountains, lions.

Interview visitors to the square, using a portable tape-recorder.

Carry out a survey of types of traffic using the flanking roads to the square.

Make a survey of all those whose business, trade or occupation is connected with the square: those dependent upon visitors; those partially dependent upon visitors; and those completely independent of visitors.

Pigeons: methods of sample counting: numbers occupying a paving slab over a given area.

Starlings: roosting places.

Buildings around the square: Canada House, South Africa House, Charing Cross Station, Charing Cross Hospital, Trafalgar Square Underground Station, St Martins-in-the-Fields, National Gallery, National Portrait Gallery.

Standard Imperial measures.

Busts of Jellicoe and Beatty. Other statues.

Listen to tape-recorded commentaries on eastern wall of the square.

Sounds of the square: traffic, pigeons, music, aircraft noises.

Art and craft
Officers and men in naval rig of the period.

Battle scene of Trafalgar – large group picture.

Portrait of Nelson.

Frieze of two squadrons of ships moving into battle positions.

Signalling flags – hang on ropes to spell out – England Expects . . .

Make a model of the *Victory* in cardboard.

On a large sheet of board, produce a model of the Battle of Trafalgar, with all ships numbered and a key provided for identification.

Fig. 23. A small hull made from balsa wood, with a paper sail attached with a cocktail stick, makes a piece for a naval war game.

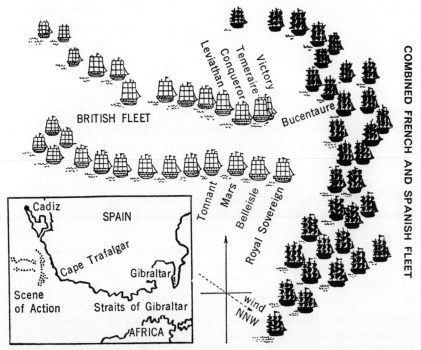

Fig. 24 The British, French and Spanish formations of ships at the commencement of the Battle of Trafalgar.

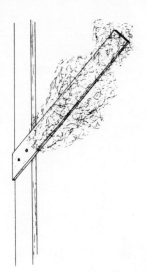

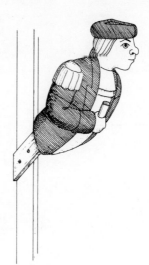

Fig. 25 Use chicken wire around a woode(armature to make th(basic shape for a figurehead.

Fig. 26 Use modellir(clay to give finer det(and then cover with papier mâché. When dry, paint with brigh(colours.

Use chicken wire around a wooden armature to produce the basic shape of a ship's figure-head. Modelling clay will be required for additional features — nose, lips, eyebrows and ears, and after these are added papier mâché is applied. After drying, paint and add other embellishments to complete the task.

Make a model of Trafalgar Square, with Nelson's Column, fountains and panoramic backcloth of the buildings around the square.

The bronze reliefs at the base of Nelson's column show scenes from his various campaigns. Prepare low relief pictures in modelling clay and cover with papier mâché.

Design a square to celebrate a more recent victory or person concerned with it.

HOMES

Man's need for shelter is second only to his requirement of food and water. Because of its fundamental nature, and the child's personal experience, this theme starts with advantages. Since it is a very large topic, each child will be able to exercise a considerable choice within the range of possibilities offered, and in topics suggested by themselves once they have been motivated. For instance the project might be divided into these broad bands:

(a) The work of the architect.
(b) The raw materials of building.
(c) Building the house.
(d) Putting on the roof.
(e) All modern conveniences.
(f) Moving in.
(g) Houses of the past.
(h) Houses in other countries.
(i) The homes of animals.
(j) Animals in the home.
(k) Science and the home.
(l) Homes of the future.

Plate 12a When sufficiently inspired a child can keep his own log of the progress of the building of a house right from the ground . . .

Plate 12b . . . up to the roof.

Special aspects

As a project, this is one which enjoys a good number of available aids to learning and so the preparation of topic cards, to go alongside these, would ensure that the class would acquire a tremendous amount of knowledge. Because of this, and the outside excursions, it would be expected that their imaginative writing would equal their descriptive and factual accounts.

INSPIRATION AND INFORMATION
Books
Because this subject is of universal appeal, it is one of those for
which there is a very large supply of general information books.
Therefore the children will be able to refer to several sources before
making any notes and drawings. In most places fieldwork activities
should be possible and some of the books dealing particularly with
architecture and design have been grouped together. But this aspect
will be found to recur in some of the other titles suggested for use.

Architecture
Barfoot, A.: *Homes in Britain* (Batsford).
Batsford, H. & Fray, C.: *The English Cottage* (Batsford).
Brown, H.: *The Story of English Architecture* (Faber).
Boog-Watson, E. J. & Carruthers, J.: *History in Pictures: Houses*
      (OUP).
Clark, E. V.: *Exploring Old Buildings* (Hollis & Carter).
Fry, J. & M.: *Architecture for Children* (Allen & Unwin).
Harston, K. & Davis, E.: *Your Local Buildings* (Allen & Unwin).
Leacroft, H. & R.: *Historic Houses in Britain* (Puffin).
Lees-Milne, J.: *National Trust Buildings* (Batsford).
Penoyre, J. & Ryan, M.: *The Observer Book of Architecture* (Warne).
Reed, G. H.: *Your Book of Architecture* (Black).
Ancient Monuments and Historic Buildings (HMSO).

General reference books on houses
Allen, A.: *The Story of Your Home* (Faber).
Anderson, G.: *Mr Budge Builds a House* (Brockhampton).
Barrett, Judith: *Old Macdonald Had Some Flats* (Longman).
Davin, W.: *Homes* (Vol. XI, *Oxford Junior Encyclopaedia*).
Earnshaw, W.: *Discovering Houses* (ULP).
Harrison, M.: *Homes* (ESA).
Horridge, A.: *Finding Out About Houses* (ULP).
Moore, W. G.: *Homes* (Hulton Press).
Morey, J.: *Let's Look at Houses and Homes* (Muller).
Osmond, E.: *Houses* (Batsford).
Thornhill, P.: *Houses and Flats* (Methuen).
Unstead, R.: *A History of Houses* (Black).
Verney, J.: *Look at Houses* (Hamish Hamilton).

Additional fact books which relate to homes

Anderson, J.: *Mr Wall, the Plumber* (OUP).

Clair, Colin: *Paint* (Gawthorn).

Doherty, C. H.: *Science Inside the Building* (Brockhampton).

Ellacott, S. E.: *The Story of the Kitchen* (Methuen).

Garland, Rosemary: *Glass* (ESA).

Harrison, M.: *Furniture* (Faber).

Norton, Elisabeth: *Hygiene in the Home* (Mills & Boon).

Tomalin, M.: *Water Supply* (Methuen).

Turland, E.: *Furniture in England* (Black).

Williams, P. H. M.: *The Young Householder* (Allman).

Stories

Atherton, L.: *Castle of Comfort* (Faber).

Baker, M.: *Castaway Christmas* (Methuen).

Dunnett, M.: *The People Next Door* (Deutsch).

Fairfax-Lucy, B. & Pearce, P.: *The Children of the House* (Longman).

Godden, Rumer: *The Doll's House* (Puffin).

Garnett, A.: *The Owl Service* (Penguin).

Harnett, Cynthia: *The Great House* (OUP).

Norton, Mary: *The Borrowers* (Puffin).

Sutcliffe, E.: *The Armourer's House* (OUP).

Wilder, L.: *The Little House in the Big Wood* (Puffin); *The Little House on the Prairie* (Penguin).

Within other stories there are some well-observed descriptions of homes. From such readings, stimulus should come for writing, art and craft.

Miss Havisham's house from *Great Expectations*.

Peggoty's house in *David Copperfield*.

Ratty's, Badger's and Toad's dwellings in *Wind in the Willows*.

The house in *Tom's Midnight Garden* by Phillipa Pearce.

A book of short stories might provide several examples. In the *Friday Miracle* (Penguin) one can find 'The Sampler' by Noel Streatfield, 'Tom Turnspit' by Barbara Picard, and the 'Dark Streets of Kimball's Green' by Joan Aiken — all with house descriptions.

Biblical sketches
The Home of Martha and Mary: John 11: 1–12; Luke 10: 38–42.
The Home of Jairus: Luke 8: 41–56.
Simon's House: Mark 1: 29–31.
Elijah and the Widow of Zarephath: I Kings 17: 9–24.
Elisha and the Shunamite Woman: II Kings 4: 8–37.

Poems
Chesterton, G. K.: *Ballad of St Barbara* (the stonemason).
Colum, Padraic: *Old Woman of the Roads.*
Davies, W. H.: *For Sale.*
Farjeon, Eleanor: *Cottage.*
Herrick, R.: *A Thanksgiving for His House.*
Hood, T.: *I Remember.*
Reeves, James: *Animals' Houses.*
Serraillier, Ian: *The Mouse in the Wainscot.*
Tippett, James: *Building a Skyscraper.*
Whitman, Walt: *Song of the Broad Axe* (housebuilding).

Traditional
The House that Jack Built.
There was a crooked man.
There was an old woman who lived in a shoe.
Three Little Pigs.

Music
Mussorgsky: *Pictures at an Exhibition* – The Hut on Fowl's Legs.

Songs
In Holland Stands a House.
Little Boxes.
Bless this House.
Over in the Meadow.

Films
Making Glass for Houses (Encyclopaedia Britannica).

Making Bricks for Houses (Encyclopaedia Britannica).
Bricks (BIF).
Chalk (BIF).
Cement (BIF).
Granite (BIF).
Building a House (BIF).
The Bricklayer (NCVAE).
Costain House (Rank Films).
Houses in History (Central Office of Information).
The England of Elizabeth (British Transport Films).
Building an Igloo (NCVAE).
An African Builds His Home (NCVAE).

Filmstrips

Building Construction: Bricks, Cement and Lime (Educational
   Productions).
History in Stone (BIF).
Ancient Stones (Dawn Trust).
The Evolution of the English Home (Common Ground).
The English House (Daily Mail).

Other aids

Water: Science Study Kit (E. J. Arnold).
Houses: set of ten charts (Wheatons).
Houses: Houses in History (Ministry of Education).
Book of House Plans: (*Daily Mail* —allied with their Ideal Home
   Exhibition).
Setting out on Site (Ministry of Works pamphlets).
Treasure in the House: free booklet from PR Dept, Dunlop Rubber
   Company, Dunlop House, Ryder Street, London SW1.
About the House; *Things to Do* by Carter, E. F. & Shaw, D. (Do-it-
   yourself booklets from Ward Lock).
1000 Years of Housing: free booklet from Dept B, The Building
   Societies Association, 14 Park Street, London W1.
Electricity and You: free booklet from the Electricity Council, EDA
   Div., Trafalgar Buildings, 1 Charing Cross, London SW1.
Architect; *Carpenter*; *Joiner*; *Bricklayer* (career leaflets from HMSO).

Useful addresses

The Civic Trust: 17 Carlton House Terrace, London SW1.

The Housing Centre Trust: 13 Suffolk Street, London SW1.

The Georgian Group: 2 Chester Street, London SW1.

National Buildings Record: Fielden House, Great College Street,
    London SW1.

The National Trust: 42 Queen Anne's Gate, London SW1.

Society for the Protection of Ancient Buildings: 55 Great Ormond
    Street, London WC1.

The Victorian Society: 29 Exhibition Road, London SW7.

Central Electricity Generating Board: 15 Newgate Street, London EC1.

Electricity Council: 30 Millbank, London SW1.

Gas Council: 59 Bryanston Street, London W1.

The Building Centre: 26 Store Street, London WC1.

The Design Centre: 28 Haymarket, London SW1.

Excursions

Try the local scene first. The environs of the school will most likely
include a variety of dwellings, and even those working on new estates
have older buildings nearby to compare with the new.

The study of one street, especially a town High Street, is one which
would engage a class in architectural drawing, an activity in which
young children enjoy a surprising success.

Local building site. With permission from the work's foreman, regular
visits might be made to watch progress, with tape-recorded, written,
drawn and photographed reports. The growing numbers of schools
possessing an 8-mm movie camera can embark on a film of the
building of a block of flats. The showing of the final results to the
new inhabitants (who might include new pupils of the school) and the
co-operative builders would be an appropriate end to the project.

Most regions have at least one important house. These might be in
the care of the local authority, National Trust, Ministry of Public
Buildings and Works, or private individuals who would be willing to
receive visitors. There are many such buildings in the country, and on

a school journey, or by making a special excursion to them, interesting work can be developed about them and the people who lived in them.

For details of places to visit, consult local county guides, e.g. *Buildings of Britain* series by N. Pevsner (Penguin). *Historic Houses, Castles and Gardens* is published annually and gives information by counties. *Let's Use the Locality* by Henry Pluckrose (Mills & Boon) includes a valuable gazetteer, and makes many useful suggestions on work connected with houses and other buildings.

The majority of museums feature aspects related to homes and home life. The Geffrye Museum, Shoreditch, has period rooms for children to work alongside.

Schools in or visiting London can include a visit to the Design Centre and the Building Centre. The Ideal Home Exhibition and the Furniture Exhibition are two national events which would be valuable to visit during a project.

In larger cities outside London, similar exhibitions are arranged, and the local press should be studied for details of these.

On some new estates, show flats and dwellings can be examined and, by previous reference to the agent, small groups can be invited.

Quarries, brickworks and timber yards should provide unusual experience and evidence for writing and other creative work.

Where information can be obtained from the local guide book, museum or master builder, arrange a walk to see various kinds of stone in use. In London the following buildings could be looked at to see various kinds of building stone: St Paul's Cathedral (Portland stone), Brompton Hospital (Kentish rag), The Wall of London (chalk), Houses of Parliament (magnesium limestone), Liverpool Street Station (new red sandstone), Covent Garden Market (Jurassic limestone), Nelson's Column (Dartmoor granite), fountains — Trafalgar Square (Scottish limestone), Albert Memorial (Italian marble), Westminster Cathedral (brick).

CREATIVE ACTIVITIES
Written work

Prepare 'A Book of Houses', in which there is an illustrated account of a series of houses in the neighbourhood.

Write a series of advertisements for property. Consult examples from estate agents' windows, newspaper adverts and *This Desirable Plot* by Thelwell (Methuen). Attempts can be made to conceal the truth: large unspoilt garden = four acres of virgin soil; near all forms of public transport = nestling under a railway bridge on a busy bus route and so on.

Prepare a street quiz for another member of the class:
    Which house has five storeys?
    Which house is named after an East Coast town?
    Which house doesn't appear to have a television set?
    Which house is being sold by the agents 'Jones and Jones'?

Write a poem about the building of a house. Give a verse to each of the workers concerned until the new family moves in.

Develop a simple poem about making of bricks from clay, and with tuned percussion instruments set it to music.

You witness a runaway lorry crashing into a house at the end of the street. Write about the next fifteen minutes.

It is a dark evening and you are on your own. It is rather a still night. An owl hoots and then from under the floor boards you hear a scuffling sound or is it something being dragged? What could it have been? Tell your story . . . to the policemen you decided to call, after ten minutes.

Make a glossary of terms associated with building work: gable, lintel, freehold, etc.

Take an interesting street in your town or city and prepare an historical trail. Tape-record this with sound effects for use on a portable machine. Prepare a marked way map.

214

Drama and movement
Mime the actions of the various workers on a building site – mixing cement, carrying bricks, laying bricks, climbing ladders, digging foundations and hammering wood. Create sound effects to go along with the various activities.

An old lady refuses to leave her home, although all around her have done so. Tell the story of all the various social and other workers who attempt to persuade her to move.

Mime the actions of removal men, with grandfather clocks, pianos, glassware, etc., arranging all the furniture in position and two flights of stairs to negotiate.

The water pipes in the loft burst; mime the action of bailing out and trying to stem the flow of water (use the music from the *Sorcerer's Apprentice* by Dukas for this).

Create an underground scene of animals who choose this region for their homes – rabbits, foxes, badgers – and mime their daily contact or avoidance of each other.

Develop a play based on the German Richfest custom or 'Topping Out'. A house is built, and as the last roof timber is hoisted into position it is time to celebrate. However, the roof timber is removed during the night, but found again in the neighbouring village where it has been decorated. It must be paid for in this old custom. When this is done it is carried back with great ceremony and hauled up with a rhythmic song accompaniment. The *Polier* or foreman asks for blessings on the house and its future occupants, thanks the builders, masons and carpenters, and they all drink three times to the owner and then smash their glasses to the ground. Then a party follows and gifts are given to the family – horses' heads carved on gables. windows decorated, pieces of furniture, etc.

Mathematical and scientific assignments
Where a good relationship has been developed with the clerk of works

on a building site, various kinds of work can be developed during a supervised visit: the quantity of bricks, tiles or slates required for one house, a block of flats or even an estate, could be calculated. It may be possible to discover the cost of a brick, and so the cost of all the bricks required for a single dwelling.

From an estate agent, ask if you might have plans of large and small houses. Compare the provision of space and facilities with plans drawn up by archaeologists of houses of other times.

After examining architects' plans, and possibly looking over the same house, discuss the provision of amenities and use of space. Suggest improvements or more convenient arrangements, and draw up a new plan for a house. (Perhaps the architect would comment on yours when completed!)

Using various methods determine the heights of various buildings. By the shadow stick method: Erect a stick of known height on a sunny day. Measure its shadow length, and the shadow length of the building to be measured. Find the height of the building as follows: multiply the shadow length of the building by the height of the stick, and divide the product by the shadow length of the stick.
By estimation: Measure the height of a brick plus one layer of mortar. Multiply this measurement by the number of courses of bricks.
By angular measurement: Sight along the hypotenuse of a 45° protractor, and adjust your position until the top of building is just in your 'sights'. Ensure that the base of the set square is parallel with the ground. Measure your distance from the point of the building immediately below your sighting point. This added to your eye height from the ground will be the height of the building.
Consult maths books for other height-finding devices.

Art
Use a rectangular form — or cut one from potato or other hard vegetable — and print brick patterns. Observe English, Flemish and Stretcher bonds and try these arrangements. Use this technique later when modelling houses.

When visiting old buildings look for masons' marks and make a pattern of these. Invent one of your own in this style.

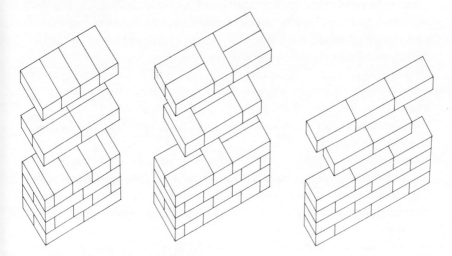

Fig. 27 Various kinds of bonds used in brick-laying: Flemish Bond, Stretcher Bond, English Bond.

Make a collage picture of houses and other buildings, using magazine and newspaper shapes.

Draw a series of building workers and mount these on stiff card and arrange against a building site background.

Make a pattern of scaffolding, ladders, lifts and joists, ropes, unfinished courses of bricks. Make this a group effort and add figures of workers.

Design an attractive house poster.

Where a derelict building site exists in the area, take a sketching party to watch the demolition of old houses. Paint a large scene showing this work and rising, almost phoenix-like, a new tower block (refer to *The Tower Block* by R. P. A. Edwards, published by Burke).

Make a series of pictures (using crayon techniques) to make a frieze, showing the different styles of regional architecture. For example, cover a piece of stout card or hardboard with wax crayon — white on the lower half, and yellow above. Cover with black crayon and then carefully cut through the black top layer to reveal the white of 'chalk clunch' building material, with a yellow thatch above.

Craft
Use a variety of fabrics to create wall hangings with houses of various types as the motifs.

Use cardboard boxes to build a town of houses. Different shapes and sizes of boxes will create a varied street pattern. Use acrylic paint to remove labelling as well as to decorate the houses attractively.
A particular style of architecture might be adopted, e.g. black and white Elizabethan dwellings with coloured tiles for a Tudor settlement, warm yellow stone for a Cotswold village of today, and so on.

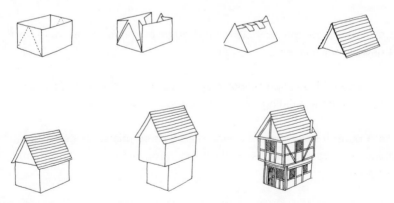

Fig. 28 A series of drawings to show how cardboard boxes can be adapted to make a model house.

Use card and a scale to reproduce a model of a house or a great hall.

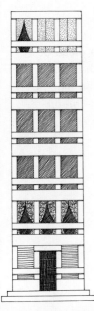

Fig. 29 A tall box is embellished with strips of balsa wood and painted to become a block of flats.

Use simple scrap materials to make furniture. Design a wall covering from paper, print patterns on material for curtains and carpets, and create rooms inside large cardboard boxes. Depending upon the scale, make and dress figures. There are opportunities to make a series of such models to show the changes that have occurred over 2000 years in the kitchen, bedroom and dining-room.

Make a series of cardboard dwellings and arrange for the fronts to open, or the roofs to lift, so that the furnishings will be revealed.

Use a number of cardboard boxes fixed to a wooden base to create a Welsh slate quarry. Smaller boxes should be fixed inside the large 'hollow' to show how the slate is removed in layers. A railway and road system can be introduced to show how the material is dispersed.

Inside a box, arranged with cardboard strips representing walls, floor and ceiling, use string of various colours to show the electricity, water and gas systems of a house.

Using kits of material inside school, or loaned by children (Bayko, Minibriks), build houses for a class town.

Design a wall decoration. This might be a ceramic picture, with decorated tiles, or broken pieces of tile, glass, stones, etc.; or a pioco of oaot ploater of Paris which has been Incised; or a piece of abstract metal sculpture; or a sundial. Or the number of the house, or its name, incised in wood, with a chisel, or burnt in with an electric soldering iron. For all such work, young children will need careful supervision.

Make a model of the Palestinian house where the man who was sick of the palsy was cured (Mark 2 : 3–5).

WATER

When a class has indicated that there is a wide variety of interest, a single word title can often be found to encompass many ideas and tastes. Water is one such all-embracing topic. One feature will be the many simple scientific experiments which can be carried out with a minimum of equipment, most of it of the jar and tin lid variety. Water supply and power are two aspects which impinge upon our daily lives, and have a scientific interest. The world of living creatures is fascinating to young children, and so within the topic, studies can be made of pond, river and sea life. Many schools have some form of weather recording equipment and the adoption of this project should activate the daily round of reading instruments and checking the rain gauge. Everyone relies on an ever-present water supply, and those peoples whose supply is often a matter of critical importance can be studied, for example, the desert nomad and the Eskimo. The importance of water to the sportsman – as fisherman, swimmer, skin diver and yachtsman – will prove to be an interest of some of the class.

Special aspects
With such a variety of subjects within the topic, the obvious method of working will be to build up interest groups in which members will make detailed studies. Each group will join in certain main features of the project and also be responsible for certain experiments to their group study. This aspect of work suggests that a Science Fair or Conversazione could be used to present the topic.

INSPIRATION AND INFORMATION
See also suggestions for North Sea; River; Trafalgar.

Books
Adams, H.: *Water and the Waterworks* (Blackwell).
Adler, I. & R.: *Storms* (Dennis Dobson).
Allen, G. & Morris, L.: *Water* (Ward Lock).
Ascher, S. J.: *Water Supply and Main Drainage* (Crosby Lockwood).
Barker, E. J.: *Junior Science*, Book 3 (Evans).

Baxter, E. M.: *Your Book of Water Supply* (Bodley Head).

Clair, C.: *Water* (Bruce & Gawthorn).

Copeland, D. M.: *The Junior True Book of Eskimos* (Muller).

Davis, Delwyn: *Fresh Water* (Aldus).

de Mare, E.: *Your Book of Waterways* (Faber).

de Vries, L.: *The Book of Experiments* (John Murray).

Gadsby, J. & D.: *Looking at Everyday Things* (A. & C. Black).

Gaylard, E. L.: *Water*; *My Water Workbook* (Arnold).

Goetz, D.: *The Arctic Tundra* (William Morrow).

Haworth, F. M.: *Aquaria* (ULP).

Holmes, B. & M.: *The Water We Use* (Methuen).

Hope, R.: *Ships* (Batsford).

Hyler, N. W.: *The How and Why Wonder Book of Rocks and Minerals* (Transworld).

James, A.: *Natural Science*, Books 1 & 3 (Schofield & Sims).

Jarvis, M. A.: *Your Book of Swimming* (Faber).

Jones, E.: *The World of Water* (Blandford).

Kinns, G. & Shaw, D.: *Things to Do: Outdoor Pastimes* (Ward Lock).

Knowles, F. G. W.: *Freshwater and Saltwater Aquaria* (Harrap).

Leutscher, A.: *Life in Fresh Water* (Bodley Head).

McInnes, J.: *Making and Keeping an Aquarium* (ESA).

McIntosh, P.: *Games and Sports* (ESA).

Murphy, J. S.: *How They Were Built: Ships* (Oxford).

Neurath, M.: *The Wonder Book of Land and Water* (Max Parrish).

Newing, F. & Bowood, R.: *The Ladybird Book of the Weather* (Wills & Hepworth).

Norman, J.: *Down to the Pond* (Hutchinson).

Nuttall, K.: *Water from the Tap* (Longman).

Parker, B.: *Water* (Wheaton).

Podendorf, I.: *The Junior True Book of More Science Experiments* (Muller).

Prud'homme van Reine, W. J.: *Plants and Animals of Pond and Stream* (John Murray).

Purton, W. W.: *Discovering Ports and Harbours* (ULP).

Rowland, T. J. S.: *Wild Things for Lively Youngsters*; *Outdoor Things for Lively Youngsters*; *Moving Things for Lively Youngsters* (Cassell).

Rolt, L. T. C.: *Inland Waterways* (ESA).

Rossotti, Hazel: *H_2O* (Oxford).

Royds, A.: *Wonders of Water* (Harrap).

Sauvain, P. A.: *Exploring at Home* (Hulton).

Sava, C.: *How to Swim Well* (Hodder & Stoughton).

Schneider, H. & N.: *Science in Our World*; *Science in Your Life*; *Science Far and Near* (D. C. Heath); *Everyday Weather and How It Works* (Brockhampton).

Scott, N.: *The Ladybird Book of Pond Life* (Wills & Hepworth).

Spoczynska, J. O. I.: *The Aquarium* (Nelson).

Smith, L. P.: *Weathercraft* (Blandford).

Stephen, S.: *Water and Waste* (Macmillan).

Swenson, V.: *Stones and Minerals* (Oliver & Boyd).

Syrocki, B. J.: *What Is Weather?* (Collins).

Taylor, N. A.: *Rocks and Fossils* (Vista).

Plate 13 A project on water could embrace a study of weather recording.

Tomalin, M.: *Water Supply* (Methuen).
Thornhill, P.: *Inland Waterways* (Methuen).
Walter, William C.: *The World of Water* (Weidenfeld & Nicolson).
Western, W. G.: *Water* (OUP).
Viallo, C.: *Windmills and Waterwheels* (A. & C. Black).
Zim, H. S.: *Rocks and How They Were Formed* (Golden Press).

Stories
Burton, H.: *The Great Gale* (OUP).
Crowle, P.: *Tales From the Ballet* (Faber).
Date, N.: *Who Built the Dam?* (Macmillan).
Davidson, G.: *Ballet Stories for Young People*; *Opera Stories for Young People* (Cassell).
Fisher, G. D.: *Fishy Friends from the Hut Man's Book* (Penguin).
Horton, J.: *Legends in Music (Nelson).*
Kingsley, C.: *The Water Babies* (Nelson).
May, H.: *The Swan* (Anna Pavlova) (Nelson).
Ross, S.: *The Lazy Salmon Mystery* (Brockhampton).
Schmeltzer, K.: *The Raft* (Constable).
The Hole in the Dyke (traditional Dutch).

Stories from the Bible
Rebecca at the Well: Genesis 24.
Elijah and the Drought: I Kings 17–18.
Jesus Changes the Water into Wine: John 2: 1–11.
Healing at the Pool of Bethsaida: John 5: 1–13.
Healing at the Pool of Siloam: John 9.

Poems
de la Mare, W.: *The Snowflake.*
Grahame, K.: *Up Tails All.*
Hunt, L.: *To a Fish*; *A Fish Answers.*
Longfellow, H.: *Snow.*
Owen, W.: *All sounds have music.*

Scovell, E. J.: *The Boy Fishing.*
Serraillier, I.: *The Hen and the Carp.*
Tagore, R.. *The Further Bank.*

Music
Beethoven, L. van: Sixth Symphony, second movement; Piano Sonata
    in C Minor, Op. 27, No. 2.
Britten, B.: *Peter Grimes*, Op. 33: *Four Sea Interludes.*
Debussy, C. A.: *Clair de lune*; *Images*, Set 1: *Reflets dans l'eau*;
    Submerged Cathedral; *Three Nocturnes*; *La Mer.*
Handel, G. F.: *Water Music.*
Holst, G.: *Dance of the Spirits of the Water (The Perfect Fool).*
Massenet, J. E. F.: *Aubade* (from *Le Cid*).
Mendelssohn, F.: *Fingal's Cave.*
Schubert, F.: *The Trout Quintet*; *The Trout* (song); *The Question*
    (song); *Whither* (song); *To wander is the miller's joy* (song).
Sibelius, J.: *Swan of Tuonela*; *Finlandia.*
Tchaikovsky, P. I.: *Swan Lake.*
Vaughan Williams, R.: *Sinfonia Antarctica*; *Sea Symphony.*

Films
Water (ICI).
What Makes Rain? (Young America Films).
Water Supply (EFVA).
Every Drop to Drink (World Wide Pictures).
Waterpower (Rank).
Underground Water (EFVA).
Ground Water (EB Films).
Physics and Chemistry of Water (Unilever).
Biology of Water (Unilever).
Frog and Tadpole (Rank).
The Stickleback Family (Rank).
From Egg to Newt (Rank).
The Life Cycle of the Newt (Rank).
Marshland Birds, Parts 1 and 2 (GBI).
Waterbirds (Walt Disney).

Between the Tides (British Transport).
Seashore Ecology (Gateway Films).
Beach and Sea Animals (EB Films).
Science and the Sea (Boulton-Hawker).
Secrets of the Underwater World (Walt Disney).
Changing Coast (EFVA).
Glaciers and Their Work (EFVA).
Setting up an Aquarium (Plymouth Films).
Pan (Contemporary Films).
Your Water Supply (British Waterworks Association).
Waterworks (British Waterworks Association).
Water for Life (UK Atomic Energy Authority).
The Watermill at Work (Paul Graham Films).

Filmstrips
Water Supply: Historical (Common Ground).
Water Supply: Industry (Contemporary Films).
Rain (Visual Publications).
How Town Folk Get Their Water (Crown).
How Country Folk Get Their Water (Crown).

Booklets
Soap; *Soap Making*; *Soapless Detergents* (Unilever).

Other aids
Six wallcharts: 1. *British Freshwater Fish*; 2. *The Fighting
    Téméraire*; 3. *Irrigation*; 4. *Water at Work*; 5. *Properties of
    Water*; 6. *Sea of Galilee* (Educational Productions Ltd).
Visual units prepared by the Central Office of Information and
    available through EFVA, 33 Queen Anne Street, London W1.
Jackdaw No. 91: *Water* (Cape).

Excursions
Natural History Museum, London (including inside trails on the
seashore and pond life).

Science Museum: sections on water power, steam power and ships.

Brixham Museum (Devon); Gloucester Folk Museum (Glos); Sailor's
Home and Nautical Museum (Great Yarmouth); Borough Museum,
Dartmouth (Devon); Doughty Museum (Grimsby); RNLI Museum,
Eastbourne (Sussex); Maritime Museum (Hull); Arbuthnot Museum,
Peterhead; Museum and Rotunda, Dundee; McLean Museum,
Greenock; Waterways Museum, Stoke Bruerne (Northants).

Visit: seashore; a port or dock; waterworks or reservoir; local pond.

CREATIVE ACTIVITIES
Write a story about two children exploring an underground river.

Imagine you are a newspaper reporter. Write an account of the floods
in your local area. Collect all the reports to make a special edition of
the newspaper — with illustrations.

Listen to the music of *The Swan of Tuonela*. Write the story of a
legend concerning a swan or a poem entitled 'The Lonely Lake'.

Write a story about a family who live on a remote farm which is cut off
from the nearest village by a snowstorm.

Collect newspaper cuttings and pictures about the sea, and then
write a poem called 'The Moods of the Sea'.

Try to visit a river or stream and find a waterfall, however small.
In the case of a small stream, build a dam to make a waterfall.
Write a poem about it.

Imagine you are a radio commentator. Describe the scene and
happenings while Elijah and the prophets of Baal are on Mount
Carmel having their contest. (This could feature as part of a dramatic
activity.)

Imagine you are one of the guests at the Wedding at Cana. Describe to a friend afterwards what you saw.

Imagine you were the blind man at the Pool of Siloam. Write a poem or hymn of praise and thanksgiving for the return of your sight.

Write the story of a family who spend their holiday on a houseboat.

Using the music by Tchaikovksy, tell the story of *Swan Lake* in movement.

Use the music by Holst, *Dance of the Spirits of Water*, and explore in movement the various moods of water and plan a dance.

Discuss and act a play about an Eskimo family and include in your play a scene involving a blizzard.

Act the story of the discovery of Moses in the bullrushes.

You are on a desert journey when your vehicle breaks down. Act out the long day's journey before night and final rescue, and what happens when at last you get water.

From the *Wheel on the School* read the chapter in which Lina and Old Janus manage to get a wheel from an upturned boat. Act this story.

Mathematical and scientific aspects
Water fountains describe parabolic paths. Experiment with jets of water in the playground area. Make stitch patterns of these curves.

Find out why ships float. Collect a number of different kinds of material — wood, metals, polystyrene, brick — and see which float.

Check the weights of various materials in and out of water. Check weight of water displaced by object.

Find out all you can about the Plimsoll line.

Make a water clock.

Make some simple weather-recording instruments. The school may feel they can invest a number of calibrated instruments to take regular readings of rainfall, temperature, humidity, wind force and direction and visibility.

More advanced activities include wet and dry bulb temperatures, maximum and minimum temperatures, cloud type and amount, air pressure and so on. Readings should be taken each day at the same time (including weekends and holidays), and charts and graphs produced. Comparisons should be made with weather reports from the daily press and attempts made to forecast locally.

Find out all you can about various forms of condensation — snow, hail, sleet, rain, mist, dew and frost.

Find out all you can about evaporation and condensation by experiments, and then the water cycle.

Set up an aquarium in class to observe the movements of water creatures. Keep an aquarium diary.

Find out which substances are soluble in water — ground-up chalk, salt, sugar, flour, bath salts, baking powder. Compare results in hot and cold water.

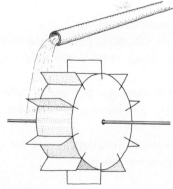

Fig. 30 A model water-wheel.

Make a model water-wheel, which will rotate when a jet of water is played upon it.

Make a simple steam turbine, using a tin with a tight-fitting lid. A card wheel, or a tin wheel in which vanes have been cut and turned, should be suspended above a small hole made in the lid. The tin is partly filled with water and heated until steam emerges from the hole.

Find out how steam engines work.

Find out how a hydro-electric power station works.

Find out about erosion. Plan experiments to find out whether plants and trees have any stabilising effect in a region affected by erosion.

Find out how sedimentary rock is formed. Try to make some, using shells, crushed chalk, cement and other materials.

Find out how stalactites and stalagmites are formed.

Make a study of plants, birds, animals, trees, fish, crustacea which are associated with water.

Carry out practical liquid-measuring work. Include a number of problems: for example, you have two containers, one holding three pints and the other five pints. How would you measure four pints of water?

Find out about hard and soft water. Check lathering of soap in tapwater and rainwater.

Investigate surface tension and carry out experiments with detergent to break this.

In winter, or with ice from the refrigerator (or a fishmonger), test action of salt; application of a weighted wire, etc.

Make a simple water purification plant.

Fig. 31 A simple water purification plant using clean sand and gravels of various sizes arranged in layers within a plant pot. Note the flat plate on the top onto which the dirty water is first poured. The water should be observed only and not drunk.

Art

Paint pictures of canals or lakes in which reflections can be seen. Sponge over area to be painted as the water area, to obtain a suitable effect. For another technique, only paint the upper part of the picture and then fold over at the waterline and smooth down with the hand to obtain the reflections.

Use oil colours or special marbling colours to learn the technique of marbling. Papers produced in this way can be used as end papers for workbooks and files.

Make snowflake patterns cut from squares of gummed paper, folded to give the hexagonal form. Mount on dark paper background.

Use scrap material to make pictures of underwater scenes. Sand and other materials such as shells and seaweed can be used in the collage.

Use a candle flame and wax crayons to make up a picture of sea creatures like sea-urchins and starfish.

Other subjects for art work: water mill, snow scene, umbrellas, water birds, water animals, waterfall.

Prepare soap solution and blow bubbles. After examination draw and colour a pattern of these.

Craft
Make a model of a Dutch scene, showing land reclaimed from the sea.

Make a model of a lock.

Make a model of a narrow boat, using traditional decorations.

Make a model hydro-electric power station.

Make a model trawler.

Make up a diorama of a reed bed with coots and ducks. Cover simple newspaper shapes with papier mâché.

Make an underwater scene beneath the model suggested previously in which fish and other water creatures are found.

Paper-sculpture fish, or those fashioned out of polystyrene, can be used and suspended from the underside of the table.

After visit to the Science Museum, model a *shaduf*, *sakia* and well from the Nile delta.

Make a series of model ships to show how their shapes have changed through the ages.

Fig. 32 A series of model ships as part of a display showing the evolution of this form of transport. (a) Model boats from cardboard.

(b) Simple galleon from balsa wood and knitting needles, paper sails and flag.

(c) Model Egyptian ship from paper and cocktails sticks.

Other outside activities

If the school has a garden or other area where there is soil, a pond can be created. A permanent school feature might be planned which will probably need some professional help (try the Parent–Teachers organisation). A semi-permanent pool can be created, using a polythene sheet (heavy duty). A hollow is excavated in the soil and lined with sieved soil or sand. Polythene is then laid and smoothed into place. The edge can be held down with flat stones, on which children can later stand without loosening the edge of the pool. Water is then put into the pool and plant and water creatures introduced. *See How to Build a Pond* – Nuffield Mathematics Project (published by W. & R. Chambers).

234

The River

'Men travel far to see a city, but few seem curious about a river. Every river has, nevertheless, its individuality, its great silent interest. Every river has, moreover, its influence over the people who pass their lives within sight of its waters.' So said H. S. Merriman in *The Sowers*. Rivers do seem to possess a personality of their own, regarded with love and devotion and sometimes fear by those who live alongside them.

By adopting the 'River' as a theme we can learn more than merely the names of these great waterways – the Ganges, Nile, Mississippi and the Thames.

Special aspects
This is yet another of the themes which most naturally invites the correlation of subjects, particularly geography and natural science. The serial story has great appeal, and one approach to this theme is to start on a river journey in the hills, and proceed stage by stage until the sea is reached. A river can flow throughout a project book, with the pupil adding relevant pieces of writing and illustration as the project proceeds.

Fieldwork opportunities in this project are seldom a problem to arrange because at least one river will be within easy travelling distance of the school. In many parks, rivers in miniature exist and these frequently display all the features of a major river – with gorges, tributaries and waterfalls.

With the increasing interest in the environment, and the dangers of pollution, animal extinction and leisure, a particular bias can be given to this topic to accommodate such aspects. There would be obvious links with other themes included in this book - for instance, Water, North Sea, Trees and Woodlands.

INSPIRATION AND INFORMATION
Books
Bethers, Ray: *The Story of Rivers* (Oak Tree Press); *Rivers of Adventure* (Longman Young).

236

Brittain, Robert: *Rivers and Man* (Longman).

Cress, R. K.: *Physical Geography of Rivers and Valleys* (Hulton).

Crouch, Marcus: *Rivers of England and Wales* (Longman Young).

Doherty, C. H.: *Science Builds the Bridges* (Brockhampton).

Greenwood, M. O.: *Discovering Rivers* (ULP).

Goodwin, Robert: *The Medway* (Constable).

Hartley, H. A.: *Famous Bridges and Tunnels* (Muller).

Ingram, J. H.: *The River Trent* (Cassell).

Lauber, P.: *The Mississippi* (Muller).

Meynell, Laurence: *Bridge Under the River* (Phoenix).

Molony, Eileen: *Maloney* (Dobson).

Painter, K. S.: *The Severn Basin* (Cory, Adams & Mackay).

Pilkington, Roger: *Thames Water* (Lutterworth); *The River* (Oliver & Boyd).

Stewart, R. N.: *Salmon and Trout* (Chambers).

Tomlinson, H. M: *London River* (Cassell).

Weingarten, V.: *The Nile* (Muller).

Rivers of the World (OUP): 1. Amazon, Murray, Ganges, Zambesi, St Lawrence, Nile. 2. Niger, Yellow River, Irrawaddy, Mississippi, Indus, Tigris. 3. European rivers.

A good geographical text-book will be useful for the relevant chapters, e.g. *Physical Geography* by P. Lake (CUP) or *The Principles of Physical Geography* by F. J. Monkhouse (ULP).

Stories

Blackmore, R. D.: *Lorna Doone* (for John Ridd's discovery of the secret way into the valley).

Bosco, H.: *The Boy and the River* (Oxford).

Buxton, Rufus Noel: *Westminster Wader* (Faber).

Dickens, C.: *Great Expectations* (Chapters 1 & 54).

Elwell, F. R.: *The Vanishing Stream* (Oliver & Boyd).

Grahame, Kenneth: *Wind in the Willows* (Penguin).

Herrimans, Ralph: *River Boy* (Collins).

Herbert, A. P.: *Water Gypsies* (Penguin).

Jerome, Jerome. *Three Men in a Boat* (Penguin).

Osmond, Laurie: *The Thames Flows Down* (OUP).

Ransome, Arthur: *Swallows and Amazons* (Cape).

Ruskin, John: *King of the Golden River* (Macmillan). See also this story set to music by Colin Hand (Novello).

Twain, Mark: *The Adventures of Huckleberry Finn* (Penguin).

Williamson, Henry: *Salar the Salmon* (Faber); *Tarka the Otter* (Penguin).

Stories from the Bible

Joshua Crosses the Jordan: Joshua 4.

Naaman Is Cured of Leprosy: II Kings 5.

John Baptises Jesus: Matthew 3.

Poems

Abercrombie, Lascelles: *The Stream's Song.*

Betjeman, John: *Henley-on-Thames.*

Bishop, Elizabeth: *The Fish.*

Blunden, Edmund: *The Pike.*

Clare, J.: *Kingfisher.*

Dalmon, Charles: *Trout.*

Davies, W. H.: *Kingfisher.*

Eliot, T. S.: *Growltiger's Last Stand.*

Keats, J.: *The Stream.*

Kipling, Rudyard: *The River's Tale.*

Grahame, Kenneth: *Duck's Ditty.*

Glover, Denis: *The River Crossing.*

Harvey, F. W.: *Elvers.*

Hughes, Ted: *Pike.*

Hunt, Leigh: *To a Fish; A Fish Answers.*

McGonegall, William: *Tay Bridge Disaster.*

Nash, Ogden: *The Guppy.*

Rieu, E. V.: *A Bad Day by the River.*

Rossetti, Christina: *Boots Sail on the Rivers.*

Scovell, R.: *A Boy Fishing.*

Southey, Robert: *The Cataract at Lodore.*

Stevenson, R. L.: *Where Go the Boats?*

Thomas, Dylan: *Over Sir John's Hill* (about the Heron).

Tennyson, Alfred Lord: *The Brook.*

Walton, Isaak: *Angler's Song* (from *The Compleat Angler*).

Watkins, Vernon: *The Heron.*
Yeats, W. B.: *The Wild Swans at Coole.*
Young, R.: *By the Tyne.*

Music
Delius, F.: *Summer Night on the River.*
Handel, F.: *Water Music.*
Holst, G.: *Dance of the Spirits of Water* (from *The Perfect Fool*).
Schubert, F.: *The Trout Piano Quintet.*
Strauss, Johann: *The Blue Danube.*
Wagner, R.: *Siegfried's Journey Down the Rhine* (from
    Götterdämmerung).

Songs
Sur le Pont d'Avignon.
London Bridge is Falling Down.
Eton Boating Song.
Waters of Tyne.
Ferry Across the Mersey.
Banks of the Ohio.
Moon River.
Old Man River.
Song of the Clyde.
Messing About On the River.
One More River.
We Are Crossing Jordan's River.
The Water Is Wide.
Ballad of London River.

Films
Louisiana River (Petroleum Films Bureau).
Forth Road Bridge (Shell Mex and BP).
Birds of the River (Plymouth Films).
Pan (Contemporary Films).
Twilight Forest (Unilever Films).
Beaver Valley (Walt Disney Productions).

The Danube (Walt Disney Productions).
Rivers (Dartington Hall – from EFVA).
Work of Rivers (Rank).
Following the River (Rank – six parts).
The Thames (BIF).
Essex River (Essex Educational Committee – Chelmsford).
The Rhine (Boulton-Hawker).
The Stickleback Family (Rank).
Amphibians (Boulton-Hawker).
The Estuary (River Thames) (Rank).
A Home In The Stream (about otters) (Wallace Productions).
Wild Life of the River (EFVA).
Caught in the Net (EFVA): based on the *Lazy Salmon Mystery* by
    Sutherland Ross).
Full Ahead, Rhine (Rank).
The Purfleet Floods (Unilever).
The Brook (a Yorkshire river) (The Brook Motors Ltd).
Bridge Over the Medway (John Laing).
Story of the St Lawrence Seaway (National Film Board of Canada).
The River Tweed (Campbell Harper).
Salmon Industry of British Columbia (National Film Board of Canada).
The River Tees (London Schools Film Society).
River Pilot (Excalibur Films – from EFVA).
The Creative Spirit (school study of the River Tern at Shrewsbury –
    EFVA).

Filmstrips
The River Tyne (Hulton).
Rivers (Common Ground).
Thames Basin (Hulton).
The Medway (Educational Productions).
The Beaver (Unicorn Head).
Beaver Valley (Educational Productions).
The Beaver (John King).
Development of Rivers (Visual Information Service).
Rivers (Common Ground).
Rivers (Stripslides Ltd).

The Kingfisher (John King).
Freshwater Fish of Britain (Tartan — from John King).
Freshwater Fish (Hulton Educational Ltd).
Bridges (Educational Productions).
Bridges (Tartan).
Tacoma Narrows Bridge (Institute of Civil Engineers).
Long Run (National Film Board of Canada).

Other aids
Charts: *British Freshwater Fish* (Educational Productions).
Leaflets and maps: The Port of London Authority, Trinity Square,
    London EC3.

Excursions
Walk alongside rivers in the neighbourhood. Where they are short
enough, follow the course from source to mouth. In urban situations
permission may be required to walk along some reaches. Some
detective work may be necessary where the river goes underground
(for instance, the Mole in Surrey). Try different banks of the river, and
the other direction. If the project is a prolonged one, go at different
seasons. If the river is tidal, explore the estuary at time of high and
low spring tides. With care, observe the river during a spate, and at
time of drought.

Where the river is shallow enough, walk in the river. Alternatively hire
a boat to experience the river in this way — keep a log on such an
excursion.

In the case of a large river, careful prior arrangement and briefing of
the coach driver can make possible a day of walking certain sections
and riding alongside less interesting stretches.

Certain rivers, e.g. the Thames, have regular steamer trips: Charing
Cross to Kew, or Greenwich: see Salter's time-tabled services up river,
or Port of London launch cruises around the docks.

CREATIVE ACTIVITIES
Written work
Write a story telling of a night row, up river, after you had been put off a ship at the mouth of the estuary.

Write a poem about the salmon on their way to the spawning grounds, and their efforts to leap over a weir.

Write a diary of your day on a river bank fishing. Talk about the things you saw, the people you met, the weather and your very big catch.

You are crossing by the last ferry — it is foggy. In midstream, the boat breaks down. Write down the events of the next fifteen minutes in this busy river.

With a friend adopt a river in this country, in Europe or elsewhere in the world, and prepare an account of it with illustrations, folk tales, statistical information, in a form agreed with each pair in the class, so that an Encyclopaedia of Rivers can be produced.

Drama and movement
You are a ferryman and are called over to take a fare across the river. Perform a mime with a companion to tell this story.

Enact the story of St Christopher.

Using excerpts from *Pepys' Diary*, prepare a play about the Fire of London, and the evacuation of some of the citizens by river.

Mime the building of a large raft of timber and the exciting ride downstream.

Use props and drama blocks to build a bridge across a river.

Use the book *The Great Thames Disaster* by Gavin Thurston (Allen & Unwin). In 1878 the pleasure steamer the *Princess Alice* crashed into a collier in Galleons Reach on the Thames with the loss of some 600 lives. Act out the whole story. Prepare sound effects on tape to go with the production.

Use the poem *How Horatius Held the Bridge* by Thomas Macaulay as an exercise in choral speaking while miming the action of Horatius and his companions holding the Tuscan army at bay on the bridge over the Tiber.

Mathematical and scientific activities
During a river excursion, find the speed of the current, at various places along its course. Use a stopwatch to time a piece of wood floating over a measured distance. Is the river faster midstream or near the banks? Note any differences in plant and animal life with different river speeds.

From the parapet of a bridge, take depth soundings of the river bottom at convenient intervals, using a weighted stone on the end of a string marked off in unit measurements. Draw a profile of the river and compare it with observations at other points on the same river.

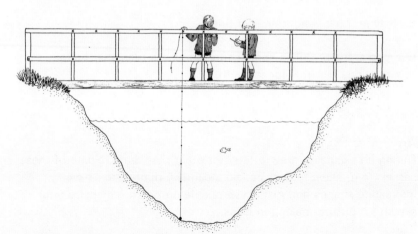

Fig. 33 Recording details of a river profile.

Where there are or have been mills on the river, use a map to comment on their siting. Measure the speed of water and if possible the force and volume of water running through the millrace. Invent a pressure gauge by combining a spring balance with a square of hardboard, held at each corner by a string.

Check the temperature of the water of a river at various points along the course. Is there any significance in the variations?

Some river bridges and even nearby buildings have flood marks. Note details of these. Examine riverside trees to see if there is any hanging debris from a recent flood, and measure the height the river must have reached at the time of full spate.

Carry out experiments with pieces of card of constant size to determine stresses and strains in bridge building:

(a) Place the card across two supports and add weights until collapse takes place.
(b) Fold the card in a series of ridges and retest.
(c) Fold card into a cylinder and retest.
(d) Try other shapes.

Each time, note weight limit of bridge.

Use geo-strips or drilled spatulas to produce a triangular bridge construction. Test this for strength.

Art
During an excursion draw a ferry (or other river craft). Some of these vessels, e.g. chain ferries, paddle steamers, punts, etc., have interesting shapes and distinctive people on board. Later use your sketch for picture-making in class.

Choose either an otter or a salmon and paint a large picture showing one in the river. Or paint the otter in pursuit of the salmon.
Prepare a river collage with creatures of the river and river bank in the scene.

244

Craft

Make a model of a water mill. Make the paddle wheel of tin strips and set it up on a draining board, so that water power can turn the shaft.

Using book illustrations or working drawings from a river excursion, make up a series of bridge models. Arrange these along a cut-out plan of a river.

Create a river model.

Make up a stretcher, say ten feet long and three feet wide. Use boxes and newspaper bundles at one end to show the high ground, and gradually make the scenery more gentle as the other end of the model is reached. Cover with sheets of pasted newspaper; when dry, varnish. When this is dry allow a trickle of water to run along the model to indicate the 'true' valley. Paint in the river and add other features: bridges, mills, docks and so on.

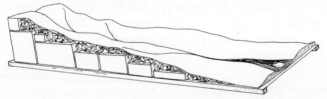

Fig. 34 A river model showing construction details of stepped boxes and newspaper packing under layers of papier mâché.

Make a river animal model. Use bundles of newspaper and string and tie securely at important places to create an approximate shape of various creatures of the river. Extra details can be added with Plasticine or other modelling material. Cover with paper mâché, and when dry, paint. Create suitable settings, e.g. reeds and nest for a coot; a holt or hole under the roots of a tree for an otter; a dam (with cut-open view to show chamber) for a beaver, with cut lengths of branches and clay.

Make a model of a hydro-electric plant. Use chicken wire to create the high sides of a gorge. Between this bend a piece of stout card or hardboard to take up the concave shape of a dam. Use card boxes to raise the level of the 'water' behind the dam. Mix plaster of Paris and use pieces of butter muslin impregnated with the plaster to cover the river bank and the water above and below the dam. Prepare 'pipes' from string or milk straws down the slope, to the turbine house. Electric pylons made from metal construction sets will complete the modelling. Paint to produce the finished scene.

With all such large models, look carefully at the size of the door if you intend to mount an exhibition elsewhere. One of the authors was obliged to re-arrange the display in his own room around a 'monster' the class had created, because it could not be manoeuvred into the corridor!

Other activities
Some secondary schools run an angler's club, and a weekend visit for this sport could be linked with this project.

Canoe building is another activity which will fit in with this topic. Rallies of canoe enthusiasts, with the correct instruction, take place on the larger rivers at various times of the year. Welsh schools can try coracle building.

School journeys on the water are also possible for older pupils. Interested teachers can contact Adventure Cruises Ltd, Union Canal Carriers Ltd, 214 Whittington Road, London, N22 (Ring 01-888 4780 after 8 p.m.). Some schools own their narrow and other boats and may be willing to hire to others without this facility.

A useful address for further information: British Canoe Union, 20 Park Crescent, London W1N 4DT.

Books for young anglers
'Mr Crabtree': *Book of Fishing* (Daily Mirror).
Gamble, Colin: *River Fishing* (Hamlyn).
Potts, W. Carter: *The Young Angler* (Black).
Wood, James: *Sport Fishing for Beginners* (Ward Lock).
Fish and Fishing: Magpie Pocket Book (Lutterworth).

The North Sea

The sea is in our blood. There can be few who, when the weather is right, do not wish to be on, in or beside the sea. And even when the weather is wrong, the sea still exerts a tremendous influence on those who live near it. The efforts of men pitting their wits and strength against the sea during storms can dominate the headlines or the television screen. A project about the sea and the seashore is an all-embracing one, full of adventure and excitement. To concentrate the study on one area, the project has been narrowed to the North Sea because in and around it can be seen examples of many facets of ocean life. However, since it would be unwise to ignore the work of composers, artists, poets and writers who have chosen to particularise about other seas, some have been included so that inspiration can be drawn from them. For instance, the *Torrey Canyon* disaster immediately comes to mind when thinking of an oil-tanker wreck, and reference has been made to this to stimulate some written work about a similar incident which could occur in the North Sea.

Special aspects

As in several other projects in the book, there are a number of component parts which inter-relate to form the whole. Teachers may prefer to adopt one or two aspects rather than attempt the whole project, e.g. fishing; shipbuilding; air/sea rescue services; invasions and sea battles; the seacoast, and so on.

INSPIRATION AND INFORMATION
Books
Money, George: *The North Sea* (Muller).

The coast
Hastings, V.: *Flood Tide* (Harrap).
Lauber, Patrick: *Battle Against the Sea* (Chatto & Windus).
Steers, J. A.: *The English Coast* (Fontana); *The Sea Coast* (Collins).

The seashore

Barrett, J. H. & Yonge, C. M.: *Pocket Guide to the Seashore* (Collins).
Beetschen, Louis: *Seaside Treasures* (Mills & Boon).
Burton, Maurice: *Margins of the Seas* (Muller).
Carson, R. L.: *The Edge of the Sea* (Staples); *The Sea Around Us* (Penguin).
Catherall, E. A. & Holt, P. N.: *Working on the Seashore* (Bailey Bros).
Cavenna, Betty: *The First Book of Seashells* (Ward).
Evans, I. O.: *The Observer's Book of the Sea and Seashore* (Warne).
Ford, V. E.: *The Seashore* (fieldwork) (Murray).
Marshall, S. M.: & Orr, A. P.: *Seashores* (Oliver & Boyd).
Matthews, Gillian & Parks, Peter: *Seashore Life* (Puffin Picture).
Norman, Jill: *Along the Edge of the Sea* (Hutchinson).
Scott, Nancy: *The Seashore* (Dobson).
Street, Philip: *Between the Tides* (ULP).
Vevers, H. G.: *The British Seashore* (Routledge & Kegan Paul).
Yonge, C. M.: *The Seashore* (Collins).
I-Spy at the Seaside (Dickens Press).

Settlements by the sea

Bradford, Ernie: *Wall of England* (Country Life).
Herdman, T.: *Coasts of Britain* (Longman).
Pringle, Patrick: *Smugglers* (Dobson).

Invasions and battles

Barclay, Brig. C. N.: *Battle 1066* (Dent).
Burland, C. A.: *The Vikings* (Hulton).
Cottrell, Leonard: *The Great Invasion* (Evans); *The Roman Forts of the Saxon Shore* (HMSO).
Dawlish, Peter: *The Royal Navy* (OUP); *Seas of Britain* (Benn).
Donovan, Frank R.: *The Vikings* (Cassell).
Ellacott, S. F.: *The Norman Invasion* (Abelard-Schuman).
Hodges, C. Walter: *The Norman Conquest* (OUP).
Proctor, G. L.: *The Vikings* (Longman).
Sellman, R. R.: *The Vikings* (Methuen).
Simpson, Jacqueline: *Everyday Life in the Viking Age* (Batsford).
Syme, R.: *Invaders and Invasions* (Batsford).

Fishing

Barker, Eric J. & McCrum, J. P.: *Grimsby Trawlers* (OUP).
Carrington, Richard: *A Biography of the Sea* (Chatto & Windus).
Darling, F. F.: *The Seasons and the Fisherman* (OUP).
Deacon, G. E. R.: *Oceans* (Paul Hamlyn).
Fleming, H. M. le: *British Trawlers* (Ian Allan).
Hardy, A. C.: *Fish and Fisheries* (Collins).
Havenhand, I. & J.: *The Fisherman* (Wills & Hepworth).
Holdgate, C.: *Netmaking for All* (Mills & Boon).
Perrott, Roy: *Discovering Deep Sea Fishing* (ULP).
Street, Philip: *Beyond the Tides* (ULP).
Wright, John M.: *Deep Sea Fishing* (Black).

Trade

Ambrus, Victor G.: *The Merchant Navy* (OUP).
Block, I.: *The Real Book of Ships* (Dobson).
Brooks, L. & Duce, R. M.: *Seafarers, Ships and Cargoes* (ULP).
Clark, D.: *Ships and Seamen* (Longman).
Cornwall, A. B.: *Ships* (ESA).
Ellacott, S. E.: *The Story of Ships* (Methuen).
Evans, I. O.: *The Observer's Book of Flags* (Warne).
Fleming, H. M. le: *Coastal Cargo Ships; Foreign Coastal Freighters;
    Coastal Passenger Ships* (Ian Allan Ltd).
France, C. R.: *Discovering Sailing Ships* (ULP).
Hoare, R. J.: *Travel by Sea Through the Ages* (Black).
Insull, T.: *Transport by Sea* (Murray).

Shipbuilding

Ellacott, S. E.: *The Story of Ships* (Methuen).
Hope, R.: *Ships* (Batsford).
Murphy, J. S.: *Ships* (OUP).
M. Simons: *A Tyneside Shipyard* (OUP).

Air/sea rescue

Ashley, Bernard: *The Men and the Boats* (Allman).
Croome, Angela: *Know About Wrecks* (Blackie).
Garland, Rosemary: *Lighthouses* (ESA).

Howarth, Patrick: *How Men Are Rescued from the Sea* (Routledge & Kegan Paul).

Jerrome, E. G.: *Lighthouses, Lightships and Buoys* (Blackwell).

Jolly, Cyril: *S.O.S.* (Cassell).

Reed, Olwen: *The Story of Lighthouses, Lightships and Lifeboats* (Wills & Hepworth).

Uden, Grant: *Lifeboats* (Blackwell).

For those in Peril: Lifesaving Then and Now (HMSO).

Oil, gas and coal
Some of the following references relate to the production of these minerals on land, but there are many similar problems facing the sea engineer.

Cooper, B. & Gaskell, T. F.: *North Sea Oil — the Big Gamble* (Heinemann).

Leyland, Eric: *Oil Man* (Ward).

Newell, J.: *In a Coalmine* (Phoenix).

Wymer, N.: *On an Oil Field* (Phoenix).

Stories

Burton, Hester: *The Great Gale* (OUP).

Conrad, Joseph: *Youth* (Dent).

Crane, Stephen: *The Badge of Courage* (the open-boat sequence — Signet).

Jenkins, A. C.: *The Golden Band* (Holland's fight against the sea — Methuen).

Treece, Henry: *Viking's Dawn*; *Viking's Sunset*; *Horned Helmet* (Penguin).

There are numerous other sea stories which will repay the reading and telling, for instance, Hemingway's *The Old Man and The Sea* (Cape). There are also many collections of stories and extracts, e.g.

'Mainsail': *Fifty Famous Sea Stories* (Burke).

Monsarrat, Nicholas: *The Book of the Sea* (Cassell).

Stories from the Bible

The waters saw thee: Psalm 77: 16–19.
They that go down to the sea in ships: Psalm 107: 23–31.
Paul's Shipwreck: Acts 27.

Poems

Arnold, Matthew: *Forsaken Merman.*
Baker, Dorothy: *Castle in the Sand.*
Beddoes, T. L.: *Song from the Ships.*
Bell, J. J.: *The Lights.*
Betjeman, John: *Westgate-on-Sea*; *Beside the Seaside*; *East Anglian Bathe.*
Clough, Arthur C.: *Where Lies the Land?*
Cunningham, A.: *Sea Song.*
Davidson, John: *A Cinque Port.*
Farjeon, E.: *The Waves of the Sea.*
Frost, Robert: *Neither out far or in deep.*
Gibson, W.: *Sail on, sail on.*
Jeffers, Robinson: *November Surf.*
Kipling, R.: *A Smuggler's Song*; *The Sea and the Hills.*
Ingelow, Jean: *The High Tide on the Coast of Lincolnshire.*
Longfellow, H. W.: *The tide's rise, the tide's fall.*
Masefield, John: *Cargoes*; *I saw a ship a-sailing.*
Mitcheson, Naomi: *Morning Herring.*
Meigo, Mildred: *Pirate Don Durk of Dowdee.*
Reeves, James: *Rum Lane.*
Rossetti, C.: *Storm Wind.*
Ross, W. W. E.: *The Diver.*
Stephens, James: *The Shell.*
Stevenson, R. L.: *The Lighthouse Keeper.*
Tennyson, A.: *The Sea-Fairies.*
Watkins, Vernon: *Sea Music for My Sister Travelling.*
Wilde, Oscar: *The Sea.*
Wilson, Marjorie: *The Gates to England.*
Wilson, Raymond: *Ghost Village by the Shore.*
Wright, David: *Shanty.*

252

Music

Seashanties:
Windy Old Weather.
Bobby Shaftoe.
What Shall We Do with the Drunken Sailor?
Fire Down Below.

Songs:
Caller Herrin'!
Hearts of Oak.
All the Fishes of the Sea (from *Merrie England*).
Big Steamers.

Orchestral
Singing the Fishing – a radio ballad by Peggy Seegar and
    Ewan McColl.
Debussy, F.: *La Mer.*
Elgar, Edward: *Sea Pictures.*

Sea and Shore Songs: Michael Hurd (Novello).
The Singing Sailor: Ian Kendall (J. W. Chester).
Music in Action – the Sea: William Bulman (Rupert Hart-Davis).

Films

Purfleet Floods (Unilever – from Sound Services).
Gale Warning (RNLI).
Tradition of the Life Boat Service (RNLI).
Shipshape (RNLI).
Troubled Waters (RNLI).
Life Boat Call (RNLI).
Life Boat Coming (RNLI).
Land Below the Sea (Caltex Services Ltd).
Having a Wonderful Time (Great Yarmouth and Gorleston-on-Sea
    Publicity Dept).
At the Sign of the Ram and the Gate (Ramsgate Borough Council).
Sunshine and Sea (Southend-on-Sea Borough Council).
Industrial Tyneside (Ford).

Modern Land of the Vikings (Caltex Services Ltd).

Progressive Norway (Caltex Services Ltd).

The Beach (Ford).

Between the Tides (British Transport).

Seashore Ecology (Gateway Films).

The Vikings (Rank).

Coast Erosion (Rank).

The Changing Coast (EFVA).

North Sea (GPO).

Sea Harvest (BIF).

Local Fish Supply (Rank).

Radar Helps Shipping (British Transport).

The Empty Sea (lobster fishing) (BP Film).

North Sea Quest (BP).

Useful addresses

Public Relations Officer, White Fish Authority: 2 Cursitor Street, London EC4. (Booklets, charts and filmstrips for sale.)

The Secretary, Herring Industry Board: 1 Glenfinlas Street, Edinburgh 3. (Information sheets and charts.)

Secretary, British Ship Adoption Society: HQS *Wellington*, Temple Stairs, Victoria Embankment, London WC2. (There is a waiting list for ships, but a worthwhile permanent link can be made and developed. Exchange visits by pupils and crew. Magazine: *Our Merchant Ships.*)

Ministry of the Environment: St Christopher House, Southwark, London, SE1. (For information about the Coastguard Service.)

Corporation of Trinity House: Tower Hill, London EC3. (For information about lighthouses, lightships, buoys and pilotage.)

RNLI: 42 Grosvenor Gardens, London SW1. (For information about lifeboat service.)

Unilever: Unilever House, Blackfriars, London EC4. (For copies of free booklet, *Sea Harvest*, and loan of such films as *Bars of Silver*, *Herrings for Sale*, and *Dual Purpose.*)

Excursions

The North Sea is probably within reach of most schools for at least a day excursion. Schools which run school journeys of longer duration, a week or a fortnight in length, can base themselves near the coast in a hotel, camp or Youth Hostel. Off season the hotel and camp rates are usually very economical.

Various aspects of this topic can be attempted even within the duration of a day, but obviously a longer period can offer the opportunity for many varied visits.

Coastal walk, to show various geographical formations.

Beach walk, at various stages of tides (seaweed, shells, birds, etc.). Rock pool study; sea marsh study; sandy beach, rocky beach.

Visits to lighthouse, coastguard station, lifeboat.

Visit to a fishing port, fish market, trawler or drifter, net-making factory, ice-making plant and so on.

Shipbuilding yard or repair shop.

Sea trip on hired boat, fishing boat or hovercraft (from Ramsgate).

Study a seaside town.

Museums on the coast: research laboratory, Lowestoft; Doughty Museum, Grimsby; Maritime Museum, Great Yarmouth; South Shields Museum; Grace Darling Museum, Bamburgh, Northumberland.

Seabird reserves: Blakeney Point; Farne Islands.

Valuable visits can also be made to such places as the *Cutty Sark* and Maritime Museum, Greenwich; Natural History Museum, South Kensington.

CREATIVE ACTIVITIES
Written work
You are on a night trip on a drifter out of Lowestoft. During your

watch, your net is fouled by another ship. Write the night's story for your local newspaper.

You are on watch above the cliffs at Whitby centuries ago and spy a Viking fleet approaching. Write the story of what you did when your homeland was invaded.

Imagine you are living in a small fishing port on the East Coast 200 years ago. Write a story of how you went to sea for the first time.

Write a poem about being on a ship becalmed in the fog.

Make a collection of shells from the beach and write a poem to include as many of them as possible.

If you have a large shell in your collection (a large whelk, for instance), hold it to your ear to hear the roaring sound. Imagine this to be the sea. Write a poem or story about it.

Write a story about the wreckers of ships and the scavengers who used to await the wrecks, e.g. the Beach company of Great Yarmouth.

Tell the story of life on a North Sea oil rig.

Make up a ballad about a shipyard when they have just begun to build a new ship.

Thames, Humber, Tyne, Forth, Dogger, Forties, Cromarty are the North Sea areas which we usually only hear about when gales are imminent in them. Write a verse using these sea areas, describing the conditions in them. Use references to the Beaufort windscale. At one time a great trade in the carriage of sea coal from the Tyne to the Thames was carried on. Here is a typical piece of East Coast doggerel:

> First the Humber, then the Spurn,
> Flamborough Head comes next in turn,
> Whitby light lies in a bight
> We'll be in canny 'owd Shields tonight.

256

Refer to a large-scale map of the East Coast and write a poem in this vein, and set it to music.

The whaling fleet was a particular feature of Leith, with whale catchers and factory ships. Find out about this type of fishing and write an account of it with illustrations.

Paul Jones entered the North Sea in 1779 with a squadron of ships. Find out about the great duel between the *Richard* and the *Seraphis* (with Captain Pearson in command). Two people can be invited to write reports of the action, from each viewpoint. Tell the story of Sir Martin Frobisher's conversion from piracy to the command of the British fleet.

Imagine you are the Greek explorer Pytheas, who journeyed into the North Sea in 325 B.C. Tell of your meetings with the sailors and fishermen of the northern tribes.

Write about your descent in a bathysphere to investigate life on the seabed — and a rather nasty scare you got.

Prepare a log of a fishing trip to the North Sea fishing grounds. For each entry, give the time on the twenty-four-hour clock in GMT and the speed and direction of travel. Make a note of estimated position, and make brief comment about weather condition, including the state of the sea. Be concise in all the entries, referring to crew members by their surnames and their involvement in the situation you are reporting.

Drama and movement
Make up a crew; perform your various tasks on the deck of the ship. A storm begins to build up and normal duties have to be abandoned as the ship runs into danger. Act this story and select suitable music (Mendelssohn: *Fingal's Cave*; *Calm Sea and a Prosperous Voyage*).

You are on a trawler. Shoot the nets; pull them in with the winch; open the net, gut the fish and store it away. Sing shanties to pass the time.

A band of smugglers land from the Continent with a load of wine, silk and tobacco. They unload their cargo and begin to climb up the cliff path, but are surprised by the customs men. Act the story with the trial of those who were not killed.

Carry out a rescue by breeches buoy of a crew wrecked on the rocks.

Read the story of the wreck of the *Forfarshire* on the Farne Islands in September 1838. Act the story of the rescue of the crew by Grace Darling and her father.

As a group activity discuss and develop the story of a Sea Witch. Select suitable music to dance the story, e.g. Dvorak's *Water Goblin* or *Noon Witch.*

Plan and set up a pirate radio station. Use school radio system to play top of the chart favourites (during wet lunchtime session), until 'authorities' send in a boarding party at 1.30 pm.

Dramatise the following Biblical stories: Paul's Shipwreck on Malta (Acts 27: 21); Noah and the Flood (Genesis 6–8).

Mathematical and scientific assignments
Make a study of the tides during a stay at the coast. Note daily times of high and low water. Note variations on neap and spring tides, and if possible make marks on breakwater or groynes to show highest point reached each day. (Note phases of moon and relate them to different tides.) Or make a line of sandpies with a code number scratched on them and time their destruction by incoming tide.

Collect (in summer) details of sunshine and rainfall figures for as many East Coast resorts as you can. Compare with other coastal areas. (Information is available in local guidebooks, but some newspapers summarise these facts for their readers.)

Make line transects up the beach at various stages of tide, and record life or remains found. Compare with various types of beach.

Make a study of a rock pool. Measure depth at various points and make plan and section of pool. Record details of animal and plant life.

Make comparative studies of animals of rocky shores, muddy shores and shingle beaches. Try counts of species. Study animal and plant forms living on a groyne. Make drawings to show distributions.

Make a collection and carry out a count of plants which tolerate the salt-laden conditions of the sea coast.

Note the direction of prevailing wind at the sea coast on a sandy beach. Check direction of groynes and depth of water or sand on either side of these.

Note high lines of debris on beaches. Why are there so many?

Mark a number of periwinkles on a rock surface, and record the number and position of these. Return later to check for movements, especially after a tide.

Make a collection of shell and seaweed specimens for identification and display work, and use in art and craft.

Discover relationships between knots and m.p.h., fathoms and feet, watches and the twenty-four-hour clock.

Geology is a subject which is becoming increasingly popular with children, and the cross-sections of cliffs reveal interesting and varied formations for study. Rocks and pebbles on the beach can be collected and attempts made to identify their place of origin. Fossils are found in many locations and add a further interest to beachcombing.

Principles of flotation and water propulsion can be investigated in the classroom.

Make a calendar map of the movement of herring around the coast.

Find out the various measures in use for different types of fish:

pounds for salmon, stones for large turbot, draughts for eels,
per 100 for oysters, dozens for scallops, bushels for whelks, gallons for
shrimps.

Art
Sketching work on field visits, especially annotated drawings of coastal
features.

Ship's flags (House and International Code).

Frieze of ships, showing development from cut-out canoes to
hovercraft.

Picture of fishermen on deck of trawler.

Beach pictures. Shell and seaweed patterns.

Portrait of a fisherman — during a storm.

A glass and concrete sea city has been proposed. It will be in the form
of a huge amphitheatre, sixteen storeys high, built around a lagoon and
positioned fifteen miles off Great Yarmouth. Model this North Sea
Venice.

Craft
Make a model of an actual size wheelhouse of a trawler with wheel,
binnacle, engine-room telegraph and radar set.

Models of various types of ship in card.

A fishing port: large model built up with cardboard boxes, showing
harbour walls, fishermen's cottages and warehouses.

Fleet of drifters leaving the harbour.

A long model, on the window-sill, showing various coastal features —
cliffs, caves, arches, stacks, estuaries, sand spits and deltas.

Model of an oil rig.

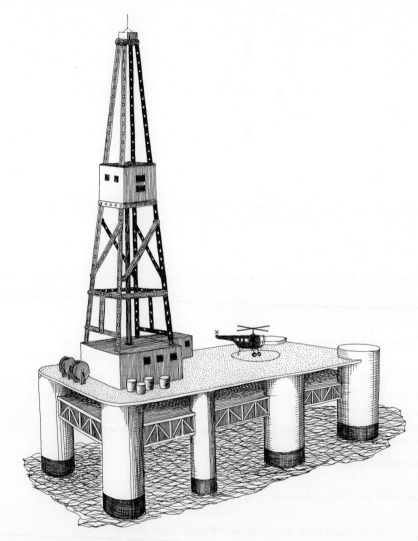

Fig. 35 A model oil rig.

Lighthouse, wired to flash.

Fig. 36 A working model of a lighthouse.

Helicopter rescue from a wrecked ship.

Breeches-buoy rescue from cliff top to vessel wrecked on rocks.

Birds of the seashore. Card cut-outs of seabirds, some suspended as a mobile, others standing on breakwater or foraging on water's edge.

Seaside resort with funfair, pier, boats for hire and shops.

Model of Channel Tunnel.

Diorama of Viking invasion.

Battle of Jutland with German and British fleets.

Submarine attack.

Models to illustrate the trawl net and the drift net (suitable for window-sill models).

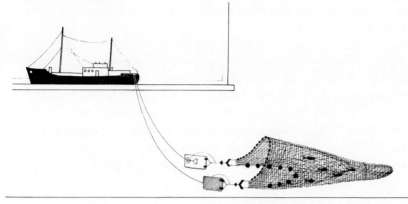

Fig. 37 Trawler and net. This model is balanced on the window sill and the net fixed to the wall, thus taking up very little space.

Full-size figure model of a fisherman in oilskins.

Model of a lightship.

Model of a hovercraft (and hoverport).

Knots; rope-laying; net-making.

Coal mine under the sea. Low-relief model showing shafts on land, and galleries under the sea.

Larger than life-size model of a Viking warrior.

In 1967 the *Torrey Canyon* hit the rocks and headlines when its cargo of crude oil spilled into the sea. Make a model of this kind of disaster in a North Sea location. (See films: *After the Torrey Canyon* (RSPB) and *Torrey Canyon* (Unilever).

Other related aspects for study: salt; weather recording.

Other outside activities

A visit can be planned to Billingsgate or other large fish market. The local fishmonger would provide another more local opportunity for an excursion.

A visit to a commercial and passenger port will give rise to the collection of much data. For instance, King's Lynn imports chemicals from Hamburg, Antwerp and Casablanca; oil from Billingham and Fawley; grain from Rotterdam and Imjuiden; and timber from Scandinavia. Wheat is exported to Emden, coal to Colchester and sugar to London. Tonnage figures, sailing times, sizes of crew and ports of registrations can be gathered together and graphed.

Aid can be given during Lifeboat Week, collections in March and displays and showing of RNLI films organised.

Organise a Festival of Sea Harvest in your local church.

A small rowing boat or old ship's lifeboat might be purchased from a shipping company and fixed with chocks in the playground. Ours was acquired for £1 and was aptly described as a jolly boat. We held an adoption ceremony in which the master of the *Cutty Sark* renamed the boat.

FIRE!

The importance of fire is sometimes overlooked, yet all industries depend on it, and heating, lighting and cooking are still closely linked with it. When we consider the many articles which we come in contact with each day, which are connected with fire, we soon realise its importance in our lives. Fire also presents dangers and here is the opportunity to study from two viewpoints, 'Fire the Friend of Man' and 'Fire the Enemy'.

Special aspects

There are many possible starting points for this project, and a choice can be made to suit the special interest of the class or age group. There are many good fiction stories set in London at the time of the Great Fire, which could provide an excellent historical stimulus; the excitement of November 5th provides another. The use of fire in industry could be approached through a visit to a blacksmith, pottery or bakery. An excursion to a fire station is usually an interesting one, and stimulates the children into realising the hazards of fire and the action to take when discovering one.

See 'A Festival of Fire', 'Halloween Festival', 'Sun Day' in *A Book of Festivals* by Derek Waters (Mills & Boon) if an approach through the visual arts is envisaged.

INFORMATION AND INSPIRATION
Books

Adams, H.: *Fires and Firemen* (Blackwell).

Adler, I. & R.: The Reason Why Series − *Storms* (Dennis Dobson).

Barker, E. & Millard, W. F.: *Junior Scientist*, Book 3 (Evans).

Baxter, E.: *The Study of Coal*; *The Study Book of Gas*; *The Study Book of Oil* (Bodley Head).

Bedford, J.: *London's Burning* (Abelard-Schuman).

Bransom, J. M.: *Fire and Warmth* (Chambers).

Brock, A.: *A History of Fireworks* (Harrap).

Clair. C.: *The Things We Need − Coal* (Bruce).

Clarke, B.: *Fire Alarm* (Epworth).

Cook, J. G.: *Look at Glass* (Hamish Hamilton).

Creese, Angela: *Safety for Your Family* (Mills & Boon).

Davey, J.: *Coal Mining* (Black).

Davies, M.: *Iron and Steel* (ESA).

Du Garde Peach, L.: *James I and the Gunpowder Plot* (Wills & Hepworth).

Epstein, S. & B.: *The First Book of Glass* (Franklin Watts).

Fawcett, R.: *Where Does It Come From — Oil* (Gawthorn).

Feravolo, R. V.: *Junior Science Book of Light* (Muller).

Finnie, J.: *Fire Engines* (Methuen).

Fox, E.: *London in Peril: 1665–66* (Lutterworth).

Garland, R.: *Glass* (ESA).

George, S. C.: *Man Needs the Sun* (Hamish Hamilton).

Havenhand, I. & J.: *The Miner* (Wills & Hepworth).

Henry, B.: *The Elements Series: Fire* (John Baker).

Hunter, L.: *Science in Industry: 1. Coal* (Burke).

Jackson, W. E.: *London's Fire Brigade* (Longman).

James, E. O.: *Seasonal Feasts and Festivals* (Thames & Hudson).

Kelly, A.: *The Book of English Fireplaces* (Country Life).

Kneebone, S. D. & Clegg, C.: *Man Finds Treasure; Man and Fire* (Hamish Hamilton).

Lacroix, P.: *Conquest of Fire* (Burke).

Ladyman, P.: *Inside the Earth* (Brockhampton).

Land, M. & B.: *Jungle Oil* (Chatto & Windus).

Lauber, P.: *Junior Science of Volcanoes* (Muller).

Manning, S. A.: *Bakers and Bread* (Blackwell).

Medler, J. V.: *A Child's Book of Mountains and Volcanoes* (Publicity Products).

Mitchell, R.: *The Study of Lamps and Candles* (Bodley Head).

Munch, T. W.: *What Is Light?; What Is Heat?* (Collins).

Neurath, M.: *Fire* (Max Parrish).

Newbury, N. F.: *Focus on Glass* (Heinemann).

Newell, J.: *In a Coal Mine* (Dent).

O'Dea, W. T.: *Making Fire* (HMSO).

Rimmington, J.: *How Things Are Obtained — Bread* (ESA).

Rowland, J. S.: *Everyday Things for Lively Youngsters* (Cassell).

Shepherd, W.: *Wealth From the Ground* (Weidenfeld & Nicolson).

Southgate, V. & Havenhand, J.: *The Fireman* (Wills & Hepworth).

Taylor, D.: *Pompeii and Vesuvius* (BBC).

Taylor, N. A.: *Rocks and Fossils* (Studio Vista).

Thompson, T. A.: *Coal and Coal Mining* (Blackwell).

Thorurmsson, Sigurdur: *Surtsey* (Cassell).

Walton, R. H.: *The True Book About Firearms* (Muller).

Unstead, R. J.: *Tudors and Stuarts; the Middle Ages* (A. & C. Black).

Wymer, N.: *On an Oilfield* (Dent).

Science in Our World, Book 5 (Macmillan).

Science Life, Book 4 (Macmillan).

Making Matches (Bryant & May).

Stories

Ainsworth, W. H.: *Old St Paul's* (Nelson).

Aldous, A.: *Bushfire* (Brockhampton).

Black, G. P.: *Arthur's Seat* (Oliver & Boyd).

Bruckner, K.: *The Day of the Bomb* (Burke).

Conrad, J.: *Youth* (Dent).

Dickens, M.: *The Great Fire* (Kaye & Ward).

Durant, G. M.: *Fires of Revolt: Boadicea* (G. Bell).

Hope-Simpson, J.: *The Great Fire* (Reindeer Books).

Lee, L.: *Cider with Rosie* (Penguin).

Leyland, E.: *Fire Over London* (Hutchinson).

Lytton, Lord: *Last Days of Pompeii* (Collins).

Miller, M. J.: *Gunpowder Treason* (Macdonald).

Nolan, W.: *David and Jonathan* (after the Gunpowder Plot) (Macmillan).

Price, W.: *Volcano Adventure* (Jonathan Cape).

Rice, D.: *Hugh Nameless* (Blackie).

Samson, W.: *The Wall* (Penguin Selected Stories).

Southall, I.: *Ash Road* (Angus & Robertson).

Strong, L. A. G.: *The Fifth of November* (Dent).

Sutcliffe, R.: *Warrior Scarlet* (Oxford).

Treece, G.: *The Grey Adventurer* (Blackwell).

Weir, R.: *The Star and the Flame* (Faber).

Stories from the Bible

Elijah on Mount Carmel: I Kings 18.

Elijah on Horeb: 1 Kings 19.

Elijah and the Chariot of Fire: II Kings 2.
Shadrach, Meschach and Abednego: Daniel 3.
Gideon's Sacrifice: Judges 6.
Moses and the Burning Bush: Exodus 3.
Moses in the Wilderness: Exodus 13.
Paul and the Fire on Melita: Acts 28.

Legends of the origins of fire: Prometheus; Hephaestus; Vesta; Hercules; The Story of Ataentsic (Iroquois and Huron).

Poems
Belloc, Hilaire: *Matilda.*
de la Mare, Walter: *Please to Remember*; *Coals.*
Dryden, John: *Fire of London.*
Ewers, J. K.: *Song of the Fire.*
Gay, John: *Walking the Streets of London.*
Gosse, Edmund: *The Charcoal Burner.*
Gransden, K. W.: *Fifth of November.*
Holmes, Robert: *The Guy.*
MacNeice, Louis: *Brother Fire.*
Milligan, Spike: *Holy Smoke.*
Reeves, James: *Fireworks.*
Rosselson, Leon: *Little Tom Macguire.*
Scannell, Vernon: *Gunpowder Plot.*
Shakespeare, W.: *Macbeth*, Act IV, Scene I.
Simpson, Eric: *Firework Night.*
Stevenson, R. L.: *Armies in the Fire*; *Autumn Fires.*

Chapter I, Fire: *English Through Experience* by Rowe, A. W. & Emmens, P. (Blond Educational).

Music
Beethoven: *Wellington's Victory or The Battle of Vittoria* (sometimes called the 'Battle' Symphony).
Cadman, Charles: *Thunderbird Suite.*
Falla: *Ritual Fire Dance.*

Handel: *Music for the Royal Fireworks.*
Stravinsky: *Firebird Suite.*
Tchaikovsky: *1812 Overture.*
Wagner: Magic Fire Music from *The Valkyries.*

Films
The Glassmakers (Crown Film Unit for COI).
Stained Glass (BIF with NCVAE).
Earthquakes and Volcanoes (Boulton-Hawker Films).
Expedition into a Volcano (EFVA).
Fire (made 1901) (British Film Institute).
Fireman (Chaplin) (British Film Institute).
Fires Were Started (Blitz) (British Film Institute).
Rig 70 (BP Library).
Forest Fire Suppression (National Film Board of Canada).
Fire under Control (Mobil Oil Co).
The Nature of Fire (Fire Protection Association).
Blast Furnace (BIF with NCVAE).
Buried Cities (Pompeii and Herculaneum) (Boulton-Hawker Films).
Buried Treasure (GBI).
Gold Beating (BIF).
The Fire Walkers of Fiji (BBC TV Enterprises).
Petroleum (EB).
Potter's World, A (BBC TV).
Pottery Without a Wheel (BIF with NCVAE).
Volcanoes (Campbell-Harper Films).
Fire in Town (National Film Board of Canada).
Fire Protection for the Home (Pyrene Co Limited).

Filmstrips
Pompeii and Vesuvius (BBC).
The Story of Moses, Parts 1 & 2 (Hulton with NCAVAE).
Volcanoes (CG).
Coal Mining (a Midland colliery) (CG).
The Steel Industry (CG).
The Potteries (CG).

Pottery (CG).
Fireman (CG).
How Pottery Is Made (CG).
Volcanic Features (Educational Productions).
Volcanoes (Educational Productions).
The First Metal Workers (Educational Productions).
Pottery Through the Ages (Educational Productions).
Ritual Fire Dance (Educational Productions).
Vulcanicity (Rank Film Library).

Other aids
Jackdaw Series: *The Plague and Fire of London.*
The Gunpowder Plot.
Joan of Arc.
Volcanoes.

Charts: *Flat Glass Manufacture* (EPC 717).
Glass — Bottles and Jars (EPC 701).
Pottery (EPC 633).
How Matches Are Made (EPC 1028).

Excursions
The local fire station; blacksmith; glassworks; brickyard; stained-glass works; ironworks; bell foundry; wheelwright.

Pottery. (The Craftsmen Potters Association, William Blake House, Marshall Street, London W1, for list of potters willing to be visited by parties of children. State radius of journey.)

Bakery; Science Museum, South Kensington, London.

CREATIVE ACTIVITIES
Written work
Write a story about a dragon who was born out of a great fire.

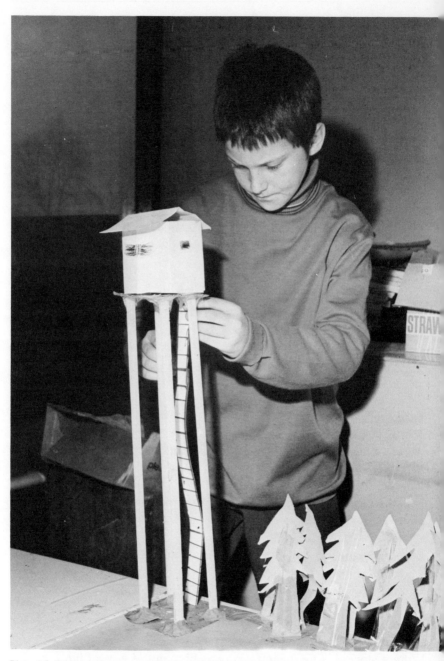

Plate 14 Perhaps the exaggerated height of the fire observation tower reflects this
young modelmaker's attitude towards this great forest danger.

Write a newspaper article with the headline 'Fire Our Enemy'.

Imagine that you lived at the time of the Great Fire of London. Describe what happened when your street caught fire.

Watch a film about an active volcano and then write a poem about an eruption which devastates the villages beneath.

Write a story about the Queen of a land of fire.

Prepare a taped commentary on the fighting of a forest fire, as seen from a control tower in a large forest.

Collect together descriptive words, poetry and noises to produce a sound picture of a firework display.

Write a poem about a thunderstorm.

Write a story about a boy who had to use smoke signals to tell his friends they were in danger.

Describe an imaginary bird called a firebird. Make a picture first, and add the description beneath.

Imagine that you are a member of a primitive family; tell how you first discovered fire and how you learned to use it.

Write a description of a witch by her fire on a windy moonlit night.

Drama and movement
Mime different fireworks and accompany the movements with percussion and other sound effects, in turn and then in unison.

Produce an improvisation on early man and his fear of and need for fire.

Dramatise the story of Elijah on Mount Carmel, I Kings 18.

Mime the activities of firemen.

Tell the story of *Firebird* in movement, using Stravinsky's suite.

Mathematical and scientific aspects
Discover the fire regulations and precautions operating in school.
Check hose lengths.

Draw a plan of the school with routes for fire drill and diversions
where exits are closed. Organise a fire drill and time it.

Find out how a fire extinguisher works.

Find out about fire and light, e.g. lamps, candles, rushlights, gas,
electricity.

Find out about igneous rocks, sedimentary rocks, and how
metamorphic rock is formed.

Find out about the treatment of burns and scalds – ask school nursing
sister for help.

Investigate gas and electricity settings and equivalent temperatures.

Find out about modern safety devices in modern buildings, e.g.
Marks & Spencer stores.

Find out about the internal combustion engine.

Locate hydrant points in local area.

Carry out tests of inflammability of certain materials under careful
supervision.

Art and craft
Make a group picture of a big fire with many firemen fighting the
blaze.

Paint a close-up picture of the blacksmith at work by his fire.

Paint a large picture of the ceremony of lighting the Olympic torch.

Paint large murals of the gods connected with fire: Hercules, Vesta, Hephaestus and Prometheus.

Paint or crayon a picture of a volcano erupting.

Make a wax-resist picture of a witch on her broomstick.

Make a picture of a forest fire, using twigs, charred timbers, steel wool and dyed cotton wool.

Make a collage design of the sun.

Design a fire safety poster.

Make wrought-iron designs in black card and mount on white.

Watch the film *Expedition into a Volcano* and then produce volcanic lava patterns, with acrylic paints on which ash is sprinkled.

Use the wax-etching technique for the following subjects: A Fire, A Storm, Fireworks and Bonfires.

Make a group painting of the Up-helly-Aa ceremony of Lerwick, Shetland.

Elijah in his chariot of fire as a paper cut-out, with simple sculpture techniques.

Make a stained-glass window of Shadrach, Meshach and Abednego, using wax crayon and then rubbing the back of the paper with olive oil.

Make a series of small models showing early man's use of fire.

Make a large head of Ra the Sun God from a block of salt, or chalk, or plaster of Paris.

Make a model of a volcano, using a flat cone of cardboard, down which plaster of Paris is poured — add dry powder and dust to the wet slopes.

Using a table, make a working model of a coal mine.

Make a large model of the Fire of London.

Make a model of a forest, showing the fire control tower.

Make a model of a large fire dragon.

Use clay to make a model of a salamander.

Make a scenic model of fire at sea caused by a fire-ship.

Make wall plaques of fire insurance signs.

Make a model of a rocket at blast-off (add a tape-recorded commentary).

Model with clay and fire the models in a home-made brick kiln, fired with sawdust.

Make and try a fire balloon.

Make a series of tableaux based on the Ladybird Book, *James I and the Gunpowder Plot.* Prepare each scene in a shoe box, all figures as flat cut-outs.

Make a mosaic of a phoenix rising from the flames (paper squares, glass or pebbles).

Make a guy and guy masks.

Cook cakes, bread and try some campfire cooking.

The Dover Road

Road systems are the arteries of a country. One might almost say that their development closely underlines the progress and prosperity which that nation enjoys. For our study we chose the Dover Road because we could most easily go there on field trips, since it was a local road. In addition, of course, it is a road along which one might say that history had marched. It would seem reasonable, therefore, for readers to choose a local road, which might be very modern, like the M3, or a very old one, like the Icknield Way. However, where the project of roads is being taken in a general way, then groups can choose highways of particular interest to them, and some of these might conceivably be abroad. For instance, the Appian Way, the Alaskan Highway and so on. Looking through the suggested lists of aids, it will be seen that many books, poems and music are of universal application. There are, of course, references to other books and aids which are only applicable to the Kentish situation. These are provided for those teachers who would find the Dover Road an ideal one to study, and also to provide pointers on the kind of local aid which is invaluable: church and town guides, people linked with roads and the places they pass through, and so on. Certainly, before such a study as this, it will be necessary to travel along the chosen road, and visit librarians, curators, and the Highways Department of the local County Council.

Special aspects
Roadbuilding and, certainly, road repairs are always going on, and observation of such work is fascinating to children.

Road safety is part of education. To do it within such a project would seem obvious even to the children!

Because of the amount of fieldwork involved, the opportunities for map reading and interpretation are enormous.

The villages, towns and cities linked by roads enable one to provide many options for children to study in such a project.

INFORMATION AND INSPIRATION
Books

Adams, H.: *Roads, Streets and Motorways* (Cassell).

Allen, A.: *Story of the Highway* (Faber).

Allen, A. & J.: *Your Book of Architecture* (Faber).

Baker, M.: *Discovering the Exeter Road*; *Discovering the Bath Road* (Shire).

Braun, H.: *The Story of English Architecture* (Faber).

Broadway, C. M.: *How People Travelled* (OUP).

Carter, E. F.: *Famous Roads of the World* (F. Muller).

Cockett, M.: *Bridges* (Oliver & Boyd); *Roads and Travelling* (Blackwell).

Cowie, E. E. & Walker, A. E.: *Man and Roads* (Hamish Hamilton).

Dance, E. H.: *Trading and Travelling* (Longman).

De Maré, E.: *Bridges and Roads* (Faber).

Deverson, H. J.: *The Open Road*; *The Map that Came to Life* (OUP).

Duggan, A.: *Thomas Becket of Canterbury* (useful for the teacher) (Faber).

Edwards, R. P. A. & Gibbon, V.: *People We Meet* (Burke).

Ellacott, S. E.: *Wheels on the Road* (Methuen).

Fry, J. & M.: *Architecture for Children* (Allen & Unwin).

Gould, J.: *Discovering the Birmingham Road* (Shire).

Greenwood, M. O.: *Discovering Roads and Bridges* (ULP).

Harston, K. & Davis, E.: *Your Local Buildings* (Allen & Unwin).

Hogg, G.: *Blind Jack of Knaresborough* (Phoenix).

Hughes, P.: *Shell Guide to Kent* (Faber).

Jessop, F. W.: *Kent History Illustrated* (Kent County Council).

Leacroft, H. & R.: *Churches and Cathedrals* (Puffin).

Lee, L. & Lambert, D.: *Man Must Move* (Rathbone).

Leyland, E.: *Road Builder* (Edmund Ward).

Madeley, H. M.: *History in the Making*, Books 3 & 4 (Pitman).

Mason, P.: *Bridges and Roads* (ESA).

Mee, A.: (King's England Series) *Kent* (Hodder).

Middleton, G.: *The Study Book of Roads* (Bodley Head).

Morris, R. W.: *Transport, Trade, and Travel Through the Ages* (Allen & Unwin).

Murphy, J. S.: *How They Were Built: Bridges*; *How They Were Built: Roads* (OUP).

Raynor, E.: *Discovering the Gloucester Road* (Shire).

Rolt, L. T. C.: *Motor Cars* (ESA).
Rush, P.: *How Roads Have Grown* (RKP).
Sawrey-Cookson, R. B.: *Roads* (ESA).
Surtees, R. S.: *Ask Mamma* (useful to teacher) (Methuen).
Taylor, D.: *Chaucer's England* (Dennis Dobson).
Thornhill, P.: *The Parish Church* (Methuen).
Treece, H.: *The True Book about Castles* (Muller).
Turnbull, M.: *Transport by Land* (Hulton).
Unstead, R. J.: *Looking at History*, 1–4; *Travel by Road* (Black);
     Story of the Wheel (Dunlop).
The Shell Book of Roads (Michael Joseph).
Guidebooks of: Rochester, Dover, Canterbury, Canterbury Cathedral,
     Rochester Cathedral, Rochester Castle, Dover Castle, parish
     churches, e.g. St Martin's, Canterbury, St Augustine's Abbey.

Stories

Chaucer, G.: *Canterbury Pilgrims* (*Tales from Chaucer*, Ed. E. Farjeon —
     OUP).
Dickens, C.: *Pickwick Papers*; *The Uncommercial Traveller*, Chapter VII
     (OUP).

Poems

Chesterton, G. K.: *The Rolling English Road.*
Drinkwater, J.: *The Tollgate House.*
Masefield, J.: *Roadways*; *Vagabond.*
Hart-Smith, W.: *Steamroller.*
Pasternak, B.: *The Road.*
Williams, H.: *The Hitchhiker.*

Music

Darling Macheath and *Let us take the road* from *The Beggar's Opera*
     (J. G. Pepusch).
O Rare Turpin.
Ben the Roadmaker.
Je tire ma révérence.

Records

The Travelling People: Argo DA 133 (about the gypsies).
Fair Game and Foul: Topic 12T 195 (about highwaymen).

Famous people connected with the road:

Bexley: The Black Prince, Paulinus, William Morris.

Blackheath: Henry V, James I, Robert Cocking.

Canterbury: Thomas Becket, Archbishop Simon of Sudbury, Henry II, Chaucer, Henry V, Charles Stuart, Oliver Cromwell, King Ethelbert, St Augustine, Christopher Marlowe, Black Prince, Hewlett Johnson.

Chatham: Sir John Hawkyns, Stephen Borough, Lieutenant Waghorn, General Gordon.

Dartford: Wat Tyler, Sir John Spielman, Anne of Cleves, Richard Trevithick, Sir Erasmus Wilson.

Deptford: Henry VIII, Queen Elizabeth I, Sir Francis Drake, Czar of Russia (Peter the Great), John Evelyn, Grinling Gibbons.

Dover: Jean Pierre Blanchard, Doctor Jeffries, Captain Matthew Webb, Colonel S. F. Cody, Blériot (Louis).

Greenwich: Henry VIII, Queen Elizabeth I, Sir Walter Raleigh.

Rochester: St William (of Perth), Henry VIII, Anne of Cleves, Dickens, Nickes Nevvson.

Shooter's Hill: Dick Turpin.

Sittingbourne: Henry VIII.

Stroud: Anne Pratt.

Roads: John Metcalfe, Thomas Telford, John Macadam.

Films

Roman Holiday (Reel 1) (Instructional Entertainments Films Ltd).
Cathedral City: Canterbury (GB).
Sir Francis Drake (GB).
Chaucer's England (Encyclopaedia Britannica).
Motorway (John Laing & Sons).
Bridge over Medway (John Laing & Sons).
Playing in the Road (Petroleum Films Bureau).
Mind How You Go (Gateway).
From Every Shires Ende (Gateway).

Filmstrips

The Castle (GB).
The Castle (CG).
The Parish Church (Hulton).
The Parish Church (GB).
The Cathedral (GB).
The Medieval City (GB).
History of Road Transport, Parts 1–3 (CG).
    A. Churches – twelve wallcharts.
    B. Churches – fourteen wallcharts.
Road Transport Chart (Educational Productions).
Queen's Highway (magazine of Asphalt and Coated Macadam
    Association, 25 Lower Belgrave Street, London SW1).
Ordnance Survey Maps (Sheets 171, 172, 173).

Other aids

Map of Roman Britain (Ordnance Survey).
Wheaton's Architectural Charts:

Excursions

Canterbury: St Augustine's Abbey, St Martin's Church, Canterbury
Cathedral, West Gate Museum, Canterbury Museum, the Weavers'
Houses, Grey Friars, Roman pavement (Butchery Lane), Castle,
Hospital of St Thomas.

Dover: Castle, Harbour, Maison Dieu (Dover Town Hall).

Rochester: Cathedral, Castle, Eastgate House (museum).

Crayford: St Paulinus Church.

Bexley: Hall Place.

Ospringe: Maison Dieu.

Royal Society for the Prevention of Accidents: ROSPA House Training
Centre, 17 Knightsbridge, London SW1.

Various museums featuring road transport: Science Museum, South Kensington; Transport Museum, Clapham; Beaulieu Motor Museum.

Other roads which could be studied
Berkshire — Wiltshire Ridgeway.

Icknield Way.	The Bath Road.
Pilgrims' Way.	Ermine Street.
Great North Road.	Gloucester Road.
M1	Birmingham Road.
The Holyhead Road.	Exeter Road.

It may be possible to make a study of some of these roads last for two or three days, travelling along the road and staying at Youth Hostels for the night.

CREATIVE ACTIVITIES
Written work
Write and record a radio programme on the life of Thomas Becket.

Imagine you are a Roman soldier; describe your arrival in Britain and your march to London. Remember Roman soldiers were trained to fight, to march and to build roads and forts.

Imagine you are a traveller in medieval times; describe the people you meet and some of the difficulties and dangers you encounter.

Imagine you are the owner of a coaching inn. Describe the arrival of a stage coach and the passengers who stay at your inn for the night.

Write a poem about a highwayman.

Describe a journey in a steam carriage made by Richard Trevithick (examine a picture of the vehicle and the road before starting).

Imagine you are the driver of the first motor car to make the journey from London to Dover. Describe your own feelings and the reactions of the crowds who see you.

Write a poem about travel on the Dover Road through the ages. Try to express the change of speed of road travel, in the words you choose.

Read one of Chaucer's *Canterbury Tales* and make a radio programme about the pilgrim who tells the tale and the story.

Imagine you were at Dover when Blériot landed after his flight from Calais to Dover; describe the scene.

Find out about Wat Tyler and the Peasants' Revolt, then produce a special edition of a newspaper on the Peasants' Revolt. Include interviews with Wat Tyler and other people, and reports of the effects of the revolt.

Prepare a series of modern travellers' tales as told in a Maidstone and District coach — add travel noises and chit-chat of passengers and conductor.

Write a modern-day *Pilgrim's Progress*, sending Christian through real cities and ending in Canterbury.

Read part of Cobbett's *Rural Rides*, and in this style 'ride' along the Dover Road.

Drama and movement
Plan and act scenes of everyday life in the past and some special happenings in the towns and villages along the road. Link these scenes and form a Pageant of the Dover Road.

Tell the 'Nun's Priest's Tale', 'The Tale of Chanticleer' by Chaucer in movement, using Beethoven's Sixth Symphony, second movement.

Simulate a road accident and the reactions of passers-by until the arrival of an ambulance.

Make up a playlet about a thoughtless boy and how he learned the rules of the road.

Prepare a story about the efforts of a village to get a by-pass (and the opposition from the traders).

Mathematical and scientific aspects
Traffic counts and traffic surveys can be carried out in different towns along the road.

Find out about gradients of roads.

Find out how bridges are built, especially any types which are found along the road, e.g. cantilever.

Explain how a caisson works.

Use pieces of sewing cotton and knitting wool to find the breaking strain of different threads. Try twisting two or more threads together and note the differences.

Use a road atlas or AA Handbook to calculate the distance between various places on the road. Then work out how long it would take to travel this distance at an average of thirty miles an hour.

Compare time taken to travel between towns when using the A2 and the M2 (persuade the coach driver to use different routes).

Make graphs to show the amount of petrol and oil used by five different cars in the course of one week.

Design and make a click wheel based on the viameter of John Metcalfe.

Art and craft
Make a wall frieze of Chaucer's Canterbury Pilgrims, using two-dimensional figures mounted on matchboxes.

Use cut-out card and coloured cellophane or tissue paper to mak stained-glass windows, or use wax crayons on cartridge paper and then rub the paper with olive oil to make it translucent.

Fig. 38 Chaucer's Pilgrims on their way to Canterbury. Simple cut-outs fixed onto a background scene.

Fig. 39 An Elizabethan coach. One of a series of models to illustrate vehicles through the ages.

Make models of road transport through the ages: Roman chariot; Roman cart; litter; horse litter; medieval wagon; medieval chair; whirlicote stage coach; steam coach.

Make a model of Canterbury Cathedral.

Make models of Rochester Castle and Dover Castle.

Design banners to represent Dover, Canterbury and Rochester. You will probably wish to include special historical or geographical aspects of the towns.

Make a large picture map of the Dover Road.

Make a model of Dover Harbour, with painted backcloth of town and castle.

Make a series of diorama scenes showing a village during several periods of history.

Paint, or crayon, pictures of: highwaymen; post-chaise; bicycles; motor cars; the Pharos; Rochester Cathedral; Doctor Jeffries' balloon; Colonel S. F. Cody crossing the Channel in a canoe with a kite; Grey Friars, Canterbury; St. Martin's Church, Canterbury.

Make a model of the building of a new road. Childrens' models of mechanical diggers, etc., can make this most effective.

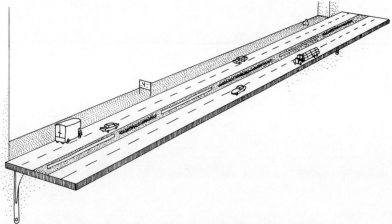

Fig. 40 A motorway model. Its straightness lends itself to this situation where a narrow shelf has been fixed to extend the window sill. A suitable background could be painted on the window or onto a backcloth roll which could be rotated to suggest movement.

Make a model of the M2 motorway showing various types of bridges, the bridge over the Medway, the service stations and road joining it. Such a model can often be built along a window-sill or similar long, narrow surface, with a frieze of the countryside in the background — an important consideration when space is at a premium.

Outside activities
An exciting way of recording the story of the Dover Road is to make a film. This can be planned in the classroom and costumes and props made, and then on one of the visits to the road the film is made.

Portable tape-recorders are most useful on visits to the road. Children will gain valuable information by interviewing people they meet on their visits, and be able to go over the material carefully in the classroom.

CANADA

It is important that children should have the opportunity to discover the nature and significance of the Commonwealth. In making a study of one member of the Commonwealth, like Canada, they will acquire knowledge which will enable them to understand this unique confederation as a whole. Such a project will provide opportunity for the study of the climate and terrain, wild life, occupations and the social integration of racial groups. Canada's history, in common with other Commonwealth countries, is closely linked with exploration and pioneering, which has great appeal for children.

Special aspects
The study of Canada is an extensive one and it could well last for more than one term. The class could be divided into groups to study each of the Canadian Provinces and then produce a class pageant of the history of the Canadian nation.

With younger children the whole study might seem too long, but a project on Red Indians or the Eskimos is an exciting and colourful shorter alternative.

INSPIRATION AND INFORMATION
Books
Berton, P.: *The Golden Trail* (Macmillan).
Bice, C.: *Across Canada* (Macmillan).
Bishop, B.: *Champlain* (Macdonald).
Bleeker, S.: *The Eskimo: Arctic Hunters and Trappers*; *The Sioux Indian* (Dobson).
Braithwaite, M. & Lambert, R. S.: *We Live in Ontario* (Schofield & Sims).
Braithwaite, M.: *Land, Water and People, the Story of Canada's Growth* (Van Nostrand, Toronto).
Brewster, B.: *The First Book of Eskimos* (Ward); *The First Book of Indians* (Mayflower).
Cabot, J. & S.: *Into Unknown Waters* (Dobson).
Caldwell, J. C.: *Let's Visit Canada* (Burke).

Campbell, A. B.: *The True Book about the North American Indians* (Muller).

Carlson, N. S.: *Jean-Claude's Island* (Blackie).

Catherall, A.: *Lone Seal Pup* (Dent).

Chisholm, M.: *Indians* (Odhams).

Clayton, R. & Miles, J.: *Canada and the Arctic* (Weidenfeld & Nicolson).

Comer, W. M.: *Wilfred Grenfell, Labrador Doctor* (Lutterworth).

Copeland, D. M.: *The Junior True Book of Little Eskimos* (Muller).

Corless, E.: *Ottawa* (Longman).

Crombie, I.: *My Home in Canada* (Longman).

Dewdney, S.: *The St Lawrence Seaway* (OUP).

Dunphy, C. R.: *The Geography of the Atlantic Provinces* (Gage, Toronto).

Goetz, D.: *The Arctic Tundra* (Wheaton).

Gorham, M.: *The Real Book of Red Indians* (Dobson).

Graham, G. S.: *A Concise History of Canada* (Thames & Hudson).

Gray, G. L.: *A Visual History of Canada* (Evans).

Grenfell, W.: *The Story of a Labrador Doctor* (Hodder & Stoughton).

Gribble, L.: *The True Book about the Mounties* (Muller).

Haig-Brown, R.: *The Whale People* (Collins).

Harrington, L.: *Ootook: Young Eskimo Girl* (Abelard-Schuman); *The Real Book of Canada* (Dobson).

Harrison, A.: *With Cartier up the St Lawrence* (Muller).

Herdman, T.: *Atlantic to the Great Lakes; The Prairies* (Longman).

Hills, T. L.: *St Lawrence Seaway* (Methuen).

Hobley, L. F.: *Exploring the Americas* (Methuen).

Holling, C.: *Paddle to the Sea* (Collins).

Howe, R.: *Cooking from the Commonwealth* (Deutsch).

Hunt, W. Ben: *Indian Crafts and Lore* (Paul Hamlyn).

Hutton, C.: *A Picture History of Canada* (OUP).

Innis, H. A.: *The Fur Trade in Canada* (OUP).

Kingsland, J. C.: *World Journeys by Land, Sea and Air* (Black).

Lamber, P.: *Changing the Face of North America: the Challenge of the St Lawrence Seaway* (Chatto & Windus).

Lay, E. J. S.: *Life in Canada and Australasia* (Macmillan).

Longley, J.: *Canada* (Penshurst, Friday Press).

Lower, A. R. M.: *Colony to Nation* (Longman).

Martini, T.: *The Junior True Book of Indians* (Muller).

May, C. P.: *A Book of Canadian Animals* (Macmillan, Toronto); *A Second Book of Canadian Animals* (Macmillan, Toronto); *Great Cities of Canada* (Abelard-Schuman).

Moore, W. G.: *The Northern Forests* (Hutchinson).

Nach, J.: *Canada in Pictures* (Oak Tree Press).

O'Callaghan, D. B.: *Canada* (Longman).

Osmond, E.: *Beavers*; *Polar Bears*; *Reindeer* (Animals of the World) (OUP).

Parker, J. A.: *Food from the Commonwealth and Empire* (Gawthorn).

Philips, A.: *The Living Legend* (Cassell).

Purton, R.: *Man in Canada* (Hamilton).

Rutley, C. B.: *Colin and Patricia in Canada* (Macmillan); *Wild Life in Canada* (Macmillan).

Scott-Daniell, D.: *Flight Two Canada* (Wills & Hepworth).

Scott, J. M.: *Hudson of Hudson's Bay* (Methuen).

Sibley, D.: *Canada* (Oliver & Boyd).

Stevens, L.: *The Land where the Beaver Lives* (Low & Marston).

Tait, G.: *Breastplate and Buckskin* (Ryerson Press, Toronto).

Tolboom, W.: *People of the Snow: Eskimos of Arctic Canada* (Chatto & Windus).

Tor, R.: *Getting to Know Canada* (Muller).

Toblon, S. J.: *The Story of Canada* (Benn).

Thompson, T. A.: *Red Indians* (Basil Blackwell).

Washburne, H. & 'Anauta': *Children of the Blizzard* (Dobson).

White, A. T.: *The St. Lawrence Seaway of North America* (Muller).

Whittam, G.: *Farming on the Canadian Prairies* (People of the World); *Fur Hunting and Fur Farming*; *Lumbering in Canada* (OUP).

Wymer, N.: *James Wolfe* (Lives of Great Men and Women) (OUP); *With Mackenzie in Canada* (Muller).

McGraw Hill Canada Series: *The Story of Quebec*; *The Story of Ontario*; *The Maritime Provinces*; *The Story of Newfoundland*; *Yukon and the North-West Territories*; *Giant of the North*.

Stories

Anderson, D.: *Blood Brothers* (Macmillan).

Ballantyne, R. M.: *The Dog Crusoe* (Peal).

292

Barbeau, M.: *The Golden Phoenix and Other French-Canadian Fairy Tales*; *The Tree of Dreams* (OUP).

Batten, H. M.: *Wild and Free: Stories of Canadian Animals* (Blackie).

Blanchet, M. W.: *The Curve of Time* (Blackwood).

Byrd, E.: *Ice King* (Gollancz).

Campbell, M. W.: *The Nor'Westers* (Macmillan).

Chaffe, A.: *The Story of Hiawatha* (Purnell).

Chalmers, J. W.: *Red River Adventure* (Macmillan).

Clarke, M.: *Mink and the Fire*, No. 11 (Rupert Hart-Davies).

Coatsworth, E.: *The Last Fort* (Hamish Hamilton).

Colbert, M.: *Kutkos, Chinook, Tyee Tales of Red Indians* (Heath).

Cooper, J. F.: *Last of the Mohicans* (Collins).

Crown, A. W.: *North America* (E. J. Arnold).

Denison, M.: *Susannah of the Mounties* (Dent).

Denny, C. E.: *The Law Marches West* (Dent).

Fairley, T. C. & Israel, C.: *The Tree North* (Macmillan).

Farrar, F. S.: *Arctic Assignment* (Macmillan).

Faulkner, C.: *The White Peril* (Dent).

Ferguson, R. D.: *Man from St Malo* (Macmillan).

Fisher, O. M. & Tyner, C. L.: *Totem, Tipi and Tumpline, Stories of Canadian Indians* (Dent).

Guillot, R.: *A Boy and Five Huskies* (Methuen).

Haig-Brown, R.: *Captain of the 'Discovery'* (Blackwell).

Harris, J. N.: *Knights of the Air* (Macmillan).

Hayes, J. F.: *Buckskin Colonist* (Blackwell).

Heker, H.: *The School Train* (Abelard-Schuman).

Hill, K.: *Glooskap and His Magic* (Gollancz).

Hood, J.: *Hunters of the North* (Phoenix).

Hulpach, V.: *American Indian Tales and Legends* (Paul Hamlyn).

Lambert, R. S.: *Mutiny in the Bay*; *Redcoat Sailor* (Macmillan).

Leitch, A.: *The Great Canoe* (Macmillan).

Longfellow, H. W.: *Hiawatha* (Macmillan).

Longstretch, T. M.: *The Scarlet Force*; *The Force Carries On* (Macmillan).

Lundy, J. E.: *The Scots Traders* (Hamish Hamilton).

McCourt, E.: *Buckskin Brigadier*; *Revolt in the West* (Macmillan).

Macmillan, C.: *Glooskap's Country* (OUP, Toronto).

Manning-Sanders, R.: *Red Indian Folk and Fairy Tales* (OUP).

Miller, O. : *Raiders of the Mohawk* (Macmillan).
Mowat, F. : *Lost in the Barrens* (Macmillan).
Phelan, J. : *The Bold Heart* (Macmillan).
Quiller-Couch, Sir A. : *Fort Amity* (Dent).
Raddall, T. H. : *The Rover* (Macmillan).
Reid, D. M. : *Tales of Nanabozho* (OUP).
Ritchie, C. T. : *The First Canadian* (Macmillan).
Schull, J. : *Ships of the Great Days*; *Battle for the Rock*; *The Salt-Water Men* (Macmillan).
Swaytze, F. : *Frontenac and the Iroquois* (Macmillan).
Toye, W., Ed. : *A Book of Canada* (Collins).
Walker, L. J. : *Red Indian Legends* (Odhams).
Wilkinson, D. : *Sons of the Arctic* (G. Bell).
Wilson, C. : *Adventures from the Bay* (Macmillan).
Wood, K. : *The Queen's Cowboy*; *The Great Chief*; *The Map-Maker*; *The Boy and the Buffalo* (Macmillan).

Poems
Diamond, L. : *A Kayak Song*.
Longfellow, H. W. : *Hiawatha*.
Lindsay, Vachel : *The Flower Fed Buffaloes*.
The Wind has Wings is an interesting collection of poems published by Oxford University Press.

Music
Junior Music Series : *Angry Arrow* (pub. J. & W. Chester).
Magic Feathers: Chippewa Song (Co-operative Recreation Service Inc).
Land of the Silver Birch (North American Indian Folk Song).
Bold General Wolfe (Sussex Folk Song).
Canada Heritage of Folk Song (Onslow Records, 61 Kingswood Road, London SW2).
Alouette.
O Canada (National Anthem).

Music for listening
Busoni, Ferruccio : *Indian Fantasy*.

Cadman, Charles: *Thunderbird Suite.*
Coleridge-Taylor, S.: *Song of Hiawatha.*
McPhee, Colin: *Four Iroquois Dances.*
Sibelius, J.: *Swan of Tuonela; Finlandia; Return of Lemminkainen;
    Tapiola:* Opus 112.
Vaughan Williams, R.: *Sinfonia Antarctica.*

Films
National Film Board of Canada Films:
The Story of St Lawrence Seaway.
Introducing Canada.
The Pre-Cambrian Shield.
Mountains of the West.
Above the Timberline.
Eskimo Summer.
How to Build an Igloo.
White Safari.
Peace River.
The Physical Regions of Canada.
Winter in Canada.
Look to the Forest.
People of the Skeena.
Fur Trade.
The Age of the Beaver.
Eskimo Hunters.
From Father to Son (farming in the St Lawrence Valley).
The Great Plains.
Bronco Busters.
Life on the Western Marshes.
River Watch (St Lawrence lighthouses).
Wheat Country.

Canada Geography of the Americas (Coronet – from Gateway).
Canada's New Farmlands: Peace River (United World Films – from
    Rank).
Salmon – Life of the Sockeye (Walt Disney).
Timberlands of Canada (Rank).
Wheat Supply of Canada (Rank).

French Canadians (United World Films).
Salmon Industry of British Columbia (Rank).
The Last Voyage of Henry Hudson (NFB).
The White Wilderness: three films (Walt Disney).

Filmstrips
National Film Board of Canada Filmstrips:
General James Wolfe.
Jacques Cartier.
Indian Life in Early Canada.
Pioneer Life in Upper Canada.
Cattle Ranch.
Discovery and Exploration

Hudson's Bay Company (VH).
Art of the North-West Coast Indians (Commonwealth Institute).
Masks of the North American Indians (Commonwealth Institute).
The North American Buffalo (Commonwealth Institute).
North American Indians (Educational Films for Scotland).
Across Canada by Canadian Pacific Railway (CPR Co).
The Art of the Eskimo (EP).
Life Among the Eskimos (CG).
Logging in Canadian Forests (Encyclopaedia Britannica).
Villages in French Canada (Encyclopaedia Britannica).
North-West Passage (Visual Productions).
Fisherman of Nova Scotia (EB).
The Story of Oil in Canada (Imperial Oil Slide Films).
The Story of Pacific Salmon: slides (NFB).

Other aids
Canadian Jackdaws (Cape):
*Confederation 1867; Riel; Canada Votes 1791–1891; Building the
C.P.R.; The Fur Trade; Louisbourg; 1837 Mackenzie; Dieppe – 1942;
Bristol and the Cabots; Selkirk; Cartier of St Malo; R.C.M.P.;
The Great Depression; Push to the Pacific; North-West Passage;
The Indians of Canada; Canada and the Civil War; Wolfe at Quebec.*

Association of Agriculture — Farm study schemes:
No. 12: *A Typical Farm in the Annapolis Valley of Nova Scotia.*
No. 13: *A Dairy Farm in French-Canada.*
No. 14: *A Mixed Farm in Southern Ontario.*
No. 15: *A Grain Farm on the Portage Plains of Manitoba.*

Macmillan Geography Pictures:
No. 81: *A Fur Trading Settlement on Hudson Bay.*
No. 86: *Loading Timber in the Canadian Forest.*
No. 93: *Hydro-Electricity in Quebec.*

Booklets, charts, posters, picture sets from:
Agent General for Alberta: 37 Hill Street, London W1.
Agent General for the Atlantic Provinces: 60 Trafalgar Square,
    London WC2.
Agent General for British Columbia: 1 Regent Street, London SW1.
Agent General for Manitoba: 1 Grosvenor Square, London W1.
Agent General for Quebec: 12 Upper Grosvenor Street, London W1.
Agent General for Ontario: 13 Charles II Street, London SW1.
Agent General for Saskatchewan: 28 Chester Street, Belgrave Square,
    London SW1.
Alcan (UK) Ltd: 30 Berkeley Square, London W1.
Bank of Montreal: 47 Threadneedle Street, London EC2.
Canadian Government Travel Bureau: 19 Cockspur Street,
    London SW1.
Canadian High Commission: Canada House, Trafalgar Square,
    London SW1.
Canadian National Railways: 17 Cockspur Street, London SW1.
Canadian Pacific Railway Co: 62 Trafalgar Square, London WC2.
Canadian Wheat Board: 5 St Helen's Place, London EC3.
Central Office of Information: Hercules Road, Westminster Bridge
    Road, London SE1.
Commonwealth Institute: Kensington High Street, London W8.
Cunard Steamship Co. Ltd: Cunard Buildings, Pier Head, Liverpool 3.
Royal Bank of Canada: 6 Lothbury, London EC2.
Royal Commonwealth Society: 18 Northumberland Avenue,
    London WC2.
Toronto-Dominion Bank: 62 Cornhill, London EC3.

Charts and pictures:
Canada: set of twelve charts (Educational Productions).
Canada: wall map (George Philip & Son).
Canada: wall map (OUP).
Canada: Eskimo kayaks (picture) (Warne & Co).
Canada: train in the Rockies (picture) (Warne & Co).
Coniferous forest region: wallchart (Pictorial Charts).
Temperate Grasslands: wallchart (Pictorial Charts).

Famous people of Canada:

General Wolfe.   Henry Hudson.
Jacques Cartier.   William Baffin.
Sir Humphrey Gilbert.   John Cabot.
Martin Frobisher.   Sebastian Cabot.
John Davis.   John Buchan.

Excursions
Kent: Quebec House, Westerham.

Devon: Ashburton Museum, Ashburton.

Cambridge: The Scott Polar Research Institute, Cambridge.

London: the British Museum; the Commonwealth Institute; the Zoo.

CREATIVE ACTIVITIES
Written work
Imagine that you are a totem pole carver and tell the story of the heads that you are carving on the pole.

Imagine you are a Red Indian boy; describe your life during one exciting week.

Write a description of a ceremonial war dance you watch from the corner of the forest.

Imagine you are a lumberjack in a Canadian forest; write about your most exciting experience.

298

Write a poem about a rodeo; punctuate with appropriate sound effects, including whoops and squeals.

Imagine you are an Eskimo on a seal-hunting expedition. Describe how you set up camp after a good day's hunting.

Write a poem about Niagara Falls.

Imagine you were a Mountie in the late nineteenth century. Describe a day in your life when you had to chase a notorious criminal.

Write a story about a cattle ranch in Canada that you inherit.

Write a poem or prose description of shooting the rapids for the first time.

Find out all you can about the travels of Mackenzie in 1789 in a birch-bark canoe to the Arctic and down Peace River and across the Rockies. Then write diary entries for the most exciting parts of your journey.

Find out about the Battle of Quebec; write a description (in the form of a letter home) as though you were a British soldier.

Drama and movement
Explore in movement the life of an Indian family, e.g. hunting, dancing, cooking.

Imagine that you are at work in a lumber camp in winter; include a snowstorm sequence and emphasise the difficulties of moving logs in the snow.

Explore in movement a group of men breaking in a horse.

Find out about Samuel de Champlain and his trading with the Indians. Act a scene between Champlain and the Indians.

Use one of the *Four Iroquois Dances* by Colin McPhee and create a ceremonial Indian dance.

Mathematical and scientific aspects

Find out about animals and the way that they camouflage themselves in the Arctic regions of Canada.

Find out about cold. Compare the coldest temperatures in Britain with those in Canada.

Find out about thermometers. Are different ones needed for extremely cold conditions?

Make a study of conifer trees which would be found in Canadian forests. Why are conifers suitable for cold climates? (Which conifers thrive in Britain's forests?)

Make a chart of distances between towns in Canada, showing how long it takes to travel, e.g. Halifax to Vancouver — one week by express train. Compare air travel now with journeys on horseback a century ago.

Find out about the properties of asbestos. How is it mined, processed and used?

Art and craft

Make masks of the Eskimo gods.

Find a suitable tree trunk, or an old telegraph pole available from the Post Office, and carve a totem pole, which can be painted and erected in the school grounds. Try a small one in balsa wood first. Young children will find it easier to nail on features — noses, eyes, wings, etc.

Make cardboard masks which can be fixed together to make a totem pole.

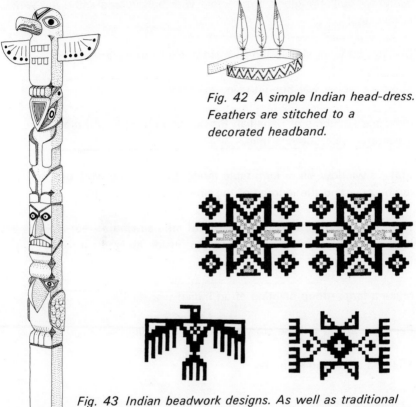

Fig. 41 Indian totem pole from the North-West Coast. Balsa-wood miniatures can be attempted, or a series of decorated boxes fixed over a central column. Where a full-size totem pole is contemplated, wooden features can be nailed on where wood carving proves difficult.

Fig. 42 A simple Indian head-dress. Feathers are stitched to a decorated headband.

Fig. 43 Indian beadwork designs. As well as traditional patterns, children could experiment with their own designs.

Use polystyrene to make a three-dimensional picture of a polar bear on an icefloe. A cutting tool can be purchased from handicraft suppliers.

Make an Indian canoe from boxes and cardboard so that children can sit in it.

Make a large tepee out of fabric or paper, and wooden poles.

Make a series of models of Indian villages, e.g. woodland, plains and so on.

Make a model of an Eskimo village in summer and winter. Dough is useful for building igloos. Experiment with polystyrene and a hot wire cutting tool.

Design and work simple Indian bead designs on squared paper.

Make an Indian war bonnet using feathers.

Paint the emblems of Canadian Provinces on shields and mount on classroom wall, above a map.

Make a window-sill or long table model to show the work of the lumberman and the journey of the timber to the sawmill.

Paint or crayon pictures of: close-up of men sawing a tree; a lumberjacks' camp; an Eskimo hunting; inside an igloo; a rodeo; the Rocky Mountains.

Make a large group painting of an Indian war dance.

Paint a frieze to tell the story of Hiawatha's childhood.

Model a wild bronco in clay.

Fig. 44 Making paper beads.

Use narrow shaped paper strips to make beads. Strips can be painted or patterned, rolled and stuck. Different forms can be developed by using various lengths and shapes of paper. Roll around a cocktail stick to maintain a threading hole.

Other activities

If sufficient snow falls during a topic, try to build an igloo or snow house.

Children may also enjoy making a sledge and altering certain features to increase speed and performance.

As French is spoken in large areas of Canada, French could be included in this project.

The Holy Land

The Holy Land has been the scene of struggles and strife throughout the ages. In the Bible we read of the many trials of the Jewish nation and in more recent history books similar activity is recorded. The newspapers, radio and television today still continue the story, the Promised Land has always been in the news. It would be impossible to separate this study from the many religious ideas which it suggests; the study of Christianity, the Jewish religion and the Moslem religion.

Special aspects

This topic is a vast one and so a central theme needs to be chosen to hold the topic together. Most of the suggestions which follow are based on the central theme of the life of Jesus Christ, but any story set in Palestine could provide the essential link. The ideas put forward can easily be adapted to a study of any Bible character. Alternatively, the study might centre on the Crusades, or a modern kibbutz in Israel. In a class which has children of many cultural backgrounds it might be interesting to study the land from the point of view of the three religions.

INFORMATION AND INSPIRATION

Books

Ackroyd, P. R.: *The People of the Old Testament* (Chatto & Windus).
Adams, Doris Sutcliffe: *Desert Leopard* (Hodder & Stoughton).
Bouquet, A. C.: *Everyday Life in New Testament Times* (Batsford).
Broadie, E.: *The Chosen Nation* (Religious Educational Press).
Clow, Rev. W. M.: *The Bible Reader's Encyclopaedia and Concordance* (Collins).
Harrington, J.: *Jesus of Nazareth* (Brockhampton).
Heaton, E. W.: *Everyday Life in Old Testament Times* (Batsford).
Hilliard, F. H.: *Behold the Land* (Philips).
Hutchings, M.: *Making Old Testament Toys; Making New Testament Toys* (Mills & Boon).
Kaberry, C. J.: *The Children's Book of the Bible* (OUP).
King, F. W.: *Pipe-Line of Power* (REP).
King-Hall, M.: *Jehan the Ready Fist* (Puffin).

Kotker, N.: *The Holy Land in the Time of Jesus* (Cassell).

Leconte, Rev. Canon R.: *In the Steps of Jesus* (Constable).

Lobban, R. D.: *The Crusaders* (ULP).

Pernoud, R.: *In the Steps of the Crusaders* (Constable).

Rostron, H. I.: *Animals, Birds and Plants of the Bible* (Wills & Hepworth).

Sasek, M.: *This Is Israel* (W. H. Allen).

Smith, J. W. D.: *Bible Background* (Methuen).

Turner, P.: *The Bible Story* (OUP).

Unwin, N. S.: *The Way of the Shepherd* (World's Work).

Welch, R.: *Knight Crusader* (OUP).

Whanslaw, H. W.: *Drawing Bible Pictures; Making Bible Models; More Bible Models; Bible Background Books, 1–6; Twelve Puppet Plays; Bible Puppetry* (REP).

Williams, J.: *Knights of the Crusades* (Cassell).

Wiseman, D. J.: *Illustrations from Biblical Archaeology* (Tyndale Press).

Youngman, B. R.: *Background to the Bible*, Books 1–4 (Hulton).

Stories

Bolliger, M.: *Joseph; David* (Macmillan).

Cocagnac, A. M. & Haughton, R.: *Bible for Young Christians* (Geoffrey Chapman).

Diamond, L.: *The Story of Joseph; The Child of the Temple; The Shepherd Boy of Bethlehem* (Wills & Hepworth).

Dingeon, J. M.: *Samuel* (Macmillan).

Duggan, A.: *Knight with Armour* (useful for teacher) (Penguin); *Stories of Crusades* (useful for teacher) (Faber).

Eldon, M. & Phipps, F.: *The Childhood of Jesus* (Collins).

Finlay, I. F.: *Joseph and His Brothers* (Macmillan).

Gill, W.: *The Story of Simon Called Peter* (Longman).

Herrman, R.: *The Creation; The Prodigal Son; The Christmas Story* (Macmillan).

Howard, A. (illustrator): *David and Goliath* (Faber).

Jones, M. A.: *Bible Stories* (Collins).

Klink, J. L.: *Bible for Children* (Burke).

König, P.: *King David* (Macmillan).

Kossoff, D.: *Bible Stories* (Collins).

Lindgren, A.: *Christmas in the Stable* (Brockhampton).
Miller, M.: *Great Stories of the Bible* (Lutterworth).
Morton, H. V.: *In the Steps of Jesus* (Methuen).
Petersham, M. & M.: *Ruth; David* (Macmillan).
Scott, Sir Walter: *Tales of the Crusaders* (Haut Robinson).
Southall, I.: *The Sword of Esau; The Curse of Cain* (Angus &
    Robertson).
Swanston, H.: *The Bible for Children Series* (Burns & Oates).
Tindall, G.: *The Israel Twins* (Jonathan Cape).
Turner, P.: *The Bible Story* (Oxford).
Waddell, H.: *The Story of Saul the King* (Constable Young);
    The Young Moses; Daniel in the Lions' Den; The Story of Jonah
    (Bodley Head).

Poems
Psalm 23.
Drummond, W.: *St John the Baptist.*
Eliot, T. S.: *Journey of the Magi.*
Hartnell, Phyllis: *Bethlehem.*
Sansom, Clive: *The Donkey's Owner.*
Vaughan, Henry: *Palm Sunday.*

Music
Bach, J. S.: *Christmas Oratorio.*
Handel, G. F.: *The Messiah.*
This is Israel (CGL 0339).
Israel Now (United Artists ULP 1179).
A Man Dies: Ernest Marvin (335X 1609).
Joseph and the Amazing Technicolor Dreamcoat: A. L. Webber
    (Decca SKL 4973, Score Novello & Co.).
Jonah-Man Jazz (Novello & Co.).
Daniel Jazz (Jupiter JEP O.C.30, Novello & Co).
Soul of Israel (Marble Arch MAL 734).
Verdi, G.: 'Va Pensiero' Hebrew Chorus from *Nabucco.*
Negro spirituals.

Films

The Holy Land (Boulton-Hawker).

Book of the Acts Series (Family Films, distributed by Religious Films).

Journey of a Lifetime: series of thirty-five films (Warner Pathé Distributors).

2000 Years Ago Series (GBI).

Birth of the Saviour (Family Films, USA).

Childhood of Jesus (Family Films, USA).

First Disciples (Family Films, USA).

The Woman at the Well (Family Films, USA).

Jesus at Nazareth and Capernaum (Family Films, USA).

Blind Bartimaeus (Religious Films).

The Wedding Feast (Religious Films).

Jordan Valley (BIF).

Israel, Land of Promise (Michael Brandt Productions).

Building a Nation (Israel) (United World Films).

Olive Growing in the Middle East (EFVA).

Filmstrips

Life in Ancient Palestine (CG).

Background to the Old Testament, Parts 1–4 (Hulton).

Palestine in Jesus' Day, Parts 1–2 (Carwal).

Life in Palestine 2000 Years Ago, Parts 1–6 (Religious Films).

Other aids

Wall Atlas of the Bible Lands (Philip).

Maps from *The Westminster Historical Atlas of the Bible* (SCM).

Wallcharts: *The Sea of Galilee* (EP); *Life in the Time of Christ* (Pictorial Charts).

Useful addresses

Bible Lands Society: 33 Museum Street, London WC1.

Bible and Medical Missionary Fellowship: 352 Kennington Road, London SE11.

Citrus Marketing Board of Israel: 122–124 Victoria Street, London SW1.

Israel Embassy: 2 Palace Green, London W8.
Israel Government Tourist Office: 59 St James's Street, London SW1.
Jerusalem and The East Mission: 12 Warwick Square, London SW1.
Jordan Embassy: 6 Upper Phillimore Gardens, London W8.
El Al Israel Airlines: 185 Regent Street, London SW1.
Trans-World Airlines: 200 Piccadilly, London W1.

Excursions
Bible House: 146 Queen Victoria Street, London EC4,

British and Foreign Bible Society: 146 Queen Victoria Street, London EC4.

A visit to a Jewish school or a tabernacle during a festival.

CREATIVE ACTIVITIES
Written work
Imagine you are a radio reporter and interview one of the shepherds after his visit to the stable. Tape your interview.

Imagine that you are Joseph, and tell of your visit to Jerusalem and how you lost Jesus.

Write a series of poems about the Nativity of Jesus. These can be set to music to form a simple Christmas oratorio.

Imagine you are John the Baptist; tell your story of the day on which you baptised Jesus.

Make a class Galilean newspaper with headlines and illustrations. Choose stories of miracles and write them as though you were a reporter at the time.

Imagine you are Peter. Write a letter to a friend telling him of your experiences with Jesus on the sea.

Imagine you are a reporter. Interview one of the crowd watching Jesus enter Jerusalem on Palm Sunday.

Write an entry for Peter's diary for Maundy Thursday and Good Friday.

Write a series of poems about the events in Holy Week.

Imagine that you are a child on the Children's Crusade. Describe your journey and at least one exciting event.

Find out about medieval warfare and then describe an attack on a city in the Holy Land from a Crusader's point of view.

Imagine you are a Jewish boy who lived in England and has now moved to a kibbutz in Israel. Describe your new life.

Imagine you are a Roman soldier on duty in Jerusalem during Holy Week. Describe your feelings towards the Jews.

Drama and movement
Act a play about the first miracle at the wedding at Cana of Galilee.

Act the story of the Good Samaritan.

Prepare and act a Passion Play which tells of the events of Holy Week, possibly in acts performed on different days.

Mathematical and scientific aspects
Find out the types of fish found in the Sea of Galilee.

Make a study of the flowers, plants and trees of Palestine.

Make a booklet of pictures and information about the birds of Palestine.

Find stories in the Bible which mention amounts of money and discover what their equivalent is in English money. The story of the

Talents is an example. (See *The Bible Reader's Encyclopaedia and Concordance.*) Make a table of equivalent weights and measures, then weigh and measure some of your friends and express the results in the Bible-time measures.

Find out why the Dead Sea contains no animal life.

Find out about the Jewish calendar.

Art
Design a picture for a calendar, for each Jewish month of the year, featuring any special feast days.

Paint or crayon a picture of Jesus calling the fishermen to follow him.

Design a stained-glass window of one of the apostles. Try to include in your design something which indicates clearly who they are. Use thick wax crayons on good cartridge paper, then rub with oil on the reverse side until the paper becomes translucent.

Paint a life-size picture of a sower with his basket of seed.

Paint a frieze of the entry of Jesus into Jerusalem on Palm Sunday.

Paint a large group picture of a Crusader camp. Remember that they carried with them pennants showing their heraldic designs.

Craft
Make a large-scale relief map of Palestine in papier mâché or plaster. Make sure that the physical features of the Jordan Valley are clearly seen. Mark on it the main cities.

Make a model of a Palestinian house with a removable roof so that the details of furniture inside can be seen.

Make a number of dolls from bottles with papier-mâché heads. Dress each doll to show the costumes of men and women of Palestine in Bible times.

Fig. 45 Bottle into figure. Modelling clay added to the neck of bottles can be tooled into a head, and into hands at the end of the wire arms. Then cover with papier mâché.

Fig. 46 Material and objects can be added to provide a realism to the figures.

312

Fig. 47 A Galilean fishing boat. By using large pieces of cardboard around wooden boxes, a boat can be made big enough for children to sit inside.

Make a large model of a Galilean fishing boat.

Make a series of diorama models of the life of Jesus Christ. Either use the base and three sides of a box or make the background and base out of cardboard.

Make a model of the Temple in Jerusalem.

Make a model of a shepherd watering his flock at a well, with a fold on the hills behind.

Make a model of a synagogue.

Make models of the siege engines used by the Crusaders in their battles.

Make a model of a typical Palestinian village.

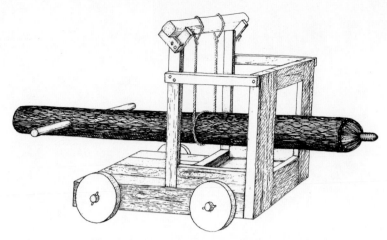

Fig. 48 A siege engine as used during the Crusades. The main ingredient here is off-cuts of timber from the local store or workshop.

AFRICA

Within a class of children there are always many diverse interests, in history, exploration, animals, science and people, to name just a few. The continent of Africa contains so many of these interests that it rarely fails to capture the interest and imagination of children. Egypt with its considerable evidence of ancient civilisations, and the emergence and development of the new African nations in this century, will interest others. Older children will be able to discuss some of the problems which face Africans today. Another interesting aspect concerns the way in which people have adapted themselves to living in deserts, jungles, mountains and plains.

Africa is a continent of mystery, with so much still to be discovered, vast mineral resources, new industries and new opportunities. It is very important that children should discover something about Africa.

Special aspects
This topic could easily last for a term, or even in more detail for a year. The age of the children and their interests will determine which aspects will be concentrated on. The geographical belts of desert, jungle, bush, veldt and mountains could be used as a plan for the topic. Countries and commodities could also be used in group or individual study.

INFORMATION AND INSPIRATION
Books
Adamson, J.: *The Peoples of Kenya* (Collins).
Budge, E. A. W.: *Rosetta Stone* (British Museum).
Burton, M.: *Animals* (OUP).
Burland, C. A.: *Ancient Egypt* (Hulton).
Burton, Sir Richard: *First Footsteps in East Africa* (Routledge & Kegan Paul).
Butcher, T. K.: *The Great Explorations: Africa* (Dobson).
Carr, A.: *The Land and Wild Life of Africa* (Time-Life).
Carrington, R.: *Ancient Egypt* (Chatto & Windus).

Chijioke, F. A.: *Beginning History: Ancient Africa* (Longman).

Compton, H.: *Chocolate and Cocoa* (ESA).

Cottrell, L.: *The Lost Pharaohs* (Evans).

Daniell, D. S.: *Flight Five: Africa* (Wills & Hepworth).

Denis, A.: *Animals of Africa*; *The Rivers and Lakes* (Collins).

Fawcett, R.: *Egypt* (Gawthorn).

Gibbs, P.: *Cecil Rhodes* (Muller).

Goudey, A.: *Here Come the Elephants* (Macmillan).

Grzimek, B.: *He and I and the Elephants* (Deutsch); *Rhinos Belong to Everybody* (Collins).

Herdman, T.: *Southern Africa* (Longman).

Hickman, G. M. & Mayo, R. E.: *Pilgrim Way Geographies*, Book 2 (Blackie).

Hogben, L.: *Man Must Measure* (Rathbone).

Honour, A.: *Men Who Could Read Stones: Champollion and the Rosetta Stone* (World's Work).

Kamm, J.: *Men Who Served Africa* (Harrap).

Latham, R. O.: *Trail Maker* (David Livingstone) (Lutterworth).

Leacroft, H. & R.: *The Buildings of Ancient Egypt* (Brockhampton).

Leakey, L. S. B.: *Olduvai Gorge* (CUP).

Leakey, L. S. B. & M. D.: *Excavations at Njoro River Cave* (OUP).

Martin, B.: *John Newton and the Slave Trade* (Longman).

Mcfarlan, D.: *White Queen* (Mary Slessor); *Wizard of the Great Lake* (A. Mackay) (Lutterworth).

Mertens, A.: *Children of the Kalahari* (Collins).

Moore, A.: *About Elephants* (Blackie).

Moorehead, A.: *The Blue Nile* (Hamish Hamilton); *The White Nile* (Penguin).

Mwangi, Z.: *Africa from Early Times to 1900* (Macmillan).

Northcott, C.: *Forest Doctor* (Albert Schweitzer) (Lutterworth).

Olden, S.: *Nigeria* (Muller).

Osmond, E.: *People of the Desert*; *People of the Jungle Forest* (Odhams).

Peach, L. du Garde: *Cleopatra and Ancient Egypt* (Wills & Hepworth).

Petkins, W. A.: *Our Continent and the World* (McDougall).

Petrie, D.: *The Nile* (Rivers of the World Series) (OUP).

Polkinghorne, R. K. & M. I. R.: *Lands of the Commonwealth* (Harrap).

Purcell, J. W.: *The Junior True Book of African Animals* (F. Muller).

317

Robinson, E. O.: *Africa* (Macmillan).
Sewell, B. & Lynch, P.: *The Story of Ancient Egypt* (E. Arnold).
Sharman, M. B.: *Africa Through the Ages: an Illustrated History* (Evans).
Shaw, H. A. & Fuge, K.: *The Story of Mathematics* (E. Arnold).
Sheppard, E. J.: *Ancient Egypt* (Longman).
Sheriff, D. A.: *Africa* (OUP).
Simon, H.: *The Young Pathfinder's Book of Snakes* (F. Muller).
Simons, M.: *Africa and Southern Asia* (Hulton).
Smiles, P.: *A Game Ranger's Notebook* (Blackie).
Sondergaard, A.: *My First Geography of the Suez Canal* (Dobson).
Sterling, T.: *Exploration of Africa* (Cassell).
Sutton, F.: *The Illustrated Book About Africa* (Macdonald).
Turnbull, C.: *The Peoples of Africa* (Brockhampton).
Webb, C.: *Animals from Everywhere* (Warne).
White, T.: *South of Suez and Panama* (W. & A. K. Johnston).
Winer, B.: *Life in the Ancient World* (Thames & Hudson).

Commonwealth Institute commodity leaflets:

1	*Oranges and Other Citrus Fruits*	15	*Tobacco.*
2	*Cotton and Cotton Seed.*	20	*Asbestos.*
6	*Cocoa.*	28	*Copper*
13	*Groundnuts.*	29	*Whales and Whaling.*
14	*Oil Palm Products.*	32	*Maize.*

British Commonwealth leaflets (HMSO):
David Livingstone.
Frederick Lugard.
William Wilberforce.
J. E. Kwegyir Aggrey.
Mungo Park.

Stories
Adamson, J.: *Born Free* (Collins); *The Story of Elsa* (Collins).
Appiah, P.: *Tales of an Ashanti Father* (Deutsch).
Arnott, K.: *African Myths and Legends* (OUP); *Tales of Temba* (Blackie).

318

Bayliss, J.: *Exploits in Africa* (Hamish Hamilton).
Buckley, P.: *Okolo, Boy of Nigeria*; *Bamburu* (Methuen).
Cavanna, B.: *Ali of Egypt* (Chatto & Windus).
Darbois, D.: *Agosson – His Life in Africa* (Chatto & Windus).
Durrell, G.: *The Bafut Beagles*; *Encounters with Animals*; *The Overloaded Ark*; *The New Noah* (Collins).
Fechter, A. S.: *M'Toto* (the adventures of a baby elephant) (World's Work).
Grant, J.: *The Eyes of Horus* (Methuen).
Guillot, R.: *Elephant Road* (Bodley Head); *Sama*; *Oworo* (OUP).
Heyerdahl, Thor: *Ra Expedition* (Allen & Unwin).
Hudson, W. H.: *Green Mansions* (Collins).
Huxley, Elspeth: *The Flame Trees of Thika* (Penguin); *Red Strangers* (Chatto & Windus).
Illsley, W.: *Wagon on Fire* (Epworth).
Jackson, H. V.: *West African Folk Tales*; *More West African Folk Tales* (ULP).
Kipling, R.: *Just So Stories* (Macmillan).
Lindgren, A.: *Sia Lives on Kilimanjaro* (Methuen).
Price, W.: *African Adventure*; *Gorilla Adventure*; *Safari Adventure* (Jonathan Cape).
Robertson, W.: *The Blue Waggon*; *The Storm of '96* (OUP).
Seed, J.: *The Voice of the Great Elephant* (Hamish Hamilton).
St John-Parsons, D.: *Legends of Northern Ghana* (Longman).

Stories from the Bible
Joseph in the Land of Egypt: Genesis 37–47.
Moses and the Land of Egypt: Exodus 1–14.

Poems
King Akhenaten: *Hymn in Praise of Aten* (1365 B.C.).
Belloc, H.: *The Hippopotamus*; *The Lion*; *The Elephant*; *The Rhinoceros*.
Carroll, L.: *How Doth the Little Crocodile*.
Carryl, C. E.: *The Plaint of the Camel*.
Kipling, R.: See *Just So Stories* (Macmillan).
Lawrence, D. H.: *Snake*; *Humming Bird*.

Nash, O.: *The Rhinoceros.*
Slater, F. C.: *Camp Fires.*
Spicer, N. H. D.: *Song of a Veld Rover.*
See also *A Book of South African Verse* (OUP).

Music

Flanders/Swann: *Mud, Mud, Glorious Mud.*
Saint-Saens: *Carnival of the Animals.*

Records

Music of Ethiopia: The Desert Nomads (Tangent TGM 102).
Music of Ethiopia: The Central Highlands (Tangent TGM 101).
African Music Anthology: Ba Benzele Pygmies (Barenreiter Musicaphon
    BM 30 L2303).
African Music Anthology: Music from Rwanda (Barenreiter Musicaphon
    BM 30 L2302).
Music of Nigeria: Hausa.
Missa Luba: Congolese Folk Mass.

Films

Life in Ancient Egypt (Gateway Films).
The Elsa Story (distributed by Collins).
David Livingstone (GBI).
Pitaniko (GB).
Nature of Things: The Camel (Walt Disney).
Nature of Things: The Elephant (Walt Disney).
Stronghold of the Wild (MGM).
How to Catch a Rhino (South African Tourist Corp.).
African Wild Life Sanctuary (Walt Disney).
South Africa (Walt Disney).
The Union of South Africa (Walt Disney).
East Africa (Walt Disney).
Surf Boats of Accra (Walt Disney).
Life in an Oasis (Coronet Films (Gateway)).
The Nile in Egypt (Gateway).

The Suez Canal (Gateway).
Oil from Nuts (BIF).
Tobacco Supply of the World (GBI).
Oil Rivers (Unilever).
Twilight Forest (Unilever).
Traders in Leather (Unilever).
Libya (EFVA).
Egypt and the Nile (EB).
How Cotton Is Grown in Egypt (BIF).
Life in the Sahara (EB).
Cocoa Harvest (Cadbury Bros Ltd).
Farming in Nigeria (BFI).
Cotton (Uganda) (Gateway).
Pygmies of Africa (EB).
People of the Congo (EB).
An African Builds His Home (Boulton-Hawker).
Tropical Forest Village (GBI).
Riches of the Veld (United World Films (GB)).
Table Grapes (BH).
Oranges (BIF).
A Hundred Million to One (Diamonds) (De Beers Consolidated Mines
    Ltd, SA).
Brilliant Fire (De Beers Consolidated Mines Ltd, SA).
Around East Africa (Brooke Bond).
Big Game Country (SA Tourist Co).
Safari South (SA Tourist Co).
Armand and Michaela Denis on Safari (SA Tourist Co).
Flight to Fortune (SA Tourist Co).
South African Encounter (SA Tourist Co).
The Majestic Continent (BOAC).
The New Traders (Unilever).
Africa Awakening (Unilever).
Mrs Humphries Goes to Africa (Oxfam).
Zambesi (Mobil).
Accra Market (EFVA).
African Crafts, No. 1 and No. 2 (EFVA).
Ethiopian Cattle Boy (EFVA).
Elephants and Hippos in Africa (Walt Disney).

Filmstrips

Northern Rhodesia (Zambia): Winter in an Ila Village (Commonwealth Institute).

The African Lion (EP).

Cocoa and Chocolate (Unicorn Head).

Everyday Life in Nigeria (EP).

Nigerian Arts and Crafts (GB).

*West Africa: In the Tropics. 1. The Savannah and Hot Grasslands;
2. The Coast and Rain Forest* (GB).

Life in Ancient Egypt (Hulton).

People in Ancient Egypt (GB).

Life in Ancient Egypt (CG).

David Livingstone (VP).

David Livingstone (CG).

Paul Kruger (Hulton).

Cecil Rhodes (Hulton).

The following filmstrips are available from EFVA:

Sumo, a Boy of Africa.

Natives of Africa.

Peoples of Africa.

Farmers of Africa.

Housing in West Africa.

Everyday Life in East Africa.

Riches of the Veld.

Gold Mining in South Africa.

Nile Valley.

The Nile (461G24).

The Nile (461G27).

Egypt Today.

The Sahara Desert.

Everyday Life in Morocco.

Other aids

Slides:

African Animals: 1. *Giraffes*; 2. *Mammals*; 3. *Water Birds*; 4. *Antelope* (EFVA).

Maps and charts:

Changing Map of Africa (Central Office of Information).

The Story of Africa in Stamps (Educational Productions Ltd).

Uganda (twelve photographs) (COI).

Gambia (eight photographs) (COI).

Nigeria (twelve photographs) (COI).

Swaziland (eight photographs) (COI).

Central Office of Information, photo-posters:
Northern Rhodesia Becomes Zambia.
Nyasaland.
Kenya Becomes a Sovereign Nation.
Zanzibar Becomes a Sovereign Nation.
Bechuanaland Protectorate.
Basutoland.
Swaziland.
Sierra Leone Achieves Independence.

Rhodesia and Nyasaland (two wallcharts) (EP).
Africans Co-operate (coffee growing) (Pictorial Charts).
Savannah Grasslands (wallchart) (Pictorial Charts).
Ghana (two wallcharts) (EP).
Cocoa Farming in Ghana (Cadbury Bros Ltd).
Junior Frieze (six wallcharts of Ghanaian village) (Cadbury Bros Ltd).
Nigeria: Camel at the Gates of Kano (Warne & Co Ltd).
Nigeria: Donkey Carrying Groundnuts (Warne & Co Ltd).
Chocolate (wallchart) (EP).
Diamonds (wallchart) (EP).
West Africa (four charts) (EP).
South Africa (twelve charts) (EP).

Excursions
Cambridge: University Museum of Archaeology and Ethnology, Cambridge.

Durham: The Gulbenkian Museum, Durham.

Hertfordshire: Rhodes' Memorial Museum, Bishop's Stortford.

Kent: Chiddingstone Castle (Ancient Egyptian Collection), Edenbridge; The Powell Cotton Museum (zoological specimens), Quex Park, Birchington.

Lanarkshire: Scottish National Memorial to David Livingstone, Blantyre; City of Glasgow Corporation Art Gallery and Museum, Glasgow.

Lancashire: Museum and Art Gallery, Bolton; Manchester Museum, Manchester.

London: Commonwealth Institute; Natural History Museum (African Nature Trail); British Museum (Egyptian Galleries).

Zoos: London, Whipsnade.

Safari Parks: Windsor, Longleat, Woburn, Stirling, Knowsley (near Liverpool) and Stapleford (near Melton Mowbray).

CREATIVE ACTIVITIES
Written work
Find out about life in a forest village in Africa, then imagine you are an African boy exploring the forest. Start your story with 'I crept through the forest undergrowth and then . . .'

Primitive Africans believed that masks had strange powers. Write a story about The Magic Mask.

Find out about witch doctors and then write a story called The Witch Doctor's Spell.

Write a story about a family in Ancient Egypt who are farmers by the River Nile.

Write a poem in praise of Ra, the Ancient Egyptian Sun God.

Imagine you are one of the slaves who built a pyramid. Describe a day in your life.

The Ancient Egyptians enjoyed hunting ducks, crocodiles and hippopotami. Imagine you are Pharaoh's child and describe one of these hunts, which is your first one.

Write a poem about an African tribal dance.

324

Imagine you are a reporter for an Egyptian newspaper in the time of
Joseph. Write a series of articles on Joseph's life in Egypt:
(a) Joseph, servant to Potiphar.
(b) Joseph the interpreter.
(c) Joseph the Prime Minister
(d) Joseph reunited with his family.

Write poems about African animals, e.g. The Elephant, The Lion,
The Giraffe. Provide linking music and sound effects to make your
own Carnival of the Animals.

The Rosetta Stone is a tablet of black basalt found in 1799 at Rosetta,
a town in Egypt. It bears parallel inscriptions in Greek and ancient
Egyptian hieroglyphics. Because of this it provided a key to the
deciphering of ancient Egyptian writing. Imagine that you were the
French officer who discovered the Rosetta Stone near the Nile in
1799, during Napoleon's campaign in Egypt. In 1822, when the
results of the study of the stone were published, tell your family how
you found this important stone.

Drama and movement
Find out about Egyptian family life in Ancient Egypt and make group
plays about everyday life.

Act the story of Joseph.

Explore in movement various African animals feeding, drinking,
sleeping, when startled, when fighting.

Use a record of African drumming or very rhythmic music, and dance
an African tribal dance. With drums, join in when the rhythm is
known.

Mathematical and scientific aspects
Find out about the geometry needed for building pyramids; the use
of the plumb line and set squares.

Find out about Egyptian measures of digits, palms and cubits.

Find out about areas of squares and areas of triangles and circles as used by Egyptians for measuring fields.

Find out about the Egyptians' knowledge of the calendar and sun dials.

Make conversion graphs to change African currency to English currency.

Find out about African plants, trees, animals, birds, insects, and produce monographs on each.

Draw graphs to show the difference in rainfall in various regions of Africa during two or three months of the year.

Find out the average rainfall and average temperature of the countries of Africa. Then express in the form of Venn diagrams the relationship between: heavy rainfall and high temperature; light rainfall and high temperature; light rainfall and lower temperature; heavy rainfall and lower temperature.

Art
Paint colourful African shields.

Paint or crayon pictures of: oasis; camel trains; Egyptian pyramid scenes; African animals; Egyptian gods; witch doctors; African birds; jungle scenes.

Paint a picture of a lion with melted wax.

Use scraper-board technique for a picture of a crocodile.

Make large group paintings or material pictures of: an African tribal dance; the life of pygmies; Egyptian funeral procession; a Watusi dancer.

African carvings have an impressive power and have influenced famous European artists such as Picasso. Try to find examples in museums, book illustrations, etc., and then make some models of people or animals in a similar style.

Craft

Make a model of an Egyptian funeral boat. This could be part of a large group model of an Egyptian funeral procession.

Make models of pyramids in cardboard and exhibit in a sand tray.

Make models of Egyptian methods of raising water from the river into irrigation channels, the *shaduf*, the *sakia* and the Archimedes screw. Make working models if possible.

Use plaited raffia to make an Egyptian lady's head-dress.

Use salt blocks or chalk for carving the heads of some of the Egyptian gods.

Make a diorama of the inside of an Egyptian nobleman's house.

Make a large model of the Great Sphinx.

Make a diorama of the Nile or the Suez Canal in modern times.

Make simple African musical instruments.

Make paper-sculpture masks (Horniman's Museum, South London, is a useful visit before this activity).

Weave colourful raffia mats.

Make a series of models of the different types of homes found in Africa.

Make a group model of an African village.

Make a large model of a crocodile.

Make a model of Heyerdahl's Ra boat.

Tie-dyeing, which is so popular now, has been known in Africa for many, many years. Try some tie-dyeing and make a wall-hanging, head-square, scarf or something more ambitious (*Tie-and-Dye Made Easy* by Anne Maile (Mills & Boon), is a book that will help).

EUROPE

It is interesting to study the history of Europe and examine the various attempts to unify it by military means. Britain has been involved throughout the ages in the power struggles and frequently it has only been the Channel which has preserved our independence. Military alliances have, in recent years, joined many nations together, but it is the need for economic unity which has been the deciding factor in bringing a closer association between countries on the Continent.

Because of the geographical closeness, it is likely that the ties felt between the member countries of Europe will become quite as strong as those of the Commonwealth.

The mass media will do much to inform and educate us, but perhaps in school we have the greatest opportunity to make Europeans.

Special aspects
The ease with which we can now visit almost any country in Europe will encourage an increasing number of schools to plan educational journeys abroad, and not only to the 'popular' resorts.

As a large class study, there are opportunities for groups of individuals to adopt particular European countries, and at the end of the project to come together to provide a picture of a community of peoples. Alternatively, a school might wish to carry out this study as a festival, each class being responsible for one or more nations. Europe Day is in May, and so there would be a reasonable chance of celebrating such an occasion out of doors, with national costumes and dances a distinctive feature.

The project would be given impetus by correspondence between classes and individuals in Europe. Useful addresses: International Friendship League, Correspondence Bureau: 16 Beaulieu Road, North End, Portsmouth PO2 0DN. International Scholastic Correspondence Exchange: Dovenden, Tipton St John, Sidmouth, Devon EX10 0AH. External Relations Dept, Department of

Education and Science: Curzon Street, London W1 (for French links).

An initial stimulus might be provided in the study by inviting children to investigate how the European influence has already infiltrated into Britain through invasion, granting of asylum, trade, politics and the arts. Language can provide such a starting point with the investigation into the derivation of words and phrases, e.g. *au revoir* (Fr), *au gratin* (Fr), *et cetera* (Latin), *ich dien* (Ger).

Dictionaries and *Pears Cyclopaedia* will provide suitable lists. Visits might be planned to places where the European influence is strong: Roman villas (Lullingstone) and the Palace at Fishbourne, Norman castles, or in the much later period to see the Italian lines of Chiswick House. Art galleries could be visited to see the work of European painters, and museums for examples of folk art from the Continent.

INFORMATION AND INSPIRATION
Books
A number of series are available for use by children.
Sally and Steve Visit: Sweden; Holland; Denmark; Italy; France; Austria; Switzerland (Angus & Robertson).
Let's Visit: France; Italy; Germany; Roumania; Greece (Burke).
Young Traveller in: Sweden; Norway; Germany; Italy; Portugal; Greece; Austria; Denmark (Phoenix).
Children Everywhere Series: *Marko in Yugoslavia; Gerdi in Norway; Manciela in Portugal; Dirk in Holland* (Methuen).
Come To: France; Denmark; Holland (Wills & Hepworth).
Getting to Know: Germany; Greece; Italy; Poland; Spain (Muller).
Land and People of: Belgium; Denmark; France; Greece; Holland; Italy; Spain; Sweden; Switzerland; USSR; Yugoslavia (Black).
Visual Geography Series: *Finland; Hungary; Czechoslovakia* (Oak Tree).
Young Explorer Series: *Greece; Holland; Spain* (Weidenfeld & Nicolson).
This is Our Country: Children of the Northern Forests (Hutchinson).

We Go to: Denmark; *The Channel Islands*; etc. (Harrap).
Shell Guide to Europe: Diana Petry (Michael Joseph).
Europa Shell Atlas: Europe (distributed by G. Philip & Son).
Nagels' Europe (distributed by Bärenreiter Ltd, 32–34 Great Titchfield
    Street, London W1).
Fodor's Modern Guide to Europe (MacGibbon & Kee).

Where teachers require further information about individual countries,
a request to the local library should furnish appropriate books.

Stories
Berg, Marie: *Tales from Czechoslovakia*; *Norwegian Tales* (ULP).
Berna, Paul: *A Hundred Million Francs* (Penguin).
Bonzon, Paul-Jacques: *The Orphans of Simitra* (Penguin).
Household, Geoffrey: *The Spanish Cave* (Penguin).
Jong, Meindert de: *The Wheel on the School* (Penguin).
Kästner, Erich: *Emil and the Detectives*; *The Flying Classroom*
    (Penguin).
Loeff, A. R. Van der: *Avalanche* (Penguin).
Serraillier, Ian: *The Silver Sword* (Penguin).
Stevenson, R. L.: *Travels with a Donkey*; *An Inland Voyage* (Dent).

In addition to these stories, we might also introduce some literature:
Church, A. *The Iliad and the Odyssey* (Macmillan).
Brothers Grimm: *Fairy Tales* (OUP).
Perrault, Charles: *Mother Goose's Tales* (it is surprising how many
    people do not know that *Cinderella, Puss in Boots*, etc., are of
    French origin).
Sutcliff, Rosemary: *Beowulf* (Bodley Head).

Poems
Anthology of French Poetry (on record RG 183).
Belloc, H.: *Tarantella.*
Browning, R.: *How They Brought the Good News from Ghent to Aix*;
    The Pied Piper of Hamelin; *Up at a Villa – Down in the City.*
de la Mare, Walter: *Napoleon.*
Drayton, Michael: *The Ballad of Agincourt.*

Housman, A. E.: *The Oracles.*
Longfellow, H. W.: *Simon Danz.*
Southey, R.: *After Blenheim.*
Thackeray, W. M.: *The Ballad of Bouillabaisse.*

Music
There is a very rich heritage of music to draw upon from the
Continent, and a search through the music books in school, will
enable the teacher to produce a programme which will exemplify the
folk song and other music of many countries.
Biquette (French); *The Bird's Wedding* (German); *The Cradle*
(Austrian); *The Little Dance* and *Andulko the Goosegirl* (Czech);
The March of the Kings (Provençal); *Paul's Little Hen*
(Scandinavian); *Festival Carol* (Dutch) – all from *The Oxford
School Music Books* (Junior).

Where the class are studying a language, then the learning of simple
songs would also be appropriate, *Frère Jacques, Sur le Pont
D'Avignon*, and so on.

With the greater availability of record-loaning facilities in libraries,
records can be borrowed and played to the children (the amount in
direct ratio to their age and musical background).
French Romantic Music (Decca ALP 1843).
Music From Spain (Ace of Clubs ACL 12).
Rumanian Folk Music (Topic IOT 12).
National Dances (HMV 7EG 8663).
The record *National Anthems* (SMVP 6105) includes many European
compositions and few children will be insensitive to the contrasts (and
particularly to our own!).

Another approach could be the systematic selection of a composer for
each nation and then listening to selections in groups, e.g. Germany –
Beethoven; Norway – Grieg; Austria – Strauss; Czechoslovakia –
Dvorak; Spain – de Falla.

Films

Introducing Belgium; *Denmark*; *France*; *Germany*; *Greece*; *Iceland*; *Italy*; *Luxembourg*; *The Netherlands*; *Norway*; *Portugal*; *Turkey*; *United Kingdom* (NATO – available from the Central Film Library and the British Atlantic Committee).

Children of Germany (Rank).

Children of Holland (Rank).

Children of Switzerland (Rank).

French Children (Encyclopaedia Britannica).

Norwegian Children (Encyclopaedia Britannica).

Spain and Portugal (Gateway Films).

Yugoslav Village (Plymouth).

Sweden (Rank).

The Rhine (Boulton-Hawker).

Switzerland and *Life in a Mountain Village* (Encyclopaedia Britannica).

Land Below the Sea (Caltex – from Sound Services).

Belgium (Caltex – from Sound Services).

Gateways to Europe (BOAC – from Sound Services).

Cross Roads: Europe (Caltex – from Sound Services).

The Great War: twenty-six films (BBC TV Enterprises).

The Lost Peace: twenty-six films (BBC TV Enterprises).

History: 1917–1967 (BBC TV Enterprises).

Factories, Mines and Waterways (Rank).

The Climates of Europe (EFVA).

Russia in Europe (Plymouth Films).

Filmstrips

Screenmaps: Europe (Hulton Press).

Farmers of Europe (Common Ground).

Fishermen of Europe (Common Ground).

The Rhine: an International River (VIS).

Europe (Hulton).

Switzerland (Unicorn Head).

Portugal (Educational Productions).

Italy (Common Ground).

Belgium (VIS).

The Netherlands (VIS).

334

Germany (VIS).
Yugoslavia (Hulton).
Austria (Common Ground).
Greece (Rank).
Norway (Common Ground).
Sweden (Educational Productions).
Denmark (VIS).

Other aids

Charts:
Europe Today: 1. *Agriculture*; 2. *Industrialisation*; 3. *Developments since 1945* (Pictorial Charts).
Europe in Stamps (Educational Productions).
The North Sea (Educational Productions).
European Adventure (Lyons Maid).

Languages:
There are several series of records available for the learning of languages, e.g. Linguaphone; Talking Book Traveller; BBC; Conversaphone. Some of these are stocked by libraries with record-lending facilities. In connection with this topic, the Schools programmes on television and radio should be investigated, e.g. ITV Learning French.
The Nuffield/Schools Council language courses: E. J. Arnold publish *En Avant* (French), *Vorwärts* (German), *Adelante* (Spanish), *Vperyod* (Russian) introductory courses.
Mary Glasgow Publications Ltd, 140 Kensington Church Street, London W8, publish magazines, recordings, tapes and courses in French, German and Spanish.

Study folder:
Workcards, study prints, pamphlets and charts. European Movement, 34 Wellhouse Road, Roundhay, Leeds 8.
Information about Britain and Europe from the Post Office or PO Box 201, Mitcham, Surrey.
Information about the North Atlantic Treaty Organisation from the British Atlantic Committee, Benjamin Franklin House, 36 Craven Street, London WC2.

Information about the Council for Europe from 82 Cornwall Road, Harrogate.
Information about the European Communities from 23 Chesham Street, London SW1.
The Stationery Office are distributors for priced publications for the Council of Europe, *European Coal and Steel Community* and *The European Economic Community*.

Useful addresses
The Austrian Institute: 28 Rutland Gate, London SW7.
The Austrian State Tourist Department: 16 Conduit Street, London W1.
The Belgian National Tourist Office: 66 Haymarket, London SW1.
The Bulgarian Embassy: 12 Queens Gate Gardens, London SW7.
The Czechoslovak Embassy: 25 Kensington Palace Gardens, London W8.
The Danish Embassy: 29 Pont Street, London SW1.
The Finnish Embassy: 53 Haymarket, London SW1.
The French Government Tourist Office: 178 Piccadilly, London W1.
The French Institute: Queensbury Place, London SW7.
The Franco-British Society: 1 Old Burlington Street, London W1.
The German Embassy, Cultural Department: 23 Belgrave Square, London SW1.
The German Institute: 51 Princes Gate, Exhibition Road, London SW7.
The National Tourist Organisation of Greece: 195 Regent Street, London W1.
The Hungarian Embassy: 35 Eaton Place, London SW1.
The Hungarian Travel Centre: 10 Vigo Street, London W1.
The Icelandic Embassy: 1 Eaton Terrace, London SW1.
The Italian Institute: 39 Belgrave Square, London SW1.
Italian State Tourist Office: 201 Regent Street, London W1.
The Luxembourg Embassy: 27 Wilton Crescent, London SW1.
The Luxembourg National Tourist Office: 66 Haymarket, London SW1.
The Royal Netherlands Embassy: 38 Hyde Park Gate, London SW7.
The Norwegian Embassy: 42 Lancaster Gate, London W2.

The Polish Cultural Institute: 16 Devonshire Street, London W1.
The Portuguese Information Office: 20 Regent Street, London SW1.
The Spanish Tourist Office: 67 Jermyn Street, London SW1.
The Swedish Institute: 23 North Row, London W1.
The Swiss Centre: Leicester Square, London WC2.
The Yugoslav Embassy: 25 Kensington Gore, London SW7.

Excursions

School journeys to one or more European countries. Possible link with
a school in France or Germany – with a view to exchange. (The
School Journey Association of London, 23 Southampton Place,
London WC1, will help with enquiries.) Educational cruises are also
available in which school parties land at various European ports.
(Central Bureau for Educational Visits and Exchanges,
43 Dorset Street, London W1, advises schools planning excursions
to the Continent.)

Day excursions are possible to France, and schools in south-east
England are well able to make such a journey.

Some towns have linked themselves with European places, e.g.
Greenwich and Maribor (Yugoslavia). Various events take place from
time to time, and schools may wish to take an active part in such an
association.

A town or city might have a French Week, or a concert featuring
dancing or other musical items presented by a visiting group.

Visit art galleries to study the work of European artists.

A visiting head of state from a European country, or a party of
students. Some interest could be taken in such an event.

CREATIVE ACTIVITIES
Writing
Travelling around Europe on fifteen pounds. Write a diary of a

fortnight spent travelling around the Continent on this limited amount of money.

Choose one of the rivers of Europe and tell about your adventures on a barge.

You join up with a group of four other European nationals, and become involved in some crime detection work after observing some people acting suspiciously. As English is not a language common to the group, there are some problems in communication. Nevertheless, write a play in which the affair is satisfactorily solved.

Write a brochure for a visit to six of the European capitals.

Prepare an information folder on different countries and, during the exhibition of work, arrange for five-minute lecturettes on each nation.

Write couplets on each of the European countries and, with tuned percussion, set them to music. (*Oranges and Lemons* might be a suitable starting point.)

Drama and movement
Prepare a number of situations to be acted in turn by the class, most of whom are air passengers, passing through customs.

Prepare a story to take place in a market on the Continent when an Englishman cannot make himself understood, and others join in to add to the confusion!

Learn a number of folk dances from various countries of Europe, and perform these in costume.

Select a folk tale from Europe and dramatise it. A weekly story such as this could be dramatised for assembly, with background information on the particular country provided as well.

Mathematical and scientific assignments

From travel bureaux obtain air, land and sea time-tables and devise various problems about routing and times to travel between centres. Compare air fares with other forms of transport and between air lines.

Use metric measures for all mathematical work. Include in the practical activities an examination of packets, tins and jars where the metric equivalents are given as well as imperial measures. Weigh all the class in kilograms and measure them in metres (and smaller units).

Compare Celsius and Fahrenheit readings.

Prepare a table of comparisons of miles per hour with kilometres per hour.

Collect a class set of European coins; prepare conversion tables for all the currencies of the Continent. (The local banks often have attractive cards with monetary equivalents on them, and papers such as *The Times* and *Financial Times* publish daily tables of exchange rates.)

Art

Prepare a set of national flags of all the European countries. These can be made as a double spread which is then folded and stuck around a set of dowel rods, which are in turn fixed into a strip of wood.

Make up a collage picture of Europe, using pictures of famous buildings, and other features taken from colour magazines, travel brochures, postcards and so on.

Develop a time-line of historical events with personalities and events over the last 2000 years. Link with short biographies written up by each child.

Make a book of maps of Europe which will show the various patterns of power which developed and changed through the ages.

Prepare a class (or school) collection of European stamps. Examine particular sets of stamps which feature historical, geographical, scientific or other features of countries. Design a set of stamps which would portray features common to every country of the Continent.

Prepare a set of illustrated route maps, with writing associated with each major place passed *en route*. This can be tape-recorded, with some national language and music. (See Travelling in Europe Series: *The Road to Costa Brava*; *Provence*; *Rome via Florence*; *Rome via Genoa*; *Salzburg*; *Venice* – Shire Publications.)

Craft
On a large base board, make a model of the Channel. This can be done by arranging boxes in two lines approximating to the shape of the two coastlines, and covering them with papier mâché. Various individuals and groups can then prepare smaller models of various forms of transport which have, through the ages, been used to cross the strip of water above, on and below the surface. Anticipate the future by creating a Channel tunnel, suspended under the base board.

Prepare a model of the landing on the Normandy beaches in 1944. Children will be able to lend model military vehicles and soldiers which should give a realism to the scene. Prepare a loop tape of gunfire to be played alongside the model.

Make a large group of models of famous European buildings – Leaning Tower of Pisa, Eiffel Tower, Big Ben's tower – and arrange them against a backcloth of a map of Europe. Some interesting display techniques might be tried with a montage such as this. For instance, postcards from various European countries can be mounted on the face of cardboard boxes which have been previously covered and painted. These can act as stands for the various models. Tape-recordings can be prepared to run as travelogues with appropriate music and language. Ribbons or threads could direct attention to wallets fixed to the front of the model providing information on particular countries.

Prepare national costumes either in miniature to dress dolls and small figures or life-size pieces for wearing during a Parade of the Nations.

Older children might collect cards on a special theme, e.g. Gothic cathedrals, medieval castles, and mix in some English examples to show the unity of culture at that period.

One area in which there is great European homogeneity, is that of industry. While there may be some very specialised developments such as lace-making in Bruges and hat-making in Luton, most of the major industries have common denominators which can be demonstrated by the use of films and by visits in this country. For example, coal, iron, steel, shipbuilding, wool, cotton, glass and so on. Prepare a set of models, as group or individual enterprises, of buildings, factories and agricultural practices to illustrate Europe at work.

The subject of Continental food opens up many situations for exploration. Discussions on the Continental breakfast – with a group agreeing to try it at home for a week, so that they can speak from experience. The availability of recipes in books and magazines and the relative cheapness of ingredients from grocers and delicatessens should make it possible for several cooking sessions to take place. An Italian day, with pasta, might be followed by a German day, and so on. Parental co-operation and the help of the school cook will be desirable elements in this work.

COMMUNICATIONS

In many ways we might consider that communication means civilisation, for without it there can be no sharing of experience, knowledge, information or ideas. As the project unfolds it will become quite evident to the group that we communicate in a multiplicity of ways, some simple and others so sophisticated that few could explain them adequately. In many ways, too, this could be considered as a history of exploration, culminating with the exciting communication between the latest moon explorers and their bases in America or Russia. This is very much a pantechnicon type of study with possibilities for many individual and group topics.

Special aspects
This project lends itself to a great deal of practical work, with opportunities for the introduction of scientific experiment and application. Because of so much creative opportunity, the setting up of a large exhibition can be envisaged with many displays inviting audience participation.

Teachers new to this way of working might select only one aspect within the project. Similarly teachers of infant classes anticipating a shorter span of enthusiasm from younger children might wish to limit their study. For instance, within this study of communications or cybernetics, it would be possible to extract the story of the postal services, or, for a simpler study, the story of a letter.

INFORMATION AND INSPIRATION
Books
Adams, H.: *Postmen and the Post Office* (Blackwell).
Adler, I. & R.: *Communication* (Dobson).
Bateman, R.: *The How and Why Wonderbook of Stamps* (Transworld).
Bell, G.: *Signs and Signals* (OUP).
Brinton, Henry: *The Telephone* (Weidenfeld & Nicolson).
Brun, T.: *Sign Language* (Wolfe).

Burton, H. M.: *Stamps and Stamp Collecting* (Methuen).
Britten, B. & Holst, I.: *The Story of Music* (Rathbone).
Comton, H.: *Newspapers* (ESA).
Corbett, Scott: *What Makes T.V. Work?* (Muller).
Cowie, E.: *Communications* (Wheaton).
Davis, D. H.: *Behind the Scenes on a Newspaper* (Phœnix).
Fabre, M.: *A History of Communications* (Leisure Arts).
Fry, Leonora: *Post and Telegraph* (Methuen).
Gass, I.: *My History of Music* (Evans).
Goaman, H.: *How Writing Began* (Faber).
George, H.: *A Daily Newspaper* (OUP).
Haskell, A. L.: *The Story of Dance* (Rathbone).
Herbert, Roy: *Over to You* (Brockhampton).
Hildick, E. W.: *A Close Look at Newspapers* (Faber).
Hoare, R. J.: *Messages* (Muller).
Hogben, Lancelot: *The Wonderful World of Communication*
    (Macdonald).
Horsley, E. & Hampden, J.: *Books from Papyrus to Paperback*
    (Methuen).
Irwin, K. G.: *Man Learns to Write* (Dobson).
I-Spy Signs and Symbols (Dickens Press: Big Chief I-Spy Series).
Jones, H.: *Sign Language* (EUP).
Juppo, F.: *Read All About It* (World's Work).
King, Charles: *Modern Communications* (Harrap).
Knight, B.: *Sending Messages* (Blackwell).
Middleton, Geoffrey: *Study Book of Radio* (Bodley Head).
Miller, L.: *Sound* (Whiting & Wheaton).
Mitchell, Ray: *Study Book of Telegraphs* (Bodley Head).
Moore, Mary: *Our Post Office* (local post office).
Neal, H. E.: *Communication from Stone Age to Space Age* (Phoenix).
Newsom, J.: *Sending a Message* (Hulton).
Page, R.: *The Story of the Post* (A. & C. Black).
Pedelty, Donovan, Ed.: *Communication and Language* (Macdonald).
Percival, R.: *Discovering Dance* (ULP).
Perrott, R.: *Discovering Newspapers* (ULP).
Reade, Leslie: *Marconi* (Faber).
Roberts, Frederick: *Radio and Television* (Studio Vista).
Rolt, L. T. C.: *Transport and Communications* (Methuen).

Robbins, A. P.: *Newspapers Today* (Oxford).

Ryan, J.: *Ballet History* (Methuen).

Ryder, John: *Study Book of Printing* (Bodley Head).

Schneider, H. & N.: *Your Telephone and How It Works* (Brockhampton).

Siddle, W. O.: *The Story of Newspapers* (Wills & Hepworth).

Simons, E. N.: *Communications* (Dobson).

Simpson, W. W.: *About News and How It Travels* (Muller).

Soucek, L.: *The Story of Communications* (Mills & Boon).

Southgate, Vera: *The Postman* (Wills & Hepworth).

Taylor, Boswell: *Here Comes the Post* (ULP).

Zim, H.: *Codes and Secret Writing* (World's Work).

Macdonald First Library: *The Postman* (Macdonald).

Oxford Junior Encyclopaedia, Vol. 4: *Communications* (OUP).

Postmen Through the Ages: A Brief History from Schools Officer, Post Office HQ, St Martins-Le-Grand, London EC1.

Stories

One might almost say that any story could come within the category of communication. For instance, some of the conversation pieces in *Alice in Wonderland*, which leave the heroine and many readers rather confused, might be explored. Folk-tale collections are now plentiful and a selection of these would be appropriate, because they represent early attempts at story telling.

This is a selection of material which is closer to the theme because of its content.

Dumas, A.: *The Count of Monte Cristo* (section where the Count bribes the semaphore signaller) (Collins).

Harnett, Cynthia: *The Load of Unicorn* (Penguin).

Holm, Anne: *I Am David* (Penguin).

Keller, Helen: *The Story of My Life* (Hodder & Stoughton).

King, Clive: *The 22 Letters* (Penguin).

Kipling, Rudyard: *How the Alphabet Was Made* (*Just So Stories*).

Stories from the Bible

The Tower of Babel: Genesis 11.

The Miracle of Pentecost: Acts 2.

Poems

Equally it can be said that every poem is a form of communication, and only succeeds if it successfully links the poet and the listener. This group of poems has close links with the project.

Auden, W. H. : *Night Mail.*
de la Mare, W. : *Double Dutch.*
Frost, Robert: *The Telephone.*
Reeves, James: *Jargon.*
Tennyson, Alfred, Lord: *The Charge of the Light Brigade* (the classic example of a misunderstanding).

Music

Teachers may well want to illustrate the way in which composers have been able to demonstrate their skill in communicating ideas, patriotism, victory, hope, a sense of place and so on, and there is a large repertoire from which to choose. In addition there are musical compositions which can be used to illustrate and stimulate work directly.

Anderson, Leroy: *The Typewriter.*
Menotti, G. : *The Telephone.*
Mozart, W. A. : 'The Letter' song from *Cosi fan Tutte.*
From stage shows: 'Happy Talk' (*South Pacific*); 'Getting to Know You' (*The King and I*); 'Talk to the Animals' (*Dr Doolittle*).

Films

Alphabet (National Film Board of Canada).
Development of Communication (Rank).
Girdle Round the Earth (EFVA).
The Telephone (EFVA).
Sound Recording and Reproduction (Rank).
The Postal Service (Rank).
The Postman (Rank).
Postcard to Devon (BIF).
The Postman (BIF).
Newspaper Story (BIF).
Local Newspaper (Essex Education Committee).

The Chinese Theatre (Gateway).
Steps of the Ballet (Rank).
Instruments of the Orchestra (EFVA).
Radar Helps Shipping (EFVA).

Filmstrips
Electricity and Magnetism: The Telephone (Common Ground).
The History of Radio (Unicorn Head).
Radio (Common Ground).
The History of Television (Unicorn Head).
Twopenny-Halfpenny Journey (Rank).
A Letter in the Post (Common Ground).
The Work of the Post Office (Letters and Parcels; Telegraphs and
    Telephones; Stamps and Savings) (Visual Information Service).
History of British Newspapers (Common Ground).
How a Newspaper Is Produced (Common Ground).
The Story of Writing (BIF).
The Story of Books (BIF).

Other aids
Records: *Communications in Animals* (BBC RESR 11).
Sound and Silence: classroom projects on Creative Music (with
    accompanying manual) (CUP).
Wallchart and pupil's booklet: *Science in Writing* and *Writing and
    Communication* from Mentmore Manufacturing Company,
    Platignum House, Six Hills Way, Stevenage.
A large series of booklets, pamphlets and charts has now been
prepared by the Post Office. For example: *The Seven Stages of a
Letter, Mechanising the Mails, Speeding the Mail, Ring Around the
World* (details from local Postmaster or Telephone Manager).
The History of Writing: five wallcharts, five filmstrips and one film
    (Ministry of Education Visual Unit).
Printing and Papermaking: nine wallcharts, four filmstrips and two
    films (Ministry of Education Visual Unit).
Communications (Penguin Primary Project).

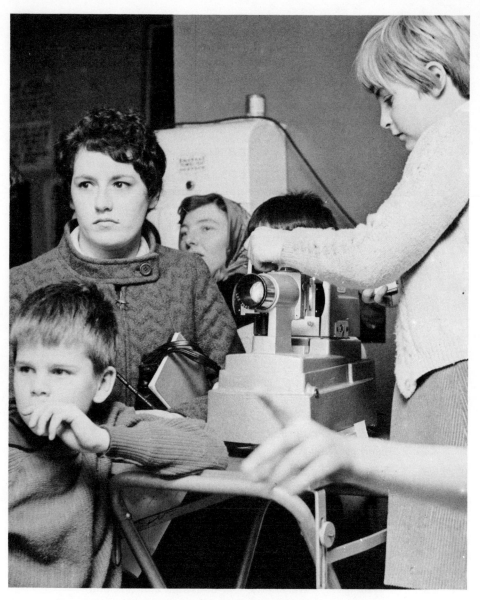

Plate 15a & b The slide-projector and the tape-recorder are valuable means of communicating ideas, both visual and aural, during any project.

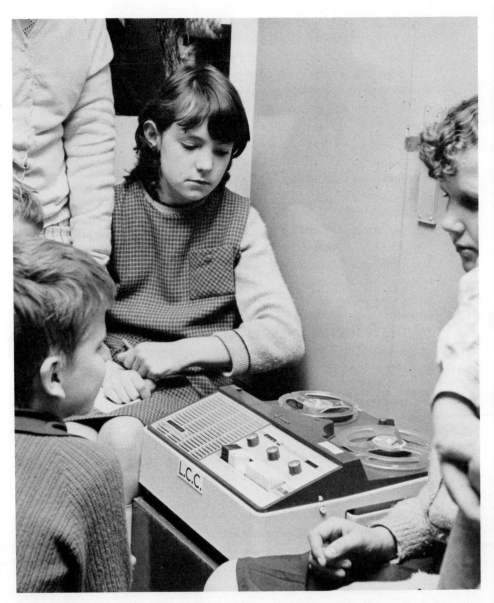

Excursions

Almost every museum reveals some aspect of communication. For example, the Transport Museum in Clapham has a Royal Mail coach (which can be entered); the Waterways Museum at Stoke Bruerne displays ancient notices warning offenders of the consequences of some thoughtless action on the canals; at the Commonwealth Institute one can pick up an earpiece and listen to voices and sounds of people at the other side of the world. One would need to consider this suggestion as an activity to include within a larger study of which this would be an integral part.

Apply to the local postmaster for permission to visit a sorting office. Schools in or visiting the London area can apply to the following addresses to make special visits:
The Controller (Room 4), Mount Pleasant Post Office, London EC1, to see the sorting office and Post Office railway.
The Controller, ES and FS (SB & A section), King Edward Street, London EC1, to visit the sorting offices for London and overseas mails.
The Telephone Manager, Long Distance Area LO/T (Gen), Godliman House, Godliman Street, London EC4, to see the telephone exchanges.
The Principal Superintendent, London Inland Telegraphs LIT/AB, Fleet Buildings, London EC4, to see the Inland Telegraph Service.
The Telegraph Manager, Post Office Overseas Telegraphs, Commercial Section TM/LC, Electra House, Victoria Embankment, London WC2, to visit the Post Office Overseas Telegraphs.

The National Postal Museum is at King Edward Building, King Edward Street, London EC1.

The Science Museum has a permanent display of machines which portray the development of photography and cinemaphotography.

Application can be made to watch the making of a television show. Apply to the Ticket Unit of the relevant ITV company, and the Ticket Unit, Broadcasting House, London W1, for BBC productions.

Visit the printing works of a national or local newspaper. The latter is a better proposition for groups of young children. A local printer may also be able to receive small parties. Some secondary schools run printing departments for their magazines and they can be asked to help in this project.

Visit art galleries, concerts, Parliament, Speakers' Corner, church, a lecture, a film, to see examples of communications.

Visit local police station, fire station, ambulance station, coastguard station, to investigate their means of communication – especially during emergencies.

CREATIVE ACTIVITIES
Writing
Prepare a series of letters: application for jobs already defined in advertisements; thanks for services rendered; complaint following some incident; congratulations; condolences; and so on.

Prepare a radio play, and tape-record it for transmission throughout the school.

Prepare a class newspaper, after some study of the layout and content of a national and local newspaper. Make this a weekly issue with regular features.

Prepare a school magazine, and give a special bias to the issue, e.g. the history of the school; the local neighbourhood; personalities in and around the school writing on some specific topic from various classes.

Prepare a poem about a conversation, and punctuate it with sound effects to heighten the effect.

Make a wall newspaper of items discovered during the project.

Prepare a series of lecturettes (three or four minutes) on ancient and modern methods of communicating.

Write the scenario for a film or a series of transparencies.

Take a situation reported in the local newspaper and prepare a ballad on the subject. Begin with the story and reduce it to sections, keeping in chronological order. Prepare a poem with a verse for each section.

Possibly include a refrain line. Use percussion instruments to set to music after saying the verse aloud to establish the rhythm pattern.

Write a prospectus for the school, with illustrations, photographs or cartoons.

Investigate the life of someone (Samuel Morse, Louis Braille) who has made a significant contribution to the world of communications. Prepare a biography and make a resource tape for others to use.

Write an individual diary or group account of the project.

Examine a number of official forms (from the Post Office, for example) to discover how clear their meaning is. Re-draft those which are ambiguous. (See *The Complete Plain Words* by Sir E. Gowers, HMSO.)

Look for howlers, oddities and misprints in the newspapers and make a class collection of these. (See *Funny-Ha-Ha and Funny Peculiar* and other similar works by Denys Parsons (Pan Books) to start off the collection.) Re-write the excerpts to make their writers' intentions clear.

Prepare telegrams to cover various situations – congratulations, news of a calamity or delay, etc. Send to other members of the class to see if they understand clearly the intended meaning (and if they could reduce the numbers of words used). Two examples might amuse the class. Telegram: No mon. No fun. Your Son. Reply: How sad. Too bad. Your Dad. In times of war, signalling must be difficult. The general transmitted the following message: Send reinforcements, I am going to advance. The signal was received at base headquarters as: Send three-and-fourpence, I am going to a dance!

If there is a child with a father in the newspaper business, or there is a local correspondent willing to help, the class could be introduced to cable-ese, and asked to prepare despatches.

Introduce other languages – oral and written. Numerous teaching records are available and groups could contract to learn one.

Esperanto is now spoken by eight million people — try this. Where there are immigrant groups within the school, their languages could be introduced — possibly with parental help.

Write the story of a castaway who is eventually rescued after sending a message in an unusual way.

When on a visit to the coast, prepare a message and seal it in a bottle and throw it out on the ebbing tide. We have had replies to such messages on a number of occasions. (The Glass Manufacturers' Federation, 19 Portland Place, London W1, issue an interesting leaflet on this use for their product.).

Prepare a story of a sea disaster, with various forms of communication used before the rescue is successful. Dramatise the story later or make an illustrated book on it.

Write a story of an exciting race between two mail packets, each anxious to get across the Atlantic Ocean first with some extremely important news.

Drama and movement
Prepare a puppet play (with puppets, costumes, backcloth and sound effects), for the re-telling of favourite fairy tales. Arrange to show to the youngest class in school, with various means of publicity beforehand.

Use miming techniques to tell a story of anger and forgiveness; deceit and remorse; failure and triumph; misunderstanding and comedy.

Prepare a number of short plays or excerpts from plays to illustrate the history of theatre with miracle and mummers' plays, Elizabethan drama, etc.

Tell the story of Sleeping Beauty, using Tchaikovsky's music.

Use the BBC series of Music Workshops and give a concert performance of the current production.

Perform Benjamin Britten's *Let's Make an Opera.*

Learn how to do semaphore, and transmit messages in this way.

Act the story of Moses returning to the tribes of Israel to find they have built a golden image.

Act the story of Samuel when he hears the voice of God.

Practise the art of conversation between small groups; with larger groups of five or six, ask for a chairman to be elected. The next stage of development would be a debate.

Make an 8-mm film of a story written and prepared by the class. (*Young Film Makers* by Sidney Rees and Don Waters (Society for Education in Film and Television) is a useful booklet as well as a series of Focal Cine Books from your local photographer – *How to Script; How to Title; How to Edit.*)

Prepare a number of sketches on the use of the telephone, with some amusing crossed-line situations included.

Use particular diaries to prepare dramatic scenes, e.g. Pepys, Captain Scott, Anne Frank.

Mathematical and scientific assignments
Take a sample of a number of pages in any book and work out the frequency of letters, and so the wisdom in choosing the simplest arrangement of dots and dashes for the most frequently used letters.

Learn the Morse code. Make up a buzzer or a light and transmit messages.

Prepare a system of codes and use these in class, between groups. Attempt, after some practice, to break codes.

Use a system of mirrors to make a heliograph and pass messages or signals when the sun is shining.

Purchase a cat's-whisker radio kit and make up the wireless receiver.

With the help of the local Post Office or the cadet corps of the secondary school, prepare a field telephone system for use between classrooms.

Find out the name of a local pigeon fancier who would allow a visit to his loft, or bring pigeons to school and talk to a group about them. Ask if a message could be fixed to the leg of a racing pigeon. If this is possible, engage in an experiment to determine the speediest way of delivering a message to a point fifty miles away: by post, telegram, telephone, pigeon, rail or personal messenger.

Investigate the use of various colours, shapes, etc., to attract attention from above.

Part of this study can be an investigation of sound: study of the ear; use of megaphone; hearing trumpet; making up a telephone with two cartons with taut waxed string between; musical instruments, especially of the home-made variety; drums; vibrating strings; echoes; recording sounds on tape and record.

Fig. 49 A simple 'telephone' device employing a carton fixed at each end of a taut waxed string.

Art

Make a class collection of postage stamps, arranged by country and thematic design. Design a new postage stamp to fit some topical occasion, achievement or centenary. (PO Philatelic Bureau, 2–4 Waterloo Place, Edinburgh EH1 1AB, can be contacted re new issues and first-day covers.)

Make a portrait gallery of 'communicators' and include in picture a significant feature of their contribution (for example, Alexander Graham Bell with his telephone).

Produce a fabric collage of communications in the pre-electric age, with bonfires, torches, flags and town-criers.

Design a poster about your exhibition on communications.

Design an illuminated letter.

Fig. 50 Design for an illuminated letter.

Choose good pens, inks, materials, and demonstrate different styles of handwriting.

Prepare a large frieze of a street scene, in which all forms of communication are shown: posters, street signs, policemen on point duty, cars with indicators out, price labels on goods and so on. (Prepare a tape-recording with a portable machine in a busy street and play it beside the picture.)

Make a stained-glass picture of Jesus talking to the multitude. Use wax crayons, and add black tape for the lead. Wipe the reverse side of the picture with cooking oil and display against a window.

Make a picture or model of the Tower of Babel. (A reproduction of the

356

Breughel in the Kunsthistorisches Museum, Vienna, might give inspiration.).

Use potato, other hard vegetables or lino to prepare letters for printing.

An old typewriter might be purchased and material prepared on this, including stencils for duplication of class newspaper. (Typewriter 'pictures' might also be attempted.)

Explore the world of signs: Indian, brands, languages, etc., and produce a large sheet on the subject.

Craft
When it was his turn as Lord Mayor of London to select the theme for the annual parade, Sir Peter Malden Studd chose communications. Prepare a number of floats to illustrate this theme and parade these around the hall (possibly a starting point for a Festival of Communications).

Use cardboard boxes, tubes, rope and other scrap material to make up a number of television cameras. Embellish a table to make a control booth and produce a television play.

Make rockets and lunar vehicles for a model showing communications with outer space.

Prepare a set of signal flags and use the *Observer's Book of Flags* (Warne) to send a message, e.g. I need a doctor, In quarantine, Dangerous Cargo. If the school is near a port or visiting a coastal or busy shipping area, identification flags for the different shipping lines and countries of registration can be painted. Probably with teacher or parental help build a recording booth for use in a spare classroom or other area within the school. Hessian or egg boxes can be used to line the booth to make it acoustically more satisfactory.

Using a long cardboard roll as a base, and pieces of corrugated card of different widths and lengths, make a model of the Post Office Tower.

Fig. 51 *Pieces of corrugated cardboard can be cut and rolled . . .*

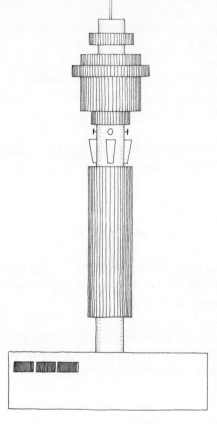

Fig. 52 *. . . and fixed around a central column, so making a model of the Post Office tower.*

Make clay tablets and inscribe a message in cuneiform signs.

Make up 'parchment' scrolls.

Fig. 53 Left: A w*ax tablet.* Right: *A paper scroll.*

358

APPENDICES

1 WORKCARDS

A These examples are for use by children whose reading is at a very elementary level. The teacher will need to introduce such cards to the children and then discuss their answers with them afterwards.

Swan   Duck   Frog   Fish

Fill in the missing word.

1. The _____ is a white bird.
2. The _____ is under the water lily.
3. The _____ is sitting on its nest.
4. The _____ is on the water lily leaf.

Further developments: larger word list to select from; missing word in different position in the sentence; more than one blank space introduced, e.g. The _____ is chasing the _____ .

B For use with simple well-illustrated books. For example, *Seven Trees* by Edna Johnson (Basil Blackwell). Find page 11, which is all about fir trees.

Fill in the missing words.

1. Fir trees grow up _____ and _____ .
2. Their leaves are short and pointed as _____ .
3. The _____ are the fruits of these trees.
4. Many small fir trees are cut down and sold as _____ .

C   At this stage of development, the pupil is given help in answering questions and responding to directions. Such devices are necessary at this preliminary stage, but can soon be dispensed with.

For example, *Looking At Nature*, Book 2, by Elsie Proctor (A. & C. Black).

Q. When does the lapwing lay her eggs?
A. The lapwing lays her eggs _____ _____ .

Q. What colour are the lapwing's eggs?
A. The lapwing's eggs are _____ _____ with _____ blotches.

Q. Why is the lapwing sometimes called a peewit?
A. The lapwing is sometimes called a peewit because he makes a call which sounds like _____ .

Q. What has a lapwing on its head?
A. The lapwing has a _____ on its head.

Draw a lapwing with a baby lapwing beside it.

Further developments: find the page about ash trees: ask questions. Where do ash trees grow? What colour are the buds of the ash tree?

These examples are suitable for use by first-year juniors who are being introduced to project workcards.

D   Based on the book *Life in the Middle Ages* by Jay Williams (Nelson), pages 20–21.

The text of this book would be too difficult for this early stage, but the illustrations and captions are excellent.

Find the answers by looking at the pictures.

1. What are the men doing to the sheep?
2. What is the man carrying to the windmill?

3. What animals did the men hunt?
4. How did the people make wine from grapes?
5. Draw a picture of a village mummer.

E Based on the book *The Middle Ages* by R. J. Unstead (Black), pages 8–10.

1. Why did William build so many castles?
2. What were the first castles made of?
3. How did the Normans cross the moat?
4. What was a portcullis?
5. Draw a Norman castle being attacked.

F Based on *Children's Encyclopaedia* (Black), Book 4.

Use the underlined words to help you find the answers.

1. Where was <u>Robin Hood</u> supposed to have lived?
2. What sort of stories did <u>troubadours</u> tell?
3. <u>Wat Tyler</u> led a rebellion in 1381. What was its name?
4. When was <u>Dick Whittington</u> Lord Mayor of London?
5. In the Middle Ages <u>windmills</u> were often built on posts. Draw a postmill.

G Based on the book *The Medieval Tournament* by
R. J. Mitchell (Longman).

The text of this book is somewhat difficult for first-year juniors, but by carefully wording the questions, and directing attention to the glossary page, the children will learn a great deal about life in the Middle Ages.

Use the <u>Contents</u> and the <u>Glossary</u> to help you answer the questions.
1. Who made the <u>proclamation</u> that 11th June was to be a public holiday?
2. What was a <u>lance</u>?
3. What are <u>spurs</u>?
4. Among the <u>spectators</u> were the King and Queen. Draw a picture of them in the Royal Box.

Workcards for slightly older children are suggested next. Now that the children are more proficient in their use, the numbers of questions can be increased, and the limits placed on pages of a book can be widened. It should no longer be necessary to underline words to be looked up in the index. After some practice at this stage, the children can be taken on to the stage where they might have to deduce the word to be looked up. For example, the answer to the question 'What fruit is grown in Malaya?' could be found by looking up 'food' rather than 'fruit'.

The type of workcard produced will be determined by the content of the book, difficulty of text, type and quantity of illustration, and the length of the account. Sometimes one aspect will be selected for study, and a few pages of a particular book will be used as in the examples given above. Other books cover the subject in a relatively simple way. Where the reading matter is easy, the whole book can be used. *The Junior True Books* (Muller) are a good example of this treatment. These workcards could be used by third- and fourth-year juniors, since they do provide a general background to the study of Red Indians.

H Based on the book *The Junior True Book of Indians* (Muller).

1. What were totem poles for?
2. How did the Indians catch the whale?
3. What was a potlatch?
4. What uses did the Indians make of buffalo?
5. What was pemmican?
6. How did Indians of one tribe speak to people of another tribe?
7. What were pueblos made of?
8. What did the pueblo Indians use maize for?
9. Which Indians built their homes on posts?
10. How did the Indians boil water?
11. Why did the woodland Indians wear masks every spring and summer?

The next stage would be to phrase the questions a little more generally, as in the following card.

I   Based on the book *Pilgrim Way Geographies*, Book 2 (Blackie).
Read pages 117–123.

1. What is a reservation?
2. What is life like in a reservation? Include information about homes,
   food and work.
3. Imagine you are a fur trapper. Describe a day in your life which
   was an exciting one. Draw some pictures to show what happened.

Some members of the third- and fourth-year junior stage may still
need workcards of the type already described. However, most
children will require more demanding work.

J   A river project.

Find out about the following water animals:
Water Vole   Otter   Salmon   Swan

Use at least three sources of information, making notes from each
before writing down your final account. Illustrate your work.

K   Use books and encyclopaedias to discover all you can about the
Cretan bull dance; a Spanish bullfight. Write a comparison of these
two events with illustrations which could be used for a dramatisation.

2 STIMULUS CARDS

1. Two pictures are shown from a magazine – one of a leafy wood in summer, the other a dark and dense wood. Write a story about the day you went into one of these woods.
2. Take the record of the *Moonlight Sonata* from the cupboard. Listen to it and build up a pattern of words. Afterwards arrange them in a poem.
3. On the cassette tape-recorder play tape number 1. This is all about African animals. After listening to it, imagine you are a game warden tracking down poachers. Prepare some notes on your adventure and then record it on the mains tape-recorder. Let me know when it is complete and some of us will gather round to listen to your story.
4. Take *The Book of Sea Shanties* from the reference corner, and choose one you like. Try to read the music and sing it to yourself. If you are in difficulty ask Jane or Sarah to play it for you on their recorders.
   Try to make up a sea shanty yourself with the same word rhythm.
5. We count One, Two, Three, Four, Five and so on. Can you find out how the French do it, and which words the Germans would use for the numbers 1 to 10?
   Try to invent a number of words which would serve for counting terms.
6. A number of pictures of snakes. Try to identify these snakes.
   Project loop cassette No. 1. Snake Movement. Try to make your body move like this. Ask one of your friends to make up a piece of music to go with your dance.
   Take half-a-dozen different lengths of string. Drop them on the floor. Use these shapes to start you off with a pattern of snakes or a snake pit. Perhaps you can write a story about being put in one and working out a way to escape.

3 ARRANGING THE ROOM

A room in an old school with inadequate facilities is here compared with an arrangement in a modern school where a team-teaching project is being carried out.

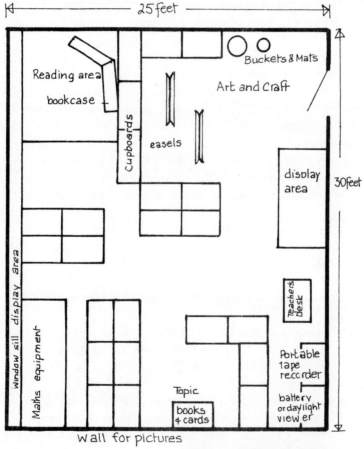

|← —————— 25 feet —————— →|

Reading area

bookcase

Cupboards

easels

Buckets & Mats

Art and Craft

display area

30 feet

window sill display area

Maths equipment

Topic books + cards

Teachers desk

Portable tape recorder

battery or daylight viewer

wall for pictures

For 35 Pupils

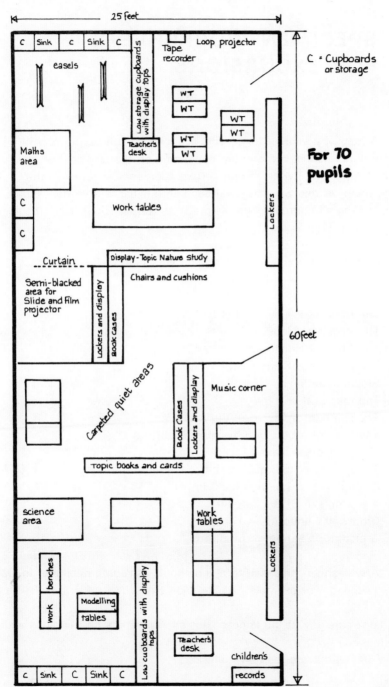

25 feet

C | Sink | c | Sink | C

easels

Low storage cupboards with display tops

Tape recorder

Loop projector

C = Cupboards or storage

WT
WT

WT
WT

Maths area

Teacher's desk

WT
WT

For 70 pupils

C

C

Work tables

Display - Topic Nature study

Curtain

Chairs and cushions

Semi-blacked area for Slide and Film projector

Lockers and display

Book Cases

Lockers

60 feet

Carpeted quiet areas

Book Cases

Lockers and display

Music corner

Topic books and cards

science area

Work tables

benches

work

Modelling tables

Low cupboards with display tops

Lockers

Teacher's desk

children's

c | Sink | C | Sink | C

records

367

4 SPECIMEN WORKSHEETS FOR EXCURSIONS

A   A map of a village, town, villa or a church can be given, with some detail added, the amount depending on the age of the class. The children are invited to plot certain additional features on the worksheet. In this way they will become familiar with certain things common to all churches, and aware of those particular to the building they are visiting.

Find and mark the following things on your plan of Rochester Cathedral, with the code letter given.

A. The tomb of William of Perth.
B. The Pilgrim's Steps.
C. The Chapter House doorway.
D. The bell of HMS *Rochester.*
E. Sloping columns.
F. The medieval vestry.
G. The painting of Christ on the wall.
H. The boss of a boy with his tongue out.
I. The plaque to Charles Dickens.
J. The tracing of the apsidal end of the church founded in A.D. 604.
K. A tomb with a pointing hand on it.
L. A painting of St Christopher.
M. Cromwell's uniform.
N. A picture of Simon de Montfort.

B   A worksheet for a visit to a zoo should encourage children to learn by observing. For example, 'At The Lion House'.

1. Look carefully at the lioness. Has she any spots on her sides and legs?
2. What colour are the lion's whiskers?

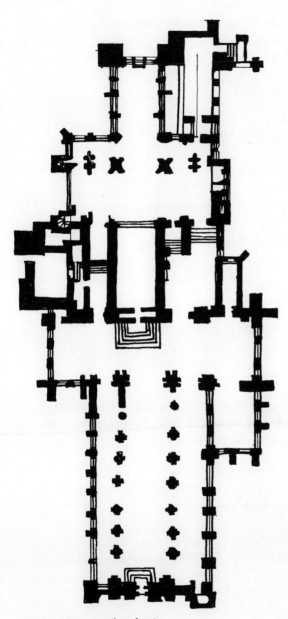

Rochester Cathedral

3. Lions wave their tails when they are angry. What is it that makes this signal obvious to another lion?
4. If the lion is eating or yawning, try to see how it is able to rip and tear the food it eats.

At the Elephant Pavilion.

1. What are the main differences between African and Indian elephants?
2. Make a list of the ways in which an elephant uses its trunk.

C   A route worksheet can be prepared which can be described as a combination of check list and time chart. Note features from each historical period in each of the towns visited.

	Pre-Roman	Roman	Saxon	Medieval	Tudor
Rochester Barham Canterbury					

D   Direct questions and instructions should be asked of younger children, or those for whom this activity is new. For example, in the Nigerian Gallery of the Commonwealth Institute.

1. Label and draw one of these people.
   (i) Hausa   (ii) Yoruba   (iii) Ibo   (iv) Msekeri
2. What is the name of the Red-walled City?
3. What is palm oil used for?
4. What minerals are mined?
5. What is columbite used for?
6. How is tin mined?
7. What do Nigerians eat for breakfast?

E   An older group visiting a museum can be asked to gather evidence on the way in which people of another race or period lived. The Roman Rooms in the British Museum.

1. Write down the kinds of food the Romans ate, and the way it was prepared.
2. Study the vases and the scene on them, and list the various activities portrayed.
3. Draw a picture of children playing with their toys.
4. Make a list of all the things which have a connection with trading.
5. On a map of the British Isles mark in those places where the Romans used the natural resources of the area.

F On a visit to a village or small town, an experienced class can be divided into groups each with a responsibility to discover as much as they can about a particular facet of the study, e.g. schools, libraries, shops, police, welfare services, post office, newspapers and so on
The sheets and follow-up work, supported by photographs, postcards, and sketches, will make up into a guidebook.

Leisure in a village

1. Is there a recreation ground or park?
2. What is its position in relation to the village?
3. Who uses the field and for what activities?
4. What clubs are there for young people, and how often are they open?
5. Is there a branch of the British Legion? How often do they meet and where? What was the last charitable service they performed? How many members have they?
6. Is there a Women's Institute? How many members are there? What were the subjects of recent talks or demonstrations to members?
7. Are there any other clubs for adults, including old people?
8. Are there any annual town festivities?
9. Is there a cinema in the village? If not, where is the nearest?
10. When was the last concert or play to be performed in the village?
11. Are there any organisations run by the church for young or old? What do they do?
12. If there is a nearby river, is it fished? Is there a careful control on this activity?

5 POETRY ANTHOLOGIES

Blishen, E., Ed.: *The Oxford Book of Poems* (OUP).
Chisholm, E., Ed.: *The Golden Staircase* (Nelson).
Clark, L., Ed.: *Drums and Trumpets* (Bodley Head).
de la Mare, Walter: *Collected Verses and Rhymes* (Faber).
Graham, E.: *A Thread of Gold* (Bodley Head); *A Puffin Quartet of Poets* (Puffin); *Puffin Book of Verse* (Penguin).
Holbrook, D., Ed.: *Iron, Honey, Gold*, Vols. I, II, III, IV (Cambridge).
Macbain, J. M.: *Book of a Thousand Poems* (Evans).
Mackay, David, Ed.: *A Flock of Words* (Bodley Head).
Parry, H., Ed.: *The Merry Minstrel* (Blackie).
Reeves, J.: *The Merry Go-Round* (Heinemann).
Smith, J., Ed.: *My Kind of Verse* (Burke); *Faber Book of Children's Verse* (Faber).
Stevenson, R. L.: *A Child's Garden of Verses* (OUP).
Summerfield, G.: *Junior Voices*, I, II, III (Penguin); *Voices*, I, II, III, IV (Penguin).
Whitlock, P., Ed.: *All Day Long* (OUP).
Wollman, M. & Grigson, David: *Happenings* (Harrap).

6 SUPPLIERS OF FILMS AND FILMSTRIPS

Films

BBC Television Enterprises Film Hire: 25 The Burroughs, Hendon, London NW4.

Boulton-Hawker Films Ltd: Hadleigh, Suffolk.

British Transport Films: Melbury House, Melbury Terrace, London NW1.

Central Film Library: Government Building, Bromyard Avenue, Acton, London W3.

Central Booking Agency (for BFI registered members): 82 Dean Street, London W1V 6AA.

Columbia Pictures Corporation Ltd: Film Renters, 142 Wardour Street, London W1.

Concord Films Council: Nacton, Ipswich, Suffolk.

Connoisseur Films Ltd: 167 Oxford Street, London W1R 2DX.

Film Distributors Associated Ltd: 37 Mortimer Street, London W1. (United Artists and Twentieth Century Fox.)

Foundation Film Library: Brooklands House, Weybridge, Surrey (including USA films).

Gas Council Film Library: 6–7 Great Chapel Street, London W1V 3AG.

Gateway Educational Films Ltd: 470 Green Lanes, Palmers Green, London N13 (including Walt Disney films).

Guild Sound and Vision Ltd: 269 Kingston Road, Merton Park, London SW19.

Hovis Ltd: 154 Grosvenor Road, London SW1.

ICI Film Library: Thames House North, Millbank, London SW1.

National Audio Visual Aids Library: 2 Paxton Place, Gypsy Road, London SE27.

National Coal Board Film Library: 68–70 Wardour Street, London W1V 3HP.

National Film Board of Canada: 1 Grosvenor Square, London W1.

Petroleum Films Bureau: 4 Brook Street, Hanover Square, London W1Y 2AY.

Rank Film Library (formerly GB Films): PO Box 70, Great West Road, Brentford, Middlesex.

Shell Mex and BP Film Library: 25 The Burroughs, Hendon, London NW4.

Warner-Pathé Distributors Ltd: 135 Wardour Street, London W1.

Filmstrips

BBC Schools Publications: 35 Marylebone High Street, London W1M 4AA.

Camera Talks Ltd: 31 North Row, London W1R 2EN.

Common Ground Ltd: 44 Fulham Road, London SW3.

Diana Wyllie Ltd: 3 Park Road, London NW1.

Educational Productions Ltd: East Ardsley, Wakefield, Yorkshire.

Gateway Films Ltd: 470 Green Lanes, Palmers Green, London N13.

Hulton Educational Publications: Alan House, 55–59 Saffron Hill, London EC1.

Macmillan and Co: Brunel Road, Roundsmill, Basingstoke, Hants.

Rank Audio-Visual Ltd: PO Box 70, Great West Road, Brentford, Middlesex.

Unicorn Head Visual Aids: 42 Westminster Palace Gardens, London SW1.

Visual Publications: 197 Kensington High Street, London W8.

Wills and Hepworth Ltd: Derby Square, Loughborough, Leicestershire.